A DRY SPELL

A DRY SPELL

SUSIE MOLONEY

Delacorte Press

Published by
Delacorte Press
Bantam Doubleday Dell Publishing Group, Inc.
1540 Broadway
New York, New York 10036

Library of Congress Cataloging in Publication Data

Moloney, Susie.
    A dry spell : a novel / by Susie Moloney.
        p.   cm.
    ISBN 0-385-31829-4
    I. Title.
PR9199.3.M592D78   1997
813'.54—dc21   97-23455
                                                   CIP

Manufactured in the United States of America
Published simultaneously in Canada

October 1997

10   9   8   7   6   5   4   3   2   1

BVG

FOR JOSH,
WHO ALWAYS BELIEVES ME

ACKNOWLEDGMENTS

No one does anything alone, and in many ways this was a group effort. My thanks to Sharon Alkenbrack, a truly human banker; Jan Huffman of the Bureau of Criminal Investigations; Gary Proskiw, who knows everything there is to know about the silos. Thanks to *The Farmer's Almanac,* to Jolanda Bock for the "road maps," and to Stephen George for demographics. Thanks to Judy Kift, who got me the books I needed. Mothers would get nowhere without special help, and for that I thank Tammy Hurst-Erskine. Mick Moloney gave me the benefit of his farming experiences, even when I had to ask for the fourth time. Josh Rioux and Mick read everything, and were lovingly critical. Michael gave me a reason to go home every day. My special thanks to Lynn Kinney. Thanks to Jackie Cantor for her patience and insight: *Get some sleep.* And to überagent and friend Helen Heller, thanks for taking my calls.

A DRY SPELL

PROLOGUE

ARBOR ROAD IS HAUNTED. THE MAN WHO WALKED THERE could not have known that, however, because it was a local legend. And he could not have known that Arbor Road was more frequently referred to as Abattoir Road, also as part of local legend. It wound crazily through bush and forest, many of its curves and dips sudden and sharp. The worst stretch, "Slaughter Slide," ran for a good five miles at the beginning of Arbor in the town of Telander, Minnesota, near the North Dakota border. Slaughter Slide had taken seven adults—two of them young mothers—and no fewer than nine teenagers since the road was paved in 1959.

The man who walked that road rounded a soft curve that opened up into a wider spot, where it then straightened out for a few hundred feet. He walked slowly, comfortably, the kind of walk that has been learned, the sloping, gentle walk of someone who plans to do it for a long, long time.

He didn't know that he was reaching Slaughter Slide. There were no crosses on the road today, no signs, and any flowers left as a memorial from the last accident had long since dried up and disappeared. He walked with his hands in the front pockets of his jeans, pushed down low, not for warmth, because it was summer, but for balance.

He was dressed too warmly for the weather, but since he rarely altered his form of dress, he was comfortable with what he was wearing—an oilskin jacket with leather collar and cuffs that were nearly black with age and the dirt of many roads, and under that, an old plaid shirt that he'd picked up two years before in a secondhand store. He had on a white T-shirt, Fruit of the Loom, the only item of clothing he ever bought new, loving the look and feel of the brand-new white cotton. This one was road-weary and gray. On his feet were thick wool socks and grimy desert boots, down at the heels. The boots were still great. As his mother used to say, "You get what you pay for, Tom."

On his back was a green canvas pack, some kid's old scout pack whose origins had long since been forgotten. A side pocket held a pouch of Drum tobacco and some rolling papers, but he was dead out of matches and his lighter was long gone, left in some bar. In the other pocket was a high school grammar guide that had his mother's name written in two different forms—maiden name, married name, maiden name, married name—on the inside front cover, nearly obliterating the stamp placed there by the high school. The book was stuffed full of receipts that he didn't need, papers, letters, empty Drum pouches with notes and addresses vaguely written and no longer necessary. Except for one. One piece of paper, the return address torn off a letter, signaled his current destination. A cotton-soft map, well used, and a page torn out of an old road atlas were stuck resolutely inside the back cover. Throughout the book, written in the spaces left by the typesetter, there were things, written mostly when he was drunk. Mean things. Sad things. Things best not written, and rarely read over.

The pack held two T-shirts, bought in the same package as the one he was wearing. There was another shirt, lighter, a bowling shirt with a name embroidered over the left breast pocket: *Don*. Not his name. His name was Thompson Keatley, Tom since birth.

There was another pair of socks and a newspaper from a couple of months back that he used to start fires when he was cold and tired and had to stop in the bush for a couple of hours of shut-eye. Also inside was an empty quart milk carton waiting for a garbage can, and floating around in the bottom were five dollars and some change, and a penlight, batteries dead. Didn't matter; he liked the dark.

Tied to the bottom of the pack with two heavy black hockey laces was a gray and threadbare army blanket, rough and scratchy, but better than bare dirt. He traveled light.

If his walk and style of dress bound him to every other drifter in America, the rest of him did not.

On his cheeks there was only a slight stubble, a day's growth of beard. He preferred to be clean-shaven, and went to great lengths to be so. He needed, and sometimes even craved, the clean, soft feel of rain sliding down his face, or the ripple of breeze against his skin. He dry-shaved mostly, or hunkered down beside a lake, river, or even a puddle, using the water to see his reflection. He was good at it, and rarely cut himself.

His jaw was emphatically square, enough to give his whole face an even, regular appearance. His skin was slightly darker than average, perpetually brown from days spent on the road. He was tall, but not remarkably so, just over six feet. He kept his hair long, and that seemed to somehow lengthen his overall appearance.

The women he met, mostly in bars, found him attractive, but unless very drunk, they would have been hard-pressed to talk to him for more than a few minutes. It was his eyes, they would have said. When company was unwelcome, as it usually was, he had only to narrow his eyes and his companion's banter would slow down to an eventual "Well, see ya." But he also possessed some other, less understood quality that could draw people to him. It seemed to be entirely a matter of his choice.

Tom was approaching the most revered stretch on the nefarious Abattoir Road, Slaughter Slide.

Its legend and danger were part of the attraction for kids out driving, sometimes for the first time, with licenses so new the photos were still wet. The thing was to pump to sixty before hitting Slaughter Slide and "get airborne." If you did it, you were juice. If you didn't, chances were you'd be well remembered by your friends and mourned by your parents.

The problem was, Arbor Road ran the distance between Telander and Oxburg and neither town was prepared to take responsibility either for straightening the road—an extreme expense, even in a joint venture between the two small agricultural towns—or lowering the speed limit already universally ignored by mature and immature alike. It was marked and stated at thirty-five miles per hour. No one drove thirty-five miles per hour. Not even in a blizzard.

Mostly it was the kids who took the biggest risks. Every time someone was killed students and friends posted a white cross that would glow eerily in the dark and serve as a reminder to the next batch of idiots who went airborne. What happened to the crosses after roughly two weeks of vigilance is unknown.

The road had taken on a new personality in the last fifteen years, however, ever since Richard Wexler and his buddy Wesley Stribe had gone unfortunately airborne just as they graduated from high school and were ready to move on to lives of desperate ordinariness.

"Dicky" was driving his baby, an enormous Mercury Montcalm that had been recalibrated to idle at tremendous speed. A set of mags on the back and a homemade spoiler gave the car a dangerous look. Mothers would not let their daughters go on a date in that car, and that was final.

Wesley had no bones about the car. He and Dicky had made careers out of cutting school and five-fingering liquor bottles and screaming down Arbor bragging about getting laid. If Wesley was sick to death of Dicky and his fart jokes, he never let on. The two boys, just eighteen, were usually the only two in the Mercury. With Wesley, Dicky could make noise about how tough he was, how he was going to kick ass, how he did kick ass, and he could punch Wes in the arm so hard his eyes would sting. Wesley could talk about how he got laid on the weekend and how big his dick was and how much the girls loved it—so much so that one actually *paid* for it—and Dicky rarely scoffed. They'd been cutting school and failing math together since grade school.

It was a Saturday night without girls, in 1980, the year that Ronald Reagan campaigned for the presidency of the United States and the long, eventless seventies were nearing a close. Cocaine was yet to be the drug of choice at Telander-Johannason High, and yuppies and AIDS were still in the future. Wesley and Dicky were in the Montcalm, pulling onto Arbor Road and screaming along with AC/DC's "Thunderstruck."

"Suck my Dicky!" Dicky screamed pointlessly. The car climbed back up to fifty after rounding the first of the worst curves. The windows were open and each boy had an arm out, feeling the hot, dry middle-of-summer breeze.

"Fuckin' school starts in less than four fuckin' weeks, and we WON'T BE THERE!" Wesley screamed.

"SUCK MY DICKY!" The two boys gave a fist-up salute to their freedom and whooped into the night air. Both had graduated with scores in the low fifties, after much campaigning by two sets of tired, exasperated parents.

The speedometer climbed to sixty. Slaughter Slide approached out of the darkness, curving to the left.

"AIRBORNE!" was the last thing Dicky said, and the last word Wesley heard.

The car left the ground at sixty and rammed sideways into a

thick-trunked oak tree. Wesley died on impact, one arm severed, both legs shattered as the door smashed inward and twisted upward. Dicky died from head wounds, having gone airborne one last time through the windshield. His spinal cord was crushed, both arms were mangled, and his skull was nothing less than smashed—the injury that would be named the cause of death.

After that, Arbor Road was called Abattoir Road. And had become haunted.

The ghost had thus far been seen by enough people to have been reported to a number of the TV shows featuring tales of the unexplainable. There had been constant reports of drivers slamming on their brakes for the sudden appearance of a young man right in front of their cars, only to have him disappear moments later. Three accidents had been reported, all the drivers blowing green on the Breathalyzer, each claiming a near-miss with a pedestrian and giving the same description.

He was a menace, this vanishing boy.

Teenagers held séances on Abattoir Road, calling back the spirit of the dead Dicky, who was widely believed to be the dangerous ghost. As often as not, the séances made the girls cry and the boys work hard to get their testicles to come back down, even hours after they were home safe in their parents' houses.

Television had yet to substantiate a ghost, but had Dicky known, he would have been front and center, rattling chains and jumping out in front of cars for them, take after take. If in life he had been vulgar and annoying, in death he had taken on a crueler quality. He might have liked to kill the people he was resigned merely to frighten. He would have enjoyed forcing those cars off the road, watching the drivers fly through their windshields, to join him in the bush, dark company for eternity.

On this cloudless night, Slaughter Slide was lit up by the moon. In the bush alongside the road there was indeed a ghost— the restless spirit of the dead Dicky Wexler. It was not in the form that those who had known Wexler would have expected.

At that moment, Dicky lay in wait over an expanse of bush as a mixture of mist and energy, an invisible haze that clung to rocks and sticks and leaves.

It felt rather than heard or saw the approaching man, as it gathered itself up and changed into a singular form. It began a slow movement toward the road as the man came on steadily, the tread of his boot heels regular and moderate on the paved road along Slaughter Slide.

The two equally restless spirits met without the man's ever knowing. As he approached the mischievous, nasty, former Dicky Wexler, its bluster and swagger dissolved. The man passed, formerly-Dicky slammed up against resistance that came from somewhere deep. It was literally scared away.

Tom Keatley passed by without ever seeing Dicky Wexler.

Arbor Road fed out into an artery of the town of Oxburg, still nearly a day's walk to where he was going. Tom Keatley, of no known address, continued onto the artery, whose name he didn't catch as he passed a group of road signs. It didn't matter if he saw them or not, read them or not, because he walked by the map in his head—memorized from the page torn from a road atlas in a small library someplace in West Virginia months before. He knew he was still heading the right way. He was blessed with an immaculate sense of direction and the necessary patience to follow it.

He walked along the shoulder, as he had for many days in a row, except for a long stretch at the beginning of the trip when, exhausted, he took the bus from Columbus to Sioux City. A milk run if he'd ever been on one, it had taken too long and he'd dumped the idea of staying on, of ever waiting to be called in a bus station again. If he was going to travel like a peasant, it would have to be on foot.

Every now and then he sent out mental feelers, by habit, and felt the rain behind him. That was good. His clothes were dry again, but if they hadn't been, he wouldn't have minded that either; he was used to the feeling of dampness and cool. The rain was behind him now, into the east.

He walked for about thirty minutes, the land opening up and allowing him to see farther ahead, and what he saw were lights. Familiar lights. He knew what they represented, even though he couldn't say he'd ever been this far north before (New York didn't count), and he had no idea what Oxburg had to offer. The lights, neon and flashing, were part and parcel of The Bar. The Bar that bracketed every town and every city in the whole big, beautiful United States of America, God Bless Us One and All.

Five dollars and change wouldn't even supply him with a decent buzz, and he had promised himself he would wait until he hit his next deal. He had never been able to keep a promise like that to himself, but he kept making them. Breaking them never did him any harm. When you're tired, you sleep; when you're hungry, you eat; when your brain is ringing death's dinner bell, you belly up to the bar and soak it in. Ever clear. Words to live by. And he did.

There was something about every bar in America that welcomed you home the minute you stepped through the door. Some kind of promise of belonging, an assurance that you could stop pretending to be someone else and just be who you are. Some cosmic sigh of relief was ready to greet you when you walked in, yours and theirs, the people inside already, glad to see another of their kind, another one who was getting by. Tired of *passing*, wanting just to curl up with a cold one and suck up tunes like vitamin pills, chock full of someone else's depression. After a couple of hours, you're ready to make up stories about who you're going to be as soon as that next deal goes through, as soon as that phone call comes. Tom walked into the bar, whose burned-out neon sign read CHARLIE CHU K S THIRSTY B Y, to begin his familiar descent, the smell of the rain very much behind him now.

The deceptively loud jukebox gave way to a nearly empty beer hall, with four guys sitting at the bar and three half-filled tables.

There was one old drunk chick in the back trying to read a novel, swaying when she turned the pages. Tom stepped up to the bar and sat a couple of stools away from the group shouting together at the other end.

The bartender nodded in his direction and Tom said, "Bud," over the music. His spirits were lifting already, the road dust settling under the stool.

He felt in his backpack for his cash and dropped the pack beside him on the floor. He paid for his beer using the change with a nickel on top, which the bartender left behind in disgust. Tom pushed it onto the beer-soaked counter on the bartender's side. Maybe he'd leave him another before the night was through. He got generous only when he got loaded, and five bucks wasn't going to do it. He needed cash if he wanted to eat tomorrow.

When the last song on the box ended, the sudden quiet was filled with voices that didn't drop in volume. The four guys to his right were shouting each other down, arguing about something somebody did or didn't do to Gage's car.

"There was no fuckin' problem with the points, I get it back and there's a fuckin' point problem, one-two-three, like that," Gage screamed, pointing a drunken finger into the face of his friend. His finger went up and down with the count, and landed in his lap, where he had a quick scratch. The baseball cap on his head said *Lansdown Motors,* and the bill was covered with grease.

Gage was the drunkest of the lot, but from the look of the bottles lining the bar, the others were catching up.

"Stupid son of a bitch," the friend cackled. Gage laughed, and a guy with a red beard said he took the Cruiser to the dealership. "Can't go wrong with no dealership," he finished. The others snorted, and they began a loud, fruitless argument about prices. The woman at the table in the back swayed over to the jukebox and began reading the lists, one eye closed.

Three men at a table by the juke were looking over at Tom, and he nodded. They nodded back slowly, sipping their beers.

Their talk was decidedly more serious, their heads closer together, their faces set and still. Tom heard only one word.

"—raining—"

The woman stepped away from the juke taking odd little mincing steps, in a parody of dancing. KT Oslin began singing about small towns. The men's rumbling talk disappeared under the music. Tom downed the rest of his beer and signaled for another. He took it with him to the juke, letting the bartender run a tab, just in case he got lucky. He was now down to a buck.

He pretended to look at the song lists and tried to listen to what the men at the table were saying. The talk he heard was broken with pretty song lyrics.

"—yesterday—Cy putting in the slew for—not since the bank—wasn't no way for—"

Between songs, Tom picked up the gist of the conversation.

"Tank says that if it doesn't get better this year, he's got to be moving them all to his sister's in Florida."

"He's kidding?"

"I don't think so. This'll be the fourth year. Four years without rain? Some guy out on Route 70's got a big wooden cross on his front lawn and he and his family get down and pray in front of it every night. That kidding?"

"Holy jeez—place like that. Makes you think."

"One goddamnedest spell."

Just before Conway Twitty began drawling on the jukebox, Tom made out one last comment.

"Makes you think it could happen here."

Tom closed his eyes, the juke, the bar, the men and their talk waning and dying out. He felt the rain. In the east. Here, in this town, it was dry right now. No rain in . . . five days or so. Maybe enough to worry folks.

His eyes opened slowly and he was looking down at the list of songs again, the men's talk rising and falling in the slow places and the bridges.

With his dollar in his pocket, Tom waited for the batch of songs to end. Then he approached the table.

He nodded to the men. All three wore working clothes, outdoor clothes that marked them as farmers. The smell of animals and fresh air clung to them and probably never went away. It was a scent Tom knew well, as well as he knew the smell of dirt after it rained.

The man who knew Tank was a big bruiser with a stubble of irregular beard and a bad front tooth. When Tom stepped up, the man leaned back on the two legs of his chair and looked at him with disinterest, except for a dismissive glance at Tom's longish, curling hair, pulled back in a tail. The other two stayed in position, elbows on the sticky table, beers half gone in front of them.

"Yeah?" said the one with a Feedmaster cap.

Tom remained standing, but looked at the empty chair between two of the men. No invitation was forthcoming. That could wait.

"I heard you talking about rain," he said.

"So?" said Feedmaster. The guy next to him had a pair of overalls on and shit on his boots. Tom could see it as much as smell it. He wondered what the man's wife would say if he tracked that into the house. Maybe that was why he was in a bar.

"I can make it rain," he said.

Three pairs of eyes stared at him blankly.

"For"—he calculated what the men might have on them— "fifty bucks."

There was a long period of silence until the man with the bad front tooth righted his chair and pulled his eyes away from Tom, with one last disgusted look at his ponytail.

"Fuck off," he said simply. The other two followed his lead and looked back down at their beers. The skinny one next to Feedmaster took a sip from his glass. A polite sip, to break the silence.

"You been dry here, what? Five days?" Tom asked, taking a risk. He was usually right, but sometimes wrong. Could've rained yesterday, and dried up some since; the winds were funny up north here, he'd found.

The three men looked up at him. He may have been right. Before they could speak again, he started quickly, glib, practiced. "I can make it rain, no shit, for fifty bucks. I'll take you outside and it'll rain."

Feedmaster said, "Weather says no rain for another coupla days, unless you know someone we don't. Why don't ya do what Blake here says and fuck yourself off into the corner . . . *hippie.*"

He spit the word out as if he were calling someone *faggot* at a Republican tea party. Tom stood there, calculating his chances. The buck in his pocket lay there as the seconds clicked by, his breathing coming shallow and fast as he both watched and felt around in the wind outside the bar for the rain. He looked from one face to another, catching an odd look, finally, in Blake's eye. The other men were looking at Blake.

Into the silence, Blake spoke. "And how do you make it rain, boy?"

Tom smiled. "I make it rain for fifty bucks."

Outside, the night was black, lit up with neon and the decidedly less colorful moon. With his heart pounding, Tom felt around and around, dizzy with a few beers on an empty stomach and the prospect of letting go.

The men followed in a close trio behind him.

Blake stopped beside a truck and opened the passenger side door, feeling around for something inside the cab. He reappeared with a bottle of Wild Turkey.

"Okay little shit, make it rain," he said, and cracked the top off the bottle. He took a long pull on the neck and handed it to Feedmaster, who did the same and passed it over to the nervous, skinny one in a pecking order.

No one offered any to Tom. "I need an open space," he said.

Blake smiled and winked to the other two. His eyes narrowed with cruel mirth. "No problem," he said. The skinny one giggled nervously.

The three men passed the bottle around while Blake led them to a clearing behind the bush, away from the road and the lights of the Thirsty Boy. Behind them, the music faded and became a vague vibration.

They stopped in a large clearing littered with the debris of mankind—tires, pop cans, beer bottles, cigarette butts and empty packages. Discarded paper bags blew softly onto tree trunks and held close.

"Here we are," Blake said, standing with hands outstretched. "A clearing. Did you need anything else? Something witchy? Eye of toad? Phone to God?" The others laughed. The skinny one held the bottle and splashed some more bourbon down his throat. Tom couldn't feel the hum of the bar music anymore, but he could sense something else in the air, another vibration. A bad one.

He ignored them, ignored their fag jokes and hippie shots, and slow descent into drunkenness. He closed his eyes, and before moving away from them, wished he'd thought to get the fifty up front. He always forgot that.

Standing on a rise of prairie grass, he closed his mind off.

Tom drifted away, up into the sky. Up high, to a dizzying space where there was nothing but air, dry, warm air. He let the sky sink into him, touching it, stroking it, bringing it closer, pushing it away, feeling around for the rain. In the eastern sky, about forty miles from where he stood, he could feel the first licks of moisture. It gathered first in his mouth, and then began to settle on his body: under his arms, down his back, at the back of his neck, setting his hair on end as his energy joined with the fat, pregnant droplets of water. He felt the rain, and tugged.

Blake drank from the bottle and watched the hippie standing still as a statue, sweating, from exertion, maybe, or drugs. The adventure had lost its entertainment value. The Wild Turkey was creating other possibilities.

The other two were staring at Blake, waiting for him to make his next move, so they could follow suit. Little yes-boys.

"Hey! Faggot! Where's the fuckin' rain, boy?" he shouted, the booze taking its toll on his consonants, so that they came out soft and slurred.

The skinny one, Gleason, giggled.

Tom didn't move from the rise of prairie grass, or even acknowledge Blake or the others.

Feedmaster, known to Oxburgers as Ben Jagger, took his turn at the bottle, feeling the familiar chest-pounding anticipation of a fight.

Blake looked at Gleason and Jagger. "I think Hippie there is on drugs."

"You bet your ass," Gleason said. Piss-drunk from five beers and a few ounces of Wild Turkey, he had found his tongue. "You bet your ass, Blake. Stoned on drugs."

"Fuckin' drugs, dope is for dopes," Blake said, grabbing the bottle back from Jagger. He drained it, and gripping the neck of the bottle, tossed it into the surrounding brush, where it landed with a thud. He muttered "druggie" under his breath and licked his lips, looking at the fuckin' hippie from out of town. Always hated those hippie types, showing up and taking advantage of a guy's wife without so much as a howdy-do. Wife-fuckers, for sure.

"Those guys are wife-fuckers," he said into the air.

Jagger smiled cruelly. That was it then. Blake's wife was a sore point with Blake. Could be the odd drifter was a better prospect in bed than a five-minute toss with Blake, who was called Minute Rice by his wife. Jagger knew for a fact. He smiled.

Tom pulled into the sky, tugged. The water poured off him now, the rain as much a part of him as of the sky. He was aware of nothing else. His arms moved up without his knowing it, his hands opened. The coming rain dribbled down his arms. His plaid shirt and the T-shirt underneath were wet right through, and began soaking into the oilskin jacket. His jeans were wet in the crotch and down the back of the legs, as though he'd pissed himself.

He caught it. It was firmly his now, and he pulled harder, the hot humid air coming closer. He held it warm and wet and solid, a mass, a body of rain. He held it high above their heads and let it go.

There was a moment of pure stunned surprise when the first issue of rain poured forth. Gleason uttered a shocked, "Hugghm?" when Blake stepped forward to the stock-still Tom.

"Holy fuck," muttered Jagger.

In the sudden rain, Blake stared stupidly into the sky for a second, one leg stopped in midstep. Then his face lost its look of stupefaction and took on one of nasty determination. He reached awkwardly into the side pocket of his jeans and took something out, working it in his hand until the light from the moon caught it and it glinted sharply.

He stepped toward Tom, whose arms were just coming down, and whose eyes were just opening up. Tom wore an expression of complete satisfaction, removed totally from the scene around him. He looked at the men in a semicircle around him, and couldn't stop the words before they came out.

"Fifty buck—" he began, and stopped, as his eyes caught the curve of Blake's raised arm, the knife flashing at the end of it. He screamed.

"FUCKIN' HIPPIE FUCKER!" The knife came down, missing Tom's head by inches. Blake's arm glanced painfully off Tom's thigh and threw both of them off balance. They fell.

Tom rolled out of the way, only to be kicked in the side by a smelly boot. Jagger smiled grimly and leaned over, slugging Tom hard in the face, catching the corner of his eye. Tom, caught by surprise, cried out in pain. Jagger pulled his leg back to kick again.

The rain came down more heavily. It fell harder as Jagger repeatedly kicked.

Blake regained his feet and bent over to retrieve the knife. All around them the rain penetrated the dry ground, with a constant, satisfying *thud thud*.

Tom saw the knife glinting dangerously in the moonlight. He stared, fascinated, as Blake stumbled toward him, glassy-eyed, filled with stupid rage.

Gleason watched with equal fascination. He shook his head and thought about calling out for Blake to stop, but the sparkling end of that knife might come toward *him* if he did that, and that would be bad, very bad indeed, he thought, before turning tail and pounding into the bush. He didn't know it, but he cried out as he ran.

"Cut you up," Blake muttered. Jagger watched, aroused. He nodded into the rain, looking up only once at the sky and thinking, *Little shit made it rain for sure*, before turning his eyes back to Blake and what he was going to do. *For sure.*

Tom leapt to his feet, his teeth clenched. If Blake saw the man's face change, the rapid exchange of fear for something darker, he didn't let on. Tom, body tensed for fight now, circled away from Blake. There was an electricity in the air that hadn't been there before. The rain was a torrent now, coming down in sheets, a nearly solid wall of water. Tom saw Blake trying to wipe water from his eyes.

"I CAN'T FUCKIN' SEE YOU!" Blake yelled over the rain.

Behind him, Tom could hear Jagger.

"Get 'im, Blakey!"

Something electric crackled in the air. Thunder, distant at first, approached more rapidly. The sky lit up with the sudden flash of lightning. Blake couldn't see Tom's face, but if he had, he would have been frightened.

Tom stood straight up in the rain, a pillar. Around him the lightning touched down. He was smiling.

Jagger ran when the lightning touched down just four feet in front of him. He felt the vibration as it hit the ground. It threw him back on his ass. He called to Blake to get the fuck out of there.

"LIGHTNING!" he shouted soundlessly through the thunder. Blake didn't even turn.

Through the downpour, Tom's form seemed to move and waver through a half bottle of Wild Turkey and the torrential waves from the sky. The man would light up with the mercurial strikes of lightning, and disappear in the dark. He didn't move, though.

Lightning crashed right beside Blake, sending current through a puddle and up into his feet. He felt it with surprise. He took a step toward Tom.

Through the rain, he saw Tom's face turned toward the sky, the odd smile playing on his lips, his eyes closed. Blake raised his knife.

Tom lowered his face and looked straight into Blake's own narrowed eyes. Lightning crashed down, hitting the end of the knife blade, knocking Blake to his knees and making him scream in sudden pain. His arm smoldered, the bolt gone through the blade and out his elbow into the ground. Like a knife.

While Blake howled in pain, Tom reached out and pushed him over with his boot. He fell, still holding his arm.

Tom's breath came in gasps and shakes; his body was drenched through. The lightning stopped as suddenly as it had begun. The rain continued, a happy downpour now.

Tom moved Blake over onto his side, ignoring his injured arm. He felt around for the man's wallet in his shit-kicker jeans and pulled it out. He tore two twenties and a ten from the mess of bills, letting some of them fall to the wet ground.

"Fifty bucks, you lousy hick," he said. He tossed the wallet into the pool of water at Blake's feet. The rain was letting up. Tom's heart still pounded in his chest. But the anger was falling away. He crumpled the bills into his front pocket and grabbed his pack from the edge of the clearing, where it lay soaking. It would be heavy. He was used to it.

He walked through the clearing without looking backward, teeth still gritted, exhaustion pouring over him as the water squished through his boots with every step. He walked back toward the highway that he came from, not worrying about the beer he never paid for, the man lying in the clearing, clutching his burned-up arm.

Served him right.

Tom walked into the night, firmly aware of the crumpled bills against his thigh.

There was a day's walk between him and where he was going.

He was pissed off. He hadn't even picked up any matches in the bar. He always felt like having a cigarette after a good rain.

ONE

Residents of Goodlands, North Dakota, were known to say that you could get anywhere you wanted in under an hour, and it was true, provided that you wanted to go either to Bismarck or onto Interstate 94. If you wanted to get to Canada, South Dakota, Minnesota, or Montana, you had better pack a lunch. Smack dab in the middle of the state, Goodlands was a town on its own. It had been incorporated a hundred years before, and its residents had long ago become as self-sufficient as they were self-contained. They had what they needed. The earth was rich and fertile, the sky was far and wide. Gas was cheap, taxes low, values high, and the lifestyle was built around family, unlike those other places where the Interstate might take you. If you took the time to ask, residents would tell you that it was the perfect place to farm and raise a family. As the sign said, at the crossroad from Oxburg into Goodlands, it was "A Good Little Town!"

Until the drought.

It started inauspiciously enough, as droughts do. Four years earlier, *The Farmer's Almanac* had predicted a wet, cool spring for the region, followed by a dryish June and July and a wet August—about what the Northern Great Plains could expect year in and year out, with slight variations on the theme. Goodlands, along with the rest of the Northern Great Plains, generally got an annual rainfall of about twenty-two inches. The first year of the drought, that expected rainfall had all but disappeared, and they averaged no better than nine inches. The surrounding towns of Avis, Mountmore, Oxburg, Adele, Larson, and Weston all reported average to just-below-average rainfall that year. In year two, Goodlands saw six inches. Last year there'd been none. The worst year they'd had since 1934. The towns around Goodlands continued to receive their rain, as promised. No disasters. But Goodlands stayed dry.

A bad season can do real harm to a community of farmers. Two bad seasons can start the balls of bankruptcy rolling. Three bad seasons can lead to bank foreclosures, family breakups, alcoholism, violence, and the death of something else, something that you can't name. The people of Goodlands were currently facing their fourth year of drought. If it didn't rain by July, they would be looking into the face of that nameless something. Many of the folks already were.

Drought wasn't the only bad luck that Goodlands was having. Lately the town had seemed cursed. There had been a series of fires out in the Badlands—the unofficial name for the only part of town that could be called a slum, a collection of trailers and tract houses whose inhabitants regularly shopped the refuse dump, picking through the discards of Goodlands' better off. The Badlands was an unfortunate place for fires, since the town's volunteer fire department was set up clear across town beside the Roman Catholic church. By the time they called everybody up and met there before heading out, siren screaming, to that godforsaken place, there was often little they could do except extinguish what was left of the embers.

Once two trailer homes went ballistic at once, their electrical systems igniting and popping hydro lines and sending neighbors flying into the dirt streets screaming and hollering for the cops. Flames took both trailers. One belonged to one of the few good families down that way, the Castles, who had four children ranging in age from two to fourteen. The other was no great loss. Teddy Boychuk was a drunk and a louse who slapped his women around and—so it was suspected—had raped his own daughter before she took off for points unknown.

There had been other odd things, not as serious as the fires, but nonetheless troubling to town fathers and the local cops. There was an increase in fender benders over the past couple of years, some of them getting nasty, with the drivers pounding each other before they could be stopped. The town cafe, Rosie's, had its freezers go out for no good reason and lost about two weeks' worth of meat, ice cream, and frozen food, at a time when money wasn't exactly floating around town. When they got Larry Watson in the next day to take a look, it turned out the freezers were unplugged. Just like that. Larry Watson laughed and charged them for the call anyway. They couldn't even make an insurance claim, although they tried.

Goodlands was having a run of bad luck. Some of the people were starting to say—only half joking—that the place was cursed. Especially the people in the Badlands. After the last fire several families moved from the area, causing a drop in the welfare rolls. As Mayor Shoop said, good riddance to bad news (it was conveniently forgotten that due to the drought many of Goodlands' better families were accepting relief). But people were still uneasy. Churches were doing a booming business for the first time in years. Every Sunday, and even during the week at the Catholic, the pews were full—and many of the faces unfamiliar. People were nervous. It seemed to folks that something was up. They just didn't know what.

* * *

Karen Grange pushed the box of Kleenex a little closer to the edge of her desk, but Loreena Campbell was having none of it. *She wants me to see her cry.* The tears ran down Loreena's face in streaks and fell—appropriately, Karen thought—on the piles of papers scattered across the desk. Karen had felt like crying, too. But she hadn't. She wouldn't.

Bruce Campbell was now sitting very quietly next to his wife, one hand on each of his thighs, as though he was about to stand. His face was still and very pale. He stared into the space across the desk. He hadn't spoken for a while.

There was nothing left for Karen to do or say; it had all been said. There were a couple more documents to sign, but since the Big Daddy of the papers, the Foreclosure, was lying crumpled-up in a corner of the office, she thought she would wait until some of the dust settled before mentioning them. Maybe she would wait a few days and bring the remaining papers out to the farm.

"Can't you talk to them?" Bruce asked again.

"I'm afraid it would do no good." She could go through the reasons one more time, but they seemed meaningless now.

She tried not to look at Loreena. The woman's nose had begun to run and Karen wondered morbidly if she would wipe it on her sleeve. Bruce sat, looking more helpless than any man should.

"You have people in Arizona, isn't that right, Bruce?" she said. He looked up.

"Arizona?" he said blankly. It had been the wrong thing to say. There was no farming in Arizona.

Karen finally stood up on legs that felt a little shaky, too.

"I can let you go out the back if you don't feel up to facing . . ." She let the sentence trail off. It was midafternoon. Coffee time in a small town. Everyone the Campbells knew would be walking around town or sitting down to a cuppa joe at the cafe. Loreena's nose was fire engine red, as were her eyes. Her makeup was askew, her nose running. For her sake at least, Karen hoped they would slip out the back door.

Loreena stood up. "No. I want them to see me," she said. "I *want* them to know what happened. I *want* them to know what you *did*." A dribble of mucus ran to her lip. Karen watched in horrified fascination.

"You could do something. You just won't," Loreena said, nearly shouting, as though she could no longer contain herself, like Bruce when he smashed his fist down on the desk.

Karen couldn't move. Bruce looked up at his wife with the same glassy stare that he'd had since he'd first heard the word. *In the beginning was the word. And the word was foreclosure. And the heavens did open.*

"Farms and Families and Commercial Farm Credit," Loreena spat. It was the CFC slogan. To Karen's horror, Loreena began to sing the jingle played every hour on Channels Seven and Nine, the two local stations in Capawatsa County: "Commercial Farm Credit knows your family needs. Commercial Farm Credit, a part of your family tree. Get to know us soon! Farms and Families and Commercial Farm Credit—a team! Commercial—"

"Loreena, *please*—" Karen started.

"No! Don't you *dare* say anything to me! You. Are"—she walked over to the door of Karen's office and opened it—"a Cold. Heartless. Bitch." Jennifer, at the counter, looked up embarrassed. She had been listening. The bank, mercifully, was empty. It usually was.

Loreena stepped through the open door. By then she'd begun crying again. Sobbing, really; most of the tears had gone out of her.

Bruce finally stood up to follow his wife. Karen looked at him sympathetically and held her hand out.

"Bruce, if there's ever anything I can do personally—"

He spat on the rug in front of her.

"No, I don't think there's anything, *Karen*." He followed his wife.

Bruce managed to slam the front door of the bank closed. He had to push it hard on its air hinge to manage it, but he did.

The bank was silent. Karen was still standing in front of her desk when she caught Jennifer's eye. Jennifer looked away. She was only a teller, with her own family's money in the bank, waiting for her own termination notice, waiting for her family's farm, the Bilken place, to be shut down; but she was a lifelong member of the community, born and bred in Goodlands, North Dakota. She was an Us. Karen Grange somehow, over the last four years, had become, immutably a Them. She leaned forward and slowly closed her door against Jennifer's accusing looks.

Automatically she went to the corner of the office and picked up the Notice of Foreclosure and uncrumpled it. She laid it out on the desk and ran her hands over it, trying in vain to flatten the paper again, even though she knew that ultimately she would just have another one typed. She stepped carefully around the dark spot on the carpet, Bruce's parting shot. She yanked a couple of tissues out of the box on the desk and squatted beside the ugly blotch on the carpet.

She dabbed at it with the tissues, at once disgusted and badly hurt. Her first week on the job, Bruce Campbell had come in to get a loan for a combine. At the time, Karen couldn't have picked a combine out of a lineup of backhoes, and said as much.

"I guess I should know what I'm approving a loan for," she had said apologetically. Rather than take advantage of her ignorance, he'd smiled kindly and said, "It's the one with the big snorting thing that sticks out the top, and the blades in front that cut the grain." He rotated his hand, wiggling the fingers.

She had laughed, then asked him conspiratorially what a backhoe was. After that first time, whenever she ran into Bruce in town, she always asked him how the combine was working out.

"Better than a backhoe would have," he always said. Two winters before, when Karen had been down a week with the flu, Loreena had dropped in to see if she needed anything. "I know you don't have family in town," she'd said, by way of explanation.

And then Karen foreclosed on their farm.

She pinched the tissue and dug it deeper into the carpet, scraping rather than dabbing, her eyes stinging, but not quite filling with tears. The worst part was that she was getting used to it.

She pushed the Kleenex box back to its regular place on the desk and started to gather up the papers. She did these things, not only because they would have to be done but because she had to do something to remove herself, pronto, from the emotions that were still free-floating around the room, threatening to become her own. Her hands were shaking. She held them together tightly, willing them to stop. She could not be upset. No emotional involvement. Company policy.

Until last year, Karen had been a rigorous professional, keeping a careful, required distance in her duties as manager in Goodlands' only bank, and at the same time maintaining a personal connection to the town. She was a presence. She sat on the committees, participated in the fund-raisers, went to the Christmas dance, to the Spring Fling, and to the Firefighters' Barbecue and Blowout. The Spring Fling had been canceled this year, and the barbecue, even if it went on as scheduled, would likely not even raise the amount required for the television set the firefighters wanted to keep for the on-call volunteer. No one had any money.

Karen was trying to maintain appearances in spite of the way things had changed. She still played the part, certainly dressed the part, thanks to a closetful of clothes. She was Bank, in and out, and if this was the bank's darkest hour, who would be able to tell?

But that rigid professionalism had been slipping, along with her branch's bottom line. In spite of fifteen years of experience, annual training sessions, and a copy of the Commercial Farm Credit Policy of Standards in her top drawer, these were the people she knew, the people she lived in this town with, the people who had changed her life for the better. They had welcomed her, made her feel like a part of things, and had all but erased $30,000 worth of bad memories from her mind. Up until the first big foreclosure, two years before, people had waved a friendly hello in the streets and asked after her health and asked for her advice, invited her to dinner, and to parties. She believed they had liked her. But company policy or not, it was not CFC that was foreclosing on the farms. It was Karen.

Bruce and Loreena Campbell might not have believed it, but Karen had gone to bat for them. Her good intentions had been rewarded with a written reprimand and the reminder that she should know better. It was judiciously added that she, of all people, should be in a better position to ease people through their "financial transitions," given her own experience. "You are one who should be able to advise from personal experience, without getting personally involved," the line read, "since your own commitments to Commercial Farm Credit are ongoing." Karen herself was into CFC for what her father might have called a shitload of money. It was, in fact, why she was in Goodlands at all.

She had tried to help. The Campbell farm had been in the same family since 1890. There were rumors that the father of the brood, John Mason Campbell himself, had paid Indians in guns and furs to move on, and kept it up until he had nearly eighty acres. The farm had grown some over the years, and when land prices went high, Bruce Campbell sold some acreage, as did many of the farmers in the area. It was a family farm.

Karen had gone out to see them two weeks before and had spent an hour and a half in the kitchen with Bruce, his brother Jimmy, and Loreena, trying to drop hints, to break it to them easily, to prepare them as much as she could without breaking any more rules. They had seen her visit as a hopeful sign. As a sign that things weren't as bad as they looked. Loreena had actually complimented Karen on her outfit. They'd all had coffee, and

Loreena had shown Karen pictures of their new nephew, living out in Arizona.

Karen put the papers, now neatly piled, into the top drawer of the desk. She checked her watch. It was two P.M. The Franklins would be there in forty minutes or so. Normally she would have snuck out for a bite to eat and a cup of coffee at the cafe, and a chat with whoever was in there, but by now the Campbells would have been all the way through the main street.

Karen had a feeling she would not be popular today. Everyone probably knew that the Franklins were next. There were no secrets in a small town. She had no interest in the glances that would come her way, only to be diverted when she tried to meet their eyes; no interest in the frightened faces, the pariah treatment. She should have thought of this and brought lunch.

The Franklins would become the fifth foreclosure since the beginning the fiscal year. A banner year, you could say. And these were not the foreclosures a normal year saw; these were not the borderline farms, the small farms, the badly managed farms. Those had come and gone at the beginning of the drought. These were the real farms, the family farms—successful operations that in some cases had been running for decades.

Left now were mostly farmers who were smart, who'd had their farms for a hundred years not because they were lucky but because they planned every move down to the dime, had business plans, used resources and studied to keep ahead of the others. Theirs were the farms with reserves, with backup. If any homesteads could withstand a few bad years, those farms could. They hung on to the end. The Campbells and the Franklins were both farm families like that. A testament to what was happening in Goodlands.

In a strange way, these were her people. They had been around when she first arrived, eight years before. They had gone out of their way to make her feel welcome, had invited her to be a part of the community. Her first community, really. The first time she had really belonged.

Last year there had been a grand total of six foreclosures or bankruptcies for the year, all at least middling-sized farms, one large one, all family-owned. The year before there had been four. All were casualties of the drought, poor planning, bad or no insurance. If Karen's intuition was on target, then another three could be expected to go under before the end of the year. These were large figures for a town the size of Goodlands. Frighteningly large figures. The bottom line was getting bleaker, and if things didn't improve, then she, and Goodlands, would lose the bank. Profits were her job, and profits this year would be nonexistent. Management might give her a year to recover, maybe more if they got rain this summer and a recovery began, but not much more. She wouldn't lose her job, of course, but she would be transferred. Forced to leave. And if it might not miss her, she would certainly miss Goodlands.

Karen heard a tentative tap on her door. She looked at her watch. It was 2:45 P.M.

"Yes?" she said quietly. Her heart began to thud in her chest.

"The Franklins are here," Jennifer said, and opened the door. Karen stood up and went to meet them. Jessie Franklin tried a hopeful smile. Leonard was behind her, blocked somewhat by his larger wife. Jessie was pregnant.

"Oh, please, sit down, Jessie," Karen said. When Leonard stepped into view, she saw that he was holding their three-year-old. So they'd brought Elizabeth with them. All three were dressed in good town clothes for their trip to see Karen the banker. Her heart sank. She wanted to bolt from the room. Slam the door against them and hide behind her desk. She wanted to go home.

"Leonard, how are you?" she said, and held the door open for them to come in. As Leonard entered, he put his hand lightly on Karen's shoulder, allowing her to go ahead of him. Karen felt herself losing control. A simple, kind gesture. She quickly moved around the desk to her chair. Her eyes stung again, and she blinked back tears, turning her head so they would not see. Leonard put Elizabeth down beside her mother's chair and gently patted her head. The child stood between them with a shy smile on her face, one finger in her mouth.

Karen tugged purposefully at the cuffs of her no-longer-quite-new cream color Liz Claiborne suit. Her favorite. She steeled herself and the moment passed.

She smiled and thanked them for coming. She said hello to Elizabeth and told Jessie she looked good, inquiring politely about her due date. Two more months.

Oh God.

She caught Leonard's glance when silence fell in the space between polite small talk and the real reason they were there. It was in his eyes. He knew. Already, he looked braced, stricken. Jessie fussed with Elizabeth beside her. She avoided looking at Karen. They both knew. It wouldn't be any harder than it had to be. They would make it easy for her.

Karen got up and closed her office door. She went back to sit behind the desk.

"Leonard, Jessie. When I was out to see you the other day, I had information . . ." she began.

Outside, the sun remained high in the sky for most of the rest of the day. By the time Karen drove home from the bank at the end of the afternoon the temperature hovered between seventy-nine and eighty, and the air seemed to waver and shake in front of her. The sun wouldn't set until nearly ten at night. It was mid-June. The longest days of the year had begun.

Karen Grange had come to Goodlands from Minneapolis, courtesy of Commercial Farm Credit. They couldn't have known it at the time, nor would they have cared one way or the other, but they had saved her from herself by transferring her.

It was meant to be a punishment of sorts, a banishment to the sticks for making the ultimate mistake. Karen Grange, bank manager, manager of other people's money, doler out of credit, had gotten herself into what was known in the office as "very serious trouble." Money trouble.

Before Goodlands, Karen had been a manager of a small branch in the city. She didn't like to talk or think about the time before the city, but it too, had a bearing on the facts. The facts being that Karen—before Goodlands, before eight years of pretty countryside, of wheat and barley farms, of open skies and sunsets that went on for hours, before she rented the little house outside of town still called the Mann House by locals, before she learned about seasons and harvests and planting and knowing your neighbors and asking after someone's garden, children, husband, and health (in that order), before learning to wait patiently in line at the Dry Goods while Peggy finished telling Chimmy about the afghan she made for the Houstons' baby (and then asking nicely about the baby herself)—Karen had been living in the middle of the city in a condo she couldn't afford and slowly, calmly, and efficiently suffocating herself under a heavy blanket of debt.

Soon after she moved up at the bank, from teller to loan officer, she was encouraged to use the bank's services herself. She applied for a small loan to buy a car. The payments were easy. She made decent money, and would, each year, make more. This was justification for moving to a better apartment. That accomplished, she discovered the joys of no-money-down. Furniture, towels, bedding, linen, kitchenware, small appliances, all required the subtleties not available on low-end items. She applied for credit cards. In the beginning, she limited her credit-card buying to what she definitely needed. When she'd filled the first card to the limit, she stopped for breath, frightened by what she saw on the floor of her bedroom closet. The line between need and want had blurred. There was a cut-crystal vase on the floor of the closet, still in the box. There was an unopened package of Monday-to-Sunday matching bras and panties that she had bought on a whim as a gift for a friend and then decided were inappropriate—for either of them. There were sheet sets, and towels—beautiful, soft, triple-weave towels so thick and absorbent that you need only wrap one around your body to be dried. There was a full-length leather coat, too heavy for a hanger, that had fallen in a heap and stayed there. Not warm enough for North Dakota winters, too warm for summer, too delicate for unpredictable spring, the coat could be worn only about two months of the year.

When she opened her bedroom closet that day and saw all that credit lying unused on the floor, she had the first of what would be many good scares. Something had gotten away from her and it had to be grabbed back. And she did grab it back. The first time.

It took her a year to pay off her debts. A year of deprivation, of paying cash, of buying on sale. But she paid off the furniture, the towels, the sheets, the Monday-to-Sunday underwear set, and the countless other purchases that littered her condo. Once they were paid off, she had to celebrate. To celebrate, she bought herself a little something. In retrospect, it seemed as though paying everything off had been surprisingly easy. Nothing at all, really. And she still had all her things.

The year of denial had taken its toll on Karen, and she celebrated the end of her financial celibacy frequently. Then it took half the time to fill up the card.

Karen didn't need a shrink to tell her why she shopped. She wouldn't have spent good money on one, even if she'd had any by that point. She could have had the answer for $3.95 from any women's magazine on the shelf, usually during the big buying seasons of spring and fall.

A lifetime of denial, growing up with parents so ill-equipped to handle their own finances, so poor that the newest thing in the house was the latest note from a creditor.

It was the newness of things. It was the look and touch and smell of things so new you could still smell the fumes of the factory on them, could still see the fingerprints of the underpaid workers who had put them together, could still, if you wanted to, preserve the newness of them by leaving them in their boxes, taking them out to admire and pet, and then putting them away, still brand, brand-new, price sticker still attached, un-marked-down, unreduced, as high-priced as ever. It was the standing in the store and holding something and wishing for it, and then having the power to buy it and take it home. It was the shiver down her back when she ran her hands over mater-ial so fine and soft that it was barely there. It was pawing through mail order catalogs from boutiques in cities far away; the thrill of filling in the card, giving her number over the phone, of asking for something "rushed," so it would be there the next day when she got home from work.

It was the way she looked in the clothes that she bought. A whole new Karen. *Tall, willowy, and dark* were her good points. Clothes, well-cut clothes, looked as good on her as they did on the models in the magazines. If Karen's beauty was quieter than the models', the clothes were the great equalizer. Her dark hair set off her fair skin, which glowed in the creams and whites, and the deep, rich earth tones that she preferred. Her brown eyes, widely set, were balanced by a straight, small nose. Her attractiveness was the kind that could go unnoticed for years, only to be sud-denly seen by surprise. Men did not swing their heads around when she passed, but had on occasion, over dinner, found them-selves staring at her. "You have a very pretty face," they'd say.

"It's the jacket," she would say earnestly. As far as Karen was concerned, the clothes made the woman. So she bought them.

It took her three years to get into serious trouble. That was after a year of applying for new cards so that she could pit one against the other in a battle as familiar to shoppers as the ring-ing of a till. She would write checks, "forgetting" to put on the date, putting the wrong check in the right envelope.

Serious trouble was litigation, and a threat to garnishee wages. By that time, thanks to cards, checks, rent-to-own, and time payments, she was more than $30,000 in debt.

Hence the letter from the CFC head office. They "promoted" her to Goodlands to punish her, and there she found her home. Goodlands, North Dakota, where, she wryly noted, there was no shopping. There hadn't been much to leave behind. The stuff, after all, went with her.

The house in Goodlands was at least ten square feet larger than the condo in Minneapolis. It was a farmhouse, new by Goodlands standards, but built and rebuilt and added on to from the one-room shack it must have been at one time. The land since then had been parceled off and sold until it was a small three-acre property retaining only the apple orchard, set off back from the house, and the yard. The last tenants had landscaped the yard with a lush green lawn and a gleaming rock garden that Karen didn't care for. Other than a darling hand-pump, painted red, also courtesy of the previous tenants, the back of the house was empty, a vast open expanse that Karen also didn't care for.

The house needed something. Some imprint that would make it her own.

When Karen was in high school her family moved to a part of town that was, if anything, worse than the one they'd left. They formerly had lived in a house in a working-class neighborhood. They were living paycheck to paycheck, like most everyone on the block. Her dad was working at the time at a factory that manufactured the plastic casings for computers. When he lost his job, they had to give up the house. The house was rented, but it had been Karen's home for twelve years.

She changed high schools and the family moved to an apartment downtown. A fifth-floor walk-up. Karen's bedroom window looked out over an alley. If she looked straight across, she could see into the bedroom window of two little kids who lived next door. She had her curtains from the old house, and she kept them drawn.

It was then that she really started thinking about a better way of life. With the noise of the neighbors, the cars, the dogs audible through the window that she kept closed, she dreamed about a big, quiet yard and the family she would one day have, sitting out on the lawn on a clean white blanket, sharing food from a bountiful wicker picnic basket.

There was always a man and two little children. The children and the man were vague and varied in her imaginings, but the yard never changed. It was wide, expansive, green and lush. And it had a gazebo. Sometimes, in her dreams, Karen would dance with her man inside the gazebo and the only sound she would hear would be the click of her sling-back heels on the floor as she swung around in his arms. Even if, many years later, she knew it was a naive and overly romantic image, the clean, warm, *new* picture of it never really left her.

Her fourth summer in Goodlands, Karen built a gazebo.

"A *what*bo?" was the reaction she got from George Kleinsel, the carpenter she hired on the advice of a lady in town to build the tiny building that would finish the yard. Karen drew it out for him, adding carefully thought-out details like the country-style gingerbread archway, and the white-pillared posts, and the low picket fencing that she liked to go around it. And a concrete floor—not mentioning that the sound of sling-back heels echoing under the shingled roof was the inspiration for that particular detail.

George was at her front door with Bob Garfield, as promised, by eight A.M. on the next Saturday, to put the gazebo up over the weekend. George said it wouldn't take more than a couple of days. "Painting's extra," he told her, with his omnipresent cigarette dangling.

The gazebo did not go up in two days, as scheduled. But it was no fault of George's.

Karen could remember the day only as a succession of scenes, vivid, but incomplete. She did remember leaning on the porch with a cup of coffee, ready for a day of watching the men work on the image that she'd had for so many years. She remembered teasing George about the legendary state of disrepair his own house was in.

"George, I hear your wife still doesn't have a bathroom door," she'd called out. George nodded, smiling, blushing.

"Oh yeah, gonna do it this year," he told her.

"You bin saying that for ten years," Garfield said.

"What in heck's name she need a door for? Something secret she's doing in there?" It went on like that about his roof, the siding piled in his yard, and the truck up on blocks behind his garage.

It had been warm that morning, the beginning of summer. The men looked hot by ten o'clock, in their overalls and shirt-sleeves, working without hats in the sun.

They spent the better part of the morning doing what George called "pissing around"—measuring, marking, adding numbers and lines to the drawing of the gazebo that Karen had supplied. It was nearly eleven when they fired up the backhoe and started breaking up the earth.

Whenever Karen thought about it later, as she did frequently, the rest of it seemed to move much more slowly that it really had. She on the porch in uncustomary T-shirt and denims, George on the backhoe with heavy headphones covering his ears, Garfield behind him waving his arms in instruction, or standing and smoking, leaning on a shovel, the classic pose of a man at work. The machine roared and screamed and clunked. There was a scrape of metal on earth, metal on metal, and finally, the oddly definitive sound of metal striking something unexpected.

Garfield waving his arms like a flag man at a race; George not understanding, his face blustery red with frustration, shaking his head no, pointing to his headphones; Garfield frantically pointing to something in the ground, trying to shout above the engine. Karen was far enough away from the machine to catch some of what he was saying.

"—HIT SOMETHING!—" he screamed. "THERE'S A GODDAMN ANIMAL—"

Karen rested her mug on the railing of the porch and stepped down the stairs, hands in her pockets, approaching the site just as George was shutting the machine down.

There was a sudden silence after the engine stopped.

Garfield, face ashen in the bright morning sunshine, pointing to the huge rent in the earth, leaning over, seeming to not want to take the couple of steps required to get closer.

He said, "There's a goddamn skull. A goddamn *human skull!*" George's eyes widening, his head moving slowly downward to look.

Karen stopped moving. From where she stood she could see only something white—gray, really, a curve disappearing into black earth, surrounded by lush green grass. But really, she saw nothing.

"Holy shit," George said. Gingerly, he crouched closer to the ground, but got no closer to the place where Garfield was pointing. His head turned and he looked at Karen.

"Better call Henry," he said. Henry Barker was the sheriff. Karen stood unmoving. "Go on, Miss Grange. It is what he said it is." It was not so much the words George spoke as the way he said them that made Karen walk woodenly to the house and dial the phone and explain and then, equally woodenly, come back out to the yard, moving no closer than she had stood before.

The weekend that the gazebo was supposed to go up turned into more than two weeks of machines tearing up her yard, looking for other bodies. The woman, and it had been a woman, clearly had been dead for many, many years. A pathologist from the city said she had been dead for maybe more than a hundred years, prompting everyone to believe there was a cemetery under Karen's yard. For two weeks they searched the yard carefully for signs of others but found none. They tore up the yard and the property beyond, which no longer belonged to the people who owned the house, and the area took on the look of a new development before they decided that the woman had been buried there alone, for reasons unknown.

The pathologist had said that the woman had been between

the ages of nineteen and thirty. She had never had a child, and her hair had been red or auburn, this last clue coming from several strands that still clung grimly to the skull the men had seen first. It was the hair that bothered Karen most of all. It had given her more of a picture of the gruesome find.

The woman's identity was never really confirmed. There were decayed scraps of fabric, determined to be from her clothes, in the ground with her, but no papers or jewelry. There had been teeth in the skull, but since dental records from the turn of the century were all but nonexistent, the teeth were of no help, except for determining an approximate age. There were also no real clues to how she died. There were no marks or scars on the bones.

People dropped by unabashedly, asking what had happened, what she knew. George, Garfield, and Karen became local celebrities for a while, with George and Garfield relishing the telling and retelling. Garfield might have seen it first, but it was George who had known enough to tell Karen to get the police.

"I said to her, 'Better call Henry,' and she stood there, scared, like, you know. So I said, 'Go on, Miss Grange,' and finally she did."

There was speculation that the woman had died suddenly, given that there was no casket or sign of one, and given the state of health evident in the remains. There was no way to prove that she had been murdered, but that's what was said in town. Even long after the yard was put back the way it had been; even long after the gazebo was built. Her identity was never discovered, and her remains were reburied in the Catholic cemetery with a numbered stone.

Talk died down slowly, and the subject still came up on occasion. Karen was asked sometimes if her house was haunted. She would always smile politely and tell them that she did hear strange noises at night, but that she was pretty sure it was the plumbing.

Truth of it was, the whole thing had put Karen in a state of unease. She had been so comfortable in the little house, as though leaving the city had changed everything inside her, rearranged it so that it was Goodlands that had always been home, the home that she had returned to, and the city a short, uncomfortable memory. Then that horrible thing happened, and it set her back.

She had tried to put things back into perspective. When the gazebo had been up for a solid month, and she still hadn't done much more than walk around it, she decided to go out there and have a sit.

She poured herself a glass of wine and took it with her into the gazebo, her sneakers not making much of an impact on the concrete floor that George had carefully, if quickly, laid down for her. No clicking heels, no swirling dance with her imagined husband.

It had been around nine o'clock. The sun was dropping in the west, and she leaned on the railing and watched. The sky was broad and beautiful, lighting up that night with pink and orange, the sun still a bright ball. Fluffy white clouds scudded across the sky.

There was silence. At that time of night, cars were rare—the ones that went by were on their way to Clancy's, the roadhouse. The sound of crickets came only when the breeze blew the right way.

Karen stood in the gazebo with her back to the house. She took a sip of her wine and relaxed into the view, the outdoor sounds blending into, and finally becoming, the silence.

She stood that way for a few minutes, her mind wandering, feeling very pleased about the place.

It lasted only a few minutes.

The light had not yet faded into dark and yet it suddenly seemed like she couldn't see. She found herself squinting into the sudden dark, her forehead crunching into a frown. As it seemed to get darker, so the night sounds got closer. If she hadn't been leaning against the railing, she might have believed she was in the middle of a wild field.

She tried to shake it off by taking another sip of wine, but even as she did, she had the feeling that she was not entirely alone.

Feeling silly, she looked back toward the house, but it was too dark to make it out clearly. It looked as if it had disappeared. Been swallowed up.

And it was cold.

Karen was in light clothes; it was July. But a breeze had come up, and she felt it run up the leg holes of her shorts, and through the fabric of her blouse. The breeze ran over her skin and she felt uncomfortably naked.

She started thinking about the woman. How she died. At that moment, Karen felt quite sure that she had died badly. She knew she was spooking herself, but she couldn't get rid of the thought. She imagined the woman's face, contorted in terror as something unseen bore down on her. Her long auburn hair grabbed from behind, pulling her down to the ground, her feet slipping out from under her, sliding along the field, wet and muddy. Karen imagined her screams.

The vision was suddenly too real, and she forced herself to stop. But her peace and enjoyment were gone. She shuddered and cast a glance behind her. There was, of course, nothing there, but by then she was thoroughly spooked.

Karen stepped out of the gazebo and hurried in the direction of the house. As she got closer, she felt an overwhelming sense of relief that it hadn't disappeared, that she wasn't standing in the middle of an empty field, even though the thought was preposterous.

She closed the door behind her and put her glass aside without finishing the wine.

Much later, she looked out the back window again. It was getting dark. An hour had passed since she'd been outside. And the house was hot, not cold. It was, after all, July.

After that, she rarely went into the gazebo. Certainly never when it was dark.

But the image of the woman and the way she might have died never left her. Karen didn't entirely stop thinking about her until things dried up, and the drought got bad.

Vida Whalley slipped out of the house unnoticed, onto the dark dirt road out front. There were no streetlights on the road. In fact, there were very few in the whole of the Badlands. Just three: one at the beginning of the road that led out of the rest of town, one at the end, that led back out onto the interstate, and one in front of the trailer park. That one was easy enough to avoid if you wanted to. You just slipped into the trailer park through the back. You had to go through some bush and, during the rainy season, a terrible, muddy, slewy area that lay between Vida's house and the trailer park. Lucky for her, there hadn't been a rainy season in Goodlands for quite some time.

She wasn't going to the trailer park tonight. She crossed the road and slipped into the minefield of the Larabees'. After that, she would cut through the Frenchman's yard. The Larabees had two ugly dogs, not fighting dogs like her old man's, but fat, lazy hounds that could bark and give her away. Like all dogs in the Badlands, and in Goodlands too, they were loose. But she had a juicy present for the hounds. A couple of rabbits, that used to be cute, she supposed. Now they weren't. Now they were dead, shot by the old man for tomorrow's supper. Or maybe for a snack when he got home tonight, drunk, pissed off, and hungry. He'd probably be screaming for her to get her ass out of bed and cook them up when he got home. Too bad they would be gone. "What rabbits, Dad?" Ha ha. Too bad.

She began a soft call for the Larabee mutts.

"Here Cashus, hey boy, Digby, Cashus," she called softly. She heard their low growls begin, until they picked up the scent of the rabbits she carried in the plastic bag from the General. There was a hole in the bottom of the bag. She held the bag out in front of her.

There was a light on inside the Larabees', but it was on the far side of the house, in the bedroom. The dogs came forward, not ready to give up their growl, but curious now, at the familiar, tempting smell. They came closer, still not barking.

They recognized Vida, and Cashus started to wag his tail. He was a little friendlier than Digby, but they were both stupid dogs.

She threw the bag down in front of her and the dogs ran to it, heads down, sniffing. They pounced on the bag and starting ripping at the plastic. She stepped around them.

"Stupid mutts," she said in the same low, friendly voice. She walked through the yard, then through the Frenchman's yard, and then out into the bush, listening to the two dogs worry and growl at each other, fighting over her father's supper. Just like home. She smiled.

Hot as it was, Vida was wearing a hat. A baseball cap, with her long, dark hair bunched up and held in place with elastics and hairpins. She had on an oversized black T-shirt that belonged to her older brother. She'd had to take it from the dirty clothes on the floor of his bedroom and it stunk. The jeans she was wearing were dirty, too, but at least they were her own. A front pocket bulged with the big box of Redbird wooden matches that she'd taken from the kitchen and would replace later. She had hours yet before her brothers, her father, and her father's bitchy girlfriend got back from Clancy's. They never got home until they were thrown out, or after last call. Since they'd just been let back in after the last time they were barred, they would be on their best behavior. She had hours. It was only ten-thirty. She had waited only for full dark. It was important that she not be seen, or at least not recognized. That's why she wore the hat, and the big shirt. Anyway, she was tiny, not much over five feet, and if necessary could roll up into a ball and hide in the dark. No one would see her. No one ever had, on these late-night excursions.

Branches and twigs and dry leaves cracked under her running shoes, stuck to her pant legs and socks, and scratched at her arms, the only part exposed. She swore whenever it hurt. Now and then she stopped and picked up nice-sized branches and deadwood. She had a lot of bush to go through to get where she was going. The shirt really stunk. She tried to breathe up.

There wasn't a lot of bushland around Goodlands, since it was wide-open prairie farmland, but what bush there was seemed strategically placed, separating the Badlands from the rest of town. After ten minutes of scratching and pawing, Vida stepped out of the bush into the wide open spaces of Ed Kramer's barley field. Of course, there was no barley. Ed Kramer had lost the farm last year and the place had been abandoned for eight months. The bank owned it. Bank owned a lot of property around Goodlands since the drought, and that was fine with Vida. She had no love for Goodlands.

And Goodlands had no love for Whalleys in general. Vida was considered the best of the bunch, but sometimes folks would add that she was the best *so far.* Meaning that she hadn't so far fucked up as badly as the others, but time would tell. The only good Whalley—other than a dead Whalley, ha ha. Whalleys had been plaguing the town, drinking and fighting, stealing and making trouble for years. Vida was the youngest Whalley in town. She had a long line of brothers ahead of her for inspiration, not to mention her father, patriarch of the clan, the Whalleys of Plum View Road. The "view" was of the garbage dump and miles and miles of useless, rocky farmland. When folks in town were forced by basic courtesy—usually involving taking her money—to speak to her, more than one had been known to ask jokingly how things were looking out on Slum View Road—following their bon mot with a chuckle and maybe a wink to a buddy. More than one of the old men in town would have to scrape their eyes away from her well-formed little body to spit this out. That was when she would smile as if there were nails in her mouth and add a polite "Fine, thank you"; then she might go out that night, if she felt like it, and prop open the door to the man's chicken coop so the hungry, driven foxes could get in. There was no love lost between a Whalley and the town of Goodlands.

At the other end of the field there was a windbreak, maybe eighty years old. About thirty enormous cottonwoods stood there, more or less dead, and dry as timber.

"Good for *me*," Vida whispered. She walked easily, unconcerned about discovery, across the open field in the direction of the windbreak.

Ed Kramer's farm was a good ten minutes from town. The nearest neighbor was another Ed, old Ed Gordon, who lived on a small patch of bordering land, no more than four acres. Ed Gordon was ninety if he was a day. She didn't expect he'd come running over. She had chosen well. She always did.

Vida had an armful of deadfall by the time she reached the trees. She hummed and mumbled a song as she arranged the deadfall in a tidy pile under what was roughly the middle tree in the long windbreak. She dragged a larger branch under a tree near the end, and set it up over some brush. She worked efficiently, taking her time. She had hours. The grass that had managed to grow under the trees was very dry. She would have to be careful.

"'Hush little darlin', don't say a word . . . Mama's gonna buy you a mockin' bird. . . .'"

She pulled the box of matches from her pocket and opened it. Redbird matches were "strike anywhere," but she used the rough strip on the side of the box. The match sputtered and flamed. She let it burn up the shaft.

She bent low and stuck the match upright in the dirt under the kindling pile. The flame flared brighter as it burned up the match. She lit another one and placed it at the other end of the pile. Then a third match, under the branch at the end.

Things moved quickly after that.

The grass caught first and the flames spread in an arc around the base of the tree. The grass lit the kindling. It took longer for the big branch to catch, but by then the grass was burning out. By the time Vida turned her back on the whole thing, the tree was on fire. Great flaming arms reached up the tree, dozens of them, like something trying to get away.

Vida loved the sound of fire, the snapping and crackling. Wood fires especially. She admired her handiwork. Wood fires were unpredictable. It always amazed her how someone could start a house fire with a cigarette burning in an ashtray, but sometimes you couldn't get a fire burning in a stove with kindling, dry wood, and a whole box of matches. Wood fires were unpredictable, sure, but they were the best. They smelled the best, too. She could barely smell her brother's stink on his filthy shirt anymore. The smoke was taking it all away. She wished there was a better breeze, although she was lucky there was anything. Things had been very still lately.

The trailers hadn't sounded as good. Mostly hisses and pops. And they burned slowly, and the smell was kind of chemical. Wood was the way to go. The lovely smell and sound of burning wood.

The spiral of smoke was a cathedral now, and she knew she had to leave. They would see it from town. Someone might have already called and the volunteer firefighters would be digging their hands out from inside their asses and hauling down to load up the truck. Soon she would hear the sirens, if she stayed any longer. But she could listen from home.

The air was thick and the heat intense. In spite of that, she was loath to leave.

She turned and broke into an exhilarating canter. She wished her hair was loose so that she could feel its weight bouncing and swinging down her back.

"If that mockin' bird don't sing! Mama's gon' set fire to your ding-a-ling!"

She took the long way around, avoiding the Larabees' because, this time, she didn't have anything for the dogs.

No one saw her. By the time she heard the siren on the town's only working fire truck, she was upstairs in her bedroom, watching at the window as the smoke curled up in the sky above Kramer's field.

Karen hung the dish towel back on the rack. The kitchen was clean, not having been very dirty. The living room was tidy. She had nothing to read; there was nothing on TV. She turned the radio on, set the volume low, and something by Harry Connick, Jr., filled the kitchen. Karen felt restless.

She wandered into the living room, picking up a glass that she'd missed earlier, and then wandered back. She put the glass on the counter. She opened the fridge. Nothing good to eat. The committees she sat on, the organizations in town she belonged to, mostly disbanded for the summer months and left a void in her social life, such as it was. She didn't smoke. There was a bottle of wine in the cupboard, but she didn't feel like a drink either. Lately at night she was restless. She blamed it on the heat, blamed it on the too-much coffee she drank every day, blamed it on the bank. The numbers lining up neatly in rows, adding up to something that she couldn't see, touch, feel, and in cases like the Campbells and the Franklins, could do nothing about. So at night she wandered around her little house and looked for things to occupy her time.

When she came home from work that afternoon, she slipped into her oldest Levi's, needing their familiar softness to take the harshness off her day. A bad day. She left her work blouse on, and let it hang out loose around her body, her only concession to the weather being her sleeves, rolled to the elbow. As she moved around the house she was aware of her clothes, of the cotton of her jeans and the way her soft white blouse moved over her midriff, sometimes touching, sometimes not, always there, shifting with her body. It was the heat.

She went over to the door and shut the light off in the kitchen. The darkness felt cooler. She could feel the sweat beading up on her back, her shirt sometimes clinging there for a moment, before moving with her. She stood at the open window and looked out into the dark of her backyard.

There wasn't much to see, although the moon, full in a few days, lit up the trees and the grass. And the white posts of her silly gazebo glowed prettily. These days, Goodlands looked better at night. Crickets broke through the music now and again.

She leaned out the window and a breeze, sudden and unexpected, came to her from behind. It slipped up under her blouse, up her back, cooling the sweat that had gathered there and sending a delighted chill through her. The hair on her neck stood on end. Her skin, so sensitive lately, seemed to swell out to meet the breeze, and she drew in a breath. She sighed with pleasure and closed her eyes. If only it were always like that. Cool breezes and dark kitchens.

Karen opened her eyes. She smelled something—suddenly, strong. Smoke. Fire. She couldn't see anything from the kitchen window: she strained her neck and looked to either side. But she could smell it, carried in on the sudden breeze.

Fire in a dry spell would be devastating. There had been so many fires lately. That poor man, Sticky, from the Badlands, had died not long ago. It was so dry.

Karen went into the living room, and even before she opened the front door, she could smell the smoke, blowing into the house through the window. She turned out the outside light, and through the screen door she could see the smoke, like thunderheads, sitting high in the sky. The fire was far away; the smoke was drifting in on the breeze.

She moved quickly to the phone and dialed the firehouse. "This is Karen Grange, on Parson's Road. I can see and smell smoke. It might be on the other side of town from here. Has someone called?"

"We got it." It was Jack Greeson. Teddy Greeson's brother. Teddy Greeson had an outstanding loan. "I think it's a grass fire. Haven't been out yet, myself. It's out at the Kramer farm. I guess not the Kramer farm anymore, huh? Too bad it didn't happen this time last year. Ed could've used the insurance." He cackled.

Karen cleared her throat. "I'm glad someone called."

"Yeah, about twenty people. We got it. Don't play with matches in this weather, huh?" He hung up.

She went out and stood on the porch, watching the smoke curl up into the sky. It did look like thunderheads, although Karen didn't expect it would rain.

Karen was still on the porch a half hour later when she saw a man walking up Parson's Road toward her house. He didn't look up at her. She could see the red glow of a cigarette when he raised his hand to his face. He paused and leaned down and butted the end of his cigarette on the heel of his boot. For good measure, he gave it a pinch, between thumb and forefinger. He dropped it.

Until he started up her driveway, she thought he must be heading out to Clancy's, a little more than a mile up the same road.

When he was about halfway up the drive she called out. "Can I help you?"

The man stopped and looked up at her for the first time. "Maybe," he said, and started walking again.

"Where are you going?" she called.

The man stopped again. "I'm looking for Karen Grange." He stood in the driveway. He wore a heavy pack on his back, and, of all things, an oilskin jacket and a baseball cap. Under the cap, his hair was long and loose.

"Why?" she said, startled. It was eleven at night. She frantically searched her mind for identification. She didn't recognize him. His voice didn't even sound familiar. Her mind stumbled immediately over possibilities.

The man smiled. He touched the bill of his hat and nodded.

"You're Karen Grange?"

Because she couldn't think of something else to say, she nodded, slightly, so small a gesture he might have missed it in the dark.

"I'm the rainmaker," he said, simply, and started up the drive again.

Karen stepped back toward the doorway as he came up the stairs.

"I'm tired as hell," he said. He nodded at her again, in greeting. With a sigh, he dropped his pack onto the porch. "Heavy," he said.

"Excuse me?"

He held his hand out to her. "Tom Keatley. I'm the rainmaker," he repeated. She didn't take his hand. He pulled it back. "I'm a little dusty from the road," he said.

"The rainmaker?"

"Yes ma'am." He nodded that polite little nod again.

"I don't know what you're talking about," she said stiffly. A small, cool breeze drifted over her, carrying the thick smell of the smoke, and a scent of something else. Something that smelled cool, and fine.

"You wrote me," he said.

Karen was leaning against the screen door, one hand behind her, fist curled around the handle. The man was no more than two feet away. She put her other hand out in front of her to keep him back.

The rainmaker. The man looked like he'd walked for miles. There were dark smudges under both eyes, one eye more smudged than the other. She realized it was a bruise. A black eye. He was dusty and dirty. She supposed he would smell if he came any closer, wearing all those clothes in this heat.

"I *wrote* you—?" she began, and stopped. Her eyes widened. The hand that she held out to stop him came up and covered her mouth. She blushed, although he wouldn't be able to see that.

"You remember now?"

Just after the horrible Mr. Blane from CFC had been down to

"discuss" the business plan for the branch. Horrible Mr. Blane, so official, so smug. Horrible day.

"That was over a year ago," she said. "I—I never expected . . . I didn't even think you got that letter. I certainly never expected you to just, *show up*. I expected you to contact me—"

He looked up at the sky and back at her. "Still dry here?" he asked, with sarcasm in his voice.

"Listen, I didn't know what I was doing. I was . . . under the influence of a mild drug that night," she said, wryly. "I don't even know why I wrote the letter. I'm sorry."

"What was the drug?"

"Coffee," she said, and smiled despite herself. She had been up late, worrying over the bank, over the foreclosures staring her in the face, over the business plan that had no place in reality. Over maybe failing, getting shipped out again, this time, maybe to a city branch. After she'd come so far. And after she had come to like where she was. She'd drunk too much coffee, and it was three in the morning and she couldn't sleep. There was nothing on TV, except for the Weather Show, a cable thing. And here he was.

"I guess you'll have to watch your consumption," he said.

They stood in silence in the dark. She was standing on her porch with a strange man. A man no one knew was here.

"You'll have to leave," she said quietly and firmly.

He raised an eyebrow. "I just got here," he answered, sounding irritated now. As though the time for small talk was finished. "Look, I've been walking for nearly twelve hours. I'm dirty, I'm dusty, and I am tired as hell. I think I said that. I need a place to wash up and a place to crash, in that order. I'm not fussy about guest rooms. A couch or the floor will do me fine—"

"You can't stay here," she said, alarmed.

"You *invited* me," he said, his voice rising a notch.

"I expected you to write, or call, or something. I didn't expect you to *walk* here from Winslow, Kansas, without so much as a phone call!"

"Good, you remember the details. If you don't, I have your letter," he said, leaning toward her. They both breathed heavily for a second. He was too close. Karen shrunk back against the screen door. She thought about her chances if she tore it open and ran inside. Could she make it to the phone before he— what? Grabbed her? She could see the headlines:

Former Junior Citizen Found Murdered in Rural North Dakota. . . . Parts of Bank Manager Found Strewn about Yard. . . . Cold-Hearted Bank Manager Drops Dead of Guilt. And the details: *Mayor Ed Shoop is quoted as saying, "Darnedest case of suicide I ever saw . . . don't know how she managed to cut herself up like that."* Or maybe a sound bite on one of those tabloid shows: *Rural Banker Karen Grange apparently did not know what she was getting into when approached by the good-looking stranger during the night of the big fire. It was a case of The Drifter and . . . The Dummy.* (Close-up of blank-faced blonde.) *Welcome to* Thirty. *I'm Angela Coltrain.*

His face softened suddenly as he let out a sigh. "Look, lady, I'm tired, I'm dirty. I don't want to hurt you. I don't have the energy even to hurt your feelings. I just need to crash. I'll camp out back." He reached over and pulled his pack up over one shoulder, with a tired heave.

There it was then. They each looked away. He glanced back over his shoulder, toward the smoke.

"What's on fire?"

"The Kramer farm," she found herself telling him. "The firefighters are out there. You must have passed it." He nodded.

"Couldn't see much," he said conversationally. "It was off the road. Lot of people heading down there. People love to watch a fire." They both watched in silence as the smoke swam above the horizon. He added, "Fire's bad, this kind of weather. Good thing the breeze isn't too strong. Could spread." She nodded.

"And your point is that you're a rainmaker?" she asked, finally.

He smiled, his teeth showing. They were small and white. "You have a drought," he said.

His understatement made Karen smile.

"And I'm a rainmaker."

"How do I know that?" she asked. He shrugged his pack higher on his shoulder, smiling, holding his hands out in deference.

"I guess you'll have to trust me." He shifted the pack again. It was heavy, still wet. "In the morning," he said, "we can talk about your drought. Maybe you'll see things differently then." He went down the porch steps, and onto the walk that led to the back.

"Maybe," she said softly, allowing him to go. She watched him walk, helpless to stop him. Apparently, the subject was closed. He did look tired. *Tired* was all over him, the way he walked.

She found herself saying, "There's a gazebo back there. It's not screened in, so the mosquitoes might bother you. Not many this year, though."

"A gazebo?"

She blushed. Not too many gazebos in Goodlands. Kinda fancy, was the way George Kleinsel had put it. She nodded. He turned and started walking again.

"There's a pump back there, too," she said. "Water's cold." This time he didn't stop. She watched him disappear around the corner of the house.

Her hand, which had been clutching the door handle, was sweating and sore. Her heart was pounding. She wondered what the hell she was doing, right up until she was inside the house, where she latched the screen and locked the front door, using both locks, the knob lock and the dead bolt. She realized she had never used that last one before.

Then she walked quickly to the kitchen, passing by the phone, and passing up the temptation to call the police.

In the kitchen she closed and locked the back door, using both latches again. She drew the door's tiny curtains closed. It would be a hundred degrees in the house, but she decided she was closing the windows. She reached over the counter to pull the kitchen window closed. Through the screen she could hear crickets. The smoke that had wafted over earlier was still there, but it was less thick now and had turned into a pleasant, woodsy smell. The radio was still playing softly. Background music. Summer sounds. Sometimes, when the wind was right, she could hear the music from Clancy's. Tonight the wind was wrong, and she was glad.

He had come around the side of the house. From a distance, by the light from the moon, she could see him better. She watched him. He was in her yard, and if he looked over at the house, he wouldn't even see her in the dark of the kitchen.

She watched as he stepped fully into the yard and paused. Karen sucked in her breath. The night and the man were so still, she wondered if he was listening for her. He seemed to stare ahead into the night. It was a minute or so before she realized he was looking not at the horizon but straight into the gazebo, as though seeing something that wasn't there. Between the darkness of the night and the distance between them, she could not see the lines slowly forming on his brow.

He wavered, his body leaning forward and then back, as though poised but not quite ready to move. Finally, he closed the space between himself and the little building and leaned into it, without touching the posts. Not hesitating, he dropped his pack into the doorway, and it fell just on the edge of the concrete.

Karen breathed.

He spotted the pump, a quaint little yard ornament as far as Karen had been concerned, and pushed the handle downward a couple of times to prime it. It hadn't been used in years and the handle gave a metal scream at first. It was alarmingly loud and made Karen step back involuntarily from the window.

He threw off his jacket, and pulled off his buttoned shirt and T-shirt in one motion, dropping them on the ground. His flesh shone in the moonlight, making him look very white and clean. His back was turned to Karen.

His shoulders were broad, and Karen saw how long his hair was, falling past his shoulders in soft dark waves. He cranked the pump handle again. Water poured out in a sudden gush and then stopped.

He pumped some more and Karen watched the muscles in his back working. He bent low under the spout and let the water spill over him, over his hair, his shoulders, down his back, wetting the tops of his jeans.

Karen stepped away from the window, cheeks burning. She worked the window down as quietly as she could, hoping the rush of water would cover the sound of the wood scraping in the frame. For one terrible second, she thought she saw him pause and look over. She couldn't be sure. She turned the latch on the window.

Without looking back, she left the kitchen and walked though the rest of the house, checking windows and doors, making sure they were locked. Just in case.

She drew her bedroom curtains and then pulled the blind down, too.

She thought about locking the bedroom door, but that would have been paranoid. The house was locked up like Fort Knox. Which was exactly as she wanted it, she told herself. After all, he was a stranger, and she was in the middle of nowhere, cut off from town. It was only good sense.

Karen undressed quickly, as though he might see through walls, and slipped into bed, covering herself with only the sheet. She lay on her back, hair lifted up and spread out above her on the pillow, to keep the heat off her neck. It was hot in the bedroom. Hot in her pajamas. She felt restless. It was probably ninety degrees out there. Which, she mused, would make it a hundred and ten in the house. Especially with the house locked up like a convent. A very hot convent.

She shut the light off beside the bed and closed her eyes, only to have them pop open a second later. She kicked the sheet off. She turned her pillow over to the cool side. She moved over onto her side. She turned onto her back. Finally she went and opened her bedroom curtains and pulled the blind up. The moon dripped in and filled the room with a pretty light. It wasn't even full yet, but the sky was cloudless and clear. Through her window Karen could see the stars, maybe even every one of them.

For no reason at all, she thought of Loreena Campbell singing the Commercial Farm Credit jingle in her office. It should have been funny. But it had been an ugly, dark scene. She wondered if the Campbells were sleeping. She suspected not.

Karen went back and lay down on the bed, on top of the covers. She wondered about the man in the backyard. Was he asleep yet? A pregnant Jessie Franklin floated up in front of her eyes. Bruce Campbell's face after he spat on her rug. The three loans she had to call up tomorrow and remind of payment. Her parents. The way people looked these days, with their eyes glazed over and their foreheads set in a permanent squeeze; the way it was quiet in the cafe when she went in. The stranger in the yard.

A rainmaker. He was a rainmaker. She remembered the bit on the Weather Show. It had seemed like a good idea at the time. He had made it rain in a place that hadn't had rain in nineteen months. Goodlands could beat that. He *had* made it rain, the show said.

A rainmaker. Could it be possible?

She closed her eyes but did not sleep.

Goodlands is a town that retires early. Most farm towns do. The work is hard physical labor that starts at dawn and rarely lets up for more than an hour at lunch, probably taken in the fields, and then an hour or so in the house at supper before people head out to do chores before bed. People turn in when the light fades, sometimes falling asleep even before that, on the sofa waiting for the farm report on the nightly news.

Lately, though, Goodlands was suffering from insomnia, and Karen Grange wasn't the only resident who was having trouble sleeping. All over town, whether the lights were on or not, people were awake.

Ed Clancy was awake.

There were no fewer than twelve Eds in Goodlands. Each and every one of them an Edward, save Clancy, who was an Edwin. He owned and operated Clancy's, the closest thing to a night life that Goodlands could boast. It was really just a plain old pub. Ed had been running Clancy's for twenty-two years and was hoping to retire soon, and it seemed he would get his wish. He stayed open now just for the few that wandered in after chores to have a few beers and forget about their troubles for a while. When he took their money he couldn't help but feel a little guilty, making a living off their misfortune, but he had a business to run, too, and he was stinging from the sudden betrayal of the land like them all. He was thinking of shutting her down next year, selling to some of the stupid city people who passed through and always told their wives, Don't you think this would be fun for a while? Running a cute little pub like this? Ed always agreed with them. Let them buy him out and go broke. He had a business to run, too. That's why he was up at night, trying to figure out what he could get for Clancy's.

Ed's best friends were Walter Sommerset and his wife, Betty. Good, steady people. They were partners in the farm; Betty was in on everything right from the start, and Walt was one to boast that she had a damned fine head for business. It was her idea to put everything on to the computer as soon as they had come out with farming programs that let you keep track of every dime, every seed, every animal, every rainfall. They'd poured nearly four thousand dollars into that computer and got it all paid for two years earlier. Just as the drought grabbed them by the balls and started its relentless squeeze.

That night, the two of them were holed up in their attic office, going over the books for the umpteenth time, trying to find money enough for their second mortgage. If they didn't pay their boy's tuition at the university next semester, they could make it all the way to November. But it's a hard row to tell your boy that school's maybe out.

Bruce Campbell was thinking about hard rows himself. He and his brother Jimmy were drinking, still sitting at the kitchen table in the house that was, technically, not even theirs anymore. They'd gone through the beer stocks that Bruce kept on hand for the hired people, and were into the whiskey that Jimmy'd got for Christmas last year. The table was littered with beer bottles, papers, newspapers, and spent tissues with Loreena's tears still drying on them. About every hour Loreena would come into the kitchen and blubber a little and ask Bruce what they were going to do. "I'm not going to Grandma's!" she'd insist, reminding Bruce that she and his mother did not get along. The kids stayed clear of the kitchen. They'd never seen Daddy so wobbly and slurry, and their mother was acting like a crazy person. She was upstairs going through closets and boxes, every now and then bringing something down and showing it first to the kids—"Do we need this? Should we let it go at the auction?" Before they could answer she would take it into the kitchen and ask the same thing of their father and Uncle Jimmy. Now and then she would pause to blow her nose or wipe her eyes. The kids hadn't even had a proper supper, they'd just fed themselves from the fridge. They'd put themselves to bed.

Charlene Waggles—Chimmy to her friends—and her husband, proprietors of the Goodlands Dry Goods and Sundry, stayed up late anyway, but every night it was Chimmy who sat and burned over the books. Her husband watched television without saying a word while she gave him a running commentary on who owed what and who was going to whistle for it and who was going to have to be paid and what exactly various suppliers could do with their demands for payment. She took vicious delight these days in filling in the ledger in red. As far as she was concerned, it was another dime the bank would never see.

Butch Simpson, who would be twelve in July and wanted a new bike, stayed up and listened to his parents fight about money, their voices rising through the vent in his bedroom.

It was not the first time that Goodlands had stayed awake to worry or wonder. Along with the rest of the nation, it had suffered through three wars and the Great Depression. It had watched its tax rolls fall as residents migrated to the cities, as children grew, and as times changed. People had stayed put through hailstorms, soil erosion, rising and falling prices in agriculture, and the advent of the commercial megafarm. They had stayed through bad times, perhaps because they felt that the bad times had been ordained by God. In some families, faith was shored up by crises, and that faith would be unshakable by even the most secular disasters.

And there had been many crises of the secular sort in Goodlands. The kind of crises that might not devastate a crop or knock down a barn but that shook the unseen moral fibers that can hold a community together.

There had been wild speculation some fourteen years before, that Paul Kelly had slowly and methodically murdered his wife, Denise, ten years his senior, with some kind of poison. It was never proven. But Paul Kelly spent most of his time away from home, and when he came back, after a couple of weeks, his wife's health would begin to fail. She would rally after his departure for a bit, only to be ill again with his next return. Eventually, she just wasted away to nothing and died. He sold the farm and moved away, no one knew to where. Rumor had given way to accepted fact. Now it was part of the town history, true or not.

Don Kramer, whose father, Ed, had had the fire, was rumored to be a child molester. Don was married but childless, and for years he ran the Wolf Cub Pack, a boy's winter club, which included in its activities a weekend camp-out on the Kramer farm. Don himself did all the cooking, and he slept out there with the boys, despite the comfort of his own bed less than forty feet away. Parents questioned his uninhibited commitment to the kids, aged eleven to thirteen, and some even pulled their boys from the club at the peak of the rumors. There was never a harsh word said about Don Kramer by a single child who went through the Wolf Cub Pack. That didn't stop a barroom fight one Saturday night a week before the annual camp-out, when Don was confronted by several drunk fathers and beat up so badly he had to be hospitalized. The camp was canceled that year, and from then on, Don Kramer did not run the Wolf Cubs. He and his wife moved off the family farm and eventually away from Goodlands altogether.

Larry Watson committed adultery with the doctor's wife. This was not widely gossiped about, because a doctor still carries weight in a small town.

Still, there had been persistent rumors about the Griffen family of doctors, to which Grace Griffen Kushner was distantly related. At the turn of the century, the Griffens were more than just a well-to-do farming family. At one point, they had four sons practicing medicine. William Griffen was the only one who stayed to practice in Goodlands.

Grace was aware of the stories about the Griffen men, each and every one of them tainted in some way. With Matthew, the eldest, it was regular injections of morphine; with William, the youngest, it was women.

It was rumored that William raped a number of his female patients. It was also rumored that he peeked in windows and was careless with his hands during his examinations. The ugliest rumor at the time was that he performed abortions.

Dr. Griffen had never been arrested or openly accused of peeking in windows, or giving abortions, and certainly never of raping or fondling his patients. It was all rumor and speculation. He had been beaten up by a husband, and once he was chased out of a house by a girl's father. The girl never married and later went soft in the head. But nothing was proven. And the man was a *doctor;* a certain amount of intimacy was expected, and if women were oversensitive or poorly informed, that was their misfortune.

Only once did the rumors get out of hand.

Her name was Molly O'Hare. She was an Irish girl who had come to America to live with her brother on his farm in Goodlands after their mother had died. She was overage to be a maiden, nearly twenty-five by the time she started telling stories. It was believed to be hysterics. The priest at her parish had even asked around about a suitable husband for her.

She started the stories herself. She said Dr. Griffen peeked in her window when she dressed. She said he followed her home one evening after Mass. But the Griffens were not Catholic and had no reason to be at the church. Molly was seeing things or making up stories, people said.

When the flu epidemic hit Goodlands hard, the O'Hares fell ill along with the rest of the town. Dr. Griffen made his rounds to all the affected households, especially those in the less affluent areas. After Molly recovered, she complained to the Father that Dr. Griffen had taken advantage of her, nearly to a desperate point. The Father, misunderstanding her, enlisted the help of another lady of the church to explain to the motherless Molly the routines of a feminine medical examination.

Not everything Molly said went unheard or unbelieved. A neighbor, returning a set of grinding tools to the O'Hare farm sometime after dark, definitely had seen a man peeking into the far bedroom window. Molly's window. He shouted, and the man ran away before the neighbor could identify him absolutely. But he did say the man carried a satchel. And on his way over he had recognized the doctor's horse, tethered to a tree between the two farms, slightly hidden from the road.

As the number of wives who had been girlish patients of the doctor began to seek their medical care in another community, the talk increased. Some of the women even began to pity Molly.

About a year after her first complaint against Dr. Griffen, Molly got a suitor. An older man, never married, from a neighboring community, began to walk her home from church.

When Molly disappeared a month or so after their courtship

had begun, people began to talk. She had vanished somewhere between church and home, a distance of two miles. When she did not turn up, people began to mutter about her boyfriend. Lucky for him, he had not been anywhere near Goodlands the night she disappeared. He had been caring for his ill father.

It was the Griffen women who first noticed that William had a couple of hours missing from his still full schedule.

Tongues wagged. William Griffen lost more patients and became an alcoholic, dying at fifty-eight from a fall.

Molly O'Hare was never found, alive or dead.

Goodlands was no stranger to bad news, in no way different from any other town in Capawatsa County. Except in this one way; about this new foe, this drought. For the first time in its history, people weren't talking. Not about the drought. They talked about bills, about kids, about what to do if things got worse. They talked about rain; they talked about selling, about leaving, about staying; they talked around it. But not directly about the drought. In their hearts, they believed it had been ordained by God, and that they were being punished. Punished for what, no one could say.

Morning light came early. The first rays stabbed into Karen's room from the spaces between the blind and the window frame. A slash of light cut across her face. She opened her eyes. It was very hot in the bedroom. She'd kicked off her covers and, during the night, her pajamas too. She lay naked on top of the covers except for panties. Automatically, her eyes went toward the clock at her bedside. Five A.M. The alarm hadn't even gone off.

She had to pee. She stumbled from the bed and pulled her pajamas back on. She opened the bedroom door and stopped. Something was wrong.

Karen snapped awake. She stepped softly, cautiously into the living room and turned to look in the kitchen.

Silhouetted in the light from the window stood the rainmaker. They stared at each other.

"Good morning," he said softly.

"How did you get in here?" she demanded.

He smiled at her. "Do you still drink coffee after your little . . . indiscretion?" He held the pot up. "I just made fresh." He poured coffee into a mug.

"How did you get in here?" Karen did not move.

"The back door."

"It was locked."

He shrugged. She took a step farther to where she could see the back door. It stood half open. There was no damage, no sign of a break-in. She looked at him. He sipped his coffee.

"I can start today," he said. Karen stared at him, then back at the door. "But I want half up front," he said, "the rest when it rains."

"Half?" she repeated numbly. The doors had been locked. Double locked.

"Half of five thousand dollars. That would be two thousand five hundred."

"For what?"

"To make it rain."

The two of them stared at each other from the safe distance of a whole room while the sun rose on what promised to be a very dry day.

T W O

Near dawn, Vida Whalley was in the middle of a very bad dream. She could not wake up. While Tom Keatley was moving with ease from Karen's backyard to Karen's kitchen, Vida's chest was rising and falling alarmingly fast with each breath. She lay on top of the covers, eyes closed, face contorted, body utterly still except for the heaving of her chest as it expanded with some very bad air.

A breeze blew in gently through the open window. Her curtains, black with dirt and ragged with age, shuddered up nearly to the low ceiling in the room, then fell back as though dropped. It was too much for the rod, the whole thing tumbled to the floor, clattering loudly. Vida didn't hear it.

"Shut the FUCK up!" her brother called from the next room. "Tryin' t'sleep, you stupid bitch," he mumbled. Vida didn't hear him.

Sweat bubbled up on her chest and forehead; her nightgown

stuck to her flesh. She sucked at the air. It filled her lungs and her body shuddered and swelled with it, but it gave no relief. Her lungs burned for air.

Without waking, she opened her mouth wide, drawing breath after frantic breath, gasping for air as burning heat seared inside her. Her body dripped with sweat. It ran off her in rivulets, soaking the sheets underneath her. Her hair stood out from her head. Pain burned inside her, as though her very organs were being shifted with knives and arrows. Her flesh felt pierced. It moved of its own accord, rippling and shifting. The moisture on her body grew cold. She could not breathe; it was as though something sat on her chest, forcing its way inside her.

"Ah, ah, ah, ah," she breathed.

"SHUT THE FUCK UP!" her brother screamed. Someone laughed.

Finally her eyes opened, wide. The something was everywhere, inside her, around her. She breathed it in, she breathed it out. It *hurt*. Tears ran down her face.

"Ah, ah—" The air was knocked out of her body in one long hot breath. Her eyes glazed over, unseeing, lids fluttering. She struggled a little. The room went dark, then darker as oxygen eluded her. Her eyes rolled back in her head. She lay still.

By the time Karen found the rainmaker in her kitchen, Vida was awake. But she wasn't feeling quite herself. Vida was not alone. Inside her body, she had company.

"Get out of here!" Karen shouted.

Tom sipped from his mug. "Have a cup of coffee. You'll feel better."

"Get out of my house!" She hadn't moved from the living room. Did not want to go as far as the kitchen. She clutched at her pajama top, holding the collar close to her throat. But Tom didn't leave. He stood relaxed, leaning against her kitchen counter. The house smelled like coffee and stale air. The house had been shut up tight all night.

"How did you get in here?" she demanded.

There was a pause of about three beats before he picked up the pot of coffee and familiarly opened a cupboard and got out another mug. He poured steaming coffee into it and carried it over to where Karen stood. He held it out to her.

"Have some coffee," he said firmly. "It's good," he added, when she didn't take the mug offered. He set it down carefully on a small, polished table. Then he walked back into the kitchen and drank from his own mug. A polite sip.

Karen's heart was pounding, her body tensed for flight. The phone was to her left, but far enough away that she would have to run to it. She wavered.

"Should we talk business?" he said.

"The nerve of you!"

He chuckled and sighed. "You've gotta relax, Miss Grange. Sorry I came into your house uninvited." He drank more coffee, making a little sound of pleasure to show how good it was. "But as they say, let's make a deal. We can make it rain and save your little town. That's what you want, isn't it? For chrissakes, you asked me to come here. I'm here. Pitter-patter, let's get at 'er." He sounded so reasonable. Still, Karen didn't want to get too close.

"I don't want you to come into my house without being asked," she said, finally.

"I'll take my coffee outside. Better? You get dressed, and then come outside. Then we can talk about the money." He smiled his wide smile and looked for all the world like a handsome, benevolent kind of guy. Just a guy.

Karen nodded. "All right," she said, not relaxing at all.

"Good." He nodded and went to the door. He pushed open the screen and stepped out onto the back porch, but not before he motioned toward the table.

"Yours is getting cold." The screen door fell shut behind him.

She stood undecided for a moment. Then, slowly, almost casually, she went over to the phone and dialed the sheriff in Weston, a fifteen-minute drive. While listening to the phone ring, she picked up the mug from the table and wiped underneath it with the sleeve of her pajamas.

Tom sipped his coffee and watched her from the porch. He knew she would call someone. Whether it was her boyfriend or the law, he wasn't sure, but he knew she would go to that phone. She stood in profile to him, and he watched her watch him. He chuckled. Sooner or later, she had to make her choices.

The call was picked up after two rings. Henry Barker's voice was at the other end. "Sheriff."

Karen opened her mouth. She didn't speak.

"Sheriff's office," Henry Barker insisted.

We can make it rain and save your little town. . . . I'm a rain-maker. . . . Pitter-patter.

Henry Barker repeated himself once more before hanging up. Karen held on to the receiver for a moment longer, then quietly slipped it back onto the cradle.

Outside, Tom smiled to himself. He looked up at the sky. Except for the drought, it was looking like a fine day.

Karen laid out her clothes carefully. She was meeting with two men from the head office that day, bad enough, but now it seemed she had another meeting to attend to. She would be dressed for it. She chose her most becoming suit, a sunny yellow skirt and jacket that had cost her seven hundred dollars. That had been many years ago, during what she referred to as "the dark ages," but it was still stylish, flattering and in really great shape. The skirt came to just above the knee and she wore panty hose, as she did even on the hottest days, because she was a banker and it was required. CFC Standards and Policies had not a single item on skirt hems, but there were definite rules.

The first and foremost rule was control. The banker held the cards. She would simply let Tom Keatley know who was in charge.

Really, he wasn't all that different from the customers who came to see her at the bank. There were certain key items of information that had to be ascertained before proceeding to the next step.

What are your assets?

Mr. Keatley made it rain.

Do you rent or own?

As far as she could see, Mr. Keatley was of no fixed address.

Employers, previous employment history, references.

She could always check him with the people in Winslow, Kansas. There were other questions to be answered, such as *What are your debts?*—from the looks of him, he was not a dealer in credit—*Who do you bank with?*—she assumed that in this particular case, Mr. Keatley would be banking with the Bank of Karen—and *When, exactly, can you make it rain?* She wondered why Mr. Keatley didn't like questions.

She straightened her shoulders when she was done dressing, and fixed on her face her banker's smile: grim, strong, all-knowing. In control.

That was how she looked when she stepped out onto the porch, her fear of the rainmaker replaced by a more comfortable, familiar tack.

"You can make it rain," she said, a statement, not a question.

"I can," he said, turning to look at her. They were a study in contrasts, she with her suit and gloss, he in dirty, slept-in T-shirt and jeans, heavy boots on his feet.

"How?"

"I can make it rain for five thousand dollars," he said, smiling at his familiar line.

"I don't have five thousand dollars," she said, curtly.

"So get it."

She snorted, some of her polish slipping, at the absurdity of the remark. "If someone—you, for example—could just *get* five thousand dollars, I don't think we'd be having this conversation."

"I don't have a drought."

It was like that, then. He turned back to look out over the yard. It was about an acre of what used to be pretty green landscaped grass, with the rock garden in the corner that Karen had set free. It was now brown and overgrown. The yard was treed-in with dry-looking lilac bushes that hadn't bloomed. Beyond was the small apple orchard, which she didn't expect to bear fruit. Everywhere, even in her own yard, were the scars of two rainless years. Smack in the middle of it all stood her pretty gazebo, with its four-year-old white paint. The whole yard had a sort of gothic look in the unforgiving light of day. At any moment you could expect Heathcliff to arrive, fresh from the moors, or perhaps Scarlett, to vow she would never be hungry again.

"I'll have to see," Karen said, her forehead furrowed.

"Fair enough."

Karen turned briskly on one heeled shoe. She had to go. "I'll be at the bank all day. I don't suppose I can keep you out of the house?"

"I'm a little hungry."

"There's food in the fridge," she said, adding, under her breath, "Don't steal anything." She went back through the house and out to her car, without bothering to lock the front door. At least this time she knew where he would be.

She got in the car and started it, backing out and turning onto the road in one smooth motion. She wished she didn't have all of this on her mind. It was a big day at the bank. Chase and Juba from the head office would be in and they wanted to go over some book work with her. They were going to shut her down, Karen suspected, although they hadn't said as much yet. Active, liquid accounts were dropping dramatically, and if it weren't for the big Hilton-Shane dairy, then they would be staring at a bottom line of zero. They weren't far from it.

The Goodlands branch of Commercial Farm Credit had been

in trouble before year four of the drought. Year three was a no-profit year. They should have shut it down then. Karen, as bank manager, was responsible for the annual business plan that gave the head office a look at what to expect in profits for the next year. Karen's business plan had predicted a recovery, with antic-ipated profits. Nothing spectacular, but enough to get them to agree to keep the branch running for another year. Television jingles notwithstanding, Commercial Farm Credit, like every bank in America, had a firmer eye on the bottom line than on farms and families. She'd fudged the business plan, although she could say that she had expected, as had everyone, a recovery from the drought. After all, *The Farmer's Almanac* had pre-dicted rain. Every other town in the area got rain. It was as if some invisible umbrella were hovering over Goodlands, and there was no scientific explanation for it. They had expected twenty-two inches. So far, there had been none. Not a drop. No rain, no crops. No crops, no harvest. No harvest meant de-faulted loans, leases, mortgages, a withdrawal of savings, and profits down the toilet.

If she was transferred it would not be as a manager. She would be sent instead to some little city branch with steady con-servative profits, where she would be in loans or something equally menial, in charge, most likely, of calling repo men on lit-tle old ladies on their way to nursing homes, asking for payment or default. *What are your assets?* would become her mantra. And she wanted to stay in Goodlands.

By the time she let Juba and Chase into her office at nine-thirty on the dot, she was documented, papers figured and ready. She was prepped, groomed, stockinged, and not wearing per-fume. Bankers interpret every smell as fear.

Vida put on her nicest dress, a light cotton flowered print, faded nearly beyond recognition, but clean, and finished her out-fit off with a pair of frayed Keds that used to be white, no socks. She sat on the edge of the bed feeling quite pleased with herself.

Her hair still had the odd feeling of being on end, and so she
pulled it down, mindful of the static electricity that seemed to
run through her fingers whenever she touched it, and braided it
into a heavy, thick coil that fell down to the small of her back.
Her hair had always been pretty. It was much prettier today.
Everything about her was prettier today, so much more *alive*
than usual. She liked the way her dress swished about her legs.
She liked to think about the way people would look at her in
that dress. Nasty men people.

The others in the house were still asleep. On the couch in the
living room, a man was snoring loudly. The coffee table, broken
for close to two years, was littered with saucers filled with cigarette butts, beer bottles—some with labels, some without—and
empty bottles of the hooch her father made and sold. Butch, the
family pet, a gargantuan rottweiler, veteran of so many fights
that her father kept him around like a trophy, lay across the
floor farting and snorting and smelling like a brewery. Her old
man and her brothers thought it was funny to get him drunk
and then laugh when he puked all day. She didn't know who the
man on the couch was, and didn't care. She hardly gave him a
glance.

Vida went through the kitchen and out the front door of the
house. Had to go. She had plans for the day.

She stepped deftly around a puddle of vomit near the stairs.
The sun was bright and in the distance she could hear the buzz
of a machine. Not many birds since the drought got bad. That
didn't matter. The drought was a *good* thing. She had thought so
many times and felt even more strongly about it today.

The drought was killing Goodlands. It was drying up and dying. Good.

Vida walked out onto Plum View Road in front of her house.
She looked up and down the street as though she had never seen
it before. It all looked different today, from the tall, dry poplars,
to the brown, dirty grass. Today, it had its own special shine.

Her sneakers kicked up dust from the dirt road onto the hem

of her dress. She would walk to town. She had to go to town. Because she was *mad*. She had business to do. Her step was light.

The Dry Goods had cut her family off credit just last week. A nasty, nasty, *nasty* bit of business.

The sun was bright and shining in her eyes and Vida hoped that was the reason she was feeling a little dazed, a little light-headed, this morning. Not unwell exactly, but not quite the same as yesterday morning. Strange things were going through her head and she mostly ignored them, and stayed on the road to town, hoping that a bit of nasty business of her own would bring her back up to her par-tee attitude. It usually did. She hadn't decided just what she would do, maybe just shoplift some candy, maybe go prop open the back door and call some dogs, unplug the freezer as she had done at Rosie's. Just something small and, hopefully, expensive. People like the Waggleses lived for money. Let them live a little.

When she got to town, the streets were bustling with people. She hadn't thought of that. She crossed the street and stood under the big old elm in front of the post office, thinking that she had missed her opportunity and that maybe she would come back at night.

The elm was throwing lots of shade on Vida's spinning head and cooling the light film of sweat that had beaded up over every inch of her body on the walk out. It was good to have the sun out of her eyes. An enormous tree, at least a hundred years old, she knew, because about seven or eight years before there had been talk of cutting it down and everybody got their nuts in an uproar, talking about *heritage* and *history*, and they had left it standing, only to see it dry up from four years of drought. After that there was talk of a plaque or a small sign. But no sign ever showed up. It was a good, sturdy tree. It stood directly across from the Dry Goods, aimed, sort of, right at their window.

It was dry and suffering like the rest of them in Goodlands. She thought offhandedly about how it would go up like a Roman candle, but burning it was out of the question. After the fire last night, not to mention the rest of them, people were talking. She'd have had to come back at night for that anyway, and she was already here.

Too bad it wouldn't just fall on the place. She would have to think of something to do that wouldn't attract too much attention. Vida reconsidered slipping out to the back of the Dry Goods and leaving the back door open for the dogs, but the back of the store faced a row of houses, all of the yards probably full of little kids and mothers by then. Distantly she could hear some little kid squealing.

Too bad. *Stupid tree,* she thought. She reached out and gave it a petulant little push.

John and Chimmy Waggles had bought the store in Goodlands three and a half years earlier. They were from Minneapolis, and so couldn't be faulted for their poor timing. They might have questioned why the Hastens were so eager to get rid of the place, but having been eager themselves, they hadn't noticed. The timing had been so poor that now Chimmy no longer stayed up nights crying, but instead had the look of someone braced for a fall. Her eyes had a permanent set of bags under them. The last time she'd cried was when she and John laid off Tammy Kowzowski, after having promised her she'd keep her job when they took over. After that, no more crying for Chimmy. She didn't sigh anymore when a local came in and bought another hundred dollars' worth of goods on credit, but wrote it on his tab with a vengeance. In the last two years she had ceased to care about overdue bills and banks and large companies wanting their due. They were the enemy, she felt. Their phone had been cut off four times. Her anger and fury at the large feeding on the small had won her points with the people of Goodlands and bought her entry into the community. When the money came in after harvest, people paid their bills (as much as they could) at the store. When she talked to the locals it was "us against them," even if, technically, Goodlands Dry Goods was one of *them.*

John, on the other hand, could not quite let go of the overdue bills and the threats to discontinue service. Three years of it was having a negative effect on his character. Never a strong man (he let Chimmy lead the way), he had lately given in to whining and complaining—and on some particularly dark nights, crying—whenever the mood overtook him. Chimmy let him. Her grandmother used to say that people everywhere felt the same things, good and bad, and let them come out in different ways. Chimmy had come from a loud, shout-it-out kind of family. The important thing was not to hold it inside.

This morning, Chimmy had come down the stairs tired as hell, around eight, to open up. In the last two years she'd put on a massive amount of weight and she was feeling it in her legs. John didn't mention the weight gain; it was their little agreement: He drank, she ate. She mentioned it herself, at every opportunity, just so people didn't think she hadn't noticed. She called her thighs "hammocks" and her behind "the only working caboose in Goodlands." She came down the stairs carefully, because when John wasn't around, she let herself feel her poor old fat legs and the pain that followed them everywhere. It shot up her thighs but was mostly in her knees. She had ripe blue veins up and down her legs from her years on her feet in the library, and working in the store hadn't brought them down. Sometimes in the morning the pain was so bad she would hold on to her leg when putting her foot down on the stair, and then pause. Getting down the stairs in the morning could take ten minutes, some days.

It was mid-month. A big day. The bank would be calling about the overdraft, wanting their money. That smart-as-you-please Karen Grange making the call herself, and wasn't she just filled with ice water and ink. But Chimmy wouldn't give them a cent until they called. Every month at this time, they would call and she would be rude; and then about ten minutes before the bank closed, she would come in with the payment. She hadn't missed a one, but waited every time for the call. She and John kept the account low enough so that the bank couldn't take it directly; they kept the rest of the cash in the store, in a strongbox. The bank could whistle, as far as Chimmy was concerned. She didn't like to think about the time, soon enough, when they would have to. The money that Chimmy and John had brought with them to Goodlands was nearly gone. Savings, retirement, nearly all. Gone.

She waddled to the door and opened the dead bolt. She turned the sign around that declared them open for business. Already the June air was heavy with heat, and would only get heavier, so she propped the door open with the little brick that always got kicked out of the way. It was those heavy boots the men wore. Like the people before them, Chimmy and John had been unable so far to put in air conditioning. Too expensive. It got so warm in the store some days that the candy bars melted in their wrappers and the gumballs stuck together. By midday, even the flies seemed slower. The produce, especially the bananas, only lasted a couple of days and then would end up in the reduced bin good only for banana cream pie and milk shakes. She used to prop open the back door, too, to get some air moving through the store, but she'd had a problem with dogs wandering in. The back door stayed closed, unless it was an emergency and the temperature rose above the nineties. That wouldn't happen until at least July.

By eight-thirty the produce was out of the fridge and into the bins, the float was counted and put back into the cash register, the front door was propped, and it was still cool. Chimmy sat behind the counter, looking over yesterday's newspapers, absently rubbing her knees while she read.

She was deeply involved in the crossword when she heard the first cracking sounds, loud enough to make her look up. Through the big front window she saw the top of a huge tree racing toward her. It hit hard, with a thunderous crash, as branches came through the window, spraying glass, flowerpots, Tupperware, and old, yellowed toys in her direction. Chimmy managed only "What in God's name—" before she screamed, falling off her stool and hitting the floor face first.

Ed Kushner and Gabe Tannac were parked on the bench in front of the cafe when the tree hit. They, too, managed only epithets before leaping to their feet. Inside the cafe, Ed's wife Grace looked up just in time to see the window of the Dry Goods implode.

"Call Franklin" was what she said to Larry Watson, the only customer at that time of the morning, as she ran out the front door and crashed into her husband. Leonard Franklin was fire chief of the volunteer fire brigade. Grace herself had her first aid certificate and she was going across the street to see if Chimmy was alive or dead.

Up and down the street people were rushing toward the Dry Goods. Trying to get in though the locked back door, Larry ran for an axe just as the door was pulled open by Chimmy—scratched, bleeding, but more dazed than hurt, and smiling to the beat of one helluva drummer.

"My insurance's all paid up! All paid!" she cackled, just before taking dizzy and dropping to the steps in a faint. Grace laid her flat as best she could on the loading bay and fanned her face with her apron.

"Go get the doctor—and might as well call up Gordon's," she said to Kush with a snort, thinking of her own freezer breaking down and her not getting any insurance from it. "Get Ben Gordon down here, not that little snake that works for him," she added. "Maybe somebody'll make some money today."

Out front a crowd had gathered around the tree and were speculating on what *could've* happened, but hadn't. The talk was nervous. It was just one more thing.

"Are we locked in to these?" Garry Chase wanted to know.

The top of Karen's desk was covered in piles of paper. Dozens of files were open and spread across other files and on top of those was a long spreadsheet telling tales of bundles of numbers, all of which added up to the same thing.

Garry Chase had taken over Karen's desk and was sitting in

her chair. Richard Juba was standing behind him, listing accounts as Chase found them on the spreadsheet and marked them off. Karen was relegated to a supporting position and sat in the extra chair, pulled up close to the desk should they need her. They didn't. They barely spoke to her. The fact that they said little meant that they hadn't turned her down. Karen's stomach churned and she wished she'd started the day with something more than coffee.

"Except for the Hilton-Shane account, we're not locked in to anything. However, I would move cautiously on the personals, just because, even with a recovery, people are going to be operating on credit. I wouldn't expect full payment on anything until after next year's harvest," she said. She wished she could just say yes, yes, yes, and get them out of the office. She wished she could read their minds. Her heart went up and down with every breath they took, thinking one minute they'd buy it, and thinking the next that they'd never go for it. Wondering if it would matter either way.

They had left the door to the office open and now and then Karen could feel Jennifer's eyes on her back. They had left the door open on purpose, letting the help see the boss in trouble. Mind games. Because the door was open, they heard a distant crash, just before Jennifer screamed.

"OH MY GOD!"

Both men looked up, but only Karen moved. Jennifer had run to the front window and was pointing out. "The Dry Goods!" she said. Karen looked out and saw that the tree in front of the post office had fallen over and crashed into the store's front window.

"There's been an accident," Karen called to Chase and Juba as she and Jennifer left the back.

Vida smiled a little at all the commotion. Her smile was like a cat's—full of feathers. She narrowed her eyes until they were almost closed, and she pictured the skies, bright, cloudless, and dry. She felt the sun on her face and tilted it upward just slightly, enjoying the heat. Her eyes closed all the way and she turned a little more in the direction of the sun, to the east. She couldn't help it: a little giggle came out before she demurely covered her mouth with her hand. Her hand still tingled from when she had pushed the tree.

All she had done was given it a little push. And it fell. Right on that fat Charlene Waggles.

The sun was hot. It had to stay that way. All day Vida kept smiling, hugging that knowledge to herself like a lover's note. She could do anything she wanted. Mostly, that day, she stayed and watched.

Henry Barker, the sheriff, came into the cafe to write up his report for the insurance claim.

"Goddamnedest day," he said. "Gimme a coffee, Gracie." Grace brought the pot over and also filled up the three mugs of the other guys sitting at the table. Ed had been insisting lately on charging for refills, since it was hard times; but she and the local populace usually forgot and she was losing track of who had paid for what, so no one was ever charged the extra fifteen cents. She had to be careful around her husband, though.

"Well," Henry started. The cafe got quieter. "Been over out at Kramer's there, and I guess Leonard Franklin's right as rain. The damn thing was surely started by someone. There's a pile of shit and ash as high as my arsehole someplace round the middle there, and Leonard says there might be a matchstick. It's burned up black, but you can see it fine enough. Took pictures," he said. He took a long slurp of his coffee.

"You know, I saw a fellow walking out on the main road when me and Gooner were heading out there to see if we could lend a hand," Bart Eastly said. "He was a tall fellow, looked pretty sneaky to me. Came in from the highway, I figure, just as smart as you please. Sneaky-looking. Long hair."

"Heard about him already," Henry said, in his closemouthed way.

"Who is it?" Gabe asked.

"Don't know. But Jacob saw him, too. He and Geena were coming out in the car to Kramer's. They passed right by him on Parson's. Geena watched in the mirror and thought she saw him turn in to Karen Grange's place." He stopped. The bank lady was living alone there, and to say more would just be gossipy.

"Karen? He a friend of hers?" someone asked.

"I never said that," Henry said, and took a nervous sip of his coffee. "Nobody jump to any conclusions," he warned. Of course, he knew people would and wished he hadn't brought it up.

"Guess that Whalley girl got a bit of a scare this morning," Henry said, chuckling, wanting to change the subject. "That tree was an accident waiting to happen. Should have cut it down a year ago." It was an old argument, and it started up again.

"Shaping up to be a helluva summer," Gabe Tannac put in, "if this is the start of it." No one answered him. Drought talk was too close to home.

While Chimmy was telling one and all about her insurance being paid off, and Karen was playing pitchman to the boys from the head office, Tom Keatley was wandering around the back property of Karen Grange's rented house, formerly home to two generations of Manns, trying to find a place to think. He had to think.

It wasn't just drought in this place, Tom Keatley was thinking. It was a vacuum. A pure vacuum of moisture. The air breathed in was hot and dry; the land was crying out for rain. As far down as he could feel in the earth, there was no water. The trees, usually a reserve of moisture, were dying of thirst. Of all the dry spells he'd been in the middle of, had fixed up, had suffered through, this was the worst. He'd never felt anything like it.

He'd felt it first when he passed by the sign announcing to the road traveler that he was in Goodlands: GOODLANDS, A GOOD LITTLE TOWN! POPULATION 620. He could feel the drought even then.

After Karen had left for work, he'd stripped down and washed in the cold water from the hand pump. Then he rinsed out his clothes and put on the clean T-shirt. He put his jeans back on wet. It kept him cool. He washed his hair out using a sliver of soap that he found in his pack and combed it with his fingers before tying it back. He laid his shirt out on the grass to dry in the sun. Anything to put off the inevitable.

Something was wrong. It didn't seem to matter where he went, although he always had his preferences.

He avoided the yard, with its brown but neatly trimmed grass, and worked his way back over to where the tree breaks had been planted. Past the trees was open prairie, where there was no relief from the beating sun, the open sky. He wandered in and out of the small apple orchard. Pretty spot. The trees— there were about forty of them—surrounded a small clearing that was just slightly raised, a little hill. The trees had likely been planted around the hill so that water would drain naturally into the orchard. The trees weren't in blossom anymore—if indeed they had been at all that spring—and it was too early for apples. There weren't even the beginnings of fruit. But the trees were pretty and their roots must have been deep and strong, because they looked healthier than most of the others he'd seen in Goodlands.

The clearing should have been the perfect place. But even there, he could feel it. It was *dry*.

Something had nagged at him ever since he walked into town. He couldn't say exactly what it was. But something was wrong. It didn't seem to matter how hard he tried, he couldn't bring in the rain. He could *feel* it out there; it was as though he were blind and couldn't see it, but knew it was there by sense. He could almost make it rain. But he couldn't bring it in.

Just as when he walked into Goodlands, he felt as though he were in a void of some kind. A vacuum. Nature and Tom abhorred a vacuum. And in Tom's case, five thousand dollars was riding on it. That was good for a lot of abhorrence.

The big rain was still four or five days to the east of him, just as it had been the night outside of Oxburg. But there were little pockets everywhere; at one point there was a half-hour sprinkle's worth only an hour or two away. He should have been able to pull in that one in a dream. He tried. He had it right outside of town and could bring it no farther. Why couldn't he pull it in?

By the end of the day, Tom had stretched out his blanket on the dry earth and lain down on it, looking at the sky. Waiting. Now and then, he would reach up and find it and feel its wetness, its fullness. Twice during the day, he could feel it open up and pour down, raining somewhere else. Then alter its course. It seemed that it was raining everywhere but in Goodlands.

THREE

THEY SAID THEY WERE GIVING HER ONE YEAR. *IF IT RAINED.*
All they were really doing was holding off shutting her down until after the end of June. If it rained in June, Chase said, they
would give her the season. If it was another washout—and he really said *washout,* Karen didn't miss the irony—then they were
shutting her down. They didn't say anything about her future
with CFC. They didn't have to. She was supposed to know how
it worked. All she had done was buy some time. She had roughly
two weeks left in June. Two weeks in which to hope, pray, beg,
maybe pay for rain. Two weeks.

And there was still the matter of the money.

Outside the bank, the freak accident at the Dry Goods kept a
constant roar of chain saws blaring. She could hear it over the
air conditioning, and for the first time in weeks people walked in
and out. Karen suspected it was for the cool air indoors. Outside
work was hot. No one stopped in to say hello to her.

She had default calls to make to three families who were
months behind in their mortgages. She spoke to Mrs. Paxton first,
and received less than a warm response. Mrs. Paxton said that
her husband was in the field and might be in later in the afternoon.

"Would you please have him call Karen Grange at CFC when
he comes in?" Karen asked.

"I don't know if he'll have time when he comes in, you
know," Mrs. Paxton told her. What she really meant, Karen
knew, was *kiss my ass*. The Paxton family had recently put a
twelve-foot cross on their front lawn and Jennifer Bilken had
told Karen that they prayed for rain under it every night after
supper.

The outer office was a mess. The files and spreadsheets required by Chase and Juba earlier in the day had been piled on
two small desks and part of the counter. Jennifer, unsure of what
to do with them until Karen said something, had worked around
them until four-thirty. Then she asked.

"Karen, did you want me to start refiling these before I go?"

"You can file the accounts if you have time, Jen," she said casually. "I still have a couple of things to cover on the spreadsheets." She didn't look up from the delinquent accounts on her
desk. She heard Jennifer open the big file drawer outside her office and begin the tedious task of refiling.

At four-forty Karen tidied up the papers in her office. The
bank closed at five.

At ten minutes to five, Karen stepped out into the outer office
and smiled at Jennifer, who was just finishing up the account fil-
ing.

"Thanks, Jen," she said.

Jennifer looked up at the clock hopefully. "I can stay and help
you with the rest of it, if you want," she said. Jennifer lived outside of town on her father's farm with her two kids and her
mother. Her husband worked in Alaska and sent money home,
but Karen thought there might be a problem there. As far as she

knew, Jennifer's husband hadn't made a trip home since Christmas.

"What about the kids?"

"My mom's off today," Jennifer told her. She stole another look at the clock. "I can stay as late as you need—"

Karen shook her head. "That's all right. I'm going to be at least another hour finishing up those spreads. You can go now, if you like."

"If you're sure . . ."

Karen smiled apologetically. "I'd give you the overtime if I could, Jennifer, but you know how things are around here," she said, with the appropriate amount of concern in her voice. She hoped.

"Okay," Jennifer said, disappointed. She added, slowly, "Did Mr. Chase say anything? About layoffs, or anything?" Karen realized how things must look to Jennifer. If CFC shut Goodlands down, Jennifer would lose her job. She would have to find work in Weston, or somewhere else. She'd have to drive, worry about child care, get up at dawn and not get home until dark, maybe. Not that it wasn't something that just about every family in Goodlands was dealing with at the moment.

"I don't know," she said honestly. She thought about adding, like a tasty little secret, *maybe it will rain,* but she didn't. Thing was, she didn't know. She knew less about rain-making than she knew about building a space shuttle. She certainly didn't know anything about her guest, other than his name and that she had seen his picture on TV once. She didn't know what was going to happen to the bank, or to Jennifer, or to herself, and she couldn't think about it anymore. She didn't know anything other than the way her heart was pounding in her chest, and the fact that Jennifer had to leave before she could do what she had to do.

"Try not to worry about it," she told her, lamely. *And go home, for both our sakes.*

Jennifer looked away. "It's just that, you know, my dad and

stuff . . ." She blinked. Her dad was hanging on to the farm with both hands, but they were doing no better than anyone else. Even if it did rain, he might not recover. It was Jennifer's salary that was keeping their heads above-water. Her mother worked at the big Wal-Mart in Avis, and that was what was paying their loan.

"Try not to worry about it," Karen repeated, firmly. She remembered the look on Jennifer's face when Loreena Campbell had called her a cold-hearted bitch. Probably the girl believed it. And would go on believing it, even after it rained. Jennifer gave her a withering look and got her purse from under the teller counter. It was five minutes to five.

"Well, see you tomorrow," she said. Karen sat down at the small desk between the safe and the counter and waved a busy good-bye. *Cold-hearted bitch.*

She waited twenty more minutes, glancing up at the clock again and again, pretending to make notes and fold up papers and put things in order and look very, very busy, until she was absolutely sure that town was shutting down for the day. She tried not to think too hard or too deeply about what she was doing. Her hands were shaking.

At twenty after five she stood up and quickly put away the papers that had been on the desk, her ruse for the last twenty minutes. There were no notes to be made (although she'd made a few mental ones).

Her heart was thundering away in her chest when she walked over to the teller counter and found herself a loan note. She stared at it for a long time.

Then she filled in a name. It wasn't her own.

Larry Watson, RR #2, Goodlands, North Dakota, she wrote. She filled in Larry's social security number, his general information, and information that only she and the tax man had access to—his account balances, assets, liabilities, and current mortgage. He owned his farm; his car was ten years old and his pickup was predrought, only five years old. It was holding up nicely.

She filled in his income for last year, fudging a little, no more than Larry himself might have if he was indeed applying for a CFC loan.

When all the information was filled in she amortized the loan that Larry Watson, one of the few liquid farmers in Goodlands, would be taking out. He was borrowing five thousand dollars. And he would never know.

Unless it didn't rain. Then everyone would know.

The first payment would be due in thirty-one days. Karen would barely be able to make it. Not much of her salary was unclaimed. What was that saying? Why is there so much month left over at the end of my money? If she got caught—if the head office so much as sent a thank-you note to Larry Watson—she would tell. They would declare her a liability and a bad debt and she would not be transferred, she would not be promoted, or even demoted, she would not pass Go, she would certainly not collect $200. She would be prosecuted for fraud. But if she was caught, she would simply explain what she had done and hope for the best. As she stood there, it occurred to her that if she told now, she would not be believed; and if she told later, she would be accused of lying to save herself. She was between a bank and a hard place.

She entered the loan into the computer. All neat and decent. Then she opened a separate account for Larry, forging his familiar and easy signature and signing all his papers. She added her own signature, a bit shaky on the loan note, but better on the account papers, which required only her initials. She thought briefly about using Jennifer's initials on the account stuff, realizing that she rarely opened any accounts for people—they were seldom that busy—but drew the line at dragging Jen into it. She was in enough trouble anyway. Forgery was probably a separate charge.

When she stood at the open drawer in the safe room and counted out $2,500 of the money, there was a sick and familiar feeling in the pit of her stomach. It was the feel of the crisp bills in her hands, the excitement of taking the money, of having the money. She was shopping. It might have been a trip back in time to the old days, a blast from her past. In spite of the air conditioning in the bank, she was perspiring badly. She could smell herself when she moved. The animal smell of fear that she had avoided so successfully that morning with Chase and Juba. But this time, no one would ever know.

If it rained.

It would simply have to rain. Karen put away the rest of the papers and filed Larry Watson's bogus loan in a dark place in her desk drawer. By the time she left the bank, the streets of downtown Goodlands were all but deserted.

When Karen saw Henry Barker's pickup in the road in front of her house, her first thought was that he knew. That Jennifer had called him. *Mr. Barker, I just left Karen Grange at the bank and I think she was up to some kind of no good. You'd better get on over there.* But that couldn't have happened, it *hadn't* happened. She tried to keep her knees from shaking as she got out of her car. He waved from the front porch. Tom Keatley was nowhere in sight. She hoped they hadn't met. Hoped he hadn't offered him a cup of his coffee, maybe told him how he felt about questions. She tried to hold her purse casually, in a way that did not reveal its $2,500 cargo among the spare tampons, lipstick, comb, wallet, and breath mints.

"Hello, Henry," she called, waving as she started up the walk to the porch.

" 'Lo there, Karen. Hot enough for ya?"

"It is that," she said. He made room for her on the porch, stepping aside to let her get to the door. But Karen didn't move to the door. She had no idea if Tom was inside or not.

She put her purse down carefully on the porch floor. It looked fat and full. For one horrible second she wondered if the catch would burst and send her contraband flying all over the yard for Henry to see.

"Don't see much of you these days, Henry. What can I do for you?" *Keep it casual.* She glanced down at her purse. The catch was, of course, holding.

Henry pulled a pack of cigarettes out of his breast pocket in an effort to look casual himself, a gesture he had seen on *Matlock*.

"Weelll," he started, then held the pack out to her. "You mind if I smoke?" he asked. She shook her head no. "Good. Never know what folks are going to say these days." He lit a match and cupped his hand around it. There was no breeze and it seemed like another gesture he'd seen on a cop show. *Heat of the Night* maybe, in reruns. "You want one?"

"No, thank you," she said. She could still smell the fear on herself. She wondered if he could smell it. Could cops smell fear the way animals and bankers could? Or was that something from television, too? She had to work to keep her breathing regular.

Henry puffed on his cigarette. "I hope you don't mind my just coming right out and asking you what could be a pretty private question, but you know the way things have been around town lately, what with all the funny things going on and all. I gotta cover all the bases, right?

"Well, last night, as you probably well know, there was a big to-do out at the Kramer place. Fire in the eastern corner. The windbreak went up like a matchstick. So dry, you know.

"Anyhoo, that Jacob Tindal and his wife Geena, I don't know if you know them or not, but they headed out to Kramer's there. Good Christ, just about everybody in town showed up to help, or so they say, but they just ended up getting in the way of the real help, you know what I mean. John Livingstone cut his hand on a goddamn fence post—pardon my language—trying to cut across and get a better look. People won't stay home if they don't have to, you know what I mean.

"Anyway, the Tindals live about five miles up the road here, thereabouts, and they happened to be passing by down here and they think they saw someone walking down this road here right after the fire. Some fella, they said. I don't suppose you saw anyone, yourself, last night, roundabouts eleven o'clock, let's say?"

Karen had listened to the whole speech with a blank stare, glancing now and again to the purse perched up against the door. She wasn't ready for the question.

"Saw someone?" she said. She thought she could feel her knees start to shake. She wished she could sit down.

"You know, a stranger. Were you up around that time?" He sucked on his cigarette, thoughtfully blowing the smoke away from Karen's face, but his eyes never left hers.

"No," she said, too quickly.

"You didn't see the fire from here?" he asked, surprised.

"Yes," she said. "I saw it. I called it in. But I mean, I didn't see anyone." She swallowed a dry breath.

He nodded. He'd finished his cigarette, but he held it in his hand, between finger and thumb, letting it burn down. The smell of the filter burning stunk up the air between them.

"You don't mind if I ask you the personal part, then?" He grinned sheepishly at her.

"No, that's all right."

"I was just wondering if you had some company staying with you these days? Geena thought she saw someone walking into your place. In the mirror, I mean. The rearview. A fella," he added.

Small towns.

"No," she lied. "She must be mistaken." She wondered why she lied. It would have been a simple matter to claim Tom was a cousin, a long-lost brother, a boyfriend, an old friend from the city. Maybe she could even have come clean and said he was a rainmaker. Then everyone in town could talk about how Karen Grange from the bank had gone off the deep end and was probably calling the psychic hotline at night to boot. But she lied.

There it was, then. Now she could add impeding justice, or whatever that would be called, on her growing rap sheet. And aiding and abetting a criminal. Harboring a witness. Was that a crime? Add it to the list. Of course, the fraud and forgery charge would be federal, whereas this was small stuff, probably state. Get in line, Henry Barker.

"Sorry," she added.

Henry nodded. "Okay then. I just thought I should stop over and cover all the bases, you know what I mean." He dropped the butt on the porch and ground it down with his toe, then he bent over and picked it up. It left a black, ashy mark on the paint. He rubbed it with his shoe. It stayed. He picked the butt up and threw it into the overgrown garden at the front of the house.

"It's out," he said. "I won't be taking up any more of your time. I'm sure you want to get your supper. It's damn near six-thirty," he said. "You always home this late?"

Karen did not look down at her purse. "A little extra work at the bank tonight," she said. At the same time she willed Tom Keatley to stay wherever he was for as long as it took for Henry Barker to drive away. She plastered a smile all over her face. "Bye, Henry, nice to see you."

"Yeah, been in town so much more these days than I used to be. Sign of the times, I guess." Henry went down the porch stairs. He walked slowly toward the pickup while Karen counted the seconds, mentally keeping Tom away.

At the truck Henry called back to her, "You let me know if you see anyone suspicious, okay?" he said. Just before he pulled open the door, he looked down at the road and stooped to pick something up. He looked at it. It disappeared into a pocket. Henry's frugality was legendary. He must have found a dime. Karen held back a giggle, wondering what he'd think if he'd checked out her purse; wondering if he'd turn her in—or split it with her.

He threw a wave and got into the truck. He pulled away.

Anyone suspicious. In a small town, that could be anyone. Including her.

She waited until the truck disappeared before picking up her purse and stepping into the house. Then, for the first time in hours, she breathed normally.

A banner day.

Karen sat in the living room until the sky started to darken. By then, she had decided that he'd left.

A con man.

He'd never meant to make it rain. He'd never made it rain in those other places, he was probably just lucky. He wasn't a rain-maker at all, he was an opportunist. She supposed he'd weighed and measured his chances of getting any cash out of her, and had decided that she was a dud. She knew she should go through the house and check for missing things—she had some very valuable things, thanks to her dark days—but she didn't do it. Hopefully a dirty, scruffy drifter wouldn't know a good piece of porcelain if it bit him on the ass. She had several.

In fact she could see her piece of Capodimonte from where she was sitting, an objet d'art from those very dark days she was thinking of. Those days that she had revisited that afternoon. All for naught. Karen was as close to crying as she had ever been, al-though she supposed the figurine's still being there was a good sign.

All for naught.

Maybe he had set the fire out at Kramer's. Maybe Henry knew more than he was saying.

She had almost begged Chase and Juba for another year. Put her already tenuous position with the bank on even shiftier ground. Made a fool of herself. Again. Maybe loans wouldn't even be the next position. Maybe she would find herself, next year, back at a teller window, calling out "Next" to people who complained about how slowly the line moved. That would be her future. And the best she would be able to afford on what tellers made, was a dime store.

The money was still sealed inside the blank envelope, tucked inside her purse, the catch now open to save the stress on what had once been a very expensive bag. The purse was on the floor in her bedroom closet, behind twelve tidily stacked shoe boxes. It would stay there until the next day, when she would take it back to the bank, destroy the loan information before it got zapped to the head office, and put the money back in the safe. Then she would put this behind her and move on.

Move on to what? she wondered. She thought back to the bit on TV where she had seen the rainmaker, the way he had looked, standing wet in pouring rain, a tilted grin moving up one side of his face, his expression one of satisfaction and pure pleasure; he brought his hands up to push his wet hair off his face, out of his eyes, as he spoke, his T-shirt plastered to his body so that the skin showed through. Behind him people walked around in the rain, looking up at the sky, drinking it in, laughing, talking fun. The people behind him, almost all of them, wore slickers or carried umbrellas. He was the only one in the rain without something to keep him dry. The last time she'd felt as disappointed as she did now was when, after three weeks, she still had no reply from the rainmaker who had made it rain in Winslow, Kansas, and she knew he wouldn't come.

She went into the kitchen and made herself some tea.

Just after it was full dark she heard him climb the back porch stairs. Without knocking, he opened the screen door and poked his head in.

The house was dark. Karen didn't speak.

"Mind if I come in?" he said.

She sipped her tea. "I do."

"Should I close the door?"

"Bugs will come in," she said. He let the door slip quietly closed. The old wooden porch chair that had come with the house squeaked as he sat down in it.

Tom rolled himself a smoke and lit it. He leaned back in the chair and propped his legs up on the railing. The smoke stung his throat. It was parched. Like the bush he'd been in most of the day, moving from place to place around Karen's property, and finally, around Goodlands itself, sticking to the back roads where it was quieter, smelling, feeling, pulling, tugging at the skies, searching for the pocket that would let him through. There was dust and dirt in the creases in his face. His T-shirt, fresh that morning, was now patchy with dirt and sweat. Even in the cool of the dark, with the sun gone for an hour, the air was stiflingly hot and thick. He was dry. As dry as he'd ever been.

"A cup of that tea would be nice," he called from the porch, trying to sound more casual than he felt.

Her voice, coming from inside the house, was flat. "Why don't you conjure yourself up a glass of water?" she said. He smiled a rueful smile.

Tom smoked in spite of his throat, and stared out into the night. Goodlands was a peaceful, quiet place. Most of the places he went were like that, and that was why he went. But here, under the peace, he could feel something else. A current of something that ran through the whole of the town. When he listened, he thought he could almost hear a steady, persistent hum. Not the kind that you would notice as you went about your day, but something that might sink into you after a while, making you a little irritable at first, and then cranky, and then, just before you cracked, you would stare into the face of it and scream. When he listened, as he had all day, that was what he heard.

"Is that what you want?" he started slowly. "A party trick? Some kind of proof? 'Give me a sign!' " he mimicked, irritated.

"I thought you'd left." He looked behind him, startled. Karen had stepped into the doorway. She had her forehead pressed against the screen so she could look at him without opening the door. A circle of her skin showed white through it.

"I was walking around, checking out your little town," he said. "These things take time, *ma'am*."

"I thought you were going to make it rain today."

He hesitated. "We have an arrangement," he said, carefully.

"I pay you, you make it rain, is that our arrangement? But you won't or *can't* make it rain without the money."

"Something like that," he said. He added, "Are you in some kind of bad mood?"

Karen laughed. She put a hand over her open mouth, to stop any more laughter from coming out, because she could feel it there. Hysterical laughter. "Yeah, I guess I am," she said after a moment. "The sheriff was here."

"What did you do, rob a bank?" He chuckled at his joke. Karen's small leftover smile faded. If he had looked at her then, he would have seen her brown eyes close. He heard her deep breath go in and come out slowly. The circle of flesh disappeared from the screen.

"The sheriff thinks that maybe you started that fire last night. Someone saw you coming here," she said, quietly. Her voice sounded tired, dead.

With the last of her energy, Karen said firmly, "I'm out of patience and time. If you *do* have a party trick to show me, then I think you'd better do it. You're not getting a dime from me until you *prove* you can make it rain." She hooked the latch on the screen door.

"And don't come in here," she added before closing the inside door.

Tom listened to her lock the bolt. He took a last drag of his cigarette.

"These things take time," he said quietly, more to himself than to anyone who might be still standing behind the closed door, as he knew Karen was. He took a last, sick drag on his cigarette and butted it on his boot, sticking the butt into the pocket of his jeans.

There was something wrong with this town, it wouldn't let him in. Why didn't he leave?

There was something here. His forehead was creased in a frown. He had felt his door to the sky closing. That had never happened before, not in as long as he had made it rain. So what was here? Tom teetered back on the chair again and thought about leaving. It wouldn't be the first time he picked up and left someplace without a good-bye. There was no reason to stay if he didn't make it rain.

He sat in the chair for a long time before he got up and walked out to the clearing in the orchard.

Sometime in the very middle of the middle of the night, Karen woke to a tapping on her window. She didn't immediately identify the sound, but searched her mind in half sleep. Bird? breeze? vampire . . . ?

"Grange?"

Karen came fully awake. "Huh?" She clutched the sheet all the way to her neck. She turned toward the window, trying to see out. It was too dark. Then she saw movement, a hand.

"It's Tom."

"What do you want?"

"Come to the door," he said. A shadow moved from the window, toward the front of the house. Karen lay back, still holding the sheet up to her neck. She shook her head to get rid of the last of the fuzzies and sat up.

She was wearing only a long cotton nightdress. She frantically searched for a robe. She had six. Why the hell couldn't she find one? She found her slippers, slid them on. She finally found a robe on the desk, slipped it over her shoulders, and held it closed with one hand. With the other hand, she removed the chair she had propped under the bedroom doorknob, and wrenched it aside.

She found him on the front porch, waiting for her. It had cooled off a little, and although there was no breeze, it was nice outside, out of the heat of her bedroom.

"Sorry," he said. "Did I scare you?"

"What do you want?"

"I didn't come in," he pointed out.

"What time is it?" she asked. It was still full dark. She felt as though she had just fallen asleep, although she had been asleep for hours, a troubled sleep.

"I don't know, late. I have something to show you," he said.

He reached over to grab her free hand, before she could stop him. She yanked it back.

"Don't!"

"Hey," he said, softly, raising both his hands to show he meant no harm. He seemed excited. "Come with me."

Karen stepped back, away from him. "No."

Tom went partway down the stairs and turned to her, motioning her to follow him. "Come on," he urged. "It's your party trick." He went down the remaining step and walked toward the back of the house.

Karen stood on the porch for a moment longer, and then followed.

He was leading her to the clearing. Just as on the night he first came, the headlines roared through her head.

Goodlands Banker Murdered in Orchard. $2,500 in Stolen Money Recovered from Very Expensive Handbag in Bedroom. Banker Found in Pieces. Finally Rains in Goodlands. Rains Bankers, though.

The sharp, dry grass scratched at her ankles. It would be worse in the clearing, where there was sharp brush. While she walked, she slipped her arms through the sleeves of her robe, letting it hang loose in front of her. She tried to keep Tom in her sights. He walked on ahead of her, glancing back now and then, smiling when he saw her following him.

Away from the sanctuary offered by the porch, Karen became aware of the darkness, the still night air, the nearly silent sound of him moving ahead of her.

He was walking toward the apple grove. She stayed a good forty feet behind him, and now and then lost sight of him, though his shirt reflected white in the darkness.

They cut across the backyard, past the gazebo with its gothic lines, past the overgrown rock garden—just a dimly glowing circle in the dark yard—past the tree line that marked out the full of the yard, and then into the first of the apple trees. Tom disappeared into the grove.

Karen stepped between two tall trees that had been planted too close together, and whose branches had since entwined, and she saw him again. He stood waiting for her in the center of the clearing. She stopped and stared, trying to decide: Should she bolt back to the house, or should she step into the circle?

Her heart pounded. It could have been the utter lack of cardiovascular activity in her life, or it could have been him.

In the moonlight that filtered through the trees, turning their poor, thirsty tops silver, he seemed to glow. It was his white T-shirt, she decided. And his eyes. She could see them, the white showing around blue irises, exaggerating their roundness. He looked as he had the first time she'd seen him, on the TV, from Winslow, Kansas. One step and she would be very close to him.

Did she still want it to rain?

Karen stepped through the trees into the clearing.

He held a hand out to her. "Come here. Stand with me." Karen stopped about four feet in front of him, and ignored his hand. She swallowed. "I'll stand here."

"Okay, sure." He chuckled, a grin, which Karen suspected wasn't for her, spreading on his face. He ran his hands nervously through his hair, pushing it off his face, the way he had in the video clip. His bare arms reflected the scant light in the clearing. She became aware of how dark it really was in the orchard. If she had to run, would she be able to see? she wondered. Or was she at his mercy? Gooseflesh rippled up her back. It wasn't exactly fear.

"Give me your hand," he said, reaching over for it. She shook her head no. He kept his hand held out to her. "Please," he said, quietly, and reached out again tentatively. "Please?" She finally let him take her hand, holding it out stiffly, not liking the feeling of his palm, beneath hers. His was large and warm. Their hands rested very lightly together.

"What is this?" she demanded, uncomfortably aware of his heat.

"Shhhh," he said. He eased her hand gently until it was cupped, and held it that way with his own. She looked up to him, and his eyes began to close slowly. He raised their arms together, palms upward, to her eye level, and held them there. She stood facing him, rigid, unyielding, only dimly aware of the sudden change in the meadow.

She watched him.

He closed his eyes fully. Then he opened them. "A party trick," he said, "by Tom Keatley. For Karen Grange." He winked and closed his eyes again. Karen smiled.

He stood very still, like a statue in the middle of the clearing.

When Tom closed his eyes, he let go of the place in the orchard. He emptied his mind of Karen, of the trees, of Goodlands, of the incredible *dryness* here that he couldn't explain. He reached up, farther and farther, and found the rain. It was there. As always he could feel the wetness inside his body; the plump and pregnant clouds that were holding it seemed to be inside him. But this time, it was as though he were standing very nearby, but not near enough. He tried again, as he had many times that day, to pull it toward him. When he grabbed at it, he could hold on. He could feel it there, letting him touch it. And he could tug it a little, as though his door to the sky was all but closed. But he couldn't bring it in. He didn't have to bring it all. He had only to bring enough over to convince her. To show her that he could do it. Just enough for a show.

He strained against the sky, teeth clenched, lips pulled back in a grimace. The muscles of his face and body stiffened with the exertion. He found a neat little pocket of rain to the west of them. He settled on it. He worked the sky through his little doorway.

The heat in the meadow was impossible. Full, sultry. Karen watched Tom's face change. His face turned upward, to the sky. One arm reached up, palm up. Nothing in the clearing moved.

The stillness moved through her, soothing her. Her eyes were locked on his face. He was motionless. He didn't seem to know she was there. Karen kept her eyes open and watched his face. Energy seemed to come off him in waves, running down through his hand to her. She could feel something change in the air around her. Her nightgown clung to her. Sweat radiated along her hairline. She became aware of the trees, their smell. Everything in the clearing became hyperreal, hyperalive. She was transfixed.

Karen was still looking into Tom's face, had watched it change, settle, relax, when she heard the first sound. A trickle as if from a stream. Something familiar filled her hand. It broke through the heat in her body and chilled the flesh of her palm. It slipped softly down her arm. Moonlight sparkled, following the rivulets. With the light splashed over her, she saw it. Her eyes widened and her lips parted as she drew in breath.

In the palm of her hand there was a little pool of cool, fresh water. It trickled down through the tiny spaces between her fingers, down to her elbow. She could feel it. See it. Smell it.

Rain.

CONVERSATION, LOUD AND GARBLED WITH WHISKEY, FLOATED
up through the grate in the floor of Vida's bedroom. Downstairs,
there was a party going on. Vida fixed the time at sometime after
one in the morning, when Clancy's shut down, and before five,
when the homemade whiskey and beer would finally shut everyone up. Other than that, time stood still.

Vida had spent the better part of the night trying to figure
things out through the fog that had been with her for most of the
day. The fog was a part of the problem that she had been working through. The fog was inside her, covering up some of her
own thoughts and intervening with its own.

The fog was a woman. The woman was inside her.

Outwardly, Vida was the same. Her thick, dark hair looked
somewhat different, maybe, and her brown eyes were cloudy.
These were not changes that anyone else might have noticed, but
Vida thought she saw them. When she looked at herself, she could

swear she saw someone else's features briefly superimposed on her own. It could have been the glass in her mirror, spotted with missing silver, and wavy. She didn't think it was that at all. She thought it was the woman.

The woman had a name, and that name seemed always to be just slightly out of reach to Vida, there and then not there, resting on the tip of her tongue, never quite coming through, like the whispered, mumbled words she thought she could hear in her head, never clear enough to make out. What was clear was that the pictures, the images, and the woman's thoughts came to Vida that way.

They were simple thoughts: *Find the man.* The man-thought, which came to Vida regularly, was particularly powerful and clear. It was cloaked in black-dark fog, like an oil slick resting uncomfortably above a water hole, the sound of thick, greasy oil loudly pouring down, like an evil rainstorm. Sometimes a smell accompanied the thought and it was foul enough to make Vida wrinkle her nose up. The foul stink of sweat and blood and feces. The impression would be brief, more visual than visceral, but nonetheless, strong enough to cause a physical reaction. That was the simple thought: *Find the man.*

Behind the simple thought was a darker notion, whose meaning was hidden from her. She had only a general idea that once she found the man, there would be work to be done.

She could not make out the woman's name, and as the party raged on underneath her feet, the floor occasionally thumping with some thrown object, she distractedly tried to listen to what was inside her.

She didn't think long on who the woman was. The woman was a friend. That was all that was important. She was a friend, and if Vida did as she was told—*Find the man*—then they would both get the things they wanted.

What did Vida want? Her mind wandered over the town of Goodlands, the town that refused to allow her to belong, to move up out of the gutter her family had dragged her into.

Standing alone in the middle of her shabby bedroom, the bare bulb hanging above her head, Vida closed her eyes and felt the presence of the woman.

Vida's arms extended from her body. She let her head drop backward, her face turned to the light. She concentrated on the electrical feeling that coursed through her body. It ran like a current from the top of her head through her neck and torso, creating an odd pool in her belly, and from there surged downward through her legs, her feet, the floorboards.

She could feel it reaching outside the house. The current raced over the town; she could almost, but not quite, see its path through desiccated fields, through the burned-out windbreak at Kramer's farm, over the slight rise on Route 55, down the main street, through the Dry Goods and over the debris from the fallen tree, through empty ditches, over tractors, cars, and trucks. The current ran over it all.

Somewhere very far from where Vida stood, the man would be. He was there, somewhere, in town. Vida had only to find him.

Above her, the light extinguished, puffed out as though it had been only a flame on a candle. The room was dark. Vida stood that way for a very long time, long after the party downstairs wound itself down, and would stand there long after the light of the next day began to creep up the wall of her bedroom. On her face was a small, determined smile.

Tom was still holding her hand.

Karen was captivated by the small puddle of water in her palm. She raised her head to look at him. His face shone with perspiration, but he was smiling.

"Do you believe me?"

"Yes."

She shook her head in wonder, in spite of what she'd said. But it *was* there, soft on her skin. The rain in her hand had all but slipped through her fingers, and what was left was now warm.

The meadow was still and quiet. The sky was clear. There were no rain clouds. She looked back at Tom.

"How—?"

In the dark, his face was indistinct. He shrugged, not returning her look. Instead he reached up with his other hand and dipped a finger in what was left of the rain. His touch was light in her hand.

They were standing very close together. Again Karen felt his heat, from his hand and from his body, so close to hers. She swallowed and leaned away from him, stepping back a little. But he kept holding her hand.

Karen was uncomfortably aware of his hands touching hers. She realized at some point that she wasn't pulling away. On his face was a look of intense satisfaction, as though he might laugh out loud at any moment. Her stomach tightened as she watched him. Her hand was hot, like a live thing that she might not be able to control. She was flushed, her cheeks warm. Her mouth felt dry and she wished, ironically, for water.

Tom looked up. They stared at each other for a moment, and for Karen the meadow's silence increased until she could hear nothing at all, not even her own breathing. His head leaned forward, closer to hers.

They stood like that for a long time. Then Tom lifted his finger from her palm and curled her hand in his for just a second, giving it a small press before letting her go completely. The moment passed.

"That was just . . ." he said, breathing deeply and looking away, into the sky.

"You won't tell me?" He didn't answer. "But it's not a trick?" she pressed.

"No."

He smiled secretively and stepped past her toward the trees. Karen stood alone for a second or two before turning and following him. The irritation that she had felt for him earlier that night returned.

"Well then," she called ahead, her voice sounding unnaturally loud in the stillness, "when will you make it rain for real?"

He didn't turn or speak. She followed him through the trees until they were in her backyard. Things seemed very different then, as though the moment in the clearing had never happened at all.

"Wait!"

He stopped and turned back to look at her. "Did you hear me?" she asked.

"Yup."

"Well?"

"I don't know," he said, and began walking again. At the gazebo, he slipped inside and dragged out his bedroll, laid it flat on the grass.

"What do you mean, you don't know?"

Tom sat on the blanket and got comfortable, drawing up his legs and leaning his arms across them. She noticed that his shirt was damp, and clung to him. His hair stuck to his neck and forehead. His skin shone in the light from the porch lamp.

"What do you think 'I don't know' means?" he said, sighing.

Karen stood above him. "Is it the money? I have the money."

Keeping his gaze away from her, he leaned back on the blanket and lay flat. His hands went behind his head and propped it up. Then he looked at her. Or through her. She crossed her arms over her chest, pulling her robe closed, feeling vulnerable and foolish suddenly, standing outside in her nightdress.

"Aren't you going to answer me?"

He closed his eyes. "You got your proof," he said. "Now you're going to have to wait."

"Wait for what?" she demanded.

Tom remained silent. She heard a bird fly from the trees. A minute passed.

Karen groaned. "Tell me what is going on, first."

His body stiffened and he sat up. His face clouded. He looked up at her, standing over him, leaning over him, her own face angry and demanding.

"I don't *know*," he repeated. "That was just a sample, like a *test* bit. Something bigger, anything bigger . . ." He thought about the skies over Goodlands and how *closed* they were, no better word for it. He couldn't say that. He couldn't let her think that it wouldn't happen. Because it would. He shrugged.

"I showed you. These things take time," he said, feeling like it was a lie. Because it hadn't taken any time before. He lay back down on the blanket and repositioned his arms. His eyes closed again.

Karen stood like that for a while, not ready to give up. When it was clear that his side of the conversation was over, she turned and walked back toward the house.

She was too agitated to sleep. The clock said it was three-thirty in the morning, and she *had* to get to sleep, had to get to work looking much as she had when she left, without any extra lines of worry or concern. She had to be *normal*.

Normal. The image of him lying on his blanket in the backyard came up before her closed eyes and forced them open.

What was he doing to her? Was it a game? Why wouldn't he tell her what was going on?

But it had really happened. She couldn't articulate it, even to herself, but she knew instinctively that it had really happened. The cool, clear water in her palm had been rain. There was something different about the way rain felt from the harsh, cold, hard water of Goodlands.

When she was a little girl, her parents had kept a rain barrel beside the house. It was special water, kept for watering the garden when it was dry, for times when the drinking water was low, and for fine washables, as her mother called her big, old-woman undies and slips. They kept a dipper hanging alongside the rain barrel, and on hot afternoons, when Karen played in the sun and got sweaty and hot, she would take a drink. Her mother didn't like her to drink from the barrel, but her father kept the dipper there for just that reason. He would come in from the fields and head right over to the barrel, scooping up a whole dipperful, water slopping over the sides of the dipper and back into the barrel, and he would put his mouth against it and slurp it up, swallowing until the dipper was empty. When she had been very little, he would give her some, because she couldn't reach on her own.

If her mother saw them, she would call out, "Hank! You're *teaching* that girl!" Privately she would scold Karen. "The birds do their business in that water, girl," she would say. "Your father doesn't know better. The Granges never had proper water at their old place, and that's why your dad drinks from the barrel. But we have proper water, and you can just go and get yourself a glass in the kitchen and run it from the tap," she would add firmly. But Karen's father wouldn't drink from the kitchen unless he was very, very tired or thirsty. He called it "kitchen water," and screwed his face up at his wife. "For washing dishes and wiping noses."

Karen drank water from the barrel. And deep in the summer, when the house was hot from cooking, her mother would some-times help Karen wash her hair outside, with the soft, warm-cool water from the barrel running down her back, soaking her clothes through the towel around her neck. The barrel water was soft as velvet and as fragrant and fresh as the way the garden smelled when it was wet from a rain. Nothing else on earth smelled that way. Nothing could.

And that's how she *knew* it hadn't been a trick. Unless Tom Keatley could also make the rain smell and feel the way it was supposed to, and make the meadow quiet the way it would get when it rained. If he could do all that, she would pay him the money anyway.

Karen was getting sleepy, remembering. Her mind drifted back to the meadow. Unconsciously, she curled the fingers of her right hand up until they were touching her palm, very lightly. He hadn't *really* been touching her, of course, he had only been holding her hand open to catch the stream as it came down. It had only been her imagination that had made it seem as if he'd held on to her hand for longer than he'd had to.

It was only her imagination that he had been close enough to kiss.

She didn't want to kiss him. She would never have closed the space between them by leaning forward, face tilted toward him, close enough that it would have been possible.

Sleep was sweeping over Karen. Her hand, with its curled fingers, relaxed and opened. She sighed.

Just as sleep took her away, she saw his face, closer to hers than before, a little smile on his lips, which looked soft and cool, as the rain had felt.

Tom's breathing was shallow as he lay on the blanket. He did not sleep, though he was exhausted. He lay staring up into the clear, dark sky while a million stars, with nothing to block them out, stared back.

His body had stopped shaking, and he was beginning to relax. He had no idea what had happened out there. But it had never happened before.

There was something wrong in this place. He'd felt it ever since he'd come. That hum that ran underneath the earth, the incredible, persistent *dryness* of the place, the way the sky wouldn't open for him, the feeling that something was blocking his view of the sky, locking him out.

It had taken everything he had to show Karen the rain. Every muscle, every nerve had been stretched open to pull down for her the little bit that had come through him. He had never worked so hard for so little. Three nights before, he had brought a downpour, easy.

The possibility that he was dry loomed inside him, but he refused it, pushed it back. He'd never considered such a thing. He'd never been dry. Not from the first time he'd called to the heavens and they, in return, poured forth.

He had been ten or maybe eleven. He lived with his mother

and father in a two-room house on the edge of town. On one side were neighbors, a gas station, and the road to town. On the other side were the railroad tracks and endless bush country, deep and thick and filled with secret places that Tom knew well.

His father worked at the mill in town and earned a decent living, if the other mill workers were any example. Tom's dad gambled his away, sometimes winning, and when he did win, Tom and his mother got presents and dinner out, or fried chicken brought in. When he was losing, the old man would stay away for days, sneaking back into the house and taking the presents back—Tom's watch, his mom's jewelry, pots, pans, whatever he could get his hands on without getting caught—and he would disappear with it. Tom knew now that it was pawned and played with again, as his father tried to win it back. The bad times—and they could go on for weeks—were days and nights with his father gone. When he was winning, he didn't stop; when he was losing, he couldn't. He never missed a day's work, recognizing that the money would dry up if he did, but when the day was over, he was likely as not at the races in the city, at a card game, at a dice game, or in the bar making bets. The stuff he brought home would be dutifully put away, but not used too much, because even Tom's toys, when he was little, might be scooped up and taken away at a moment's notice.

Tom couldn't forget the way he was, even though when things were going his way he was happy and laughing and generous. It was all only temporary. Things would be bad again just as soon as he got back into the game. From the age of six, Tom learned not to trust the good times, and would avoid his father when he was home.

His mother, though, drank up those good times like sweet water. Dancing with the old man after he brought the record player back, heartily eating his restaurant-bought fried chicken, licking her fingers and laughing at his lame jokes, trying to get Tom to join in. He wouldn't.

The good times were accompanied by a parade of good intentions. Late at night, when Tom was in bed, he'd hear his father telling his mother what he was going to do with the money he'd won, always claiming he had a new scheme that was going to make them rich.

It was a cycle of win and lose.

By the time Tom was ten, his mother was lined and old-looking, worn out from work and worry.

When he was losing, the old man beat her. Tom, too, if he got in the way, or tried to stop him from hitting her. His mother would scream at him to run, get out of the house, and Tom would run into the woods behind the tracks and wait, sometimes hearing them, but more often not, the whole thing taking place almost in silence, his father grunting with exertion, his mother muffling her cries.

By the time he was ten, he was nearly as tall as the old man. He stopped running into the woods. He fought back. No match for his father, who was still bigger and stronger, he would end up getting the worst of it. But Tom had rage that his father didn't have, and that made up, some, for the difference.

His mother would beg for her husband and son to stop. She would pull Tom away, dragging him by the waist.

"Hit *me*, Bart, leave the boy. Hit *me*," she'd beg him.

In the middle of August the year Tom was eleven, the old man had been gone for a week. They hadn't seen him in seven days and nights, although there were signs that he'd been around, either sneaking back in the night when they were sleeping, or coming in when they were out in the bush picking the fat berries that Tom and his mother would sell in town for cash. His mother's silver brush, comb, and mirror set, treasured for a little while, had disappeared; the big oak mirror was gone from the wall by the door; the cookie jar money—back up to four dollars from the last time—was gone. His father's buck knife with the bone handle was gone. The next thing to go would be the deer rifle, pawned and retrieved so many times there was still a tag hanging from the barrel. After that it would be his mother's wedding band, forced from her finger, just as it would be put back on when the old man was flush again. Not always the same band, either, but his mother took it back all the same, with the same enthusiasm and pleasure.

That August, when the old man hadn't been home in a week, Tom and his mother wandered around the house in silence, did the berry picking in silence, and walked to town with the full baskets in silence. They both knew it was just a matter of time.

He tried, once, to talk to her.

"Let's just get out of here before he comes home," he said.

"Hush" was what she answered.

Another time he told her that he could get a job. They could live somewhere else.

"Maybe he's had a run," she said. They both knew he hadn't, or he would have been home already. Showing off the winnings. Fanning out a wad of cash that would be his stake. Bringing home baby chicks, or beads for his mother to string into jewelry. Or a wedding band with someone else's name on it.

It was nearly midnight on a Sunday when the old man came up the road. Tom heard him through his open bedroom window. His step was fast.

His mother was still awake, even though he had heard her open the pullout bed. They had each lain awake and listened to the other breathe. Something was in the air that told them he would be home soon.

By the time he heard the front door thrown open, the rage in Tom was rising like a tangible thing, from inside his body. Black, red, hot rage.

"GET UP!" the old man hollered at his mother. Tom heard the springs in the pullout scream and his mother's feet hit the floor.

The next thing Tom heard before crawling out his bedroom window was his mother's muffled *"oof!"* and the sound of her body hitting the floor.

Young Tom slipped out of his window and out to the back shed, where he got the deer rifle, still tagged with the pawnbroker's tag, and checked the chamber.

The front door was still open. As he walked up he could see his father standing over his mother, kicking her as she clutched at her stomach.

He raised the gun. He and his mother locked eyes. Hers widened.

"NO!" she screamed. His father looked at the door and saw Tom with the gun. Tom fired. The old man never made a sound. Except for his *"oof!"* when the shell hit him.

Then his mother was screaming. "You killed him! You little bastard, you killed him!" she sobbed, calling out her husband's name over and over.

Tom ran to the woods, his heart thundering, his blood in his ears. He ran until he thought his chest would burst. In the middle of the woods, with nothing but trees surrounding him, he threw the gun aside and howled into the sky.

Rain exploded with a crash of lightning that seemed to come from his chest. He could feel the thunder when it cracked, the lightning breaking up the skies with blazing light. It came from *him,* an invisible cord that he pulled but couldn't see. It was his and he knew it right from that first time. He would keep it forever after that night, making it rain at first when he was tormented, angry. Then later, when he was older, he gained some control over it, though never seeing the cord when he pulled it, never looking into the door that he knew he could open at will. He never knew if it had always been his or if it became his after his father died, but he always connected the two events with the night he first made it rain.

Until he came to Goodlands and something shut his door.

That night, in Karen's backyard, it took Tom a long time to fall into a light sleep.

F I V E

I N THE HEAT OF THE MORNING SUN, HENRY BARKER WAS BACK IN Goodlands, in the far northeast corner at Dave Revesette's ranch. He found Dave out by the barn, dragging a big black horse inside. He stopped at the gate to the barnyard and waited a respectable distance away. He'd never liked horses. As far as Henry was concerned, they were the most unpredictable animals God made.

The barnyard, usually full of horses in the morning, was empty except for an old yellow nag that was the kids' pet from childhood, fifteen years old if she was a day. She wasn't tied or haltered but just stood at the water trough quietly, dipping her head every now and again to take a sip. That was more Henry's idea of a horse.

He strolled cautiously into the yard when Dave came out of the barn, wiping his forehead with a hanky.

"Sonofabitch wouldn't mind," he said, jabbing the hanky back into a pocket and putting his baseball cap back on. "She's little Anna Best's horse, and spoiled rotten. Kid comes over and feeds her sugar till she's ready to bolt and then goes home for another month. No one rides her except us, and I don't know how little Anna'd feel about that, but that horse sure as hell needs some discipline in her life. Both of them do, frankly, to my way of thinking." He reached out and shook Henry's hand. "How're you doing, Henry?"

"'Better than you, I hear. Missing some horses?"

"Shit, I come out here this morning, about six-thirty, and the yard's empty, except for Daisy. The animals don't go in this time of year, it's cool overnight, but I checked the barn, and sure-as-shit it was empty. I got on Daisy and did a walk around and found the fence like it was. Come on," he said, and turned on his heel for Henry to follow him.

Dave pointed to a spot on the horizon too far away for Henry to make out, but he knew it marked the end of the north side of the barnyard and the start of the highway that ran past.

"You lose any on the highway?" Henry asked.

"Not that we've seen so far, but we still got four missing. A couple of the roans we seen out as far as Nipple Creek, and Mike and Bobby Laylaw's boy are out there. There's still four we haven't spotted," he finished.

"You can see it from here." He pointed and Henry followed his finger to a post rising out of the ground all by itself. Where the next post should have been there was nothing.

"Had to be a goddamn near-hundred feet of fencing cut down," he said, his voice rising. "Goddamn metal fence. This is the only spot where the yard hits the highway. Whoever done it wanted those horses to get onto the road."

Up the highway Henry saw Mike, Dave's youngest, sitting sad-dleless on a chestnut and leading a darker horse behind him. A couple of hundred yards behind him was another kid with two more.

"How many you boarding these day, Dave?"

"There's still twelve, but now four of them are for sale.—I'm handling the sales, if you hear of any interest.—I have a feeling that Lester Pragg's going to take his two home. Can't afford it anymore. Things are—you know how things are around here, Henry," he said.

Henry stepped back to let the boys go past with the horses. One of the horses snorted a complaint over losing his brief freedom and Henry jumped.

"Shit!"

"He won't bite you." Dave chuckled. Both boys waved at Barker. "Take them right in, Mike. You see Brian?"

"Nah," Mike said.

"That Bobby Laylaw's boy?" Henry asked after the boys were past and the two men had started walking again.

Dave nodded. "Yup. Name's Joe, but he wants to be called Chance now," he said. "Wants to be a cowboy, for chrissakes." Henry laughed.

"You got anybody mad at you, Dave?"

"Can't think of anyone. Been trying all morning." He shook his head.

"What about kids?"

"This goes beyond devilment, Henry."

Henry nodded. The two men were about fourteen feet from the fence before Henry got a good look. The fence was cut on both sides, about a hundred feet of chain-link fencing with wooden posts, was lying on the ground, bent and twisted from the hooves of twenty or more anxious, free horses.

Henry bent down and looked at the part of the fencing that had been cut.

The ends weren't flat, but rounded.

"Isn't that a sonofabitch? They don't look cut to me. They look like they were snapped clean, or something."

He rubbed his thumb along the edge of the wire. It was smooth. He fixed the wire between his thumb and two fingers and put some pressure on it. It bent, but not easily. He sighed.

"Whaddya think?" Dave asked.

"Well," Henry said, having nothing at all to say except *sorry about your fence and sorry about your horses,* "is there a tool that you know of, could make this kind of a break? Something that would maybe snap it off, instead of cutting? Anything like that?"

Dave shook his head, frowning.

"Nope, nothing that I know of, and I've been fencing for thirty years," he said. "Can't you dust it for fingerprints, or something?"

Henry gave him a withering look. "Have to have pretty tiny fingers to leave a print, wouldn't you say, Dave?"

Dave stood up and took his cap off, smacking the fence with it. Dust flew up into the air. Then he hit it again.

"Goddammit! Somebody's done this and somebody's gotta pay for it! I'm still missing four horses!" He spun around and pointed a finger in Henry's face. "I know for a goddamn fact that I'm not the only one who's lost animals this way, Barker. There's been a real bundle of these going on. Someone's doing it deliberately, and what the hell is the sheriff of this county doing about it, exactly? Are you waiting to catch someone red-handed, for chrissakes? I know for a fact that someone went in and cut open the chicken yard out at Boychuk's and foxes got all his chickens. He said it looked like goddamn chicken Vietnam in that yard the next day." He smacked his hat on the wire part of the fence, and it shook. "So this time the horses just got out. What are you waiting for, the next time, when they get hit by a semi? Or maybe you're waiting for the time when my horses get into someone's yard and trample a garden, and then maybe you can come and arrest *me*!" Out of breath, he smacked his hat one last time, against his thigh.

Henry took his own hat off and wiped at his forehead with his hand, pushing his hair back, and replaced the cap. He hooked his thumbs in his belt loops underneath his impressive stomach.

"I guess I'll just have a look around here then, Dave, and be on my way. Maybe it was kids. School's out and God knows there's not much to do around here. But usually the thing to do

is go out and get stinking drunk. Sometimes they'll knock over a
couple of cows, but kids like horses."

"They're valuable animals, Henry," Dave said. "Thanks for
coming out, and I'm sorry about that bit, there. I'm obliged." He
held his hand out to Henry and the two men shook.

Henry stepped over the fence and started poking around in
the ditch, not expecting to find anything. He didn't.

The county seat is located in Weston, the largest of the seven
towns that make up Capawatsa County. It was a nice-size jurisdiction and Henry Barker had been sheriff for going on four
years, having come into office just after the drought in Goodlands had begun. At that time, it was considered just a bad spell,
one of those things that, unfortunately, are as familiar to farmers
as falling wheat prices.

He'd run for the office when old Ed Greer retired at sixty-
seven, telling people he was too old to chase dogs and break up
fights. He told Henry on the day they traded places that the real
reason he was calling it a day was that he was more and more
tempted to pull out his firearm and shoot the buggers—dogs and
drunks both—than arrest them. Henry, at fifty-two, was by no
means in the shape that Ed had been in at sixty-seven, but he had
more patience, and in the four years that he'd been sheriff, the
only time he'd pulled his firearm was to finish off a deer that had
been hit by a truck, something he would have done as a civilian
anyway.

He chased dogs and broke up fights and helped the meds
scrape kids off the highway, usually on Arbor Road, which was
supposedly haunted. As far as Henry was concerned, the only
thing haunting Arbor Road was that goddamn hill the kids liked
to get airborne over. He gave out speeding tickets and warnings
for broken taillights and tickets for dogs running loose, and he
went out on domestic disturbances when a neighbor called the
cops.

He could divide every community into two parts: good parts

and bad parts, and never the twain shall meet. With one or two exceptions in all of them—usually some smart guy in any of the good parts was pounding on his wife, and over in Avis, one wife regularly pounded on her husband—but for the most part, you had your goods and your bads. The good neighborhoods got burglarized, and the burglars were living in the lousy neighborhoods. A couple of times of year, usually in the summer, a couple of privileged, bored kids from the middle class burgled their friends' houses (usually with the friend), and they were caught easily enough, after hiding the stuff in their bedrooms for their mothers to find on laundry day.

In fact, as far as Henry could see, crime in Capawatsa hadn't changed much since he was a kid. The stuff that kids took was more expensive, but more people had it. There was more vandalism because kids had less to do. For the most part, crime was still kids acting out in the last days of summer.

He went about his days negotiating feuds and writing reports about broken fences and showing up at fender benders. Every year someone got shot, usually over women, dogs, or liquor, but there hadn't been a murder in ten years. With the odd exception, crime was still minor stuff, and usually property offenses to boot, and Henry could easily say that there was no better place to live in the world than Capawatsa County.

Unless you lived in Goodlands.

Although it boasted some of the richest soil in the region— hence its name—it was the worst place to be a farmer right now. There was no accounting for what was going on there, and Henry's part in it all was increasing with the drought. People were getting tense, and when people got tense, trouble got to people.

And it was getting weird. Carl Simpson, as far as Henry knew, a normal guy with a hundred some-odd head of cattle, was—like everyone else—suffering the butt end of a bad season. He had a wife and a son, a good kid named Harold but called Butch for obvious reasons, who was just about to step into the abyss of adolescence. Carl Simpson had come to see Henry a few weeks back and wanted to go into his little cubbyhole office and talk all hush-hush.

"Henry, what I got to tell you is going to sound strange at first, but I need you to hear me out. With an *open mind*," he'd said at the start. When someone told Henry to listen with an open mind he tended to sigh inwardly and wait for some exaggerated tale of neighborly woe. This time, he sat behind his desk and took out his notebook and pencil. He was just licking the end of the pencil to get started when Carl told him to put it away.

Glancing over his shoulder at the court secretary's empty desk, he said, "I don't think you should write any of this down. Might cause more trouble." Henry put his pencil back in his pocket and closed his notebook, giving himself the pleasure of one of those inward sighs. He settled in his chair to listen with half an ear and maybe plan his vacation at the same time. He set both eyes on Carl, though, not wanting to seem rude.

"What's on your mind, Carl?"

"Well, I've been thinking about the drought lately, about how it's only Goodlands, and how even Oxburg, butt up against Goodlands, is still getting its normal annual rainfall, and Goodlands *isn't*."

Henry nodded. There was little else to think about when you were farming in Goodlands.

"I was watching this show on the satellite the other night," Carl continued, "and they were talking about this place out in Arizona called Groom Lake. It's not a lake anymore, just a dry bed in the middle of the desert. It's not a town, either, but you can see the sign out on the highway just the same.

"What it is, is a top secret military installation"—he looked at Henry for a reaction and Henry, in keeping with his public-service accountability, raised his eyebrows—"and it's so secret that it's not listed on any military maps. I checked. Don Orchard's on the Internet, you know, and we looked like buggers for it.

"Anyway, the locals all know it's there, and there's always talk and speculation, and what people say is that it's a place where they keep crashed flying saucers. UFOs, right?"

"UFOs?"

"I know what you're thinking, I don't think I put much in the whole UFO thing myself, but what I'm getting at is that this place is kept so secret that there's signs up all along the road out there, with warnings that if you pass *this* point you're in a restricted area, and if you pass the *next* point you're being watched, and you'll eventually come to a sign that says 'If you pass this point, you can be shot under the jurisdiction of the United States Military.' "

Henry nodded. He wondered just how bad things were over at the Simpsons'; maybe Carl had taken up the bottle, or worse. He didn't look stoned or drunk, but there was a look in his eye that didn't seem right. He looked scared.

"You worried about that, Carl?" Henry asked gently. Sometimes people got into a state about the state of the world and Henry, like anyone with a uniform, served as a sounding board, counselor, or scapegoat.

"Not so much that, Henry, but I was thinking about Goodlands and the drought, and maybe what goes on in those silos," he said. The missile silos were of concern to everyone in North Dakota, although people had pretty much become used to them over the thirty or so years they'd been there.

"The silos are mostly zipped up, now, Carl. You know that. They're not pointed anywhere anymore, and they're all coded down so that it would take a big to-do to set them off. They're safe," Henry reassured him. And he believed it.

"Yeah, that's what they tell us, but seeing that Groom Lake on television, I was just thinking about all the things the government doesn't feel the need to share with the American people, and maybe the silos are being used for something other than defense now," he said.

"Like what, Carl?" he said, letting a sigh escape.

"Like maybe weather experiments." He leaned back in his

chair, relieved to have it out, finally, and rested his hands, clenched into fists, on his legs.

Carl went on to explain his theory of the government doing experiments with the weather—a better defense against the Russians, the Iraqis, the Cubans, and Canada than any missile. "Wrap them in winter for ten years in a row," he offered, "and send them hailstones the size of baseballs for a week or two, or," he added, pointedly and ominously, *"dry them up for four years."*

Henry had listened with concern and compassion, and he got Carl out of the office after extracting a promise that he wouldn't start writing the government or—most important—inspecting any of the silos himself, until Henry could look into it. They shook on it and Henry walked him out to the street and said good-bye at his pickup, wondering the whole time what Carl's wife Janet, a levelheaded, hardworking woman, was thinking these days.

It was a story four years old. The night after he'd talked to Carl, Henry did something he rarely did, and that was put on the Weather Channel and sit in front and watch, missing his favorite shows, watching for several hours while the clock ticked away over *NYPD Blue.*

He sat through the highs and lows of nearly every state in the union before they got to the Dakotas, and there was the weather picture, dragged in by magic and satellite, a pretty picture of thin white clouds moving over the state like cigarette smoke in a bar. Right around, through, and inside of Goodlands, rain fell, according to the picture on the tube. Rain was predicted and recorded, and the lack of it, through ignorance or denial, was never mentioned. Goodlands was a small dot not even listed on the high-low map, although Weston got a nod and they were right about the weather that night. Goodlands never came up.

You didn't get UFO and government conspiracy stories from perfectly respectable citizens unless things were really bad. Things were really bad in Goodlands. Some days, even Henry wondered if they needed a cop, or an exorcist. Goodlands was getting more than its share of misfortune, including the freak accident down at the Dry Goods and, lately, the fires and such, along with the usual rise in petty crime that comes along with bad times. People needing things and stealing to get them, when there was no cash to be had. In fact, it was a different place entirely that Henry was looking at these days. So different as to make him think twice about anything that happened in it.

Driving in his car back to the office, Henry absentmindedly felt around in his breast pocket for the little sandwich Baggie that he had in there. In the Baggie was a cigarette butt, found in the road in front of Karen Grange's house the evening before. She said she hadn't seen anyone suspicious the night Kramer's field went up. But right there in the road was the butt end of a half-smoked hand-rolled cigarette. Tobacco. He was pretty sure Karen didn't smoke. He'd never seen her smoke. Yet there was a butt in the road at the end of her driveway and, really, too far away to have been tossed—people were darned careful about their butts when things were this dry. And it was *stubbed,* as though someone might have stooped over and rubbed it in the dirt. It was dropped there by someone standing in the road. Could she have not noticed someone standing before her driveway? Possible.

But there was something hinky about the whole thing. Like the way she stood with him on her porch like that, not inviting him in for something cold to drink on a day when the temperature had stayed in the high eighties for twelve or more hours, them being on more than just a first-name nodding acquaintance. Could be she was tired, rude, thoughtless, or had an empty fridge, but he didn't think so. Not like her. She was a nice woman, a woman who had worked hard to become a member of the community.

It seemed more like she was hiding something.

Even if she did have someone staying out there with her, it

didn't mean it was the drifter who'd been seen by the Tindals and Bart Eastly and Gooner. Maybe she had a boyfriend shacked up with her for a few days and didn't want the banking public to know it. Or she was a closet smoker, or a bad housekeeper. Or maybe she was just lying to him. When someone like Karen Grange lied to the law, there was a good reason for it. And he didn't think it meant she hadn't paid her taxes.

Goodlands was giving Henry an ulcer.

Dave Revesette wasn't the only one with vandal problems that morning. Before Henry even left the Goodlands town limits, there were four more messages at the office for him to return.

Larry Watson went out early to check on a piglet that he thought he might lose. In fact, he expected to find her dead. She was a runty little thing who wasn't suckling, that his wife and the kids had formed an affection for and had been feeding by bottle. He'd put up with it as long as he could bear, but if it was going to die, he was a firm believer in letting nature take its course.

He went out to check on the piglet—which he half hoped had finally expired so he could get his family out of the barn oohing and ahhing all the livelong day and get his work done like he was supposed to—and went out early, before they were up.

The sun had risen and he could hear the birds—few enough of them came around anymore—and it was still cool enough to be beautiful. It was a good time of day.

He was just coming up beside the barn when he saw something odd, very odd, and for just a second his heart stopped and he thought the unthinkable.

There was a wide puddle on the ground.

Maybe it had rained. Miraculously, overnight, without anyone hearing, and only over by the barn. But that didn't make sense. He really got to wondering then, and jogged over to investigate.

"SHIT!" he screamed. "SHIT, SHIT, SHIT!"

The water came from the water tank. From the looks of it, the entire tank had emptied and the water was fast soaking into the ground.

The tank was about six years old, just starting to show some age. He'd gone over it regularly, checking for weak spots, but it had been fine. It was a quality tank. He had four of them, located in various places on the property, all on trailers so they were easy to hook up to the truck and fill. You had to have a quality tank.

Like everyone in Goodlands, the Watsons rationed what was left of their near-to-dry well, and picked up water in neighboring Avis, Oxburg, or Adele, whichever was next on the rotating list of communities who were helping out. Baths were verboten. Everybody showered, even three-year-old Jennifer. Everybody cleaned up in the same washbasin in the sink, and then the dishes were washed in that water. They used water for cooking, but they drank milk. Probably they were going to extremes, but Larry was a saver, and saving hadn't steered him wrong yet; so even when the family grumbled, they rationed hard. It had paid off. The well wasn't dry.

"Shitpiss!" He bent down in front of the tank.

The spout was gone. Confusion spread over his face. He checked the ground under the tank, stuck his hand into the puddle, realized he was crouched in water up to his ankles—water that was quickly soaking into the parched earth. He felt around under the water for the spout, but couldn't find it. The spout was gone.

There wasn't time to look, or even think about where the hell the spout would go, or how the hell it had come off, even. He stood and stared into the distance at the other end of the barnyard to the second tank. He couldn't see much, but he suspected the worst.

Mad as hell, he walked back toward the house to get in the truck. He had to check the other tanks.

* * *

Jack Greeson, who served under Leonard Franklin at the Goodlands Volunteer Fire Brigade, was backing out of his driveway, thinking about whether he'd have pie or some of Grace Kushner's homemade doughnuts, fried in lard and weighing in at a half pound each. At the end of the drive his car hit something with a sudden wrench, throwing him into the steering wheel, where he hit his nose hard enough to make it bleed. He wasn't wearing his seat belt.

Cursing, he slammed the car into park, thinking he might have hit something big, like a deer. Pinching his nose to stop the blood, he fumbled the glove box open, found a hanky, and held it to his nose, checking the flow. Wasn't too bad, but hurt like a bitch. He swung the rearview mirror over so he could look at his nose, and that's when he noticed something strange.

The road was very close to the back of his car.

When he stepped out of the car, his legs, hit the ground with a *whack!* sending a painful shock up to his knees.

"What the hell—" Looking down, he saw that the ground very nearly met the car. Whatever it was, he didn't think he'd hit a deer.

There was a fissure in the earth where the driveway met the road. The car had backed into a deep hole, burying the back wheels up to the axle.

Jack walked to the back of the car and stared down into the hole. Dark, dry earth, roots and rocks, stared back at him. The asphalt of the driveway had separated, somehow, from the road.

He stood like that, staring. His wife opened up the front door and called out to him—was everything all right?

"Call Grease," he called back. Grease, his brother, worked down at the garage with Bart Eastly. "I'm going to need a tow." His eyes never left the back of the car.

Terry Paxton, who was called Teresa only by her husband, was vacuuming the living room when she glanced out her front window. She sometimes took comfort in the big cross that her husband had erected on the lawn, even though the signs of their despair were all around it, in the brown, dry grass and the vast empty field that would not be planted that year. If she looked properly, kept her eyes correctly focused, she would see only the cross, standing tall and high amid the wretchedness, and she would take comfort. Plain, sturdy wood, rough hewn, scarred and bare, it was a source of supreme unction, and was the only thing that could banish the sinful thoughts she often felt come over her when she let her mind wander over their terrible situation.

She lifted her eyes to receive the blessing.

But it never came. Because the cross was gone.

Further inspection revealed that it was lying in two pieces more than twenty feet apart in the yard.

The family spent the day praying away whatever evil had been present. Mr. Paxton took a break around noon, however, and called the cops.

Henry and his deputies were kept hopping like frogs in a French restaurant. The only clue they had, out of all the bizarre occurrences that would go on through the rest of the day, was one small, sneakered footprint in the wet mud beside one of the water tanks out at Larry Watson's.

Henry would never get the other connections.

It was payback.

Vida was running on little sleep, but could hardly tell the difference. Adrenaline surged full throttle in her veins. She was on a high like she'd never been, not even after she started the first fire. This was overload.

Her elation over the havoc she had wreaked among her Goodlands neighbors was short-lived. The voice inside her reminded her that there was work to be done. The voice was sobering. It frightened her a little.

She had woken that morning with the distinct and hopeful feeling that the night before had been little more than a dream. That she had only dreamed of the other face in the mirror, the one that flickered across her own features. She had only dim memories of standing at the end of her bed and letting the feeling, like a buzz, run through her body. She remembered the strange vibration it made between her feet and the floorboards, as though she were actually standing on top of it, the tingling feeling of hundreds of tiny bugs, like larvae or maggots, buzzing and moving under the soles of her feet and spreading out across the floor.

And out the window, and over the town, through fields and barnyards, across roads and dead, dried creeks, it had spread out and covered the whole of the town.

She had hoped it had all been a strange, unlikely dream. The result of bad meat at supper, her dad slipping something into her water. Whatever.

But in the morning, her arms were sore, the muscles cramped and tired, as though she had held them up for a long time. The undersides of her feet were black with mud. Even though she had worn sneakers, even though she had bathed the day before. Even though to have feet that black, with the dirt smeared up nearly to her knees, she would have all but had to wade through thick, muddy troughs.

She woke after a long, restless night, feeling as if she had just dropped into bed, and then had been shaken awake. Though she didn't notice at first, her feet had muddied the sheet. The remnants of her dream stayed with her as she stumbled out of bed. Horrible dream. Running, being chased. Caught, and then the dark, as black as the mud on her feet, dark and wet and scratching its way into her lungs. Then, morning.

For the longest time, she avoided her reflection. Until she couldn't stand it any longer, felt stupid. So she stared at herself. Like a fast trick of the light (or a ripple in the glass), something flickered across her face, eyes superimposed over her hair pulled back, tiny, freckled nose, none of it her own. The horror of the nightmare came back.

It had only been made better by the voice. Which told her that it was her turn, first, and then the business of the man.

Her turn first.

As for the other thing, the tether, it came from somewhere in her belly and led to a place unknown. She could feel her new strength inside her like a hot coal. She could do anything she wanted. The water tanks, the crack in Jack Greeson's driveway, the pathetic two-by-four cross at the Paxtons—those were her things. Her things were over. Now she was to follow the tether, reaching out over town as it had the night before.

Vida walked, but she didn't seem to have a clear path. She walked sometimes on the road, sometimes in the ditch. She followed it because she was supposed to, and because she was afraid not to.

S I X

KAREN GRANGE HAD LEFT A NOTE FOR TOM PASTED ON THE
back door. It was the first thing he saw when he opened his eyes.
The note said simply "Today," underlined with a thick stroke.
He supposed that she was getting the fidgets. It pissed him off, a
mood he didn't appreciate first thing in the morning, and he tore
it off the door and crumpled it before jamming it into his pocket.
The door was locked, but he went in anyway. He needed a jolt of
caffeine and maybe a nice hunk of that yellow cheese she kept in
the fridge. He hadn't slept well.

A drink would be nice, too. A shot of whiskey or rye would
have gone down smooth, taken the edge away. A splash in his
coffee, with a chaser to follow, and then, maybe, the rest of the
bottle. Just to take away the incredible dryness he felt in this
place, a dryness that had sunk into him.

Sleep had been filled with bad dreams.

He'd had the one about rainmaking again, a dream he had

frequently, but this one had gone bad at the point when it usually went *good*. In the dream he stood tall in Karen's backyard, where the foolish-looking gazebo was, except that in the dream the gazebo wasn't there. Nothing was there—it was a wide open field. He stood with his arms upraised, calling out to the rain. And it fell, first softly and then harder. The sky was dark, like night, and the rain began to chill him. It turned icy cold, sinking through his flesh like millions of tiny knife blades, freezing him to his core until he could stand it no more. But he could not stop it. He tried to find shelter, and could find only a deep hole in the ground, like a trench. When he stepped in, the icy rain filled the hole to his knees until he couldn't move. That's when he realized it was a grave, and woke up, a scream on his lips.

It took only a moment to realize he was drenched with sweat. He opened his eyes and what he saw was that goddamn gazebo. It was giving him the heebie-jeebies. After that, he pulled his bedroll a little farther away from it. It had taken a long time to fall back to sleep, but there were no more dreams after that. None that he remembered. Tonight, he thought, he would maybe move his bedroll out to the clearing.

It was time for Tom to do a little walking. Walking had a way of forcing him to think. The rhythm of his steps, the quiet on the road drained his mind of extraneous things and helped him to concentrate. Besides, he had something in mind.

He cleaned up the coffee mess he'd made, but purposely left his mug, unwashed, in the sink. To let her know that he'd been inside. The thought of her finding it brought the first smile of the day to Tom's lips. No note, just the mug. And the cheese missing. He chuckled then, and felt a little better.

He would follow the road in front of Grange's house until he found the place where Goodlands stopped and some other place began. He had a feeling that the difference would be very conspicuous.

When he'd first walked into town he had felt the change, the difference. Like Alice walking through the looking glass, he had

taken a step into another world, a matter of a few feet between
where it rained and where it didn't. *Or couldn't.* That was where
he would go. He had to find the place where the rain still was,
and follow it. He had a feeling that the town limits and the place
where the rain stopped would be one and the same.

Rain, in Tom's experience, was funny, maybe unpredictable,
but it wasn't picky. It didn't choose one place over another for
personal or political reasons; it was uncanny, but not magical.
There was no reason why it would rain everywhere but Goodlands, as far as he knew, and he'd been in the middle of more
than one drought. That wasn't the way a drought worked.

But there was something different about this one. It didn't feel
right.

He passed a bar, Clancy's, on his left and continued on the
same road. It was wide open prairie, and he could count hydro
poles until they were no more than an inch high in his eye. Miles
and miles of flat land and hydro poles.

Here, you could see the sky touching the ground and there
was nothing in between that could be hidden from the eye. The
landscape was more rugged and daunting than anything he'd
known. Nature was closer. Everything was more vivid—the sun
beat down harder, the wind was fiercer, color was more intense.
There was no escape from the sky. As though it had to be seen,
demanded that you stand up and take notice.

The only other place he'd been that could compare to the
prairie was the desert, another hard, relentless place. If it was sim-
ilar in beauty and breadth, it was night compared to day in its ac-
commodation. The prairie invited, embraced; the desert spurned.
Its beauty didn't belong to humanity, and didn't want you there. It
was beauty for its own sake, not to be shared. Crossing Nevada
had been a rehearsal in death: the long expanse of nothing, the
frightening, glaring heat, the deathly night chill, the stark *alone-
ness,* the feeling that you were the only one left on earth, and earth
was dry and dead. When Tom walked out of the desert for the first
time, and into the little town at the end of it, he had been *hungry*

for people. He'd stayed at a little hotel, using his last hundred bucks for a chance to feel like a part of the world again. It had taken a long time to recover from that feeling.

He'd taken a woman for the time that he'd been there. Her name was Wanda. They'd spent a week together, an all-time Thompson Keatley record, because after the time he'd spent alone, he needed the feel of flesh against his flesh, the feel of blood and bones and moist breath after the hard ground and hot dry air of the desert. For a week they'd been together, most of it spent in the narrow bed in his hotel, having sex, eating, getting drunk. In the dark, she told him her secrets. She told him about her life, most of it spent in the same town. He had been so immersed in his desire that he would have been surprised to find that she saw him in a very different light. He had slipped out of his room while she slept and hadn't left so much as a note. He felt bad about it later. The only one he'd ever felt bad about. Now he couldn't even remember what she'd looked like, although he remembered clearly what she had felt like. Warm. And moist. When they'd made love, they drenched themselves in sweat and Tom suspected later that that was his doing. He had brought it out of her. He had needed that moisture, that water, that drink of flesh. She was his walk back.

He knew well enough why he thought about his trip through Nevada as he walked the road to the end of town. It was like that here. A vacuum, devoid of everything. He could feel the need in this place, and along with it, his own. Dry inside.

It was up ahead. Already, as he approached, he could feel the change in the air.

Up in the sky, at the end of the line, there was a cloud. A small, thin cloud that held rain. It was tiny and hung like mist above the horizon, invisible to all except him. He picked up the rhythm of his steps and headed for the cloud like a moth to flame.

As if crossing through the looking glass, he stepped from one world into another, out of the void. He dropped his pack to the ground. Standing directly under the cloud, he reached up with his hands and felt inside the sky. He touched the rain. He buried himself in it, fat and wet, as it filled his nostrils, his pores. Then he closed his eyes and pulled on it. A little tug. And a light drizzle fell on the spot, fell on Tom, rolling down his face. The tiny droplets ran over his eyelids, his face, slipped into his mouth, where they tasted sweet, and down his throat and into the neck of his shirt.

So there was rain, somewhere. Thank God, it wasn't his well that was dry. It was the place. Tom stood there for a long time after the tiny cloud had spent itself, breathing in the moisture that simply existed. He breathed deeply, wanting nothing more than to just stay in that spot forever, a part of that sky, and not the sky that hung over Goodlands, malevolent and arid. He stood feeling the rain all around him until he was renewed.

Then, because he had to, he stepped back into the void, and walked on.

Butch Simpson stood quietly in the archway between the living room and the family room. He had his baseball glove on and was holding his cap in his hand. His mother didn't like him or his father to wear a hat in the house.

He watched his father watching television. Watching his tapes more accurately, the shows he taped overnight. They were all about weird stuff. His dad had tried to get Butch to watch them with him before, but his mother intervened, saying firmly (more firmly than she usually spoke to his father) that she didn't think such programs were appropriate for children Butch's age. That got him intrigued, and the next time his parents went to town and left him alone, he'd put one of his dad's tapes in the VCR and turned it on, expecting to see gross pictures of dead bodies, or people being burned alive, or at least some naughty sex stuff. All it was was junk about the end of the world and flying saucers and some guy named Ed Cayce or something, talking in a trance. Dumb stuff. He didn't even watch a whole show.

He was waiting for his dad to turn around so that he could
entice him out to the yard to throw a ball around. Butch thought
if his dad just turned around and saw him there, maybe he could
be *forced* to come outside, *willed* to come outside. He concentrated.

Soft steps behind him made him turn around. It was his
mother.

"Hey, buddy. You wanna go outside and play some ball?"
Butch looked at her, appalled.

"With you?"

"Yeah, why not?" She touched the top of his head and
thought about how fast he was growing up. He pulled his head
away.

"You can't play ball," he said. His dad, though he must have
heard them, didn't turn around.

"Come on, I'll show you," she said.

"I want Dad to come."

"Daddy's thinking, honey," she said. "Let him be." She said it
quietly and led Butch outside.

They threw the ball back and forth, his dad's glove big and
clumsy-looking on his mother's tiny hand, but she surprised him
with her catching and throwing. She wasn't bad, for a mother. In
the middle of a throw, he asked her suddenly, "What's the matter
with Dad, anyway? Why's he watching that stuff all the time?"
Janet Simpson detected much of her own concern in his voice.

She caught his throw in the big glove and tossed it back. She
tried to choose her words carefully.

"Remember we talked about the drought?"

"Yeah."

"Do you remember that I explained about how things work,
about the bank, and mortgages and—"

"Yeah."

"Well, now that the farm isn't doing well, Daddy's . . ."
Janet's own face tightened with the desire to choose the right
words, knowing the true words were not appropriate for a child.

"Daddy's having a hard time getting used to the way things are. And he's very worried," she said.

"So why does he watch all those stupid shows about ghosts and aliens and stuff?"

Janet caught his pitch and tossed it back. They threw the ball back and forth while she thought.

"It's just his way of dealing with being worried, Butch. People deal with things in different ways. When I'm worried, sometimes I clean the house. It clears my head. Daddy's just watching TV."

She felt satisfied with her explanation, even though the look on Butch's face told her that he didn't believe it. It was the truth as far as the truth went, but Janet knew Carl was captivated for deeper reasons than that. He was searching for a secret truth in those shows. He was trying to learn something esoteric and secret about farming during a drought. Those horrible television programs, with their dark tales of the supernatural, had captured in him something alternately spiritual and conspiratorial. He was starting to frighten her at night with his recounting of his day's viewing. He tried to get her to watch. He was obsessed with the government and What They Weren't Telling. And lately, the stories were getting more bizarre. He could quote what he called "modern-day prophets," all with their own doomsday predictions. He was starting to give her the creeps. He was driving all the way over to the bookstore in Bismarck and loading up on ridiculous books with titles like *Surviving the Millennium* and *The Doomsday Calendar,* spending all kinds of money when they could barely keep their heads above-water. *So to speak,* she thought wryly. Their bedroom was starting to look like the inside of some kind of dark library. In spite of the morning heat, she shuddered.

"So," Butch said. He caught the ball and held it, looking down at his glove. "Is the world going to end?"

"Where did you hear that?" she asked sharply. Seeing his mother's startled look, he said apologetically, "That's what Dad's shows are all about." He lowered his eyes to the ground. "I watched one when you guys went out. I didn't mean to."

"Those shows are not for children," she said.

"But is it?"

She shook her head firmly.

"No. Never. Someday soon it's going to rain and everything is going to be all right," she said. Butch tossed the ball. She caught it and tossed it back. They played for a couple of more minutes, politely, but the fun had gone out of it.

By silent, mutual agreement, they avoided the house. Instead Janet sat on the hard, dry ground while Butch played in the tire swing that Carl had put up for him before he was big enough to walk, and talked of other things.

Around noon they listened to the old pickup start on the other side of the house. Then they gathered up the ball and gloves and went into the house for some lunch. The first thing Janet did when they went in was turn off the TV.

Tom stopped around noon and walked into the field beside the road where someone had thoughtfully planted a row of trees. Served to block the wind, he suspected, but for his purpose it would block out the worst of the sun. He dropped his pack on the ground and sat beside it, leaning up against one of the tree trunks.

There was no irrigation where he sat, he figured, because the trees were dry and dead-looking. Leaning up against one of them, he could feel that horrible, desiccated feeling that he was getting all over town. Until you slipped into what he was starting to think of as the rain belt, and then, suddenly, everything felt all right again.

He reached inside his pack and felt around for the rest of the cheese he'd slipped out of Grange's fridge. He washed it down with water from his canteen, the warm, stale taste of it in no way spoiling the way it felt going down. He closed his eyes and swallowed deeply.

He'd been making his way around Goodlands for more than two hours already, and most of the fields he had passed were empty. Some were tilled and waiting, probably a goodly number of them had been planted, but he had yet to see anything growing. Four years of drought; he doubted that people still had the hope it must require to work the land anymore.

One thing he hadn't thought much about was Karen Grange's part in things. He'd passed more than one empty house, with wide, yawning eyes for windows, the glass broken and paint peeling; more than one For Sale sign hanging limply; more than one abandoned farm, and he wondered about that. Karen Grange being the banker and all, he wondered about her shutting people down. Foreclosing, that would be her word for it, clean and distant sounding, *foreclosing* was the word to use when you stopped the heart of a town.

Karen Grange would be the forecloser; the town, of course, the foreclosee.

Tom took another swallow of his water and screwed the cap back on. He pulled out his tobacco and rolled himself a smoke.

So he'd solved that little mystery. Grange had written the letter because she was the bad guy in this story. He allowed himself a little smile, thinking of her pulling out a pen and writing that letter. At first, he'd thought she was the wife of someone, a farmer, most likely. Wives or daughters will ask. Farmers themselves, very rarely. There's something in the heart of a woman that will stretch a little farther past boundaries than the heart of a man. Maybe they get desperate sooner. On the other hand, he'd been found by town officials, usually on the sly, but they were politicians for the most part, and it doesn't get more desperate than that. He'd never been called by a banker.

The way it usually happened was, Tom found them. He would find himself on a road that led somewhere, and when he got there, find it was a place that needed his services. As often as not, he didn't get paid, even if people knew what he'd done. Folks didn't like to admit that the rain was something that could be brought on. And if it did get "brought on," they would believe it was because of a machine, or a pill, or a spray that commanded the rain to fall. Tom's way was too hard to grasp.

Winslow, Kansas, had been an exception. He had been called. The fellow there, town clerk by the name of David Darling (and didn't he just bet the kid inside that man had grown up tough and scrappy), had heard that Tom had made a hundred dollars in a bet in a bar one night in Topeka. It was a rain bet. There were four guys sitting around, shooting the shit, and Tom heard them talking rain. Tom was just passing through, stopped in for a couple of beers to take the edge off things, and went into his pitch. They hadn't had rain in a month and it was dead summer. Nothing to worry about, Tom had walked into the place and knew that rain was only a day or so off. But he took their money and gave them a show. Everyone bought round after round that night, leaving the door open while it poured so they all could see it. "Ain't that just the *damnedest thing!*" He'd taken the smacks on the back all night long and felt like a goddamn hero, especially after the sixth or seventh round. Tom got about as piss-drunk as he'd ever been and spent the night in the back of some guy's pickup, under the cap, falling asleep listening to the sound of the rain echoing inside the back of the truck. He woke up sometime in the afternoon, head pounding and mouth tasting like something had died inside, and had dinner with the guy who owned the pickup. Turned out that he had a friend in Winslow who was in kind of a bad way. He'd called and told him about the bet and the rain.

"His name's Darling," the guy said. "I went to school with him. He's town clerking in Winslow and we keep in touch," he told Tom, sheepishly. "I told him all about what you pulled off and he would be very grateful if you could go down there and see what you can do for them."

Tom did, thinking that he wouldn't be doing it for no hundred bucks, either.

Darling had been a little worried about keeping it hush-hush.

He didn't want his boss, a self-important, tight-assed type, to know that he'd called in a rainmaker.

Winslow had been dry for eighteen months. Tom made it rain the next afternoon. Took no time at all for people to find out what had happened. Darling couldn't keep his mouth shut about it long enough. Someone called a TV crew and they did a story about it, talking to Tom and everything. That's when Karen had seen him.

Turned out the people of Winslow were glad to have the rain, but were a little skeptical about where it came from when it was time to pass the hat. Except for Darling, who slipped a hundred bucks into Tom's hand, people were tipping him as if he was a slow waiter. He got less than five hundred dollars. It might as well have been a bar bet.

Tom dragged on his smoke, and thought about Goodlands. Goodlands had been different from the start.

For one thing, it was funny as hell, if you thought about it, how that letter got to him at all. It found him, even as he moved around, almost as if it were chasing him.

Passed from hand to hand, through people who didn't know him, for the most part, finally getting to him from a fellow who knew a guy who thought he'd heard something about this man who made it rain on a bet. The guy who gave it to him had carried the letter around with him for a good six months, and it was crumpled and stained and one corner was all but torn off, but it was readable.

"I don't even know why I kept it. Bartender gave it to me because I travel. I also drink"—he laughed—"and you've made your way through a few bars, from the sound of it. Hey, can you really make it rain?"

"Yup," Tom had said. The guy stared at him, sizing him up. Tom was wondering how much cash he had on him. *Wanna see? I make it rain for fifty bucks.*

"Aren't you gonna open it?"

"Later, maybe," Tom said. The guy looked disappointed, like

he figured he was owed something, carrying that letter around as long as he did. And Tom supposed he was owed something, but still he didn't open it. The paper was cool and smooth in his hand, but he got a small buzz off it. Not that that meant anything in particular. He got a buzz off a lot of things. The writing on the letter was clearly feminine, and to Tom that meant some kind of bad news, a letter from someone still crying or finally pissed off. He'd wait until later, when he was a little more lubricated, and would get a good laugh out of it, instead of the tweak of nasty conscience.

"So," the guy went on, "how do you make it rain?"

Tom smiled, thinking about the guy's worn overshoes and the shiny seat on his cheap suit.

"I make it rain for fifty bucks." He did, too.

That had been nearly a year before. He'd read the letter late that night, lubricated with the other guy's beer, as predicted, in the bush between the bar and someone's house on the other side. He'd laid out his bedroll, had a small fire going because it was fucking cold, and he'd read the letter by the light of the fire. He still had it, pressed carefully in the pages of his mother's old grammar book.

It had been formally and carefully worded, a business letter. No wonder she had looked at him with that blank face, then the suspicion, when he showed up on her doorstep. She probably expected a fellow in a suit, driving a truck with "Rainmaker" on the side. Maybe a catchy slogan, like "Rain without Pain," under that. She would have expected him to call first, and make a neat appointment to meet on neutral territory, maybe in the coffee shop in town. She would have shown up in one of her little suits, with a briefcase, probably, and would have kept it all very formal and businesslike, like the letter. Details would have been discussed, a few papers signed, and he would have come through with a torrent of rain to save the town. He frowned. A torrent of rain.

Karen's face came to mind, not the face of the previous morning, in her banker's suit and expression, but the one from last

night. Her big eyes, wide open like a kid's. The surprise and delight.

It had taken nearly a year for him to get to her, but he had
spent part of the winter in the South, where a man could sleep
outside and not wake up dead.

As soon as he read her letter, with its muckety-muck language
and neat signature at the bottom, he knew this was a different
job. Hell, the letter getting to him at all meant that there was
something . . . different about this place. As though he was supposed to get the letter, supposed to come to Goodlands.

Supposed to make it rain.

So why couldn't he? When the cash, the woman who wanted
him to do it, the conditions, everything was ripe for rain, why
couldn't he just open up that door and let it pour from the heavens, as he had almost nightly for mere chump change in every
highway bar in the Midwest? Why couldn't he make it pour for
Goodlands?

The money was good. Enough cash to allow Tom to go away
for a long time, to someplace warm and wet and loose. Someplace so infused with its own moisture that you could wake up in
the morning and drink the dew off leaves on trees. Tip the leaf
just so, and it would run down into your mouth, your body sop-
ping it up, without so much as a muscle moved. For five thousand dollars he could do that for a long time. He closed his eyes
and pictured the place, a sigh passing over his dry lips. He could
taste it: sweet, wet, cool.

The only other option was to cut his losses and leave. Go on
to the next place, score big off them. Goodlands could be a place
he'd been; passed through.

Tom's mind clouded over with the options. It was too hot to
just sit around; he had the distinct feeling that if he did it any
longer he would fall asleep. And there was a childish fear, as of
something under the bed, that if he did fall asleep he would dry
up and die, become a part of the lifeless landscape.

He was sorry to leave the shade of the tree and even sorrier to feel the way the sun beat down on top of his head, making him sweat under his cap. But it was better than that feeling he got when he stood still. What he needed was a little red meat to get the blood going. He decided then and there that he would pick up a couple of thick, juicy steaks and—what the hell?—treat Karen Grange to one of them.

She was a funny one. Good-looking in a quiet way, something he hadn't noticed until last night, when her face lost its stiff, unyielding look. When she stared down at the small puddle in her hand, she'd lit up like a lightning storm, the smile on her face reaching all the way up to her eyes. In that moment, she'd looked so open, almost vulnerable, something Tom didn't usually find attractive, but did last night. It had been attractive enough for him to slide his eyes down to her mouth, and wonder briefly how good she might taste. Lucky for both of them, the moment had passed. Then the curt note on the door this morning. The soft hand he'd held and the quick jerk of her arm that pulled it away. Quiet good looks. Nice. If she'd been a woman in a bar along the way, he would never have noticed her.

The opportunity of her being there had not escaped him. It crossed his mind every time she was close enough to smell. There was someone under those banker clothes, and whoever it was, smelled fine, like flowers a day or so after they are cut. But he was determined not to find out who. It would just be trouble for both of them.

A new woman was working her way through Goodlands.

Vida was walking on the road that started out as Plum View Road and became Highway Drive at the end of the Badlands. It was known as Route 55. Larry Watson and Dave Revesette both had farms on Route 55. It was a long walk from there to where the road forked. You could stay on the paved, state-maintained Route 55, or you could veer off onto the gravel road that led halfheartedly around the outer eastern corner of Goodlands. The less-traveled gravel road would take you past the Paxton place.

It was getting on to noon, and Vida had been walking since dawn. She did not feel like stopping, because her body wasn't her only source of energy these days; her new energy was coming from another source entirely—an *inside* source.

As was the way in a small farming community, especially in the early morning hours when there were chores to be done, the road was empty. Vida had seen no one. And no one had seen Vida. Even if they had, she wasn't altogether sure she would have noticed them.

Her walk had always had something athletic and aggressive about it, a stance and movement born of necessity, a step that warned of her approach. Now it had softened, was more a sway, something more feminine and come-hither than she would have liked. She looked as though she were dancing while she walked, her hips moving lightly from side to side, her hand scooping the skirt of her dress (the same one from yesterday, a little the worse for wear). She didn't know if anyone else would have noticed the small changes in her, but she knew they were there. She was focused, and she walked with that focus as she never had before. She had her work to do.

The voice inside her was something different, though. She wished she could still the voice. It was insistent, constant; it gave her a slight headache as it rambled on and tried to make her listen. She did listen: she found herself stopping on the road sometimes to hear it. The voice wanted her to follow the tether. To find the other. The other had to be found.

It would take all of Vida's will to drag herself away from the sound of the voice and begin to move again. Sometimes she stopped for a long time, a look of absolute blankness—many would have said it betrayed her as a Whalley—on her face as she listened. But always she was able to drive by the part of her that the voice had discovered, her darker side. The side of Vida that wanted to *hurt back*. Vida and the voice worked in perfect sync in that regard.

In sync, the two of them inside the one body, followed the tether.

The Waggleses had hired Tammy Kowzowski back temporarily, since Dr. Bell thought Chimmy should take a few days to recover from her injuries, however minor. She had a mild concussion from her head hitting the floor during the tree incident. She also had numerous bruises, one bad slice across the bridge of her nose from a piece of glass, and a couple of smaller, though deep, cuts on her hands from the broken window debris. The doctor also told her, in no uncertain terms, that it was time for her to lose some weight. "A layer of fat is important for arctic animals and pregnant women," he'd told her sternly. "You are neither." He made some dietary recommendations, which did not include eating the ice cream pops and other goodies from the freezer during the hottest part of the day before they got soggy. It did include exercise, however, and Chimmy started right away, climbing down the stairs just after Dr. Bell left, and Tammy Kowzowski arrived.

Tammy didn't mind coming back, exactly; Chimmy was fun and talkative and it made the day go by faster. But she was also a little worried, because Chimmy had a concussion, which certainly *sounded* serious.

The power was off again, and so Chimmy was sitting on her stool doing sales slips by hand. Concussion or not, she wanted to be in the store, where the action was. Folks came in to chat and check out the new awnings and larger window.

There was quite a lot of news that morning.

Jack Greeson had come in to buy a pack of smokes and told Chimmy about his driveway near snapping in half. He'd just asphalted that drive last summer and was giving serious consideration to suing the company that had done it for him, a place from over in Weston. His rear axle had been shot to shit, and one of his tires was sliced clear through from the edge of the road.

Tammy suggested that maybe there was a fault line running through Goodlands. She'd seen a show on television once that said there were fault lines running everywhere, even in Canada.

"Well, I don't want to make you feel bad, Tammy," Jack said, "but this was no fault line in the earth. This was a fault line in the asphalt. That crack was right smack along the drive where the asphalt ended and the road began. Some kind of damage was done when those boys laid that down. And someone, by God, will have to answer to that, and correct the situation." Chimmy wrote out his sales slip and handed it to him with his cigarettes, making change from a tin box they were using until the power was back on.

Jack pointed to the cash register. "Now you see, that's the problem with things. You can't even run your cash register without power. People are too much in a rush to do things in a new way. There's nothing wrong with writing out a receipt while I wait here, but people got to have a machine to do it for them. Here we are having a nice talk, because it's taking longer to do, but if you had that machine up and running, we'd be done and I'd be across the street already, and we wouldn't have spoken any more than a how'dya do," he said. *Point taken,* Chimmy thought. Except Jack Greeson was never one to just have a how'dya do; he would have said his piece anyway, just would have lit up a smoke to pass the time.

"Same goes for the asphalt situation. Those boys brought their machine and did her up in no more than a couple hours. In the old days you would have done it by hand, and by God, you can bet dollars to doughnuts that it wouldn't have bust up like that. People don't care anymore. It's fast, faster, fastest," he finished.

"Well, you might be right, Jack," Chimmy said, shifting on her stool, "but I have a feeling that the cash register is a little more accurate than I am."

She chuckled a little when Jack surreptitiously checked his

sales slip once he was outside the door. Now see, she pointed out to Tammy, if she had been upstairs resting, she would have missed that.

The other thing they heard about that afternoon was Larry Watson's water tanks having been drained. That was a little more sobering than Jack Greeson's driveway being on the receiving end of a fault line. They heard about it from Gooner when he came in to buy a can of pop; he was heading out to weld the spouts back on.

"Damnedest thing, I went out and had a look. I don't know what the hell could have happened, make them pop out like that. It's like it happened from inside. I was asking him if he maybe had some kind of gas mixed in with that water, or something—you know, build up some pressure—but he says the animals have been drinking it all week. Damnedest thing." For once Gooner didn't make any of his lame jokes. He was in and out in minutes.

Tammy was cleaning up under the counter when Gooner left. She shook her head. "Just seems like everything's going crazy, doesn't it, Chimmy?"

"Well, my grandmother used to say things happened in threes. There was the storefront, Jack's driveway, and the water tanks. If you just count those, then things are about to get back to normal for a while," Chimmy said.

"What about the fire?"

"Inflation," Chimmy said. "Things are happening in fours."

Around three o'clock, Tammy was on the stool behind the counter and Chimmy was standing to stretch her legs when the two of them saw, nearly at the same time, a stranger—a handsome stranger, both women thought—heading right for the Dry Goods.

"Who's that?" Tammy asked.

Chimmy stretched her neck to get a better look, since her view out the window was blocked by George's scaffolding. She shook her head. "I guess we'll find out."

* * *

Tom was well aware of the curious eyes on him as he walked down Goodlands' main drag. Still, people were polite and friendly, nodding and trying not to stare. He was used to it. He had spent most of his life being the stranger in town.

The main street reminded him of an Old West movie set, seemingly plunked down in the middle of nowhere. The town itself had been built on a grid, and houses and buildings were set in rows straight as arrows, roads crisscrossing at ninety-degree angles, nary a mound or hill to nudge them to one side or the other, no leanings, no curves, just the gradual rolling up and slight decline of the land itself. It had a strange, organized, futile beauty, a combination of the awesome power of the omnipotent sky and man's insistence on markers. If Tom had felt better about the place, he might have been able to respond to the beauty, let it take him away, instead of feeling that he would be taking it *on*. All he needed to really get going on it was a shot of Scotch. Or tequila. With a pinch of salt and the tang of fresh lime. A vodka chaser, topped off with a couple of cold beers. Instead, a juicy steak would have to do, and a little vino to wash away the road dust.

He found a grocery. The building was in the midst of destruction or construction, it was hard to tell which, but the sign leaning up against the building, sideways, read GOODLANDS DRY GOODS AND SUNDRY, and under that it listed, MOVIE RENTAL, BEER AND SPIRITS, GROCERY. All that modern man could want.

The door was propped open with a brick, and Tom went in, under the curious gaze of a man on a ladder.

There were two women behind the counter. Tom nodded a hello and they smiled and nodded back in unison. The bigger one had a bandage across her face, over her nose. She asked if she could help him.

"You gotta couple of nice steaks?"

"We've had a bit of trouble lately, as you can see, we're under construction," she said. "We're keeping the perishables across the street there at Rosie's, the cafe. You go on over there and tell them that Chimmy sent you." She pointed out the window. "Tell them you want the fresh stuff that came in yesterday. They'll fix you up. You tell Grace."

"Good." Tom looked above the counter where the bottles, the "spirits" mentioned on the sign, glittered in the dusty light. It was all there, the Scotch, the rye, the vodka. No tequila, though. He itched for one of the big bottles of the cheap rye, and a hole to drink it from.

Karen Grange didn't strike him as a rye kind of lady. *None until this was over.*

"I guess a bottle of wine will do me," he told the big woman.

"Red or white?"

Karen struck him as a *white* kind of woman, but Tom was compromising as it was.

"Red."

Chimmy frowned into the space between her and the bottles. "We have some such Californian thing in red. Gallo. That do?"

"If that's what you've got," Tom said. Chimmy lumbered over to the far end of the counter where rows of bottles stood high on the shelves.

"We don't carry much wine. People around here like spirits and beer, spirits and beer. Christmastime we get more in. Then at New Year's we sell some champagne. Can't drink champagne myself, makes me gassy. Don't mind a beer once in a while, though," she said. She dragged a step stool over to the shelf and climbed it, her bulk leaning precariously as she reached and stretched up for a bottle on the top.

The younger woman grimaced. "Chimmy, maybe I should do that—"

"I'm fine, I'm fine," Chimmy said, grunting and straining. She got the bottle and came down off the step with a *huh*! "There," she said, breathing heavily. "Got it." She brought it back to where Tom was standing, smiling, waiting.

"You just passing through, or you staying awhile?"

Tom broadened his smile, "Little of both, I guess," he said. Chimmy nodded and reached for the receipt book.

"We're out of power until the front's finished. Had a freak accident yesterday. The tree across the way fell over and crashed into the front of the store. Imagine that. Insurance was paid up though," she said, and wrote out the wine and the steaks on the sales slip.

"Anything else, mister?"

Tom shook his head. Chimmy started adding up the prices, punching the numbers silently into the hand calculator beside the register.

"You just here for the day, then? Visiting someone for supper?" she asked. Tom ignored the question.

"You got a map of this town?" Tom asked.

"A map? Sure, we got maps. How about a state map?"

"Actually, just the town."

"Well, now, I don't think we do, do we, Tammy?" The young woman hadn't spoken since trying to help, but she'd hovered around the counter while Chimmy did the sale. She blushed full red in the face when Chimmy spoke.

"Um, no, I don't think so. But what about those ones Mr. Shoop had made a couple of years back?"

"Right. Right. They're those silly maps, supposed to be funny, you know, with all the drawings and such of the people and the businesses on them. We did a hunting-fishing thing here about two years ago, trying to drum up a little tourism. Didn't have much impact, if you ask me; same people who've been fishing and hunting here for years came back. But there are those maps. You'd have to go to the town office," she said, and leaned over to point out the window at an angle. "Someone should still be there. Cost you a dollar. I don't know how accurate they are as far as the streets and such, but the rest is pretty good. We put the Dry Goods in on there. Cost us twenty-five dollars."

"Does it mark out the town limits?" Tom asked.

Chimmy looked at him curiously. "Yeah, that at least it does."
She stared at him for a second before looking back down at the
sales slip and double-checking the tax.

"That'll be eleven-sixty for the steaks and the wine."

Tom pulled out one of the twenty-dollar bills that were still
crumpled in his front pocket. Blake's money. It was dry by then,
but when Tom touched it he could feel a slight burn. He uncrumpled it before handing it to Chimmy.

"So, a map, huh? You looking for something? Maybe I could
help you," Chimmy said, unable to contain her curiosity.

"I'm taking pictures," Tom lied. "Just like to know where
they're from. Like a souvenir."

"Oh, I love taking pictures," Tammy said. The two of them
looked at her and she blushed again. "I do." It was news to
Chimmy.

"Pictures of what?" Chimmy asked the man.

"Oh, barns, fields, that stuff," Tom said, flashing an even bigger grin. All the smiling was beginning to hurt his face and he
wanted to leave without being rude.

"Oh! Like that guy in the book about Madison County? I
loved that book!" Tammy said, blushing again. Chimmy's eyes
shifted slightly. Tom noticed.

"Let's see your camera," Chimmy said suspiciously. "Tammy,
you'd like to see his camera, wouldn't you?"

Tammy tried not to, but she giggled. "Sure. I love cameras!"
Later, disgusted with herself, she would repeat this to her friend,
mocking herself: *Oh, I love cameras!*

Tom had his pack on the counter and was slipping the bottle
of wine inside. He narrowed his eyes until they were nearly
closed. He nestled the wine in between a couple of T-shirts for
protection and stuck his hand deeper into the pack. A second
passed. He pulled his hand out of his pack.

"Here it is," he said quietly. In his hand was a small camera.
The name on the front wavered and shimmied. Then settled.
Nikon.

"Oh, it's so tiny!" Tammy said. It rested in the palm of Tom's hand, not quite filling it.

"It takes great pictures," he said. Suddenly, he tossed the tiny camera into the air and caught it easily with the same hand. His face broadened in a happy smile and he chuckled. Just as suddenly, he slipped his hand back into his pack and the camera disappeared.

Chimmy stared down at the place where the camera used to be. When she raised her head, her eyes looked glassy. She rubbed them, looked blankly up at Tom.

"Ladies, thank you very much for your time. Lovely town you have here. A little dry, though." Tom shouldered his pack and nodded a good-bye.

"Bye," Tammy said.

"Bye," Chimmy said, but by that time, he was gone. Chimmy watched him walk up the street to where she had pointed. She watched until she could no longer see him.

"Strange guy," she commented.

"I thought he was cute," Tammy said, sounding wistful.

"Never seen a camera like that," Chimmy added, more to herself than to Tammy, who was back under the counter, dusting.

"Gawd, Chimmy, there's twigs and everything under here, too. That tree must have split wide—"

"Tammy, I think I am going to go upstairs for a little bit. Feeling tired," Chimmy interrupted. She rubbed her eyes again.

"Sure, Chimmy. You go ahead, everything will be fine," Tammy answered, concern in her voice.

The woman at the town office was alone. She didn't ask him any questions, and sold him the map for a dollar, as Chimmy had said.

"Is it accurate?" Tom asked her. He laid the map flat in front of him. It was small, no more than eleven by seventeen when laid out. But what it lacked in size it made up for in color. The fields were a bright yellow, presumably lush with growing wheat; the roads were a polished gray, the signs were blue and large, and, dotted along the roads, particularly in the middle of the map, where the town was located, there were whimsically depicted buildings, with smiling large-headed people waving from their places of business.

She pulled the pile of maps around so she could see it better, nudging Tom's hand off the pile as she did so. "Everything is accurate, except for the dimensions of the buildings in the town center there. But I supposed that's obvious," she said. She ran her finger along the outer circle of the map. "This is Goodlands," she said. She stopped at the end of the state highway where a sign indicated "Oxburg," with an arrow pointing off the map. Smaller and less colorful, Tom supposed. "If you want a map to drive by, I'd pick up a state map," she said, peeling one off the pile to hand to Tom.

Tom stared down at the map. He ran his hands over it, as though smoothing it down.

"Thanks," he said, not looking up at her.

"Don't mention it," she said. "You visiting from somewhere?"

"No." He handed her a single from the change at the Dry Goods. "Thanks again."

Donna Carpenter watched the man leave. He was a good-looking guy, and Goodlands did not exactly have a plethora of young, good-looking guys. It might have been nice to flirt a little with him, but he hadn't exactly been up for conversation. She sighed when he disappeared out the door, taking a deep breath first. As she exhaled, she thought she tasted something tantalizingly familiar. And then she smelled it. A clean, cool smell, wonderful. It took a moment to place it. Rain. She smelled the wet smell of rain. Then it faded away.

Odd. She shook her head, smiling. She ran her hands over the pile of maps still on the counter. At one corner, where the man had rested his hand, the paper was slightly warped. She pushed her fingers into the spot. She was sure, for just an instant, that it was damp.

Her brow furrowed, and she slipped the pile of maps back under the counter.

By the time Tom picked up the steaks and was heading back out on the road that led to Karen Grange's, he had been seen by thirty or more people, some of them just passing by on the street.

He'd walked through town, plain as day, and everyone who passed by noticed him. He was a stranger, after all. A few people made note of the fact that he was on foot. A number noticed where he turned on the road. Ironically, one person who didn't see Tom in town that day was Karen Grange.

He walked as he always did, easily, nothing in his stride or his expression ever once betraying what was going on in his mind. He had a strange feeling that he was not walking through a town at all, but through a citadel, and that he was being watched. By whatever it was that had closed off the town. By then, he knew that wherever he went he was no longer the rainmaker. He was the enemy. And he was challenging the skies and whoever held them in this place.

His bag was heavy with the wine and food and it dragged his shoulder down. He had an uneasy feeling in the pit of his stomach, unfamiliar, but identifiable just the same.

Vida Whalley was standing at the junction of Parson's Road and Main Street, contemplating dropping in on the Dry Goods and maybe having one more go at someone, maybe that *smug* Charlene Waggles who apparently was still standing, maybe wiping that *smug* smile right off her stupid face, when the stranger passed by.

Her attention had been diverted by the memory of the tree crashing into the front of the Dry Goods, that first sound of the wood cracking, the scratch of splinters against her legs, the rush she got, seeing that *huge* tree hover for just a second before coming down. Her attention was focused on that moment, and so before she noticed the stranger, there was the sudden force of his physical presence that pushed her back, like a gust of wind.

The blood rushed painfully to her head, sending her hands up over her ears to block the terrible roar that started from inside her. As the power welled up, it silenced every other thought.

She turned her head in the direction of the thrust. Time seemed to slow down as people moved and swam in front of her. She blinked hard to focus, the roar in her ears louder, so loud she wondered if it could be heard by others. Her heart pounded. The black place inside her grew hard, like a rock. In her belly, the tether tightened.

Far, far up the road, she saw him. As he walked, and grew smaller in her sight, the pounding in her ears lessened, her heartbeat slowed. The voice began a wail, shrieking, not allowing Vida her own thoughts.

It was him. He was the one.

She watched him walk away, and felt the pull of the tether. She followed.

SEVEN

KAREN HAD BEEN A MEMBER OF THE GOODLANDS BUSINESS Council for four years, ever since it was founded in the winter of what would become the first year of the drought. It had been a dry winter, but in the cycle of seasons and years, that wasn't cause for concern. At the time, Goodlands was prosperous, a place that had always maintained a status quo, not much affected by politics, social disaster, or the fast and furious booms and busts of other towns. It was constant and sturdy, affected only by the mercurial temperament of weather, which for the most part had been good to them.

The council had been formed, in fact, because of the sturdy, unchanging nature of the town's long-term economy. They met on matters of tourism, snickered about at first, and business planning, such as trying to convince the town to add a couple more festivals to their short list of excitements: the Ice Festival in mid-January, the July Fourth picnic, and the Sports Day Rodeo in August. The first year the council sat, they were instrumental in organizing and funding an Arts and Crafts Fair and Bake Sale at the end of November, which had been very successful, and they had added an extra day to the rodeo. There had been plans to add a community "End of Summer" barbecue to September, but by the time they met on that, the drought was in full swing, and they had decided not to move until the following year. By then, it was the beginning of bad times.

Every six weeks, on a Wednesday, the council met, satisfied an innocuous agenda, and finished up the evening with gossip cloaked as open discussion, and had coffee graciously provided (for a ten-dollar annual members' fee) by Rosie's Cafe. Occasionally, Betty Washington came down to represent the county and brought something she'd baked. The meeting was chaired on a rotational basis.

In past years, Karen had enjoyed the meetings, held infrequently enough that they weren't a burden on anyone's time. It was a chance to catch up with people she normally saw only in a banking capacity. Also, because of the good-natured work of the council, the meetings tended to be fun. Ed Clancy, for one, usually had a new joke to share, he being in the best position to hear them. Karen suspected he cleaned them up thoroughly before telling them at the meeting, but they were always good for a laugh.

But, during the last year, council members had begun to feel they were meeting in vain. "Business" was not exactly booming, and the very idea of introducing anything that required fundraising was absurd. Some on the council were all for disbanding until the end of the drought, and Karen had a feeling that if things didn't get better over the summer, the meetings would not resume in the fall.

This Wednesday meeting couldn't have come at a worse time for her. She wanted only to go home and find out what had—or rather, hadn't—happened.

In the first year, the meetings had been officiously termed

"supper meetings," and had met every sixth Wednesday at the cafe, where Grace would whip up an evening's special, invariably served with French fries, and there would be more eating than meeting. That stopped after the first dry year, when the members decided that it looked bad to eat while talking about the declining fortunes of the town. No one, however, had thought to change the original time of the supper meeting so that people could go home and grab a bite before the council met. It made for a quick, if sometimes noisy, gathering.

The June meeting was the last of the year before breaking for the summer, when those who could afford it would pack up and go away for at least a couple of weeks. Those who couldn't would go through the motions of the rituals of summer, usually involving a backyard barbecue or two and a trip to the man-made lake in Weston on the weekends. There would be few families filling the children's pool this year, or setting up a sprinkler for the kiddies.

Worst of all, the rotational chair, according to the mailed agenda, was Leonard Franklin. If she could only disappear, or think of an excuse not to be there. But it would have looked worse if she hadn't shown. Karen took a seat at the far end of the long wooden table, wishing that she hadn't had to show up. For all the reasons.

People trickled in during the ritual part of the agenda, the roll call and declarations, and there were mumbled conversations and sometimes two seconders for motions, without any movers. The real part of the meeting started just as the last member— Larry Watson—arrived, and Karen realized that she was running out of places and people in the room on which to lay her eyes.

"Okay, ladies and gentlemen, the first item on the agenda is the Fourth of July picnic," Leonard said. In spite of the mock enthusiasm he put into the announcement, it was met with silence. "Okay, as far as I know, everything is still going ahead—" he said, looking questioningly over at Ed Shoop, who gave a small nod "—and so we have this lovely sign-up sheet to pass around for volunteers to man—oops, pardon me, to *person*—the council's booth. Sign up, hour at a shot, you'll be there anyway, *comprende?* This year we are right next to the pie tables, so the eating's fine. Some incentive for you," he finished, and he absently passed a piece of paper to Larry Watson who signed it and passed it on.

"Next item is—"

"Wait a minute," Chimmy interrupted. "Aren't you going to call for discussion?"

"On the booth? Booth was carried two meetings ago, Chim."

"I don't think we should have a picnic this year," she said. "What the hell are we celebrating? We're going into what will probably be our worst year ever, no one has any money, and personally I don't think anybody feels like celebrating anything." She leaned back in her chair, arms folded over her chest.

Karen closed her eyes. Chimmy, no friend of hers, in spite of numerous overtures and a paycheck spent almost entirely in her store, was going to hold up this meeting with a petulant complaint about a done deal. Karen wished she could just stand up and leave. In some ways, she wished it were still two o'clock that afternoon, when she had looked up from her work and thought she saw, through her little office window, a tiny wisp of cloud. For one special moment, her heart had leapt up into her throat and she believed it was going to start. That any second from that moment on, the skies were going to send their most beautiful manna. But it hadn't been a cloud at all, just a funny trick of the light between the window glass and the sunshine, and then her heart landed in the pit of her stomach and she knew with absolute certainty that it wasn't going to happen that day. She stared at the window for a few more minutes, *willing* a cloud to appear, but it didn't.

And now Chimmy Waggles, with her pout and her bandaged nose, was going to turn this into a philosophical discussion about whether or not they should celebrate the birth of their country during a drought. Karen was torn between letting out a deep, annoyed sigh and remaining as invisible as possible. One glance at Leonard kept her silent.

He ran a hand through his hair. "Well, I was going to save this for the end of the meeting, but since it's up for discussion, I'll say it now. I guess we won't be here for the Fourth picnic. But I'd like to take this opportunity to invite you all to our auction sale, to be held in just under two weeks' time, out at the farm," he said.

"What?" Dave Revesette said, shocked. A couple of people looked over at Karen. She was blushing.

Two weeks? Why couldn't he have waited? They had a grace period until August. If the rain came before they left—as it surely would—they could have worked out a lease deal and maybe even something better. Dave shot her a sharp sideways look.

"Well, you know, we got a break. Friends of ours in Minnesota are going to Europe for a year"—he chuckled slightly—"and said it would be good if we took over their house while they're gone. It's a nice big place, close to a hospital, and Jesse's happy about that, with the baby and all, and I have a lead on a job out there. So's everything is working out fine. We have to do it now, is all, because they leave in a month, and we've got to be ready when they go."

There was an awkward silence. Karen's cheeks were hot and obvious. She wished for nothing more than to stand and shout, "But it's going to rain! Maybe even tomorrow. And anyway, *it's not my fault!*" But instead, she sat stiffly in her chair, waiting for someone else to speak so that there would be something else in the room to look at.

"I'm sure-as-shit sorry to hear you're going, Leonard. You're a helluva citizen; helluva farmer, too," Dave Revesette added.

"It's a bad sign," Ed Shoop said, shaking his head. "Our best people leaving. You sure there's not another way?" He looked directly at Karen. Several others followed suit. It became clear who was expected to answer the question. It was the first acknowledgment of the position she was in in the town. As though she had any real power over the decisions made by a faceless head office. There was no way to explain that.

"Um . . . there's always another way. Leonard, I wish you had spoken to me before you made your arrangements. Can you see me before you do anything final?"

Leonard's eyes narrowed. "I won't be a tenant on my own land."

Karen felt a terrible rush of guilty despair, rising up like a stone in her throat, an overwhelming sorrow. She, author of the quick trip into credit hell, knew that the next step in the chain of disaster was a desperate measure; in her case it had been a saving grace, being sent to Goodlands. In Leonard's case, it would not be redeeming. Her blush deepened on her cheeks instead and she felt embarrassed for having spoken at all. There would be no winning, no matter what she had said.

"I'm so sorry, Leonard," she said quietly. For a moment, she thought she would cry.

The awkward silence descended again, and for a time no one's eyes were raised from the papers in front of them. Beside her, Dave Revesette made some notes on his papers. Finally, Ed Shoop spoke.

"This isn't the time or the place to discuss personal issues," he said, in his mayor's voice. "So, are we going to table a motion on this picnic? Because if we are, I so move that the picnic go on as planned."

"Hear, hear," Larry said. "People gotta get out, Chimmy."

Leonard cleared his throat and continued as though nothing had happened. "Item two: does anyone want to talk about the pool before we move on it?"

Karen only half listened to the ensuing discussion. No one wanted to pay for the pool; no one, frankly, had the money—nor did the town of Goodlands. And there was the small fact of there being no water to fill it.

Karen's eyes narrowed. *If they only knew.* She thought about the rainmaker. The money. The town. If only she could tell them. She supposed people blamed her now, looking as people do for a place to lay blame. Her friends. Were they still her friends? She guessed they believed that the foreclosure was her own doing, in spite of the reality of her position—that she was a peon for a larger body that didn't live in Goodlands. The bank's only perception of the place was as a rapid drain on their resources, and their only vision of the town was through the window of her office. Even if it did rain, they could never know her part in it. She shot a careful, slanted glance down the table and across at Larry Watson. It had to be that way, and really, it didn't matter to her at all. Her reputation would heal along with the town. *After it rained.*

The meeting dragged on, Karen's emotions zigging and zagging until she was barely able to say her good-byes.

Karen didn't get home until nearly eight o'clock, a new record for the business council. Her eyes and nose were red, her face felt swollen. She had finally cried in the car on the way home. She had been completely unable to stop herself and she decided, firmly, to blame her period, still two weeks off. Her tears had slowed down to a trickle by the time she was pulling into the driveway, and by the time she had parked the car, she was wiping her nose on a tissue and declaring the crying spell finished. Too many things going on and no escape from any of it, either at work, or at home, given the nature of her house guest. Yard guest. Too much free-floating emotion and no release for it. Not a pretty crier, she checked her face in the rearview mirror before getting out and confirmed that she looked awful. A splash of cold water might help.

Her stomach hurt from being empty so long past its usual hour; her feet ached from being squeezed into a pair of lovely, if deadly, pumps for twelve hours; and she had the beginnings of a tension headache. The first thing she did upon entering the house was to slip those awful shoes off and kick them aside. The floor on her poor aching feet felt flat, and lovely, and cool. She very nearly groaned with the pleasure of it.

Even as she did that, she wondered if she would find her guest somewhere inside. The house answered back stilly. The drapes blocked out the worst of the light in an attempt to keep the place cooler, and at that time of day, the sun slanted in on the other side of the house, in the kitchen. The living room was as she'd left it that morning, the pillows on the sofa in the same position she'd left them, the remote for the television set still carefully aligned on the side table, the silk flowers—replacing the fresh ones that were no longer available—still exactly centered on the table, the magazines, out-of-date and unread, still precisely fanned out next to the flowers. Everything was as it always was, untouched.

So he wasn't inside.

The light in the kitchen at that time of day was just starting to turn pink as the sun moved down on the horizon. It filtered through the square panes of glass, falling on the table and far wall. In a couple of hours it would be dark.

She tilted her head and glanced casually into the kitchen before going in, not sure what her reaction would be if he was there, going through her cupboards or whatever it was he did when he came into her house. The kitchen was empty, unoccupied, ordered; like the rest of the house.

There was a note on the table.

"Miss Grange," it read, "I'm in the clearing with a couple of steaks. One's for you." The note wasn't signed. She looked out the kitchen window, squinting into the dropping sun, and saw smoke rising in a curl from the clearing.

"He's crazy," she muttered. Her mood lifted with the prospect of food—and food cooked by someone else. And he would tell her what happened. She went into the bathroom and ran the water. It was tinged with brown. The well must be low again. Time for a call to Grease, who hauled it for her. She splashed some water over her face anyway, feeling the grit in it.

In the bedroom, after making sure the curtains were drawn, she pulled a soft white T-shirt over her body and tucked it into a pair of light, but belted, shorts. She was slipping into "something more comfortable," she realized. The phrase kept playing in her head as she changed, making her flush even though she was alone.

When she stepped out the back door into the yard, the first thing she noticed was that the smoke was gone. She looked quickly at her watch. It was eight-thirty. She wondered if he'd decided she wasn't coming and had put it out.

She walked as quietly as she could, glad she'd slipped on her sneakers instead of her walking shoes. The sneakers made almost no sound as she walked.

Karen slipped through the first of the spindly trees that blocked off the clearing from the house. The few leaves that were left on the ground under the nearly naked trees crackled with her steps, and she moved slowly. Just before the trees stopped and the clearing began, she paused. From there, she had a clear view of the rainmaker through the branches.

He was sitting on the ground cross-legged, staring into the small fire. The minimal smoke rising up dispersed before it got to the top of the trees, which explained why she couldn't see it from the house. The pit was surrounded by a double row of big rocks, which held what looked like a grill.

I bet it's my grill. From where she stood she could smell meat cooking. Her stomach rumbled—carnivorous origins revealed in spite of current aggressive campaigns against eating meat. He did not look up in her direction, or change his position. He sat as still as the air, staring into the pit.

He would tell her why it hadn't rained today, while she had waited all day for it at work. She remembered the moment when she had thought she'd seen the cloud outside her window, and the utter joy she'd felt, until it had disappeared, a trick of the glass. He would have a reason why. Weather conditions, maybe.

Ha ha, she mused. She should be angry. And was. But somehow, she didn't have the energy for very much anger, and in spite of herself, she was glad that she wasn't facing the evening alone. She watched him from her vantage point in the trees. He just sat there, staring into the fire, his expression unreadable.

He was handsome, in his way, but she couldn't put her finger on what it was about him that made him so. He was not boyish, or bookish, with glasses and a briefcase, like the men at the bank whom she had found attractive over the years. He had none of those qualities. His hair was long and uncombed, for all that he kept it held back in that tail. His body, equally long, was hard—from all the walking and traveling, she supposed—and he had broad, muscled shoulders and forearms. His face was tanned and square, with a strong jaw. He was very male-looking, whatever that meant. It was something in the way he looked at things, the expression on his face that betrayed an as-sumed ownership—and the willingness to discard it all. But that wasn't where the attraction was, either.

She watched him shift and lean forward, reaching for some-thing in his bag. When he settled back, he had a yellow brick that he sliced a piece from and ate. Cheese. Very familiar cheese.

Karen tried not to smile. He was a taker. It was more than just the cheese, of course, more than just the way he walked into her home without knocking, or if he did knock, with a deliberate-ness that brooked no argument. He existed in her imagination the way that most men did, their ways and means so different from her own, their sense of responsibility removed from hers, somehow more remote. She thought she knew what he was like, his type, that is. If she found him attractive she put it down to that type of man, and knew, firmly, resolutely, that the attraction would pass.

She remembered last night in the clearing when he had made it rain in her hand. It was the look on his face, the pure joy, that came back to her; his straight, even teeth, white against his tan. The direct way he spoke, and the softening of whatever he said with that smile. The classic con man, handsome, smiling, lying, smelling like rain.

"You coming out of there?" The sudden shock of his voice startled her.

"Of course I am," she said, annoyed. She took the few steps up to the two trees that were entwined and into the clearing.

"We have an ordinance against open fire, you know," she said. How long had he known she was there?

"It's a deep pit," he said.

"If you wanted to barbecue, you could have used the whole thing."

"This is barbecuing, Grange."

She stood awkwardly beside the pit, arms crossed over her T-shirt. The smell of roasting meat surrounded her. Her stomach growled loudly, to her embarrassment.

"You're hungry," he said needlessly.

"Late meeting. I haven't eaten."

"These will be done in a minute. You like it rare?" She looked for a place to sit. He sat on the open ground. He finally looked up at her.

He stood. "Oh, allow me," he said gallantly. He pulled his bedroll from the other side of the pit and swept it open with a flourish. His eyes were laughing as he let it fall to the ground. He smoothed it down and held his hand out. "There you go. Uphol-stery."

She didn't answer him, but sat on the blanket regardless. He watched her sit, the same mocking smile on his face.

"Better?" he asked.

"This is fine," she said, trying to get comfortable without sit-ting cross-legged. She settled on keeping her knees together, and resting them to the side. He sat down on the blanket beside her. She looked at him, annoyed. He answered with another smile, this time without showing his teeth.

She grimaced as he picked up a stick and moved one of the steaks closer into the middle of the grill.

Without seeing her grimace, he seemed to anticipate it. "I took some plates and forks from the kitchen. I figured you weren't an eat-with-your-fingers type."

"How thoughtful," she said through slightly clenched teeth.

"Relax. This is dinner out." He laughed. "Like a date," he teased.

She laughed tensely. "This is not a date."

"Not for you, maybe," he said, seriously. She shot him a look and he smiled. It was a joke. She did not relax.

He moved the other piece of meat closer to the center with the stick. Sitting so close to the fire's heat, Karen could feel her T-shirt beginning to cling and could smell the dampness rising from her skin.

"When I was a kid," Tom said, "we had what's called a summer kitchen. You know, off from the house so it won't get so hot? But I always liked it when we cooked outside. It's like eating a hotdog—it tastes better when there's a ball game in front of it."

The speech surprised her. It was the first time he'd said anything about himself. She supposed he was being charming. She knew she should have none of it. She smiled secretly.

"I think we'd better talk," she said.

"It didn't rain today," he said for her.

"No, it didn't." She dropped her voice carefully. "Is it going to? Ever?"

She felt him tense beside her. He was no more than six uncomfortable inches away. Close enough that she could feel his heat, and smell his peculiar scent, even over the barbecuing meat, and her own smells, a mix of nervous perspiration and laundry soap.

"Now's the time to tell me to leave. Unless you want to eat first," he said, only half serious.

"I want you to do what you said you would do," she said firmly. She was afraid to turn her head to look at him. But everything she knew about control told her she must. If this was a business deal, and the dealer wasn't coming through, she had to remain in control (CFC Standards and Policies, Chapter Three: Dealing with the Public). She had to *make* him see the control. She finally half turned and looked at him sideways, just for a moment, and then turned away. The most control she could muster while sitting so close to him.

He didn't answer. Instead he pulled a bottle from his bag and fiddled with his knife, pulling up the corkscrew, cutting away the seal and opening the bottle. Karen's face burned as they sat in silence. He was ignoring her.

And yet.

He hadn't asked for the money. It seemed fine with him that she said she had it, even though she might be lying. He hadn't wanted to see it, even, the way these deals always seemed to be done in books, the way things were done at the bank. Cash up front, collateral on the table, cards out. He hadn't made her do that. The money was still in the bag in the closet.

Unless he had taken it, she thought suddenly. It had been there that morning, she checked it about every ten minutes, her hands itching to take it back, her indecision rising as she got ready for work, imagining herself taking it back, leaving it there, taking it back. Finally leaving it where it was. Putting her faith in a dirty, dusty, scruffy wanderer from points unknown. She suddenly wanted to bolt from the clearing, run into the house and look for the money. However, she also suspected that it would still be there. For one thing, if he'd taken it, he would be gone.

"If you have dinner with me, I'll tell you all about it, after," he said, cutting off her deliberations.

"Why are you so mysterious about it?"

He raised his eyebrows at her and took a drink of the wine right from the bottle. "It's a mysterious business," he said. She looked into his face, deciding.

He offered her the bottle. "No glasses," he apologized.

"And what stopped you from taking mine?" she asked, only a little angrily.

"Too much stuff to carry," he offered. He continued to hold the bottle out to her. "No germs, I promise. And it's not bad. Something from California, I believe. None of that old stuff, this is fresh as hell. A very good afternoon," he joked.

She reached out and took the bottle, still not sure if she would drink from it. She stared at him, deciding. If she did this, then she would be accepting his terms, his dinner. Finally she raised it to her lips and took a small, delicate sip. She handed it back.

"Very fresh," she agreed. The moment had passed. She was accepting his offer of later. He nodded and smiled.

"Good," he said. It covered a lot of ground.

"Well, these beasts have stopped hollering, they must be done," he said, and deftly holding a plate beside the grill, he stabbed one steak with a fork that had appeared out of nowhere, and slapped it onto the plate. He handed it to her, with the fork and his own knife, the corkscrew replaced by a small blade.

"*Bon appétit,*" he said. "That's French for 'start chewing.' "

She laughed.

Karen had dinner with the rainmaker.

Henry Barker sat down in front of the television and flicked it on. He surfed channels until he found the Weather Channel. Then he leaned back and undid the top button of his pants and sighed out some of the pressure from his dinner.

Lilly joined him in the TV room. "You're not going to force me to watch the weather again," she said witheringly.

"Just for a second," he said absently.

She stood beside the couch and looked down at her husband. A good man. The sheriff job had been her idea and she had had occasion to regret it a dozen times over. This last year, especially. She looked at his face—furrowed brow, tired eyes, bagged and ringed from not sleeping well.

"Want some pie? Donna had some rhubarb up already."

Henry groaned with his full belly. "Sure," he said. She turned to go into the kitchen and he called after her, "Bring me a Bromo with it, Lil."

The satellite picture came up over a map of the northern central states. He picked out Goodlands easily, although it wasn't marked. The clouds rumbled animatedly over it.

The perky weather girl, Debbie something, called for rain. Equally perky, smiling little suns were half covered with gray, fluffy clouds. Cloud cover for all of the county, with rain showers overnight. He bet when he drove into Goodlands later, the sky would be clear as crystal.

As he did every night, Henry shook his head, his face darkened. He shifted on the sofa and pulled his zipper down for a little more comfort in an uncomfortable situation.

Most people had stopped watching the Weather Channel long before the fourth year of the drought. But not Ed Shoop, mayor of Goodlands. Although he had long ago stopped calling the weather bureau and the State Department, he could not keep himself from watching the weather, checking nightly to see if Goodlands was going to make the news.

He stood in the doorway between the kitchen and the living room and watched through the nation's temperature update, through a news bite on wildflowers, and waited for the state-by-state at nine.

Once, two years before, he had finally called the newspeople over in Bismarck and told them about the drought. They had come out and done a little story, but they turned it into a joke. It was the last piece of the show and was mostly silly references to something eerie going on in the town of Goodlands. They never came back, even though a couple of people had told Ed they'd called the story in, too. Assholes. That's what newspeople were. Nothing more.

When he heard his wife coming in, he quickly switched channels to the tabloid show she liked to watch after cleaning the kitchen, missing the North Dakota satellite picture by seconds.

There was no help for it. She got pissed off at him for watching the weather. Pissed off enough that sometimes she went into the bedroom and bawled her eyes out.

At the end of Parson's Road, kitty-corner to the Mann property, where Karen Grange lived, and down a ways yet from Clancy's Road House, there was an empty building, originally a farmhouse. Converted in the mid-eighties to a flower shop, and then, briefly, to a honey house, the building had been empty since before the beginning of the drought. Its neglect was starting to show. It had been listed for a while with one of the big real estate companies, but there was no longer a sign out front. The windows, back and front, were broken. Some thanks to occasional high winds with flying debris, and the rest probably due to the boredom and hormonal changes in young people, also given to propelling debris. The door still closed, but was no longer locked, its latch long disappeared and never replaced.

It had been nothing for Vida to sneak in, unnoticed.

It was growing dark. The streetlamp down a ways, in between the Mann property and the derelict flower shop–honey house, would come on automatically when the sky was dark enough. Until then, Vida had to make do with the dull light that filtered in through the broken panes, casting shadows on the far wall. That was fine. She had nothing to see inside, had only to avoid the broken glass that littered the inside of the building, and she had swept that away with her sneakered feet when she took up her post at the front window.

She stood in the shadow offered by the corner of the house, beside the window. She looked out, in the direction of the Mann House.

There was nothing going on. But she knew he was there. She could feel him. Not like the way she had felt him when he walked past her in town; that had been more like a shock, the kind you get when you touch a doorknob after walking across

the rug in slippers, except all over her body. This was more like
the way it would feel to put your hand on a beehive.

Vida realized with certainty that that was exactly how it
would feel to get any closer to him. From the outside, you can't
tell the bees are in there, but you can hear them. If you reached
out and put your hand on the hive, you would feel them inside
there, the buzzing under your hand making the hive itself feel
like some live thing. After a while, the slight casing of the hive
would start to seem a pitiful defense between you and the bees in
there. If they got out—and they would, you would start to believe in no time at all—there would be no getting away.

For now, the house stood between her and him. She would
wait and see. That was the best. Considering her hand was still
only outstretched toward the hive, and had not yet touched it.
She was afraid. Eventually, the one inside her would tell her
what to do.

After Henry's wife went to bed and he flicked the television
back to the Weather Channel, and after Carl Simpson had made
a few notes on paper about what he thought was *really* going
on in Goodlands, the streetlamp came on between Karen
Grange's house and the empty house.

Vida, meanwhile, waited. And watched.

The wine and the steak, but especially the wine, had made a
nice warm bed for themselves in Karen's stomach. She relaxed.
She sat more comfortably now, cross-legged, in front of the low
fire.

Neither she nor Tom had mentioned putting it out, and neither
had moved to pour on it the half bucket of precious water that sat
beside the pit. It crossed her mind that that half bucket might well
have been what had pushed the well over the edge. It might have
been worth it though. She was still, through the fuzz of the wine,
deciding. The fire added heat to an already hot evening, but the
color and look of it was satisfying: hypnotic and good.

They had been mostly silent since finishing their steaks and the last of the cheese, both lost in their own comforts and full stomachs, both thinking their own thoughts. Karen felt good. She didn't drink often, and she was thinking that the wine had been what she needed. She could suddenly see the reason people on those television shows came home from work and walked right over to the liquor cabinet. Her earlier self-pitying tears were far away. The rainmaker had leaned back and was resting on his elbows beside her, his right arm close to where Karen's hand lay. Even though she was very aware of his closeness, she did not move away. It must have been the wine but the feel of him next to her, so close, was . . . companionable. Two comrades in a foxhole. She closed her eyes. The wine felt fine, but it was making her head light.

"It's too warm," she whispered.

"What's that?" Tom asked. He sat up, closer to the fire. They were side by side then, he resting on his hand, right beside hers. Just barely, she could feel his flesh.

"The fire. It's so warm."

"I like a fire," he said. Karen shot him a look. She thought of Henry Barker coming out to the house that day. The fire. She dismissed it. It was ludicrous to think of Tom Keatley starting a fire for no good reason. Not without steak and cheese. And wine from California. She successfully stifled a smile. She did not want to move; not even the muscles on her face.

"Water, air, earth, and fire," she said suddenly. "Ancient al-chemists used to believe that everything that exists was made up of all four elements. Some things had more of one than another. Like people."

"What are you made up of, Grange?"

Karen thought about it, staring into the small fire. "I'm earth," she said. "And you're . . . air. I guess I should say wa-ter." She eyed him critically, as if to confirm it. "But you're not. I think you're air."

Tom laughed softly. "Air?" he said, raising an eyebrow. She refused to play. The wine was getting into her head, but there was a logic to her choice. He *was* like air. Dealing in the clouds above the earth. And when he was done here, he would just disappear and be somewhere else. As though she were breathing him in right now, and if she exhaled for just a second, he could be gone.

"You drunk, Grange?" he said, his voice light.

"Of course not," she said, annoyed with herself and her flight of fancy.

"I think you are."

"I am not," she said, sitting up straighter, wanting to make some cutting remark and thinking better of it. She didn't want him to think it was so easy to get a rise out of her, because it wasn't, really.

"Why don't you tell me what you were going to tell me?" she interjected, changing the subject. "Dinner's over." She brought her knees back up to her chest and wrapped her arms around them. Somehow this brought her body closer to his, and his arm brushed up against hers with the motion. She ignored his heat, stronger than the fire.

It was a long time before he spoke.

"Your town here reminds me of a place I've already been," he started. "There was this place in Iowa, an old man's house, just inside the state line, can't even remember the name of the town now, has to be ten years since I was there last. Never went back. About two years ago I was passing through Iowa, and I skirted around that town. No good reason. I just didn't want to go back there." Tom picked up the wine bottle and took another pull on it. He offered it to Karen, who declined with a sharp shake of her head. He took hers for her.

"There was this old man, seventy at least, and he had this young wife. Not that young, by some standards, but young for him; she was no more than forty at the time. They had eighty acres, dry as a bone. The old man caught me on the property and walked me back to the house with a rifle. So there was not much choice in going." He chuckled.

"I don't even know why I was there, on his land, I was just passing through, walking on the road and I was . . . *drawn* in. There was something about that land that pulled me to it. It was dry, simple as that.

"Stayed with the old man and his wife for a week. Rifle got put away just about as soon as I told them who I was, and what I did. After that, the old man wanted me to stay, and I did. I did what I could for them, and went on my way."

Tom took another drink out of the wine bottle, now nearly empty. This time he didn't offer any to Karen. She was looking sideways at him, listening intently.

"And?" she said.

He tilted his head and said quietly, "A very strange place.

"The woman's name was Della. He called her Dilly. Kept saying, 'Ain't she a dilly!' and cracking up. He'd make terrible, tasteless remarks about her, under his breath sometimes, sometimes when she could hear him. Talked about her and him in bed. Kept reminding me she was his wife. She seemed, not in love with him, but *devoted* in a way. They kept pigs, most of them dead by the time I showed up. You could smell the rot all over the place. After a couple of days you hardly noticed. He was an all-round bastard, as far as I could see. Just a bastard, deserved everything he got. His name was Schwitzer. She said he changed it, Anglicized it. She called him the Burgher when he wasn't listening." Tom didn't add that Della had come to his bed the first night he showed up, or that the old man had drunk himself into a stupor so she could do it, too, or that there seemed to be some kind of agreement between the two of them that Della could go ahead and get what she wanted from Tom. Tom and Della had made love in the attic room right above where the old man was sleeping. They made love silently, completely without words or sound, except for a sigh of release when Della climaxed. A sigh, like a great rush of air coming out of an overstuffed balloon. She left him as silently as she had arrived, and came back every night after that. During the day, when the old man was around, it was as though they were casual acquaintances.

"So what happened to their drought?" Karen broke into his reverie.

"It was a peculiar kind of drought," he said. "One that you might be interested in. Drought was only on their land. Just their place. Rest of the town was more or less fine."

Karen gasped. "So it's happened before. What's happening here must have an explanation!" She leaned forward, excited, pleased. "What happened?"

"I made it rain." Tom's voice was soft, so soft Karen almost didn't hear it. She didn't understand.

"So it could happen here. You could do it again . . ." she prompted.

Tom rolled a smoke from the works in his pack. He didn't answer Karen while he did it. He rolled deliberately, lost in thought or concentration, each move of his fingers slow and loving. When he was done he stuck the cigarette in his mouth and lit it from an ember on the end of the stick he'd used on the steaks. He blew smoke out.

"End of the week, I made it rain. I left the next day," he said, not adding that Della had come again to his bed in the attic room, and that time had whispered something in his ear just before she left.

"Like I said, I was going through there a couple of years ago and I stopped in a bar the next town over. Della and the old man were a regular topic of conversation. They'd had a real run of bad luck, I learned. There'd been the drought, which everyone still remembered. After that, they had a blight, killed off their crops. Then what animals they had left—an old horse, if I remember, and couple of cows, not much—they caught something and they all died. One after another. That same year Della got sick and died, too. Apparently the coroner said it must've been some kind of encephalitis. But the old man lived through it, and he would have been nearly eighty by then," he finished.

"Jeez," Karen said.

Tom chuckled softly. "Yeah, *jeez*. But I found out something else about the old man and his Dilly."

"What?"

"He was her father." Tom threw his cigarette into the fire. His mouth tasted bad. He reached for the bottle and drained it. "Wine's gone," he said to Karen.

"Oh God," she said, thinking of Della and the old man. She thought of her own father, and how kind he was. She shuddered. "Why did you tell me that story?"

"You know that expression 'when God closes a door, he opens a window?' I think it works just as well on the flip side. When God slams a door shut, if you pry open the window, he can shut that too. I think there're some places that are doing some kind of penance. For whatever reason," he finished.

"And you think that's true of Goodlands?" she asked, angrily. "You think Goodlands is doing penance?" Karen turned toward him, her brow furrowed in anger.

"I walked all over this town today. You know, if you stray even ten feet outside the boundary, the invisible line between your town and the rest of the world, the rain is right there."

He shifted so that he was even with her, and he looked deeply into her eyes. Her anger was still there, and some confusion.

"Why is that?" he asked.

She sputtered. "How would I know? *Why* would I know?"

"It's your town, Grange. You know better than I do." He stared into her face.

"Well, I don't know what you're talking about. All I know is that we have a drought here, and that I've hired you to fix it. If you can't fix it, and you're going to blame it on some crappy mumbo jumbo, then we can just call it a night." She stood, angry. He followed.

"What's your stake in all of this?" she said, red spots flaming up on her cheeks, her voice louder than it should have been in the little clearing. "Why do you care if it ends or not? You can just pack up your fancy bullshit and leave. But I'm not leaving!" She swung away from him, arms stiff at her sides. Tom rose and reached out for her, grabbing her by the arm and pulling her back. He swung her around to face him.

"Grange—*Karen*—" he said more softly, an apology on his face.

"What are you implying?" she asked, the anger leaving, replaced by a hurt look. "Do you think that it's something about *me*? That I have something to do with this?"

"No." He loosened his grip on her arm, but did not let go. "I'm not saying that. There's something wrong here. I think something's been keeping the rain away. I've never felt it like this before, not even on the old man's place. This place is like a graveyard, full of dead things. Look around you. It's not natural. I don't *know*—" He wanted to add that he didn't know if he could fix it. But he didn't. Somehow couldn't put that into words. "I'm looking for the reason."

"Well it's not *me*," she said. They stood close together. Tom raised his other hand and lightly ran it up her arm. He could see the doubt in her eyes, as though she did believe it might be her.

As if reading his thoughts, she said, "It started after I came. I don't have anything to hide. I like it here. This place . . . did something for me," she said, squeezing the words out.

"Okay," he said softly.

The hurt was still there, in her eyes. Now he wished he hadn't said anything, hadn't told her the story of the Schwitzers. They stood silently, Tom still holding her arm, Karen making no gesture to have him remove it. Her breath smelled like wine when she exhaled. He was close enough to feel the soft flutter of it and to hear her breathe in.

He had the urge to kiss her and he thought she might let him. Once more, the opportunity of her claimed him.

"I'm going inside," she whispered, but did not move. She

stayed a moment longer, and he thought he saw the same debate in her face, but then she gently pulled her arm away from him and slowly turned to go.

"Tomorrow," he said.

She turned back to him. "Tomorrow?"

"I think I might have an idea. I wish I could say more, but it's going to happen," he said, firmly, wanting to take that look off her face. "I'll make it happen." She stared at him and then nodded slowly.

Karen turned and slipped through the trees. She stumbled on a piece of deadfall and reached out to grab something for support, her head light with wine and the remnants of her anger. Her hand grabbed a branch and she felt it on her skin as though feeling it for the first time. The *deadness* that the rainmaker spoke of. She righted herself but did not let go. Under her hand, there was a vibration. Hardly felt, like a pulse point. She let go with a twinge of disgust, as though she'd touched something *awful*, like a corpse. When she broke through the trees into the darkness of her backyard, she felt a little shiver up her back. She wanted nothing more than to be out of the yard, out from under the sky. She looked up. It looked as it always did, but this time she wondered what was there. She felt watched.

The shiver was like the one her mother used to get that she swore was a premonition of something bad. Her mother had an expression for it.

" 'Someone walked over my grave,' " Karen muttered. She broke into a run, and ran all the way to the house.

Then she stood still for a moment, waiting for the feeling to fade. She wondered where he would sleep, in the clearing or in the yard. She didn't lock the door.

Tom poured the half bucket of water over the fire, carefully extinguishing the embers that were left. The moon cast blue light over the clearing. From his bag he pulled out the map he'd bought earlier in the day. There was just enough light to see the outline of Goodlands, really all he needed to see.

He closed his eyes and traveled around the boundary, as he had that day, imagining the farthest places, the ones he hadn't walked over. It was there. The rains were all around Goodlands, and all he had to do was bring them as far as the boundary and see what kind of power they could bring to move in on their own. The call of the land, the pull of the vacuum. He didn't know what else he could do.

He folded the map into four and put it back in the bag. The heat from the fire and the day was still all around him. He suddenly wished he hadn't extinguished the fire. It would have been a kind of company.

Karen was in his head. His mind played over the moment when they had stood close, his hand on her arm, just before she went back to the house. Her mouth in soft contrast to her pale face; her lips for once not pursed in disapproval or worry, but soft with doubt and maybe fear. He should have kissed her. Was glad he didn't. If he had, he might not have stopped until that look on her face was completely gone. He would have kissed her until they both felt better about him.

His eyes caught the glint of the moon on the glass of the wine bottle. It was empty. The sight of it lying useless on its side filled him with despair. He wanted more. Another drink. Just a beer. Take the edge off sleep. Let him sleep. One beer. Maybe two. He pushed the thought reluctantly from his mind, before it had a chance to take serious hold over him. What he needed was to walk. To think. Feel it out.

Tom slipped silently through the trees and into the open space of Karen's backyard. The lights were off inside and he wondered if she slept.

From the edge of the orchard he had an open view of the yard, the center of which was blemished with the somehow flawed pagoda, gazebo, whatever the hell she called it. If the buildings on the prairies looked as though they had been dropped from above, this particular structure looked as though it had sprung, weed-like, from the earth. The soil around the foundation still had the look of having been recently dug out; the ground, patchy from the drought, and dried, had crumbled and broken around the outside. Winds had blown the dry earth upward in a tiny drift around the base.

He walked over, his gait slow and even, thinking of penance.

Tom crouched down at the edge of the little building. The earth around it did seem newly broken, although that couldn't be. His eyes swept around the edge of the gazebo as far as he could see, and the earth was broken, raw. He touched it. The ground was warm. He dug his fingers into it, soft, and scooped up a handful. He stood, the earth clutched loosely in his hand.

From the east, a breeze picked up, blowing coolly over him. It swirled lightly around his head, strong enough to ruffle his hair and to blow some of the dirt from his hand. He watched as the dirt trickled over the pad of his thumb and was carried away.

His hand grew warm. Then hot. Inside his hand, the dirt began to move. His hand opened reflexively, repulsed.

He was holding a palmful of something that squirmed.

He jumped and shook his hand violently and the things fell to the earth. He wiped his hand hard on his jeans, inwardly shuddering as he crouched and looked at them. Tiny, white, formless ovals, they writhed on the ground, digging their way back under. In a moment they disappeared. Maggots.

Standing again, he dug at the earth gingerly with the toe of his boot. Nothing turned up. He backed away from the gazebo until he stood between it and first trees of the orchard. The wind that had come up so suddenly faded down to nothing. Just before it did, he swore he heard a voice.

He swiveled toward the house. It was still dark. He looked into the kitchen window, but could see nothing other than the glass. He couldn't see inside the house.

Then he heard it again. A thin, high voice, a woman's voice.

The house remained silent, guarded. His eyes were drawn back to the gazebo. It stood relentlessly, equally silent, but somehow more sentient.

Under his feet, the humming feeling that he had noticed earlier, returned.

After a moment's pause, he turned and walked away from the gazebo. Tom very much needed a drink. Maybe more than one. He walked out onto the road, and turned in the direction of Clancy's.

EIGHT

CLANCY'S ROAD HOUSE WAS HOPPING. THE BALL GAME COM-
ing over the satellite was the reason. Cincinnati hit another run
off Montreal and the crowd went wild, making Ed Clancy kind
of glad that there were no Canadians in the bar that night.

By the third inning, the crowd was buying lots of beer. Ed
Clancy was damn glad he broke down and bought the satellite
dish, even though it had set him back the price of a riding
mower. He wished he'd waited and got one of those little
eighteen-inch jobbers that everyone was buying now, since his
massive dish was vulnerable to the rocks of kids—and one brave
asshole who'd climbed the roof and spray-painted "Say Maybe
to Drugs" across the top of the dish, misspelling maybe, and
leading Clancy to believe it was someone who was in a position to know. They were scrambling more channels on the
dish and sometimes it was impossible to get anything that
would draw a crowd, beyond the soaps, without paying for it.

Some days, it wasn't much better than cable. But once in a while there was something useful you could pull in, like the games and some of the fights. If he figured it out on paper—something he left to his accountant—the dish had probably paid for itself in beer and side bets. And while he wouldn't admit it to too many people, Clancy was a faithful follower of *The Young and the Restless*.

The jukebox was quiet tonight because of the game. It was always a good game when Canada played. It was so good for business, Clancy usually made up a little sign and stuck it up over the bar advertising a Canadian game a few days before it was on. He had two color sets, both twenty-seven-inch and costing a pretty penny when he got them but still holding up all right. One was mounted at the corner of the bar, where he could watch while he drew beer, and the other sat in the far corner by the pool table. Ball games drew a drinking crowd.

Clancy's was at the end of Parson's Road in Goodlands, in the northwestern corner of the town boundaries, well inside, but close enough to the abutment with Telander, which didn't have a bar, and to the southern towns of Avis, Mountmore, and Washington, which had bars without satellite. Mountmore had gambling, which probably sucked a few bucks from Clancy's on the weekends, but on fight nights or game nights—especially if Canada was playing—he drew folks in from all over.

His capacity was about a hundred, the building a former ice warehouse, built in the fifties and empty for twenty years before he bought it and put in taps. It had concrete floors and pillars and was hard to heat in the winter, which was a bitch, but in the summer it stayed cool without air conditioning, and that was a definite plus. Clancy had gutted the place and put his own hand to the design. The end result was more rec room than fancy bar, but folks liked it. It was, in a way, like home. Outside, the place still looked like a warehouse. Every now and then a tourist would remark on how the place had possibilities. There had been no offers. If there had been one, Clancy would have leapt at it and driven his old Ford station wagon all the way to Florida without stopping.

Business was bad everywhere, but Clancy's was still doing all right. Beer holes do. Last winter had been tough and tight, but he'd still come through it in the black. Summer would be better with students home, and tourists passing through. It was depending on the locals that gave Clancy his gray hair.

Tonight he had what he called "a good crowd," mostly locals coming in to have a few beers and watch the game. Saturday nights he had the scum in, young guys who worked out of town and came home on the weekends. With little enough to do at home, they came in and drank themselves stupid. Mostly out-of-towners and the Badlands crowd. He kept a cattle prod behind the counter and people knew it, too. He'd never actually pulled it out, but he kept telling himself he would, even though it was probably illegal and he ran a clean store.

Kreb Whalley got drunk one night—Kreb Whalley got drunk every night, truth be known, but sometimes he got stupider than usual and it was one of those nights that Clancy was thinking of—and tried to sell Clancy some of his homemade. Clancy'd told him in no uncertain terms that he'd better keep his mouth shut or he'd turn him in just as soon as look at him. He expected something to happen to the place after that, but nothing had. On the other hand, the case was still open on who had defaced the dish, but he didn't think there was a Whalley who could spell even *that* well. He had gone to school with Kreb Whalley, and he was a badass on his way to being a loser then. Now he was a badass loser, and Clancy guessed that Kreb had at least fulfilled himself that way.

Kreb was in the bar. The Whalleys were all present and accounted for tonight, every last one of them except for the girl. She never came in. Ben Larabee was sitting with them tonight. Not a bad sort, really, but lately given to hanging with those bad actors. The drought had been tough on the worm-picking business, and his wife had moved away to her sister's someplace. He guessed Ben was working things out for himself. He didn't figure that association would last too much longer.

People were coming in and out of the door, and it was turning into a real party. It was a good crowd. One whole half of the bar given over to "the boys." Teddy Lawrence, Larry Watson, Leonard Franklin, Teddy Boychuk, Bart Eastly, Ed Kushner, Henry Barker, Jeb Trainor, and the rest of them had come in to watch the game and shoot the shit. They'd get louder as the night wore on, and their waitress would get some outrageous tips, but so far, except for Watson, they weren't drinking much. If Watson got too drunk, his boy was working in the bar and could drive him home. They were the guys a man liked to have in his bar, even if they weren't drinking much. Besides, everyone else was drinking just fine. The *cha-ching* of the cash register made up for the fact that Ed was having to pitch in on the floor, since Dave and Debbie were getting run off their feet every time Cincinnati scored a run.

"Hey! Clancy! Another round over here!" Bart Eastly called out in the direction of the bar. Then he continued what he was saying.

"Helluva thing," he said. "The goddamn road was down here"—he gestured with his hand on the table and raised the other—"and the goddamn driveway up here, had to be an eighteen-inch difference. Wheels were hanging over the edge like a little kid dangling his legs in the river, just happy as you please. Course, Greeson wasn't too happy, the goddamn rear axle is shit now, bust up like that. Gonna cost him a pretty penny, and I don't think he's got it." Bart drained the dregs in his bottle just as Larry's kid, Dave Watson, came over with replacements.

"Who's paying for the round?" Dave asked, looking at his father, who had snuck in a couple between rounds.

"Mine," Bart said loudly, producing a handful of bills. It wasn't. It was Leonard Franklin's official turn, but no one was going to let him buy. Dave left after sneaking another peek at his father's increasingly florid face and grim smile. Watson wasn't a regular drinking man, but it had been a helluva day.

Henry Barker was having his second beer and trying to let go of some of the tension in his shoulders. Though officially off duty, he was never really off duty and so he was limiting himself to four beers. He was a large man, both height and girth, and four beers were unlikely to do much more than make him piss every half hour—beer went through him something fierce—but it was sociable if not relaxing. Officially, they were watching the Canadians get tromped in full color. Unofficially, no one but Teddy Lawrence and Teddy Boychuk was really paying any attention. The rest of them weren't doing much more than checking the score once in a while and shooting the shit, if that was what you could call it. Henry thought maybe you could. It was shit. The whole day had been shit.

"So, how do you explain that?" Jeb asked.

"How would *you* explain it?" Bart said back.

"Well, roads do crack. I guess the road cracked. Greeson just had it paved, maybe it had something to do with that," Jeb said.

"I'll tell you, I'm a road man," Bart said boastfully. Having an audience listening to another car story was about the best thing that could happen to Bart and he was glad to oblige.

"I wouldn't know about that, Bart. I'm a leg man—" Kush interrupted, and got a laugh.

Bart ignored him. "If it was the middle of January, I might say 'Yeah, road cracked 'cause of the weather,' but it being June in the hottest goddamn summer on record, I don't think that's it."

"So, what happened, then, road man?" Henry said.

"Don't know," Bart answered, frowning. "I guess it was a freak accident."

"This whole fuckin' town is a freak accident, you ask me," Larry slurred. The whole table shut up and everybody turned toward the game. Watson was drunk. But he had a point, Henry thought.

Before he'd come to Clancy's, Henry had checked the weather

picture one last time. Lilly had actually *encouraged* him to go
out drinking so he would quit watching the bloody Weather
Channel. It was the same as always. Rain showers had been
called for tomorrow and the next day, cloud cover and rain.
Right there in Goodlands, but Henry would have bet the farm,
as it were, that they wouldn't be getting any.

The Expos hit a run off Cincinnati and the crowd screeched
its rage.

Thing was, most of what had happened that day could be explained. On The Surface. You could claim that the driveway between the road and the house did some kind of geological shift
or some happy-shit because of heat retention or something, and
cracked Jack Greeson's driveway. You could say that someone
was involved in cutting the taps off of Watson's water tanks and
drained them out for whatever reasons, same as you could say
that some asshole had gone and snapped the fence and set
Revesette's horses to wandering on to the road. You could say
that persons unknown had gone over to the Paxtons'—nice
enough folks for their odd ways—and in a spirit of unparalleled
meanness, tore up their cross and scattered it over their brown
and dead front lawn. You could say all those things, On The Surface. You could say that it was Persons Unknown.

But the Paxtons' cross, for instance. Henry had taken a good
look there. The thing had to be over twelve feet tall. The cross
beam was cut and bolted into the stand, and the whole thing had
been buried more than four feet in the ground and packed. In cement. Even with a couple of guys armed with a tow rope and
some digging apparatus, the operation would have taken an
hour and busted up the cross. Getting the cross beam off would
have taken a drill at least. And the cross was unbroken except
for being in two pieces, and no one saw or heard a thing.

Then there was Watson's place. The taps weren't open, they
were *gone*. They had been pulled out from the tanks and they'd
disappeared. He said he'd spent the better part of the day looking for them, even going as far out as the road to see if someone

had taken them with him and dropped them. He found nothing. Nothing more than that tiny sneakered footprint. Like a girl's. Too big for his little daughters, and too small to be his wife's, not that they would have done anything like that (not that they could have, but On The Surface . . .), but it might at least have explained away the footprint. Unless whoever did it had his little girlfriend with him, like Bonnie and Clyde.

You still could explain away what happened over at Greeson's, Revesette's, Watson's, and maybe even the Paxtons', if you didn't look very hard at the facts. But the boys didn't know, as yet, about what happened over at the Bells' place. There was no way to explain a car lying on its back like a little red turtle in the middle of a family's pretty, fenced backyard, forty-two feet from the carport where it had been the night before. There was no way to explain that, not even On The Surface. There would be tire marks in the grass, quite possibly the only green grass in Goodlands—they were buying water for their goddamn grass, but that was another story. There would have been marks from the Mazda, and marks from whatever tow truck had dragged it out of the carport and into the yard. But the funny thing about that was, there was just no room to do it. That tow truck would have to be made by Tonka, and Henry didn't think even Tonka made one tough enough for the job. Even if they'd put the car in neutral and rolled it into the yard, it would have taken at least four men to rock it until it was on its back. Henry had been to more than one party where it had been done, truth in fact, but it never took fewer than four guys, and it was never done silently, or sober. And even if that was what happened, there was the remaining question of why.

Leonard Franklin stood up and dug into his pocket, then dropped a fiver onto the table. "Thanks for the beers, you guys, I gotta get home. Jessie's not feeling good," he said.

"Got room in the truck for me, Len?" Ed Kushner stood. The question was hypothetical.

"Yup," Len said.

"What the hell, you walk here?" Boychuk asked.

"Had to leave the car for Gracie. Bad enough I came out. I gotta go help close up at least."

"You leave the car for a woman who's working all night? You're whipped, Kush."

"I'm a *peach*," he said, following Leonard with a wave.

When they were out of earshot, Jeb said, "Franklin's auction is the weekend after this. Wish I had some money. Had my eye on his John Deere for some time."

"Someone from Oxburg'll get it," Boychuk remarked casually, and turned back to the game.

"Franklin and the Campbells gone," Larry said into the silence. "How long before me, Dave, the Turners, how long before we're out? Not too goddamn long, that's when." His words were slurring and Henry caught Jeb's eye.

"Oxburg, my ass," Larry continued, loudly. "Oxburg, don't know anything about farming." He looked at Henry and pointed into his chest. "You don't know fuck-all about farming until you've had to make it through four fucking years of it without enough water. Right? Right? You know I'm fucking right."

"Keep your voice down, Larry. Bert Maule is right over there," Henry said. Bert Maule and two of his buddies were over from Oxburg. Maule sold real estate in the county. He was a bit of an asshole at the best of times, and probably didn't need much provocation these days for a fight. His wife was rumored to be interested in real estate elsewhere.

"Screw that," Larry said, but in a normal tone of voice.

Bart turned back from the game. "Hey, Henry," he said, "who's been doing it all?"

"How the hell should I know, what am I, psychic?"

Trainor laughed. "That's a good way to breed faith in the system, Henry."

"Faith shit," he said. "At this point I know as much as anybody else, and probably a good sight less. Not that I'm bragging." Jeb laughed and stood, heading for the can. Larry had missed the joke, but looked up and watched Jeb walk away. Boy-chuk and Lawrence were watching the game. Larry reached over and grabbed Henry's arm, looking deeply at him with blurred red eyes.

"I'm sunk, Henry," he whispered. "The well's dry. I spent it all. I spent Dave's school money, I spent the savings, I spent everything. All gone. Now I need new tanks or the animals will die. What the fuck am I going to do? What are any of us going to do?" His eyes were pleading, naked; his fingers dug into the flesh of Henry's arm. Henry thought of the weather picture, the fulsome clouds floating, moving, swaying over the state, over Goodlands, right in the middle. Carl Simpson, riding around in his pickup looking for black-hatted government men crawling into silos and doing weather experiments.

"I don't know, Larry. What about insurance?"

"Insurance?" He laughed, but it came out cruelly, spittle flying hit Henry's shirt. "Stopped paying on it last fall, for chrissakes. Nobody's got insurance anymore." He snorted again. He let go of Henry's arm and leaned over the table, closing his eyes. Henry wondered if he was going to pass out or throw up.

Bart stood up. "I'm outta here. I'm at Greeson's in the morn-ing. Taking Jack a loaner. Gonna help him break up the end of the drive, too. Ain't I nice guy?" He dropped a single on the table. "That's a tip. Don't you guys take it."

"Why don't you give Larry a ride home, Bart," Henry said. Bart looked at him disgusted.

"Come on, Watson. No barfing in the car my mother just vac-uumed it." Larry didn't argue, just stood up and fumbled around in his pocket. He threw some change on the table. "Now that," he slurred, raising his voice in an imitation of Bart's, "is a tip. Don't none of you guys take it."

Larry leaned down beside Henry and said wetly, "This whole town is in some kind of freak accident, Henry. You should just stay away from it, before it gets on you, like shit." Henry looked up at him. Larry winked, his face grim. He held his hand out, wavering, and Henry shook it. He winked again and swayed toward the door.

Henry should have taken him home. Eastly would just drop him at the end of the drive. At least Henry would have come in for a minute, helped smooth things over with his wife. Thing was, he just wasn't ready to leave. It felt like one of those nights when something was going to happen. Something in the air. Like a fight was about to break out any minute. He should be there if it did.

Jeb came back to the table, looking worried. "Larry didn't drive, did he?"

Henry shook his head. "Eastly took him."

"That's a heavy bag of crap, those water tanks. That's hitting a guy where he lives."

"Yup."

Jeb pulled his chair in a little closer. He looked over at the two Teddys. They were talking about the game, as though everything was business as usual. Maybe it was for them. Henry knew that Boychuk was on welfare, even if no one else knew. He also knew that Boychuk made regular trips out of town, and that the family was leaving as soon as he found work somewhere. They lost their farm a year or so ago and were living with his wife's mother. The Boychuks, maybe, had dealt with all of it already and were just biding their time.

"Something's got to be done, Henry," Jeb said.

" 'Bout what?"

"All of it. The town. This place is dying and we're all sitting around on our asses waiting for rain," he said. "Someone is sure as shit pissed off about something, to run around town hurting folks for no good reason. I heard about the Paxtons and their cross being torn up. They're weird as hell, for sure, but no one earns that kind of trouble. Someone's walking around mean, and I don't think it's one bit surprising, given the circumstances."

"I know what you're saying, Jeb. Just no help for it." Jeb

Trainor was what they used to call, in Henry's family, "good people." Steady, dependable, respectable, if a bit of a braggart in his way, Jeb was quick to lend a hand and no dummy. Henry had known him nearly all his life.

"I dropped in at Revesette's before I came here. It's not looking good down there, Henry," he said, shaking his head. "I'd almost recommend your stopping in there, if I could be sure you wouldn't get your head blown off."

Henry stiffened. "What are you talking about? I saw Dave this morning."

"I know that. He's got the boys set out all around the ranch. They're loaded up and sitting watch. He was dead set on it. I told him he was just asking for trouble. I said to him, like a joke you know, 'You wanna see some ID?' and he didn't laugh. He said he was trusting nobody. He also said he wasn't waiting for you to solve any of his problems, either, but that's besides the point."

"Shee-it."

"People are getting hot. Carl Simpson's taken to driving real slowly down the roads, looking out his window kind of strangely. He drove past my place the other night and shone a flashlight out the window into the yard. I was out there having a smoke—Lizzie thinks I quit—he didn't answer my wave at all. Just looked at me. And my wife saw Janet down at the post office and said it didn't look like she was getting much sleep," Jeb said, quickly adding, "who is?"

"I saw Carl a couple of weeks ago. I've been meaning to drop by," Henry said lamely.

"I don't know that you noticed, but the Gordons have been avoiding town like there's plague, lately. I don't know to say, but I think they're going to cut their losses. Saw Old Ed Gordon on the road and he just stared ahead. Everybody's doing it. People are starting to act crazy, like they're seeing ghosts." Jeb shook his head. The Gordons were the local insurance agents, and Henry wouldn't be surprised if things were starting to dry up for them. But when an insurance agent starts avoiding people, then times are strange indeed.

"I tell you, we put the place up about four months ago—that's to be kept under your hat, Henry, I don't want people around here thinking I'm deserting the ship—and I've been looking at my options. I'm not a young man anymore, but I'm starting to think that starting over can't be any worse than staying here. I don't think I'm alone in that. I saw more than a few familiar faces down in Weston. All near or around the real estate office there. Could be a coincidence, but given what I was doing there, I'm not so sure."

Henry nodded. Jeb was right. There was a feeling in Goodlands that never used to be there. The optimism was gone, which was to be expected, but it was something more. Like most farming communities, the people in Goodlands were pretty self-contained, self-reliant, but the feeling lately was not so much one of doing for your own, as it was protecting your own from everybody else. He hadn't been there, but he'd heard about a little fight breaking out at the water station in Telander last week. Nothing major, just a pushing scuffle over who went first, one that ended quickly and with nothing worse than embarrassment and hurt feelings, but that wasn't the Goodlands way. The Goodlands way was a basic love-your-neighbor thing. That was changing.

"I know what you mean, Jeb."

"You know Greg Washington shot his two dogs a couple of days ago? There's no more work for them on the farm, Greg sold what animals he had. Had to shoot the dogs. That big black one had to be fifteen years old. He was the kid's dog. Things are ugly if a man's shooting his kid's dog."

The two men fell silent in the noisy bar, and their eyes automatically went to the tube in the corner. The game was nearly over and Cincinnati would win. Dave Watson came over and offered everyone another round.

"Not for me, I'm leaving," Jeb said, and stood to go.

"My dad get home all right?" Dave asked him.

"Bart took him. You'll have the car tonight, I guess." He took some bills out and gave them to Dave. "Here, the round's on me, and there's a little something for you, Dave. You make a real fine waitress. Your legs are kind of skinny, though." Jeb said his good-byes and took off, leaving Henry alone at the table with the two Teddys. They turned politely around, but kept watching the game as though it was interesting, and didn't make a huge effort at conversation. Henry noted that Boychuk's cheeks were a little flushed and wondered how much he'd had to drink. Both of them had an unnatural shine to their eyes and dark circles underneath. Everyone was having his sleep problems.

Dave brought the beers and Henry was starting to think about going home after all when the door opened and a stranger walked in. Henry's blood pressure jumped about ten notches as he watched the guy walk across the floor and up to the bar, squeezing in between two fellas from Avis.

Could be anyone. But he had a feeling that was Gooner's sneaky-looking guy. The guy the Tindals saw. The cigarette butt guy.

Henry watched him, and swallowed another mouthful of beer. It went down in a lump. Sweat beaded up on his forehead, even though it was comparatively cool in the bar.

He watched while the guy ordered a beer off Clancy, looked up uninterested at the television mounted above the bar and then back down again. Clancy brought him his beer and the guy paid for it. Henry stared.

He matched the description, right down to the boots on his feet.

It could be anyone. Not even Henry knew everyone in Capawatsa County. He noticed a couple of other folks looking up at the man as if he was a stranger. Henry wasn't alone.

Absentmindedly, his hand went to his thigh and he felt around the pocket in the front of his pants. Inside was the Baggie that should have been in the evidence file at the office, but was still in his pocket. The Baggie with the butt from the road in front of Karen's.

The man at the bar reached into the back pocket of his jeans, and from Henry's point of view, blocked by a few heads and a couple of bodies, it looked like he took out a pouch of something. Henry got a peek as Cincinnati scored another hit and everyone leaned forward. With his elbows on the bar, the guy started rolling a smoke.

The two Teddys barely took their eyes off the game when Henry stood and said, "I'm gonna stretch my legs," and left the table.

Tom took a sip of his Budweiser and looked around the bar briefly, scanning the crowd more out of habit than expectation. He rolled his cigarette the way he walked; slowly and deliberately, enjoying the action as much as he would the smoke.

He felt very aware of the palm of his right hand where he had held the earth from Karen's backyard. It still felt warm.

He stuck the cigarette in his mouth and lit it with a match. Dragging, he opened his hand and looked at it, interested. The palm was callused; in the deep lines, there were traces of dirt. He rubbed it on his pant leg again.

The beer tasted good after the too-sweet wine. He was a beer man. The hard stuff was dark for him. It was something saved for when the nasties came crawling up his spine and he ceased to be able to keep the bad thoughts out of his head. Sometimes when he was walking and the dark feelings would come, he would buy a fifth and carry it around in his pack, drinking from it at intervals. He had almost ordered something stiff. But he didn't.

Out of habit, he checked out the bar patrons. If he had been passing through, he might have been able to make a few bucks in this place, although a lot of the people in the bar had the haunted look of people getting too close to the edge of something. You could almost draw a line between the people who were from Goodlands and the people who were from other towns. It was in the postures of the men sitting, in the bottles littered on the tables, on the faces of the men. The big drinkers, he would bet, were local. Funny that, about bad times.

Whatever the something was that was keeping Goodlands dry, he had a feeling it was in the earth itself. That was why he could feel the faint vibration under the ground. It was muffled and distant, and that was why no one had noticed it. Tom had made a life out of noticing.

"Hello there," a voice said just behind him, startling him, but not so anyone would notice. Tom turned his head and met a pair of bloodshot eyes.

Tom nodded in reply and shifted over, thinking the guy was trying to get to the bar. The man didn't move. He had a beer in his hand.

The man stuck out his hand to shake. "Henry Barker," he said, smiling.

Tom shook. " 'Lo."

"You a baseball fan?" Henry asked, gesturing toward the set above the bar, with his beer.

"Not much." He turned back toward the bar, tapped the ash off his cigarette into the ashtray in front of him, and stayed facing the bar. Henry noted that the cigarette was rolled skinny, like a joint.

"Me, I like the Orioles. Not sure why. I guess a man just finds his team when he's a kid and sticks with it. You get guys that swear by the Yankees and won't let go." He chuckled. Tom didn't respond.

"I didn't catch your name," Henry said.

"I didn't give it."

"Seems only civil—"

Tom cut him off. "I guess it's a friendly town, but I'm not really looking for conversation, Mr. Barker."

Henry's eyes narrowed briefly. "I just happened to notice you were smoking a cigarette there, and I don't think you're from around here," he said. "We've got some dry weather, and people are being careful about their smoking."

"You've got no weather at all, if you don't mind my saying so, but point taken. 'Scuse me," he said dismissively.

"Friendly town, it is. And like they say, it's the finest bar within twenty miles." Henry chuckled again. "You just passing through?"

There was a long, silent pause. Tom turned his head very slowly toward the man. As he did, Henry felt something change in the air between them, as though a cool wind had come up from his feet. There was a smell in the air, a familiar smell. Something pleasant, in spite of the look on the man's face. Tom smiled hard, teeth bared.

"I'm having a beer, is what I'm doing," he said. "Do you have some business with me?" He spoke clearly, slowly, deliberately, his eyes turned directly on Henry. "Otherwise, I would like to drink my beer. Like I said, I'm not looking for conversation."

The cool breeze fell away and Henry felt hot. Beads of sweat formed on his forehead. His scalp under his cap felt sweaty and itchy.

"I'm the local sheriff," he said, finding it difficult to get out.

"Is this official business?"

"Mebbe," Henry said, his voice cracking. He had the urge to cough, his throat dry with the sudden warmth in his body. "I just like to know . . . who's around."

"I'm just passing through, then," Tom said, still smiling, not shifting his eyes from the man's. The smile was still hard. He turned with a small nod, back to face the bar.

Henry stood awkwardly behind him, hardly noticing that the man had turned away. The conversation seemed to be over. Henry's throat felt closed, it was so dry. He took a therapeutic swallow of his beer. It helped some. The scent he'd noticed earlier wafted up again from the floor. He couldn't place the smell. Something very familiar. It conjured up a picture of hot Saturday mornings when he was a boy, cutting the lawn. The voice of the perky girl from the Weather Channel. It was on the tip of his tongue. Then it disappeared. Henry drank again from the bottle.

"Enjoy your beer. Nice talking to you," he said, getting his voice back. He felt funny, slightly dazed. Mechanically, he walked back over to the table where the two Teddys were still sitting. Not quite losing that dry feeling for the rest of the night, drinking not his requisite four beers, but finally, five.

He watched the man from the table, waiting for the next step.

Karen lay awake in bed, not ready to sleep, the pleasant warmth of the wine still there, but beginning to fade, the way it would just before it turned into a headache. She wanted to fall into a deep, thoughtless sleep, but instead had a restless feeling that made her want to get up, maybe have a shower, watch some television, vacuum the house. *Or maybe run up and down Parson's Road in my nightgown until I've spent some of this energy that is running in me. Maybe run until the sweat pours down my body, washing away everything like a good, hard rain.*

She did no such thing. She lay awake and let her body hum, the conversation with the rainmaker going around and around in her mind, like a piece of video that kept rewinding.

Karen couldn't seem to get control of it all. Like that ride at the fair in the summer, where they strap you into a slot along the round wall, and the ride spins and spins and spins until the bottom drops out and there you are, groundless, while the world dances under your feet. You don't have the good sense to fall, centrifugal force holds you powerless to the side, and you cling anyway, probably because it is the only means of control you still have, to hang on. Karen had never gone on that ride or any other ride, actually. You had to be "this tall" to get on that ride, and how they got anyone more than four feet tall, and presumably then cognizant of the consequences, to get on that ride at all was beyond her. But they did. People lined up to get on, and came off with red faces, shining with excitement, still laughing, thrilled, sometimes lining up to go on again.

That was how she felt: as if the ground were dancing around under her feet while she stood perfectly still.

The drought and its remedy were beyond her. Someone at CFC (or worse, Larry himself) finding out about what she had done, was beyond her. Keeping her job with or without the drought was beyond her. The man sleeping on her property with his con artist smile and, somewhere, a big bag of tricks, was beyond her. For better or worse, she was on the ride and now she had to wait until the rainmaker pulled the switch to let her off. When that happened, she promised herself, everything would go back to the way it was. For better or worse.

He would go away and she would stay. It would rain and Goodlands would go back to the way *it* was. She would get back her position in the community, people would wave to her as they passed by, they would meet her eyes in the Dry Goods. People in town would begin to call her again and ask her to sit on their committees, to bake something for the sale, to donate an item for auction, to help out at the door at the annual firefighters' fund-raising dance. He would go away and she would stay and in a couple of years some stranger would move to town, maybe a vet, maybe a lawyer working in Weston, living in Goodlands—not a farmer, that would be too ironic for her, too many steps back in a life spent taking careful, long strides forward—and they would meet and have a friendship that would quietly move into courtship and they would marry and have children, settling in Goodlands and staying there, forever. That was what would happen. And the memory of this week in June, the fourth year of this legendary drought, would begin to seem like something that hadn't really happened, just a story that would come up at parties when the old and the young got together.

She would wait for that time, and the wait would make it worth it, because it would be earned. The truth of the matter was, if anyone, or anything was doing penance in Goodlands, it was her. Her sin was covetousness and she was paying for it.

* * *

It had started, of course, with the persistent grinding poverty of her childhood and youth. It had not ended when she got her first job, or when she'd built a small bank account while she was still in high school. It had not ended when she finished school and moved away into her own apartment. It had not ended with her parents' death; it had not ended when she filled her home with the fine, expensive things that had finally sent her to Goodlands. It had not ended until she got there. Then, finally, some of the hard-edged desire, the desperation, had slowly passed on, leaving her with something that approached contentment, that had grown with the peace and tranquillity of the little house nearly at the edge of town, where she could sit on her back porch and finally, finally look out into the world and not see something else out there that she wanted.

Even as a small child, she had wanted. She had gone to school with literally dozens of children like herself, children whose parents were scraping out a living on a farm, who were dressed in secondhand clothes washed too often, who had scruffy home-cut hair, rough lunches brought to school in brown paper bags used and reused every day until they fell apart. They were all pretty much the same, and yet the girl that Karen had wanted to be was Becky. She couldn't, even now as she tried, remember the girl's last name or anything else about her, outside of the fact that she had things that Karen had wanted.

The Sears catalog that year had featured a kilt skirt, red-and-navy plaid, woven, with a delicate, soft fringe and an open flap on the side. The flap was secured with a long silver pin, an over-size safety pin. Becky had a kilt. She wore it to school and all the girls loved it, made a fuss. But none of them loved it the way Karen did. She *wanted* it. That night she'd begged her mother to buy her one. Her mother had looked at it in the catalog.

"That skirt is twenty-seven dollars!" she'd said, and the case was closed. So the next time Becky wore the skirt to school, Karen waited until they all changed for gym class and stole, not the skirt, that would have been impossible, but the shiny silver pin. She kept it for years, right up until high school, never wearing it, or letting anyone else see it, hidden in her box of secret things that she kept in the back of the closet in her room under her good shoes. The shoes changed annually (sometimes more often, as in high school, when she began to grow and grow until her parents were given to remarking that she was never going to stop and her food and clothes bill was going to send them to the poorhouse, as if they weren't already halfway there on their own); but the box they sat on top of never changed and had, years later, been used to house other contraband such as cigarettes and a can of beer that had sat in the hot corner of the closet so long it went skunky.

She kept the pin, the theft of which had nearly broken Becky's heart, even though she had it replaced within a week. The child had thought she lost it. Karen, of course, had never said a thing, and had shamelessly commiserated with her after gym class that day.

The pin had never been used to jauntily hold down the flap of a kilt skirt, had never been used to decorate a blouse, and that wasn't the point at all. It had been used to *have*. She would take it out of the box sometimes and just hold it, opening and closing the clasp, listening to the crisp efficiency of it, poking the sharp end on the ball of her finger, sometimes running it through a piece of cloth to admire the way it would sparkle in the light from the bare bulb in her room.

As an adult, when Karen thought of the pin, a feeling of recklessness and shame filled her. But she could also remember the feeling that owning it had brought her. A tightness in her scalp, the dry mouth, the heart-pounding, and the warmth in the pit of her stomach when it was finally hers. It was all still familiar from her dark days. It was the Becky pin on a much larger, more expensive scale, but it was the same feeling.

She had thought she'd escaped it when she left home and went to work and live on her own. She had achieved what her parents had not: independence from living bill to bill, regular money coming in. Karen could count on food and clothes; however modest, they were things she could afford. The mistake had been in getting ahead of the basic necessities into the larger arena of wants. The buildup of all those years of desperate wanting had culminated in the financial mess she'd made of her life, the mess that had led her to Goodlands. Then finally she was there, at what seemed at first to be the end of the line, where shame and despair and desperation were not about what she didn't have, but about what she had done.

The rainmaker was wrong if he thought she didn't have a stake in all of this.

What had finally cured her was building the gazebo. When George had dug up that poor woman, buried under there all those years, the building had all but completely lost its charm. She had been cured. Building the gazebo, spending the money, had been, in a way, a test. One last spree to see if the need was still there. It hadn't been, not really. Her palms had dampened the check when she wrote it; her heart had pounded with pleasure. But it had all turned up empty when the gazebo was built. That time, there was little pleasure in owning, even though the gazebo itself was a small step into fantasies of a different kind. The romantic fantasies of someone swirling her around the concrete floor, the click of their shoes in rhythm with music drifting in from the stereo in the house. The gazebo had made no dreams come true. The gazebo itself was just an empty building in her backyard, weatherworn now, in need of a paint job, and tainted by another woman's misfortune.

It wasn't as though Karen thought that building the gazebo was going to magically bring her the rest of the quota that was needed to complete her life. If it fulfilled anything in her life at all, it was by ending once and for all that need to have, the have-to-haves. In a way, it had brought her the one thing that she had really wanted; it had brought her to contentment.

She had been content. There had been that peace in her days that all the things she'd bought hadn't brought her. The contentment had just begun creeping over her, lulling her. Goodlands had given her a position in the community, friendly neighbors, a good job, an opportunity to leave the past behind her and start over. Then came the drought. And the slow erosion of it all.

She was doing penance. And the restlessness was beginning again. The wants. The have-to-haves. This time, however, she coveted something else.

Karen coveted the rainmaker.

The place he'd held her on her arm was as obvious to her as if he'd burned his handprint there. Had she stayed in the clearing, by the fire, by the man, she might have completely lost whatever control she had finally gained over herself and the world around her. Such a transaction would be the most expensive one she could ever have made, and it would be for one of those things she bought and paid for that ended up empty and unfulfilling. And she would have to pay dearly.

That was not the way it was going to work. Her plan was to wait until a nice vet or lawyer with soft hands and good manners moved to Goodlands and decided to stay. Their nice friendship would grow quietly into courtship and then they would get married and have children. That was the plan.

The plan was not to lose everything to a drifter who strode into town with a lick and a promise, who also, she suspected, had something hard inside him that showed through his phony con man smile—a mean streak.

It was all being disturbed, first by the drought, and then by the man she saw on TV, standing hatless in the rain, wiping the hair from his eyes, water running in rivulets down his arms, smiling into the camera his pure delight. She could not give up her control, the way it was supposed to be, to that man. It would be giving up everything. She was waiting for the right time, the right man. She had a lot to give, a lot to give up.

There was no rainmaker in the plan. Even if she only slept with him—a laughable prospect at the best of times, given her lack of experience with men. She had never been one of those girls who slept with their dates on the fourth dinner out, or third movie, or whatever the rules were now. She had been careful with her choices, and felt comfortable with them. In her mind, filled with figures and equations, rows of numbers that added up to something, she had her own set of rules. Boy number one had been her true love in high school. Boy number two was only slightly removed from manhood, and probably her only regret. Boy number three was a real, grown-up man. She met him at the bank, slept with him after two months of dating—the last month serious enough to convince her—and had continued a year-long relationship that ended when he wanted to move in with her. He joked too much, took life too lightly, had none of the desperate seriousness that Karen had. It would have been a bad match.

Not as bad perhaps, as the rainmaker. Of course, boy number three had never made her feel as though the bottom was dropping out of the ride. In spite of everything she tried, the last bit of control was slipping through her fingers, and the earth was dancing underneath her feet. Karen coveted the rainmaker. An expensive proposition.

NINE

VIDA REMAINED RESOLUTE AND VIGILANT AT HER POST INSIDE the falling-down old flower shop–honey house, except for when she fell asleep. Her body, as much as it was a vessel for the voice, was still a body. Tired and battered from a day of crawling through fences, barns, yards, and after walking long distances— across the entire town—it had slackened the way a clock will when it hasn't been wound. Without food or water her body was finally calling it quits.

When Vida had first arrived in the little building kitty-corner and down the way from Karen Grange's place, she had stood at the window, watching for the man. As time went by, she changed her position to squatting, her chin perched on a spot on the sill that she swept clear of broken glass. She'd cut her hand in the process and had not bothered to do much more than wipe it distractedly on her dirty dress. It was a small cut, but it had begun to throb. It wasn't long after that, that her chin had slipped from the sill and she hunkered down on sore feet under the window and slid in and out of sleep, in spite of the discomfort of her position. Even when her body sagged against the rough board wall, she didn't wake. By the time Karen Grange and the rainmaker were arguing about penance, Vida had fallen into a deep sleep.

It was many hours later when the ground underneath her began a persistent vibration that ran up inside the very core of her. The voice inside her shrieked her awake, a sharp, piercing shriek that could be heard nowhere except inside herself. Vida's hand flew to her ears, accomplishing nothing. Disoriented, she felt her sneakered feet slide outward, slipping on pieces of glass, and she fell on her butt. Her ankles screamed in pain, her feet, as deeply asleep as she had been, filled with pins and needles when they moved. She groaned.

Quiet, quiet, she said to herself.

She stood stiffly, obediently, but no more. The adventure and fun had long gone. The voice was persistent, no longer a partner of sorts, but beyond that; jailer, master. Vida was sometimes afraid. She could feel herself slipping in and out of control, her body not hers entirely; a vessel.

Hidden in the shadows of the building, she looked out without being seen. Her eyes adjusted to the dark, with only meager light coming from the streetlamp.

The moon by then was up high and one day from full, for all intents and purposes as full and bright as it would get.

Fully awake, her body tensed. Her belly rolled around empty and tightened with anticipation. The hair on her arms stood at attention. He was coming. She couldn't yet see him, but distantly, echoed on the long, broad, empty road, were his footsteps, regular and slow. She could *feel* him, his peculiar energy as much a part of the air she breathed in as the odor of decayed and dead things outside the building. She breathed through her mouth. Waited.

What will I do? she spoke inside herself. There was, oddly, silence inside her.

"What will I do to him?" she said out loud.

Make him go away, the voice said from inside. Vida frowned. The thought came not in words, but in meaning. Go away, how? Her eyes darted down the lane. The man had not yet come into view. In the silence, she could hear his boots.

"How?" she whispered. Another odd silence.

Vida could feel her lips being tugged in an involuntary smile; she was not making the smile and it felt strange and horrible on her mouth as she heard inside her:

Kill him.

Vida shook her head from side to side. Her mouth was still held fast in the smile that belonged to the voice, and would not let her speak. *No,* she thought over and over, while the voice held her silent.

I can't, she insistedly thought, trying to force the voice away. *No.* She tried to make it a loud-think. Tried to shake her head again, and found her neck stiff and tight. She panicked. She struggled against her own body. She tried to pry her hands off the sill of the window and found them held fast. Her lips would not part. Her feet were rooted. She fought, her muscles rippling impotently, until from deep in her chest, a pain, sharp and burning, like a knife, bored through her. Inside, she screamed. Outside her body, the silence remained, except for the sound of her own breathing, hot and shallow.

The voice kept silent until she stopped fighting. Vida sank deep inside herself, and stayed there while the body stayed upright and alert, the eyes lit with an energy not entirely natural.

The man stepped into the pool of light cast by the streetlamp.

The rainmaker walked through the light. Tiny balls of dust puffed up under his boots and fell back to earth, his steps having a rhythm to them. Vida's eyes watched him, but it was the woman inside her, the source of the Voice that Vida heard, who saw him. The eyes were narrowed.

Vida stood in the void between action and motion while the man's soft steps faded and the sound curved with him into a driveway up the road from where Vida watched. She leaned her head out the window for a better look in time to see him disappear into the backyard hidden by the house.

Indecision left her still leaning out the window. From down the road where the man had come came another set of footsteps, these louder and less practiced. Her head swung in that direction and when she recognized the interloper, she drew back into the shadows again.

Henry had waited until the fellow from up at the bar got to the door before saying his goodnights.

"I'm outta here," he said to the Teds. The game was in the ninth, a done deal. Cincinnati had kicked ass. The mood in the bar was in contrast to Henry's, the patrons buying each other beers, yukking it up; few collected bets, there not being a Canadian in the place, or at least none who would own up.

"Helluva game!" Boychuk said. "Lemme buy you a beer, Henry."

Henry shook his head. "Nah, I gotta get home. Got enough beer in me now that I'm gonna have to stop every other mile to piss in the ditch." Henry's bladder was legendary. Boychuk and Lawrence laughed.

"Well, stop by my place and piss on the fields, will ya?" Lawrence chuckled. He raised an arm and screamed Dave Watson over. "Another round—'cept for Henry!" The last part was slurred, spoken through a couple too many beers that night, and would probably be missed by young Watson. Henry figured one of them would be drinking his beer.

"Last one, Boychuk," Henry said sternly. Drinking and driving was not unknown in the area, and a couple of years back some guy drove into a tree just outside of town, but there were few accidents anyway. Lawrence might have blown over, but he figured Boychuk was still okay.

"That official, Henry?" It was the second time Henry had been tagged as an official that night. He was tired. Tired of the whole damn day.

"That's official." He sighed. He picked up his off-duty baseball cap off the floor, where it had fallen, and pushed it down
low on his head to give himself a menacing look. He had a big
head, and even on the last notch the cap was snug where he had
settled it. Out of habit, he pushed it back up again, virtually
erasing any menace that might have been there—not much, he
suspected—and replacing it with the harmless look of a round-
faced, round-eyed, slightly overweight farm boy who'd maybe
been kicked in the head a time or two. Didn't matter, people who
knew him, knew him. Anyone else was generally thrown off
guard by what his wife liked to call his "boyish good looks."

Henry left.

He looked up the road to spot the man, hoping he hadn't gotten into a truck and driven off. He had a feeling, though, that the
man was on foot. If the man was who Henry thought he was, then
he was heading northwest on Parson's, just up the road a piece to
where the old Mann place was, where Karen now lived. Henry
walked that way with the assurance of a man with a hunch.

Henry hadn't been "law" very long, but one thing he'd found
since he had been more or less in charge of the legalities of the
good citizens of Capawatsa, he had an instinct for things, just like
the cops on the television shows. He read true crime books as if
they were manuals, studying them as much as reading them for
the gruesome details. It was the discovery of things that he loved,
the methodical, systematic figuring out that came from studying
the facts from back to front. In the crime stories, they always
caught the killer. While he knew in real life that wasn't always the
case, he also knew that if you looked at the facts, things happened only one way. You worked backward from what you had,
and then you found your answer. Henry could do that. He could
figure things out—from where the unaccounted-for hundred and
fifty bucks went from the anonymous "withdrawal" in the joint
bank book, to a tiny footprint in wet dirt, to a hand-rolled ciggy-
butt left on a nonsmoking banker's road. Right now he had an

eyewitness description of a fella seen going *on foot* past a fire, and a whole slew of strange happenings since he was first spotted, and a hot-damn, real-life clue in the form of a hand-rolled, mostly smoked cigarette. The fella in the bar tied them both together, and damn, if the two didn't fit together like a glove, then Henry'd be a monkey's uncle and no better. But things were looking just as he thought.

It was only a moment before he spotted the guy, way up ahead on Parson's. Henry followed him, staying a careful hundred and fifty feet behind him, easily keeping him in sight—one of the few benefits of a long stretch of prairie road.

They walked that way for five minutes, the man never once turning around. At first Henry was confident that he didn't know he was being followed. The lighted parking lot at Clancy's was fast disappearing behind them. The streetlamp outside Clancy's was also left behind. Then they walked in the darkness of the night, the only light coming from the moon. The road glowed. There were no painted lines to walk by, just the vague outline of the shoulder that slid off into a dark ditch. Henry began to think that the man in front knew exactly who was behind him and what he was doing there, and at any moment would turn around and maybe . . . *do something.*

As odd and out of place as that thought was, it had the power to stop Henry in his tracks. The thought was so strong that Henry had an urge to squat down and make himself as small a target as possible, maybe slip down into the ditch and watch the man from there, his head the only thing poking up aboveground. He had no fix on what exactly it was the man would *do,* just that hard knot in the pit of his stomach that told him, whatever it was, the man could do it. His mind wrapped itself around possibilities, and he began to feel foolish. When the man was an additional hundred feet ahead of him, and Henry himself had become, by virtue of perspective, a much, much smaller target, he began following again.

The man in front never did turn around.

When the drifter entered into the light thrown by the street-lamp up ahead, Henry paused again. They were nearly at the Mann farm; the drifter had only to walk forty or fifty feet to the end of the driveway. Henry stood and watched, feeling safer for the distance between them.

About midway into the puddled light from the lamp, something fluttered out from the man. It literally *fluttered* through the air, the way an autumn leaf will tumble and fall. In spite of the stillness of the hot June night, something danced away from the man and drifted slowly to the road, landing in the circle of light. From where Henry stood, it looked like a piece of paper.

His heart pounded. He stayed put. He waited.

The man approached the driveway of Karen Grange's place, and as Henry knew—just *knew*—he would, he turned at the edge of the gravel driveway and walked up, never changing the cadence of his step or pausing to look back.

When the man disappeared behind the house, Henry waited a few minutes to see if he would come back out. When he didn't, Henry walked on legs that felt rubbery with excitement and trep-idation to a spot just outside the circle of light. He fixed his eyes on the object, trying to decide if it was some kind of trick, some kind of trap, something booby-trapped, like the dollar bill on a string that is yanked away, once you reach down for it, making you look like ten kinds of fool.

Except, he didn't think that it would just be a dollar on a string; he didn't believe that if he reached for it, it would simply be yanked away. He had the feeling that if he reached for it, something else would happen. What, he didn't know, but he thought it would be *awful*.

It was a small rectangle of fine paper. From where he stood, it looked about the size and shape of a business card. Nervously, very aware of how naked he would be, how vulnerable when he stepped into the light, he glanced several times toward the place at the side of Grange's house where the drifter had disappeared. The space remained empty, quiet and in shadow.

Henry stepped into the light and picked up the piece of paper. It was indeed a business card, soft with age, the corners curled some, as if it had been in someone's wallet for a long time. It read:

THOMPSON J. KEATLEY

RAINMAKER

Under the bold black letters, in smaller print, still in black, there was a slogan:

RAIN WITHOUT PAIN

Henry frowned, turned the card over. The back was blank. There was no handwriting on the card, nothing distinguishing at all, except for a smudge of dirt on the bottom right-hand corner.

Nothing distinguishing at all, except the card was warm. And damp. He raised the card to his nose. Holding it there, he closed his eyes and sniffed deeply. The image from earlier of hot Saturday mornings came off the card in waves. This time he recognized it.

Fresh-cut grass . . . new-mown hay . . . the heady smell of rich, wet earth.

Henry stood in the light and puzzled over the card for a long time, feeling as though someone had just made him look like ten kinds of fool.

If Carl Simpson was unaware that someone else had been sitting up on the night watch, as Vida was, he had something in common with her nonetheless. He was bleary-eyed with a need for sleep.

He had been gone from his house all day, and for most of the night so far. He had no idea if his wife knew of his whereabouts. It wasn't that he didn't care. Even through the fog that had become his mind over the last few months, Carl cared deeply about his family. They were, in a way, why he was doing what he was doing. What he was doing, was watching.

Carl had spent the day and night driving fruitlessly all over the back fields of Goodlands doing surveillance. If he didn't have anything more than a vague idea of what he was looking for, he had a firm grasp of what he was surveying. He was watching over the silos. He had an idea that the silos were the answer.

The Goodlands landscape was virtually covered in silos, as was much of North Dakota. As an area, Goodlands had more silos than any other town in the Great Plains region, and that was what made it so sinister. They just picked Goodlands, Carl supposed. Drew a name from a hat, eeny-meenie-miney-mo'ed, tossed darts at a map held up on a wall with tiny red pins that had, in another time, been used to pinpoint the very silos that they were using now for their experiments. Carl figured that Goodlands had simply been picked at random and the meanness of it all was overwhelming to him.

He didn't know how they were doing it, but thought maybe somebody had sneaked into Goodlands under cover of night four or five years before and opened a small vial filled with a chemical produced, not in the Great North Country, Home of the Salt of the Earth, but out East someplace, or in Texas, or California, or another of the big states Carl and hundreds like him held in vague suspicion. And whatever was in the vial had been sent into the skies and had dried them up. Just over Goodlands. And Carl figured that down in one of those silos, even as he watched, there was a government man or two, pushing buttons on computers and measuring things like how long it took the sky to dry up, how dry the land got, how much seepage there was from the regular, steady, predicted and delivered rain that fell on all the towns around them. He wondered if they were measuring the other things that a drought brought. Measuring how long it took a farm worked for a lifetime to drop off and die, how long it took a man to stop sleeping with his wife because of the things on his mind, how long it took families, stores, schools, businesses to finally shut down and call it a day. He wondered if they measured that with their computers.

They were down there somewhere, and they would have to come up sometime. When they did, Carl would see them. Then there would be something real to punch into their computers. The world would know.

He had felt, if not good, then *active,* for the first time in weeks, doing what he was doing: driving around Goodlands, instead of just sitting around and watching it all happen to him, to his family, to his friends. It wasn't just that, either. Driving around Goodlands had brought back memories that Carl hadn't had in years.

Like the time he and a couple of buddies from school took their girlfriends down to the quarry outside of Ed Kramer's, where the big fire was earlier this week, and attempted the oldest trick in the book. "Liquor is quicker," they'd joked that night on their way over to pick up the girls, laughing with a wonderful combination of anticipation and terror. "Liquor is quicker"— they must have said it a million times. To ply them with liquor until they gave in. None of them did. Carl's girlfriend, Sharon Gilespie from over in Telander, hadn't had more than one drink. She tried it and promptly spit it out. "That tastes *awful!*" She drank unspiked Coke for the rest of the night and didn't let Carl do much more than feel her breast through her clothes. Draker's girlfriend had been less offended by the taste, but after punching back about four drinks, threw up the rest of the night and they had to sneak her into her bedroom through the window with her sister's help—and her sister blackmailed her for a month.

Carl smiled with the memory of it.

When he finally did get a little, it was with his wife, Janet. Before they were married, of course, because by then it was the sixties, and everybody was doing it, even nice girls from Goodlands.

Carl had grown up with Janet, had gone to grade school with her, knew her about as well as any little boy knows any little girl, and had never given her a second look. It was like that in a small town, where you were side by side with someone so often, they were more invisible than family; they were just always there, more a part of the scenery, like the grain elevators and railroad tracks—and silos. He and his buddies couldn't wait to go to the high school in Telander and see some real girls. They spent freshmen year dating all the girls who were as fresh and new to them as the clothes picked up in Weston for the first day of school. Funny how most of them ended up with hometown girls, anyway. Carl with Janet, Draker with Peggy, Andy with Marg Bell, whose brother was the doctor.

He and Janet did it twice, not in the same night, but the second time a few nights later. And even though Janet said it was "nice," she didn't let him do it again until three weeks before they were married, and he'd worn her down. She said she didn't want him to "get used to it." At the time he thought she was right out of her tree, how could anyone get used to such a glorious, divine, inspiring experience? How could he ever want to stop? She said that if they waited, it would make their wedding night that much more exciting, for both of them, and she had been right. By the time they got through the ceremony, he was ready to scoop her up and drive right over to the little hotel in Weston where they were going to stay until the next morning, when they would be driving to Bemidji, Minnesota, for their honeymoon. Instead there had been the reception, the dinner, the speeches, and the dancing to get through. He'd done just fine, hadn't even gotten too drunk, although Janet had three champagne orange juices and was a little high, that adding to the excitement, loosening her up some, giving the whole thing a more illicit air than it had had in the back of the truck with the broad, open sky above them.

He didn't "get used to it." The first year of their marriage was spent almost entirely in the bedroom. Once, when her parents dropped over unexpectedly, they had to scramble to get dressed and rush out of the bedroom. His in-laws had walked right in and the next few minutes were embarrassing and terrible. Her parents never, ever came over without calling again. He and Janet had laughed like hell afterwards, and had gone right back to what they had been doing when interrupted.

The only dark point to their early married years had been Janet's inability to get pregnant. By the time the first year was up, with everyone constantly asking when they were going to start a family, Janet had begun to worry. Carl would tell her that sometimes those things took time. She would look up at him with her brown eyes narrowed as though she didn't believe him. He would convince her. He would point out how young they were and say maybe God was waiting for them to grow up a little before giving them a baby to take care of. And they waited.

It took ten years and three miscarriages to make Butch, and you would have thought the heavens had opened up and God himself had brought Butch down to them. By that time the farm was running in the black every year, and they had survived the little tragedies of marriage, like going out with the boys too often, and spending too much on stuff for the house, and Janet wanting to adopt and Carl saying let's wait and see what happens, and of course the terrible days each time a baby fell out Janet's womb unformed. They had gone through boredom with each other, and for Janet, the boredom of being a farmer's wife and doing all the things expected of a farmer's wife. The hard bend-over work, the animals, the gardens, the canning, the field work. She had known what it would be when she married him, and in truth she loved it as much as he did, but she went through her paces, and put him through his. One year she went to live with her sister in Minneapolis and worked at a grocery. She lasted four months before realizing that that wasn't what she wanted. She came back to him with a new attitude, a contentment that was to last forever. She made her choice.

They'd been through everything that a marriage goes through and had come out shining. They had it licked, they'd been tried by fire (so they thought) and had survived. Then the drought came. And now things between Janet and Carl were getting tense again. More than tense, he knew, but he didn't give it much thought. Sometimes, just as he told her, a man's gotta do what a man's gotta do.

He should have sold off some of the land the first year it was bad. But he hadn't. He thought, along with everyone else, that it had been a freak year, and that the next year things would be better. They were still in the black, thanks to the hogs; there had been milkers, too, but the big dairy had killed that enterprise, although they usually kept a couple of cows around and bred for their own milk and meat.

She didn't believe him when he told her what was going on. Not even when he told her that that was exactly what the government was counting on, that the public won't believe it, that the public will sit with their heads in the dust until the whole world comes crashing down and all they'll have to eat after that is dust. He'd shouted that last part and Janet clammed up. Before they fell asleep, they'd each listened to the other breathing, lying with their backs to one another, far apart in their bed.

She had no argument to offer other than that she was worried about him, and maybe he should find someone to talk to. That was when he'd gone and talked to Henry Barker, who'd listened well enough. But Carl was no fool, he'd gone all through high school and then some, and he knew when he was being patronized. Privately, he thought Henry Barker could go to hell with his head buried in the dust. *He* didn't understand, either.

It was all being destroyed while they sat around and waited for rain that was not going to come. It was too late to sell and be gone, and unless you had someplace to go, you were stuck with what you had. What Carl had was being taken away from him— would be taken very soon, maybe not this month, but he was expecting the call from Karen Grange at the bank maybe next month, or God willing, the month after—and by that time he wanted to know. He wanted to prove to them all that it was being done to them by people, not by God. By their own duly elected people. That this was a Three Mile Island, a Love Canal, in reverse. Instead of something flying out into the air, something was being sucked away. He would prove it. He would wave papers, or pictures, or whatever it took, in the bank's face and then see what they would do.

A man could not sit around and let his family eat food bought in another town with secret food stamps. That was not a man. A man took action.

Janet didn't understand that this wasn't about Minneapolis, or food stamps, or waiting ten fucking years to have a baby. This was about being a man. Taking care of his family. By God, he was doing it.

Carl pulled his pickup into a dry, dead field and shut off the engine. He reached beside him and pulled out his binoculars. It was time to take another look.

He was parked on the far side of town, in a field that at one time was all Johannason land. The son had married a Telander girl and moved out there to farm, later going on into government and becoming a state senator. They renamed the school after him when he died, calling it Telander-Johannason High School. The land had been sold and the family moved off long before that. Now it was broken up and owned by a variety of folks, some who stayed and some who'd gone off when things got bad.

He sat on the back of the pickup, on the door, and watched, swiveling around to check each silo in turn. He wondered if there were bathrooms in the silos, and decided there must be, or he'd have seen someone coming out to take a piss by then.

From his vantage point behind the north fence at the end of what was now the Mann property, Carl Simpson shifted on his butt. He rubbed his eyes at intervals, blinking them to get some moisture back into them, knowing they were red and sore from the dust thrown up into his face through the open window and the endless, endless looking.

Then he spotted something.

Through his binoculars he watched some fellow he didn't recognize—a bad-looking character if he ever saw one, suspicious,
kind of a commie-looking guy, longhaired and up to no good
was how he looked to Carl—walk up Parson's Road. He saw
something fall off the man, not so much seeing what it was as
seeing the shift between light and shadow as the thing fell, and
he decided then and there that he would have to check out what
exactly would fall out of the pocket of a commie longhair bad
character. When the man moved out of his sight line, beyond the
Mann house, Carl assumed that he'd continued on down the
road. Carl intended to check him out. He would wait a couple of
minutes and then gun up the truck and head out that way, expecting, since the man was on foot, to catch him at the junction
of Parson's and Concession 5. Concession 5 being a little-known
route that Carl himself felt he had discovered, though in reality it
was just an old field road not much used anymore, since the two
farms it ran between were no longer in operation. Not that many
farms at all were in operation anymore.

Then something very, *very* interesting happened.

He was just about to put aside the glasses when none other
than Mr. Sheriff Henry Barker stepped into his line of sight and
picked up what the man had dropped. Better yet, he picked it up
and *read* it.

Henry Barker, local law enforcement.

Henry Barker, the man who was in a position to know everything that was going on in any given community. A man with
contacts in government, however minor. The man who pretended not to believe Carl when he told him about the silos.

Carl waited until Henry turned and walked off in the other direction before carefully returning the binocs to their case. Then he
started up the truck hoping to hell no one could hear him, knowing that no one could, and ultimately, that no one would give a
shit if they did. That was how people like Henry Barker operated.
No one gave a shit what was going on. Except for Carl. Carl knew
what was going on and Carl cared. He cared a lot.

He drove with his lights out down Concession 5 until he saw Parson's Road, never going above ten miles an hour. He wanted to give Henry time to get back to his car. He didn't want Henry to see the truck and be alerted. He wanted to find that other guy first. Then he'd see what Henry had to say. Maybe tonight. Maybe tomorrow. First, he would see.

Carl headed for Parson's Road.

For all his casualness as he walked the road leading to Karen's house, Tom knew that he was being watched. He could feel the eyes on his body as fiercely as the eyes were focused. There were at least two people watching his progress, and he thought there might be a third, one who was hidden in shadow, both figuratively and literally. The image was ungraspable, beyond the ordinary and beyond his perceiving. The man behind him was the cop from the bar; he could see him as well as if he had turned around and looked at him. There was an almost comic nervousness about the man, and Tom hadn't been able to resist playing with him a little.

The other one, also a man, was deeply troubled. His image was shrouded in a black cloud of distress. He was wrapped in confusion and fear, miserable, looking for something that wasn't there. He'd seen Tom. There was no help for that. Tom couldn't control the universe, usually not even his corner of it. He didn't think either man would be trouble, no more than he could smoothly handle. Besides, it would all be over soon.

The third, the one that Tom couldn't quite see, was in shadow. Standing in the dark edges of his mind and not allowing itself to be seen. Whatever or whoever it was, was shut out to him.

He was halfway to the clearing when he stopped. He stood in the half dark of Karen's backyard.

Some kind of circle was closing. His spirits were low. He had hoped the couple of beers would help. He had hoped the dinner in the clearing would help, but neither had done much more than pass time. Something dire had followed him all day—

maybe the whole time he was in Goodlands—and it was as though it had finally caught up with him. He was overwhelmed by a feeling of impending doom. The circle was closing.

There was the trio of watchers. In itself, that probably didn't mean much. It could be nothing more than curious hometown folk, with little enough to do and too much time on their hands given the circumstances of their lives. The troubled fellow was probably out for a drive, working through those very troubles, and just happened to see him. Nothing. The other guy, the cop, was doing his job. In a small town, every stranger is suspect, even if they live in town. Goodlands had its share of problems, and the cop was just making sure Tom wasn't adding to them. The third watcher, phantom that it was, he couldn't say.

In themselves, they couldn't account for Tom's feeling that something bad was about to happen, and that he was powerless in the face of it all. He should have felt good, high even, the way he always did before he made it rain. It should have been just him and the rain, and the magnetic connection that made him who he was. The anticipation of opening the skies and letting the torrent loose, setting free the animal held captive in the sky for so long, should have elated him. He should have felt damn good, knowing that by tomorrow Goodlands would be once more under open skies, the barrier fallen, the lock struck open. But he didn't.

Winslow, Kansas, had had a good rain. The little town had been waiting, ready for the rain to fall. Tom couldn't explain nature's ways, but as often as not, he simply acted as a catalyst, a locksmith, a navigator locating the problem and pointing it out. Redirecting. They had a good rain.

It wasn't always that way.

He had told Karen about the Schwitzers. They were a case in point. There had been others.

About ten years earlier there had been a little town, whose name he couldn't recall, but south of the Dakotas, in the Midwest.

Walking along a highway, sometimes hitching, he had become increasingly aware of the dry skies. And he would be in a place, maybe having some food, and it would come in him in a flood of bad feelings. It had been unexplainable at the time, and he was beginning to think he had something wrong with his gray matter, the washes of feelings he got were so contradictory: hot dry, cold wet. It kept on like that as he walked, all of it coming from the direction in which he was headed. He was walking east then. As soon as he hit town, he knew he'd found the place he'd been feeling.

A little place, bigger than Goodlands but more isolated, the nearest "next" place a good hour away by car. He walked a lonely stretch for a long time before hitting town, but as soon as he crossed that line, he knew.

He'd come up under cover of night, looking up the road and following a set of lights that turned out to be an all-night diner. He thought he must have been coming up on a city, given the all-nighter, and had gone in for a cup of coffee, glad to have a place to sit down that the bugs didn't know about, and a cup of something hot to go with it, and interested to know what the place was about with its hotdry/coldwet.

It was dry enough, all right, and he could feel that well enough. But a place in the Midwest can throw off a dry feeling without actually being in any kind of trouble. Storms there come up overnight and overwhelm a place, when there'd been no sign of rain for days, even weeks. Tom's own radar got confused in the middle of the country because of this, and sometimes he couldn't trust his feelings. He had to rely on what people told him. If they wanted him, somehow, wherever he was, they could sort him out from the crowd. They wouldn't even know they were doing it.

The parking lot had no more than three cars in it. From the time he'd spent walking since he'd last seen a clock, Tom judged it to be about one A.M. Just past the witching hour, as his mother used to say. Still, the place was brightly lit up, like a carnival, every light on, and he could see through the windows that it was business as usual. A woman at the counter was cleaning things up and a fat guy in cook's whites was gabbing with an old man at the counter.

Tom sat down at the counter, and when the woman came over, he ordered a cup of coffee.

"Didn't see you pull in," she apologized, dropping a mug of coffee, with the spoon already in it, in front of him.

"Walked in," he told her.

"From *where*?"

"Been walking a time, I guess," he said. The woman nodded politely and asked nothing more. She went back to what she had been doing, keeping her back to him. In fact, the whole place went on as it had been, without the eyes on him that he was used to having, being a stranger wherever he went.

The guy in cook's whites kept talking to the old man. He had done nothing more than glance up briefly when Tom opened the door. He hadn't even nodded. The old guy hadn't looked at all. Another guy, in the back, kept his eyes on the table, and Tom never saw if he looked up or not. If he had, his curiosity had been satisfied, because he didn't look up again.

As he drank his coffee, the waves of what he'd felt earlier had come over him again. Hotdry/coldwet. It came off the people, off the land, and if he wasn't mistaken, it was coming off the diner, even, this feeling of contradictions.

When the waitress came over and offered him a refill, Tom said, "You been dry here?"

"Some," she said. "No rain for a month or more. Not that unusual for us, I guess. You a farmer?"

"No."

She poured him another cup. Tom watched her. Her face was blank. There was no emotion in her look, in her eyes. She smiled at him, and the smile seemed mechanical, the sides of her mouth pulled up by imaginary strings.

He drank only half a cup more, and paid for it at his stool. He couldn't wait to get out of there. Passing through, Tom brought some rain to them. It had been easy, had come as easy as if it was on its way, even though he didn't think it had been.

Just about twenty minutes on foot outside the diner, a car picked him up, some salesman on his way to the next place, gave Tom a ride that lasted all night. Tom got off in a place called Bellston and waved good-bye.

He remembered Bellston, because by that time he was ready for some food and had stopped at the first place he found. This diner was so different from the one the night before, he felt rewarded by the suspicious stares and meaningful-polite questions from the waitress, an older woman who had once been very pretty and was not letting go of that with grace, dyeing her hair an odd yellow color to cover what was obviously all-the-way gray.

The radio was playing, and could just vaguely be heard over the conversation and the clanking of dishes. It was breakfast rush and the restaurant was full. Then, very suddenly, another waitress screamed for quiet and cranked the radio.

The news was on. There was a tornado watch.

A tornado had touched down in—Wellesby? Wellbee?—and killed a dozen people.

"Harsh rains and tornado are predicted for the rest of today, and all towns in the area are currently under tornado watch for the rest of today and tonight. The weather bureau predicts—" Tom didn't catch the rest because the diner began clearing out. Chaos ensued.

He knew without checking that the strange diner of the night before had been hit by the tornado, and he would have bet the farm that the folks inside it were among the dozens killed. It had been in their eyes. That's what it had been, the blank faces, the lack of emotion. They wouldn't even have known it, but they were already dead.

Tom walked out of the town unscathed, and as far as he knew, no tornado had hit Bellston. They did get some rain. It was hard rain, but nothing serious. Nothing deadly.

Except, Tom knew it was his rain. There is no way to define

how he knew, there was no difference in the drops, no signature way the rain fell, he simply *knew*. What he also knew was that whatever it was that happened in the town near Bellston was none of his affair. That was between them and their town. Tom was only a catalyst.

But sometimes there is a price attached to the rain, and Tom could no more predict that price than those people in the diner could know they were dead that night he walked in.

Nature makes its choices. There was the feeling he got in waves from the town before he was anywhere near it. Tom was no psychic. If he got impressions of a place, it had nothing to do with the future; he couldn't predict what was going to happen in a given place. He felt only what was already there, and even that was not something to be relied on. So whatever he felt was already there, existing among them, and nature makes her choices. His own choice was whether or not to take responsibility for the rain, which was the catalyst. It wasn't the first time. And it wouldn't be the last.

The Schwitzers had already been set up for their end. The rain had been the catalyst. Their price had nothing to do with Tom's making it rain. It was already on the books.

If Goodlands was doing penance, he had no way of knowing. Just as he had no way of knowing if his rain was setting something else into motion, as it had with the unnamed town, and with the Schwitzers, and with others. Maybe nothing would happen. Maybe it would rain and the people would be happy and everyone would get their farm back and Karen would keep her job and get back whatever it was she was missing since Goodlands had turned bad for her. Tom would move on and leave behind the way the town was sinking underneath his skin, the persistent hum under the ground, and the feeling of doom.

It was the way it used to be, just a day or two before his father would come home from one of his benders. He and his mother would be fine until the last couple of days, when something would hang over the house. The two of them would get snappy at each other without knowing why; food, if there was any, wouldn't sit right in their stomachs. At the least provocation, they'd both look up at the door, even if they couldn't actually hear anything. For a day or two, it was palpable in the air, this doomed feeling. Then, every time, the old man would walk through and there would almost be a sigh of relief when he did. At least they would know what had been coming. It had been him.

"You get what you pay for," his mother used to tell him. Sometimes firmly, in warning, sometimes with a sigh. As a child Tom had thought it was just one of those ambiguous statements adults make to children that someday would become crystal clear. By the time Tom was twelve, he thought he knew what she meant.

She had got what she paid for.

By the time Tom's mother had hit high school, she was a wild child. In whispered conversations after his father's "accident," Tom had picked up some history. One of the things he heard whispered by a woman from town was that his mother had spent her life setting herself up for trouble just like what had occurred, and that as a teenager she had "gone with boys." The meaning was unfathomable at the time, even if the phrase wasn't. Whatever it had been, at twelve he knew it was bad. It tainted them all. In the same conversation, the woman had said that Tom would be trouble, no matter where he went or what was done with him. His mother had further closed the door by picking "that one." Meaning his father. His mother had once told Tom that his father was her last choice. She had laughed when she said it, but he knew, even at the time, that it wasn't really funny.

"You get what you pay for" could be applied to so many things. Drought being one of them.

If Goodlands was doing penance, then Tom couldn't stop it. He also couldn't stop the rain once it fell.

He had no concern for Goodlands. It was not his place. But it was Karen's.

It was for her that his spirits were low. If something was going to happen, he didn't want it to happen to her. She was good. In spite of what he'd said earlier, he didn't think her motives for calling him into the town were dark, or selfish. She was searching, trying to close circles, like him. She was more like him than she would ever know.

He liked her enough that he didn't want anything to happen to her. Liked her enough that taking off before morning was still an option. Maybe the status quo was the best thing he could give to her, and to the town that was closing her circle. Let nature balance its own books, without him.

Right then, standing in the darkness between the house and clearing, he wanted to see her. To see what was in her face. To see if there was a blank, emotionless look to her, the way there had been to the people in the ill-fated diner. Just to see.

He turned toward the house. He just wanted to see her. On the back porch, Tom tapped at the screen door. The inside door, he noted, was open. He heard her after tapping a second time.

"Just a sec," she called, her voice thick with sleep. He'd woken her.

When he saw her coming out of her bedroom, with her hair mussed and robe tied crookedly around her, he felt sorry that he'd woken her, and wasn't even sure what he was hoping to see.

"What is it?" she whispered.

The screen stood between them.

"I just wanted to say good night," he said.

She nodded, looking into his eyes. She raised a hand and pushed lightly on the screen. The door opened and Karen stepped out onto the porch. The door slipped closed behind her.

They stood in silence on the porch, looking out into the night.

If you looked in the right direction, you could see miles of flat, uninhabited prairie from the porch. The sky was omnipotent above them, clear nearly as far as the eye could see. In the distance, about an hour's drive away, there was cloud. Someone, tomorrow, would get rain. Everywhere else, it was a brilliant indigo, lit up and electrified by the round white moon.

"The sky is so clear," Karen said incredulously. Tom nodded. He looked sideways at her, seeing her profile lit by the moon. She was beautiful in that light, the light flooding across the one side of her face, with her hair tousled and her eyes heavy with sleep.

She turned and found him looking at her. Her eyes widened.

"Tomorrow there will be clouds," he said.

"Yes."

He had the urge to touch her face. Her eyes slid off him, but she did not turn her head. She looked down, as though embarrassed.

"I'm not going in to work," she said. "I thought I would call in sick. Do you mind?"

He shook his head no. She nodded, looking into his eyes. Then she grabbed the handle of the screen door and pulled it open. She was going to go in.

Tom leaned forward and kissed her, very lightly, on her lips. In the second that he pressed his mouth on hers, he could hear her heart beating, louder than it should have. When he pulled away he saw her eyes, wider than they were, her face surprised.

"For luck," he said. She was still before nodding.

"All right," she said. And she turned into the house, disappearing into the dark kitchen without turning back. Tom heard the door to the bedroom close softly. Then he went down the stairs and started toward the clearing. He needed to sleep.

Because tomorrow it would rain, and he would be able to put the strange karma of this place behind him and move on. Forget Goodlands, forget the woman. Take the money and hole up someplace where it was always wet, where you could drink the air, it was so thick with water. Someplace where he wasn't so aware of the sky. The sky here was too big. He wanted to be in a place where you could tip the leaves on thick, lush trees and drink the dew as it ran off in tendrils.

In her bedroom, Karen moved in a daze. She'd pushed the door lightly, not listening to see if it fitted smoothly into the jamb, and not caring. Her fingers moved up to her face and she touched her mouth. He had kissed her.

She had felt it with her whole body, and her body was still feeling it. It was alive with excitement. The surface of her skin alert, her heart still pounding.

Tomorrow she would stay home from work and pull out the rock garden in the corner of the yard. It would give her the excuse she needed. She would in reality be waiting for the rain— and for . . . him. But she had never liked the garden, never liked rock gardens in theory or in practice; it was a tortured, groomed thing to do to both rocks and earth. And the garden had become overgrown, then dry and dead-looking, so that all there was to see were the rocks themselves, layered in a fashion that nature never intended. She might have just thrown them haphazardly around the yard and let nature take them over, let green overtake them after it rained and the earth drank it up, and the plants that had been waiting under the earth for just that moment could spring up around the rocks and eventually overwhelm them.

It had just been a very light kiss. For luck, he'd said. But Karen could feel the ground swirling underneath her as the ride spun her farther away from control.

For the first time, she let herself spin.

For once Carl's timing was good. He pulled onto Parson's Road and drove slowly, lights out, meeting the Mann property from the front just in time to see the longhaired fellow cross the yard and slip into the grove of trees beyond.

He had expected to see the man walking along the road. What had caught his eye was the white roof of the gazebo in the back of the Mann yard. It caught his eye and he turned his head reflexively. Then he saw the guy, moving from the house to the trees. It was him. It was the guy he'd seen earlier. He was sure of it.

Carl drove to the end of Parson's, slowly, with his lights still out, until he found a deserted driveway to pull into. Then he shut down the motor and sat. He waited, checking behind him every couple of seconds, to be sure he wasn't followed. To be sure he was alone. Then he got out of the truck and headed to the Mann property on foot. The lights were out; he didn't think he'd be seen. If he was careful.

He had to see where the guy was going.

There was no silo on this part of the Mann property, he knew that much. But that didn't mean that they didn't have something else set up. He knew enough to know that the banker lived there. Bankers were always trouble. Their hands were always dirty.

He slipped unseen through the darkened yard. There were no lights on in the house, and he assumed whoever was in there was with the dirty-handed banker. They were all asleep.

Carl walked as quietly as possible through the yard and up to the trees at the edge of the orchard. Trees that hadn't borne fruit in many years now, thanks to the drought that had pulled the life out of everything. He squatted down low at the tree line and tried to see through the branches and brush. He could see nothing but shadows and trees, unable to distinguish which was which. He wished he had thought to bring his binocs with him, but they were stashed in the truck. But from where he squatted, he could see no movement. That meant either the guy had moved on to somewhere else or he wasn't moving. Either way, Carl had to see.

He stepped into the trees and walked as softly as possible in his heavy boots. He made very little noise.

Something began to take shape as Carl got closer to the clearing. First, he saw a long shape on the ground. In the moonlight, Carl could see it was a man.

The man was lying on his back, on a blanket or sleeping bag, with one arm thrown over his eyes to block out the moonlight, which was bright. When Carl was a little boy and wanted someone to walk him to the outhouse at night, his grandfather would say, "It's as bright as a sixty-watt bulb out there, boy." And in truth, it nearly was. The man's eyes were covered, the moonlight blocked it out so he could sleep. Carl stayed still in the trees, waiting to see if the man was really sleeping or playing possum, just waiting for Carl to step into the clearing, waiting to blow his head off with some kind of government-issue gun that would leave no trace of the farmer from Goodlands.

When he was absolutely sure that the man was asleep, he moved forward, very slowly, very silently. He stepped through the trees and into the clearing. Not a branch had snapped, not a twig moved. Neither had the man.

It was the fellow he'd seen on the road. He hadn't even taken his boots off. Carl looked around.

The guy was camping out, it looked to him. There was a pit with blackened branches in it, and if nothing else the man was a fool having a fire out here in this weather. He could smell the smoke lightly in the air as he stepped very quietly closer. At the man's head there was a knapsack, didn't look like too much was in it.

A piece of paper stuck out from the corner of the bag, the flap part, and it was facing away from the man.

That was it. Carl moved silently over to the knapsack and knelt down beside it, praying his knees wouldn't crack and wake the guy up. He pulled at the corner of the flap and the bag opened easily. He tugged at the paper. He didn't have to pull it out very far before he saw what it was.

It was the map of Goodlands that the mayor and his staff had made up a couple of years earlier. Janet had had one stuck on the fridge with magnets until it got so curled up it was garbage. They finally burned it in the stove. It was junk anyway, everyone knew that.

Carl suppressed a chuckle. In the corner that he held, he could see the smiling caricature of Bart Eastly down at the town garage, holding up a crescent wrench and pointing to their sign.

What saved him from laughing was the black line drawn heavily around the town. The line demarcating the boundaries of

Goodlands. It was clearly drawn around the edges of the silly map. A border of sorts.

It was accurate. He watched the sleeping man carefully for a few seconds. He put the map back as it had been in the bag, stood, and walked out the way he'd come, just as silently as he'd entered, checking back every couple of seconds over his shoulder. The man never stirred.

He walked to his truck, the night getting on toward morning. He rubbed his eyes before starting up the truck. He would head for home. He was tired.

And now, he was afraid.

He should have looked deeper in the pack. He should have gone through everything in it. He should have coldcocked the guy and gone through his pockets. He should have tried to find out why the longhaired, dirty-looking stranger had a map that marked out the boundaries of what was essentially the drought zone, and why he was camping out in the banker's yard. And why Henry was picking up his leavings.

But Carl was scared. No matter what he'd thought he would find, he was afraid now. His hands shook, and he grabbed the steering wheel in a hard grip.

Tomorrow he would call Henry and get to the bottom of it. First thing in the morning he would get that smug, patronizing asshole on the phone and find out who this guy was and just what Henry had to do with him. He would get to the crux of the matter.

Tomorrow the whole town would know. Because Carl was going to tell them just what was up. If they thought he couldn't figure things out, they were wrong.

With his lights out, he drove to the center of town and looked around suspiciously. There was no way to know who was suspect. Everyone might be in on it—although he didn't think that the ordinary folks, his friends, the farmers, the businesspeople, with too much to lose, would be in on it; it would the Officials. Officials were the snakes.

He drove home, not turning his lights on even once. He drove by the light of the sixty-watt bulb in the sky. He snuck into the house and into bed beside Janet.

"Where were you?" she said as soon as he was under the blankets. She sounded frightened.

Carl switched the light on beside the bed, and told her everything.

TEN

TOM WOKE JUST BEFORE DAWN. FOR A LONG TIME HE LAY STILL, flat on his back, and looked up at the sky. When the indigo night began its slow turn to day, he turned his head to the side and, through the leafless trees, watched the sun rise.

The sun was a linear glow at the edge of the earth. The change was nearly imperceptible, yet the night disappeared all the same. Squinting, Tom watched as the sun moved waves of light, like flames burning the dark away, pushing it up. Ocher, rust, sienna, a sunset in reverse, faster, the whole sky changed in a matter of minutes. He'd seen sunrises all over the country, from California to upstate New York. He'd watched the sun come up in Virginia, Florida, Texas. Every place had its own beauty.

Over Goodlands the sun came up like a monster, not rising so much as overwhelming the land, swooping over it like a vulture. Dark beauty clothed in light. By noon the heat would be unbearable.

By noon, he hoped, it would be raining.

He closed his eyes and sent out his feelers. It was not there. All around him, beyond the boundaries of Goodlands, there was rain and cloud. He felt them. There was rain. Not far, he reminded himself. Not far away. He pulled the wrinkled map out of his bag and spread it on the ground in front of him. He ran his fingers along the black line that showed the boundaries of Goodlands.

His deep, dreamless sleep had not erased his feelings of inevitability and doom. He rose and stood in the middle of the clearing, his view of the sky not obstructed by the trees that surrounded him. It was, suddenly, day. The day.

He cleared his mind of everything extraneous. When the trees, the little house several hundred feet to his right, Karen, stories from his life, and the parched land around him disappeared and all that remained was Tom and the sky, he was ready.

He began with a picture of Goodlands in his head.

He closed his eyes and from the recesses of his memory pulled up images of the boundary as he had walked it. He did this carefully, methodically, until mentally he was walking the distance again. Shrubs, fences, highways, dirt and gravel roads all became mental pictures of the ends and beginnings of Goodlands. Along the way, memories of how the earth, the dirt, the air, the sky, the sun had felt all became a part of the image, until it was no longer only pictures in his mind, but smells, sounds, tastes, voices, textures, all in the context of the sky as it covered those places, all conjured in relation to the nearest drop of rain.

When Tom held the whole town in his mind, he reached farther up.

It had been more than eight hours since Vida Whalley had first climbed into the old building on the abandoned property kitty-corner from the Mann place. It had been twice that, or more, since she had last eaten. Her exhausted sleep had been shallow and disturbed. She was thirsty, her throat nearly burning with the need for water; she was hungry. Her clothes, now three days worn, were covered in dust and dirt; there was a tear in her skirt from a stray nail that protruded from the fence at Revesette's, when she'd set the horses free. Her body was a mass of bruises, scratches, smears, and the cut on the bottom of her palm was red and swollen.

Vida's lush dark hair was now tangled and matted, and dulled with a layer of grime. Her eyes were ringed with shadows and puffy from a lack of sleep. What was remarkable was the wild look that shone out, coupled with the half smile, both knowing and cruel. Vida, in her own right, had a look that would instill fear in the people of her town. Without the power, without the entity inside her.

A long scratch across her chin that she could not recall getting had begun to itch. She stroked it absently.

She had fallen into a rough sleep out of self-defense, her body needing the rest, if her mind would not allow it. Not altogether her own mind.

They argued, the two of them, locked together in one body. By morning, Vida had stopped communicating. She could not, however, stop listening. All night the entity battered the girl with images of rage made flesh. The voice connected the fury Vida possessed, all on her own, with the place across the road, and the man who was there, until Vida's heart pounded with it, and she was blinded to all but what lay in front of her.

It was then that she was ready to move.

It was after eight in the morning when Vida stepped out into the yard of the old building where she'd spent the night. Years of neglect had left the wild things to grow over the concrete slabs that had been the sidewalk. The drought had taken its toll; what remained were dried-out stalks and leaves burying the debris from the building itself and the garbage that had blown into the yard from the road. Vida blinked into the sunlight.

Her stomach growled hollowly when she moved. The voice

competed with the emptiness in her belly, filling her head with pictures.

Vida walked primly along the concrete slabs toward the road, taking mincing, odd little steps like a marionette. Alongside the building was a gravel drive, also given over to the weeds, the gravel hammered into the ground from years of tires, but still visible. Brush had grown up around it, and the building. It provided a minimum of cover.

At the end of the drive, she stopped and looked down the road to the Mann place. There was a red Honda in the driveway, the banker's car. Dust covered the car in a thick layer, as it did everything else in town. The front yard of the Mann place was empty and still. The curtains at the front of the house were drawn. Nothing moved. The road, too, was empty at that hour, and not a bit of breeze blew, so that the whole road had the stillness and silence of the middle of the night, except for the blinding glare of the sun. She could see nothing else; not the man and not the banker. Just the car and the house, standing sentinel.

Vida stepped out onto Parson's Road and began walking slowly toward the house, the anger that had been there since she woke up creasing her face. Dust flew up behind her heels as she moved, settling around her in a cloud. The only cloud visible in Goodlands.

The voice whispered incessantly. *Find him, find him.* When it got to be too much, Vida spoke again. No sound passed her lips.

You shut up, she said. But she smiled as she said it, the prospect of what was in front of her beginning to curl up inside her like the warmth of a cat. Satisfaction for the burning anger inside. It was good. She licked her lips, her tongue nearly as dry. What was inside her yanked at something. Whatever it was, it caused pain and Vida's eyes squeezed shut for a second, and her step faltered. Then, as though nothing had happened, she was moving again. The voice and the pain, temporarily quelled.

"Don't hurt me," Vida said angrily, this time aloud.

It took no more than a couple of minutes for Vida to reach the end of the driveway where the Honda was parked. In that time, no one had driven by, no one had come out of the house. No one had seen her. Everything was as still as it had been.

She stopped and watched, again unsure. Knowing what was expected, unsure not only of how to go about it, but of whether she would entirely perform for the voice.

From the outside, the house was ordinary. Painted white, it could use another paint job, but would have held up nicely for another year or even two. The paint was not peeling or chipped, just dull. There was a pale blue trim around the windows and the door frame. The open wooden porch was painted cellar gray, a style from the old days, and it showed the most wear. The three steps leading up to the house were worn where feet landed, going up and down, maybe many times a day. The back steps, where people who came calling would usually go, would be worse. She would go to the front door.

The house was so ordinary. What could be in there that frightened the power, made the voice so insistent, so afraid? Was he inside?

Standing behind the car, she had a sudden attack of lucidity and she stopped. Her hand went to her mouth and her fingers rested on her lip, pressing in. Her eyes darted wildly to the door, the windows, the back, as far as she could see. Standing behind the car, she could see the beginning of the orchard trees, fruitless and practically leafless, and still.

Do it.

"Shut up," Vida told the voice, whispering, in spite of being alone.

She dropped to a crouch behind the car, her mind flitting over why she was there and what she would do.

The voice was little help.

Find him, it demanded. Vida did not know what she was to do if she did find him. The voice's *him* had retreated in her mind to a vague figure that she had followed. His exact looks no longer lodged there, just the outline of a man that she did not want to get close to. She sensed that outline as the image of something that could hurt her, the way a child is keenly aware that the stove is hot, the knife sharp, the stairs high. Even if he wasn't inside the house, someone would be. The car in the driveway, the early morning, told Vida that.

She could *make them*. Vida smiled cruelly. Make them do what? She could make them. She could make them do *anything*.

Vida did not know the banker, only that she was a woman. She had glimpsed her walking from bank to car, but always at a distance. All she could recall about the woman was her hair, dark like Vida's, but straight and smooth; and her clothes, like a magazine picture. Clean, groomed, well fed; that was the banker. What would she make her do? See her in the dirt, maybe. But hurt her? The woman had not ever even looked at her. Even to Vida's twisted morality, *having* was not enough to do harm.

The house and the car were worlds away from whatever Vida might own in her lifetime. The little red car was nothing fancy, even with its phony sporty look; Vida knew it wouldn't even be a fast car. It was just a car, late model, but brand-new. The house was the same house that could be found anywhere in Goodlands, or Weston, or Fargo, or anywhere else you wanted to point to in the wheat belt. It was not so different from the Whalleys' house, if the Whalleys' house had been painted and repaired over the last two decades. The Whalleys' house was even bigger, with a second floor.

She had no grudge against the banker, whom she had hardly even ever seen; she had no reason to fear her, or to think twice about her, really. If the woman stayed out of the way of the man, Vida would do her no harm. The voice did not comment.

Vida squatted uncomfortably behind the red Honda, her ankles complaining. The voice continued its one-track demand. Vida picked at the scab that had started to form over the cut on her palm. It bled where she picked.

The lawn was short, if brown, like all the lawns around town. The Whalley lawn had never been cut, not as long as Vida remembered. All the better to hide the crap that had piled up in front of the house over the years—the car radiators; the spools of cable, coiled rope, wire; the bags of garbage that somehow never made it to the dump; the countless empty beer bottles that lay hidden from whoever was desperate enough and thirsty enough to go searching for the pennies they afforded. Pieces of clothing—hats and gloves that fell off stumbling forms when they came home drunk in the middle of winter, socks and underwear from the barflies the brothers brought to the house. Beer caps, cigarette butts, pieces of broken glass, candy wrappers, and dog crap, all buried under the rest of the shit in the yard. Then there was that geographical differentiation. Vida's house was on the other side of town. The *wrong* side. The banker's house was respectable.

As close as they might have been in construction, Vida's house was miles away, literally and figuratively, from the banker's little house. And Vida didn't want to go in there.

It wouldn't be like sneaking into Watson's yard and draining the tanks; or cracking Greeson's driveway. For one thing, she'd known those people all her life, and had her own reasons for doing the things she did. And they weren't quite so far removed from Vida and her world—a bath, a paycheck, and a road or two. The banker, on the other hand, was one of Them. There was an authority, a door that was locked, opened only to consequence.

Vida's excitement over the power, over the previously unimagined ability to get even, had waned. At that moment, she longed to go home. To do that, she would have to get this over with. Satisfy the voice and her own, waning aggression.

Then she heard something.

Karen's alarm had gone off at six-thirty, as it did every morning. During the ten minutes offered by the snooze button, she lay on her back and gathered her thoughts.

Her sleep, as far as she remembered, had been dreamless, except for the moments just before the alarm went off. In those moments, she had been on the ride in the amusement park. The spinning ride. Under her, the ground shimmered, not really there, just a blurred, rotating image that never came into focus. There was no dizziness, no sickness in the pit of her stomach, just an exhilarating thrill.

She showered, blow-dried her hair, and dressed for the dirty work of tearing into the rock garden, in jeans and a T-shirt.

She called Jennifer at home and told her she wouldn't be coming in, then loaded up the coffeepot and turned it on.

She pulled a mug from the cupboard.

She looked out the window, tapping her fingers on the countertop as she waited for the coffee to brew. She wiped the counter free of water spots and tried to remember where her gardening gloves were. She looked out the window. Then she pressed her lips together and thought about their kiss.

There was no sign of him in the yard, and she couldn't make out anything through the trees.

Karen poured herself some coffee and went outside to work on the destruction of the overly groomed eyesore in the corner of the yard. Busywork.

The first thing she did, once freed from the confines of the house, was to look up into the sky. It was cloudless.

Karen waited.

Vida's head swiveled around at the noise, her fingers curling into talons, her body on the alert. She stayed crouched behind the Honda, listening keenly trying to identify the sound.

It was a door opening and swinging back on a chain or spring. The sound was hard to place at first, because it was so familiar and innocuous, like when you lie in bed awake at night and try to name the sounds you hear, wondering if the tired hum of the refrigerator is the low growl of something malevolent.

But it was just a door. Just a wooden door at the back of the house. Someone had opened and closed it. Footsteps on stairs.

She tried to make sense of it. If someone had opened the door, someone had left.

She carefully raised up and tried to see through the dusty windows of the Honda. There was no movement that she could see in the space between the side of the house and the clump of trees nearby.

Everything was quiet again. She waited expectantly, her eyes leaping from the side of the house to the trees and back again, thinking that, at any moment, the man or the woman would come from the back of the house into the driveway, and finally, to the car.

If that happened, she would hurt them. Above all, she wanted the element of surprise. Her decisions.

No one came.

After a while, she had herself convinced that she hadn't heard the sound at all. She was back to thinking she was going to have to walk up the steps to the door.

The voice was strangely quiet, muffled under the racing of Vida's heart. There was only the pounding, driving force that was always there. Without the voice, there was still the urgency to find *him*.

There was no moment of resolve, no epiphany. There was only the gnawing in her belly, and the persistent feeling inside her that she had to move. Finally she stood and walked over to the house, pausing just briefly at the bottom of the porch stairs before going up. When no one answered her knock after a second time, she pulled quietly on the screen door and found it open. She tried the knob on the inside door. It turned easily in her hand.

She went inside.

Karen had pulled the pitiful array of gardening tools from under the crawl space hatch at the back of the house. There was a hoe, and a small hand spade, along with a broken tool handle.

The sun was hot and beating down her back, but she knew it would get worse as the day wore on. She wondered if it was hot in the clearing.

Every now and then she paused and took a sip of her coffee, kept tepid by the sun. She hadn't eaten any breakfast and the coffee felt hard in her stomach. She felt strangely energized in spite of the heat. In a little while, she would go inside and get a hat.

Mostly Karen did not think about anything beyond the rain—how it would feel when it came, how it would sound beating down on the ground, hitting the hard, dry earth; the dust flying up from each drop as it hit, the cool spray against her face, her hands, her ankles. The difference it would make in her life. How it would be when things were green again. When water wasn't hauled every week. How it would be when she could shower without shutting the water off to soap up, then turning it on again only long enough to rinse off and wash her hair. (How the rainmaker would look when it was over; how he would look when he was leaving, his back to her.) She closed her eyes and imagined she felt the rapid beat of drops on her face, the water rushing from her hair and streaming down her body. How it would taste, like the sweet coolness in the dipper her father used to hand her from the rain barrel.

She bent back over and hacked away at the layers of dried, settled dirt so she could scrape the top layer of one of the big rocks, and drag it off. All the while, she watched the sky and cast glimpses into the trees. In both cases, she saw nothing.

Dust motes floated in the beam of sunlight that Vida let into the house. For a second, she was blinded by the contrast between darkness and light, and while she waited for her eyes to adjust, she felt a moment of perfect fear, uninterrupted by the voice, or reason, and she wanted to bolt. She held the doorknob in a grip so tight that her knuckles were white.

But nothing happened. While her focus slowly returned, she stared into the neat living room of the banker's house, seeing only the silent shadows of furniture. The whole house was silent and still, except for her own raspy breath.

She let go of the knob, and felt a little better for it. She pushed the door so that it was almost closed. A shaft of light beamed in through the crack. She found that she was standing in a small foyer. In front of her, to her right, was a closet. She stepped around it, taking a full step into the living room.

Her rasping breath stopped, caught in her throat.

The room was beautiful. Like in a book.

Her eyes widened and swept the room as she stood, motionless, mouth slightly agape. Everywhere, there was something to behold.

There was a chest in front of the window. On top, a lace cloth beneath a silver tea service that gleamed even in the shaded room. A large chair stood beside the chest in a bright paisley print. Next to the chair was a table, nearly as tall, with a delicately stemmed lamp and a small picture framed in the silver design of the tea service. A sofa stood in the middle of the room, and had a table of equal height running the full length of it. In the Whalleys' house the sofa was pushed up against a wall, where a sofa belonged. And yet the sofa here didn't look odd or wrong, it looked as though it was made to be set in the middle of the room.

A round rug sat on the floor, the edge of it under the sofa, and on the rug were two more chairs close together, exactly matching. A low square coffee table sat between them. A stack of thick books was on the table, along with a huge glass vase filled with silk flowers. There were more framed photographs, in various frames, all of them so pretty and perfect together, even though they didn't match. Some kind of sculpture or art, not of anything Vida could recognize, just tall and black, stood on the corner of the table.

The woman had everything. She was surrounded by beauty and wealth—if not a king's treasure, wealth such as Vida would have imagined it.

There was not a thing out of place; each and every item looked carefully arranged. There was nothing random. Even the magazines were fanned resolutely on the square table parallel to the sofa. There was no litter or junk, no hairbrush in the middle of the table, no beer cans, no stack of newspapers, no overflowing ashtrays, not even clean ones, no glasses or sticky marks on tables, no dog hair, no dust.

It was perfect.

Vida stood in the center of the room, surrounded by the emblems of how other people lived, and she was offended. The feeling came up over her in a rush.

The unfairness of it all.

It can be fixed.

With a whoop, she reached down and swept her arm across the low table that served as a coffee table that, she bet, had never, ever showed a coffee ring.

The magazines, the framed pictures, and the high crystal vase flew out from the table and landed on the floor with a crash. Paper skidded across the floor. Shards of broken glass sparkled.

She upended the table. It did not crack or break. It was, however, very loud.

That the woman who lived in the house had everything was no more than an accident of birth.

This is an accident, too, Vida thought as she picked up one of the pretty matching chairs and raised it as high as her shaking arms would allow and brought it down hard against the floor. The floor shook for a moment. One of the chair legs cracked— she heard the wood splinter, but the leg did not fall off. The chair tumbled against a bookcase. Books fell.

The power of the room lessened in the destruction. Vida spun around and pulled at the top of the bookcase until it tilted and crashed down, sending books and figurines and more pictures skidding across the floor. A little porcelain girl lost her head and shattered her skirt. Vida giggled, delighted.

She raised her foot, poised it above the tiny head of the figurine, and with a studied motion, smashed the head. She applied her weight and listened to the satisfying crunch.

She worked her way through the room, slashing out at the memorabilia of a life lived far away from her own. The power that surged through her was rage, her own—separate for the first time in days from that of the voice inside her, a voice still strangely silenced and, apparently, in wait.

Karen heard what she first believed to be a car backfiring, a sound coming from the direction of her house. She looked to the Honda and the road behind it. Waited to hear it again. She paused in mid-stroke, the clang of metal on rock halted, the hoe held out from her body like a spear. She heard something else, this time the sound of breaking glass, and this time there was little doubt that it was coming from the house. Then, she thought she heard a distinctly human sound.

A whoop.

For no reason, she looked in the direction of the clearing. She squinted and tried to see past the trees. With the sun still not at its highest point, the light was in her eyes, and she could see nothing. Another whoop sounded from inside.

She lowered the hoe to her side and without bothering to take her gloves off took a few steps toward the house.

Another crash, the sound of something very large falling, came from inside. Karen ran.

By the time she reached the porch steps it was clear that someone was inside and that something terrible was happening. Without thinking twice, without considering what that terrible thing might be, Karen pulled the screen door open and flew inside. In the dim light of the living room, she could make out only a small, indistinguishable silhouette, a woman or a girl, arms raised, holding something above her head.

"*Stop!*" Karen screamed. "Stop!"

The woman's back was to her, and above her head she held Karen's heavy oak silverware chest. The woman's head pivoted only slightly to the sound behind her, and Karen saw a curve of one cheek, raised in a smile. Then the box came crashing to the floor, the hinges splitting and the silverware clattering out in all directions.

Karen's hands flew to her mouth, her eyes fixed in horror on the cutlery glittering all over the floor. Fifty-six pieces, on the gleaming hardwood, already scratched from the debris of her living room.

She screamed.

"What are you doing? Stop!"

The woman swung violently around to face Karen, her arms swinging in the air around her body. Karen had to drag herself away from the ruins to look at the author of it, as the woman stepped into the archway between the living room and the kitchen.

She was a monster. Wild hair framed a face flushed red and shining with perspiration. The eyes were red, shot through with veins. Dirty neck, hands, and a dress, if that's what it had been once, torn and filthy. She looked like something that had crawled out of a dark hole.

The monster happily smiled a toothy grin.

"WHOOPS!" it said, loudly. Karen realized she was just a girl. Not a woman yet, and not a monster. A girl.

"It's all junk now!" she said. Her hands went to her hips, one on each side, jaunty. "JUNK! JUNK! JUNK!" she screamed, emphasizing each word with a kick, scattering pieces of silverware, pieces of the beautiful chest, a picture frame. The girl's breathing was the only sound then, heavy with excitement or exertion. She presented a frightening figure.

Karen, overwhelmed by the sight of her things in ruin, crossed the several steps' distance to where the girl was standing. Her sudden movement took the girl by surprise and she stepped back, her smile fading for just an instant.

"How could—who *are* you?" Karen cried, her arms swooping around her to encompass it all. "*Why?*"

The girl stared back blankly, chest still heaving.

"I'm calling the police." Karen leaned over, where the phone table had been, and realized there was none.

Without taking her eyes from Karen, the girl stooped down and pulled the phone up off the floor. She tore the cord of the receiver from the telephone and handed the receiver coyly to Karen. The cord dangled.

"Here you go," she said politely. "Call!" Then she laughed, doubling over with giggles.

Karen stood wide-eyed, afraid. The girl still held the receiver out to her, giggling.

"Changed your mind?" she asked, and dropped the receiver. It fell with a clatter between them.

"How dare you! Who are you!"

The girl finished snickering and stood straight up, a shy, mocking smile replacing the hysteria. She began her answer, "I'm the cat in the—" and stopped dead, her eyes flying open widely, face suddenly contorting as though struck with sudden pain.

Out of her mouth came a wail that only Vida knew was coming from inside her. The sound forced its way out of her open mouth, twisting her head up, like the howl of a wolf. The girl's hands went to her face and grabbed on to the flesh of her cheeks. The fingernail made raw red lines as she pulled the skin down. Still the sound came out, even as the girl visibly shrank.

Horrified, Karen took an unthinking step toward her. One of the girl's hands flew out and pushed Karen back.

"NO!" screamed the girl, the voice that came out of her so unlike the one she had previously used, Karen started and withdrew. The voice she used seemed to echo out of her, blasting forward like a gust of wind and sounding not quite human.

The girl pushed past Karen and lumbered awkwardly to the back door.

"NO! It comes!" she screamed again. Out of the same body came yet another voice, distinctly different from the last, a small, whining sound, like that of a child. It spoke no words but sounded more like that of a girl. "Uh, uh, uh," it wailed.

The girl's hands darted out in front of her and actually pushed the door open in front of her, knocking it off from the top hinge so that it hung without closing. She stepped through the narrow opening and out onto the porch.

"It comes! IT USES ME!"

Karen, unable to move, shook her head, trying to clear it, to make sense from the senseless.

It comes?

Both hands gripped the door frame behind her, where she had been pushed by the force of the girl's passing.

She didn't lay a hand on me, yet pushed me into the wall. Karen could not grasp it. Around her the things in the living room, her beautiful things, lay in ruins.

It comes? The girl's screams came now from the yard and Tom immediately came to mind—the thought that she was heading for the clearing.

It comes.

"Ohmigod—" Karen pushed herself to standing, at that moment feeling the persistent vibration that seemed to come from inside the walls of her house, and realizing in the moment that what was coming had to be—

Rain.

Tom stood in the clearing, the balls of his feet planted firmly on the ground. The rest of him stretched upward in supplication to the vast clear blue of the sky above.

Both hands were clenched in fists. His knuckles were white against the tanned flesh of his hands, clenched not in anger or fear but in retention. He held the rain in his hands.

Sweat poured off his body from the heat of the day and from the beating of the sun, with no respite given by the trees. The sun was above his head and still to the east. It was long past mid-morning, but Tom had no consciousness of what the time was, just as he had no knowledge of the human drama that was being played out a scant hundred yards away. All he knew was the pull of the sky above and the tug of the earth below, each fighting for dominance.

For an hour he'd stood in that way, the gentle hum under the earth, which he had recognized from the first, having grown until it was a hollow screech in his ears, coming from the ground itself, running up through his feet like an electrical current. Still he held on.

He had spent the morning gathering the clouds from as far away as the Minnesota border and as close as Telander. Slowly, he pulled, tugged, yanked, cajoled, and nudged until he held it all. He began the slow work of bringing it closer, as the purr under him grew to a roar. By the time Vida and the thing that possessed her had pushed their way out of Karen's house, it was all he could do to keep his work in his slick, sweating hands.

He held on. Then there was a shift in the earth.

Vida was entirely suppressed by the entity when the first rumble had begun in the sky. The thing that possessed her wailed and lumbered gracelessly in a circle in the backyard, at once dazed and confused by the odd vibrations in the air.

They were from her.

This was the place. The man was very nearby. She could not quite find him, could not see him, could not hear him, could only feel the drain as he almost *tugged* at her, taking her strength away, pulling it upward. He was there; he was not there. She rumbled and moaned, dragging her host's sneakered feet along the dry, deadened grass, keeping Vida tightly bound inside the body, keeping her down, even as her own strength faltered. Why couldn't she find him? What held her away?

She stopped and screeched out of sheer frustration, all the while sending Vida's body into tremors. Out of Vida's mouth came alternate voices.

"Leave me!" Vida said, the vibrations that came from inside her painful and disorienting until all the nerves in her body demanded that she move away from the source.

"*HE USES ME!*" screeched the voice.

Karen watched, terrified, from the doorway. She crouched

low, hidden from the girl's view by the inside door. Her body was rigid with fear as she listened without understanding the screeching words, knowing that the "he" the girl cursed against could only be Tom. Karen crouched unmoving, torn between her fear of the thing that raged over the deadened earth and her need to get to Tom. If the woman started toward the clearing, she would go.

In the meantime, she did not move, but watched, struggling to understand. There was something about the girl that was . . . *wrong;* something disconnected, as though her eyes, so wild, were untethered to her mind. Released from her control. A play of conflicts over her face, brutal and afraid. In the split second before the girl careened outside, Karen had seen something flicker in her face, a fear followed by a contortion that made Karen think of terrible things, of horror and violence.

A tiny slip of a girl, she had upended Karen's enormous solid oak coffee table, the one that two men had barely been able to carry into the house when she had moved; she had nearly broken the leg off a chair that had to weigh fifty pounds.

Still in a crouch behind the door, Karen reached slowly behind her, feeling along the floor without taking her eyes off the mad-woman, until her hand closed around the only thing she could reach without moving. She felt in her palm the rough wood of the hoe handle, dropped at the door when she had first come inside and seen the girl. Her fingers curled around it, holding tightly. If the girl moved toward the clearing, Karen would use it.

She pulled it noiselessly toward her, moving her hand closer to the middle to get a better grip. She felt a resolve filling her, a strength that replaced the tension and fear. Her lips pressed together. She began to stand.

When fully erect, she slipped past the broken door and quietly stepped onto the porch.

A moment passed when she felt terribly exposed. Lost in madness, Vida did not notice her. Karen left the porch—taking care to jump over the last, squeaking step and landing with a gentle thud on the ground. She stayed crouched, terrified but strong. Too afraid to move farther, she held her meager weapon in both hands and watched the girl to see what she would do. As soon as she was ready, she would move.

There was something so achingly familiar about her to Karen; it was not so much a physical familiarity as some kind of connection she was making in Karen's memory. Like an old acquaintance, someone she *should* know, but didn't remember.

In the moment that followed, two things happened nearly at once. The girl stopped dead in her tracks and turned slowly in Karen's direction. Their eyes locked on one another. The girl's face was still contorted in that horrible rage, but when her dulled eyes met Karen's, and Karen raised the metal edge of the hoe just slightly, as if poised, her face changed. The girl's eyes narrowed, and she smiled. She took a halting step in Karen's direction, her mouth open, as if to speak.

They both heard it.

A distant but distinct and familiar rumble, coming from the sky. Vida's head jerked upward toward the sound.

The hum that hurt her ears so much was widely outdistanced by the screech that followed. She threw her head back and opened her mouth wide, a wail rising from her throat and filling the air, drowning out the rumble from above. Forgetting Karen, Vida reacted to the same command from two sources.

I can't find him. Vida looked toward town. There was another way.

Karen thought for one terrible moment that the girl was coming for her, and she raised the hoe above her head, ready to strike. But Vida turned away from Karen and jerked in the direction of the road, the jerking motion increasing until she ran, disappearing around the side of the house. Karen heard her steps on the gravel drive, and then could hear no more. Her arms, shaking from adrenaline and the weight of the hoe, dropped to her sides, but she would not relinquish her hold on the handle. The hoe hit her thighs and bounced up. She let go of the breath she'd been holding, and gulped for air again, her breathing, after that, shallow and fast, and her head light. She squeezed her eyes shut and opened them, hoping the girl would still be gone. She was.

With her heart pounding in her chest, the smell of her sweat wafting up, she dropped the hoe. It lay on the ground in front of her and cast no shadow.

The odd thought reverberated in her head. *It casts no shadow.* She looked up. The sky was clear, cloudless, but the sun had gone. She stood on shaking legs, took a tentative step as graceless as the girl's, and moved toward the clearing. Where had the sun gone? Her mind was a jumble of confusion. Where was the sun? She had to find Tom.

Then something caught the corner of her eye.

At the far end of Goodlands, over where Clancy's began and where the road went on to Weston, she saw something very familiar.

A cloud. Fluffy and gray. Dense and full, it had moved to cover the sun.

As she watched, another moved into view.

Thompson Keatley was completely unaware of Karen's dismay, and finally her delight; he heard neither the commotion from inside the house nor the careening steps of Vida's exit. He was far, far away from all of it.

His body was bathed in sweat. He was naked from the waist up and his skin glowed with perspiration that beaded up and trickled down him. It ran freely down from his hairline, over his closed eyes, into his mouth, down his neck to his torso.

Every muscle was tensed. His chest bulged and contracted with hard breathing. His eyes were clenched tightly, furrowing his brow, wrinkling the skin on his temples into tiny fans. His mouth was held taut in a grimace. He might have been a statue, a living, breathing, sweating statue, if not for the animation in his hands.

His arms were held out, parallel to his shoulders. His fingers gently opened and closed, opened and closed. His arms bent at the elbow with each movement. He was coaxing. Releasing, fastening. With each motion he pulled and tugged at droplets of rain, from outside the boundary that held Goodlands captive. He pulled, coaxed, cajoled, implored, clutching hard at each bit of rain he brought forth, gathering it around the town's circle.

Tom Keatley was many, many miles away from the clearing in the back of Karen's house in Goodlands. He was, in fact, not in Goodlands at all. Therefore, he had no way of knowing that war had begun.

E L E V E N

CARL HAD LOCKED JANET AND BUTCH IN THE MASTER BED-
room for their own protection.

"They keep secrets from the people, Janet," he tried to explain.
"They hide behind national security and throw us crumbs of information, *misinformation*, and they keep the rest to themselves."

"Who are *they*? Have you lost your mind?" Janet had tried, at
first, to talk rationally to her husband, but he barely heard her.
By the time morning had come, he was ranting. There was no
other word for it. And it frightened her more than his crazy TV
shows and midnight rides through town.

"Why do you think the government throws so much money
into AIDS when more people die of cancer every year than of
AIDS? I'll tell you why." By that time he was yelling. "They
throw that money at AIDS because the disease belongs to them.
They *invented it* and somehow it got out of their labs and into
the population and now they have a hundred million people as

their guinea pigs. We're just one giant lab to them." His face was close enough to Janet's that she could feel the spittle flying out of his mouth.

"The goddamn cold and the goddamn flu are mutating viruses. Isn't that so fucking interesting? You think the flu and cold medicine companies don't have something to do with that? You think that maybe the government is getting some nice kickbacks? They distract us by telling us that it's SMOKING that's bad for you and then you drop dead from the fucking cold that's mutated into a flesh-eating disease.

"The Internet!" he yelled. His arms flew up in the air. "The Internet is just one big spy organization. You think that some guy sits down at his computer and starts plugging in UFOs, the Cuban missile crisis, dead presidents, and organic farming, you think the government just sits around *wondering* what's going on on the Internet?" When Janet tried to interrupt, he stuck his hand over her mouth. Not hard. Just a physical suggestion that she decided prudently to mind.

"You wanna take a look at Kirstie Alley's boobs on satellite TV, and on the way you look at UFOs, and a list of missile sites in your area, and they're going to think you're playing around? They write it all down under your name and then they start investigating why you're so interested in missiles. There's no benefit of the doubt, Janet. There are no secrets anymore. Only lies."

"Carl, why are you doing this?" Janet had been careful to modulate her voice, bringing it down considerably from her normal speaking voice to calm him. By then he wasn't listening to her.

"You write a letter to your congressman about how maybe you think abortion should be legal. You think the congressman reads the letter and sends you back a form saying he's grateful for your support and please send a hundred dollars to blah blah, to reelect him? You think that's what happens? No! They send that letter down to the CIA and you get put on a list of possible communist baby-killers.

"It's too late now. They'll know what I've been watching, what I've been reading. I've been a goddamn Democrat all my life, and I'm goddamn sorry for it now. I'll be on so many fucking lists and when The Big Change comes, they'll be at my house faster than you can spit at the cat and I'll disappear along with thousands of other Democrats while my wife and son get sent down to the work farm for retraining, or debriefing, or whatever they're going to claim it is. Do you understand? Do you understand how many lists I must be on by now?"

"The Big Change? Carl, listen to yourself!"

"You think Goodlands is dry because the gods dictated it be so? You think it's some goddamn cosmic mistake, the stars weren't aligned with Jupiter and now our karma's fucked? Or do you think some asshole in a suit walked over here one day with a brand spanking fucking new weather deflector and parked in one of those silos, or ten of those silos, or just turned a knob somewhere and now we're dry as a bone. Which sounds more fucking likely, Janet?

"The buck stops here." He ground his point in, poking his finger forcefully into the air, into some imagined official's chest. "There's a fucking undercover agent living at the end of Parson's Road and Henry Barker knows something about it, and the FUCKING BUCK STOPS HERE!"

The last speech took place that morning. As far as Janet knew, Carl hadn't had any sleep at all, although there had been a couple of hours when the house had been very, very quiet and she wondered if he had fallen asleep. None of that mattered. The only thing that did matter was that she and her son were now locked in their bedroom where the child had been conceived, and it was "for their own protection."

He had spent some time in the bedroom with them. He'd spent it writing things down. She knew it was to calm them. He wasn't angry with *them*. He told her he was writing down everything he'd said, along with a few other things he thought he knew, and that if he never came back again, she was to turn this over to the ombudsman on Channel Seven. She had been tempted to ask him if he didn't believe the ombudsman was in on it. The ombudsman on Channel Seven was a skinny little guy about fifty who mostly investigated things like whether or not municipal officials were getting parking tickets at the same rate the "little guys" were. He was big on "little guys."

Carl had ripped the telephone extension out of the wall and brought them a gallon of milk and the fixings for sandwiches. They were instructed to stay put and not worry.

"I'm protecting you," he told her gently. He'd kissed her, too, and Butch. Then Carl carted the TV into the room for them to watch. He reminded her that if she didn't believe him, there was a good show on on the satellite at eleven called *Secrets of the Government*, all about conspiracy theories. They'd been sued twice and had had to run retractions. She didn't bring it up. Eleven o'clock was miles away, anyway.

Butch hadn't said much, just looked at his mom with wide eyes. When it got quiet in the house, he whispered to her.

"What's he going to do?"

"He's not going to do anything to us," she told him firmly. And she firmly believed that. She firmly believed that he firmly believed everything he'd told her. Two things could happen: Either he would call Henry Barker and Henry would calm him down or Henry would call the authorities—(the proper authorities)—and Carl would be in therapy until she could get him out. She firmly hoped for the former.

Janet put the TV on for Butch and made him a bologna sandwich for breakfast. She made herself one, too, and made a show of eating it, but it wound up in the garbage beside the dresser. She also made a show of watching *Scooby Doo* with Butch, but she didn't believe that either of them was doing anything more than watching the pictures go by.

Fascinating show, *Scooby Doo*. There was always a ghost trying to scare someone. Except it always turned out to be fake. The monster was always very human by the end of the show.

The ghosts in the closet were people pulling strings, rattling chains, and doing it for very human reasons, usually greed. And the bad guys always got caught and sent to jail. Or they apologized and went on to have pizza with the gang.

Janet found herself rethinking some of Carl's theories. The common cold did not mutate into a killer disease and it *was* bad to smoke, and they were spending money on AIDS because it killed people. But the Internet could be watched, and if it was as loose and free as everyone said it was, then there was a golden opportunity for disaffected groups to spread their words to the population at large (or at least to those with the wherewithal to own a computer, no small expense).

And if there was anything at all that Carl made sense about, it was the drought. Goodlands was in the middle of the worst drought in history. Worse than the drought in '88, worse than the drought in the thirties—even if people weren't talking about it, there were enough old-timers around who'd scraped out their living through the Depression who said this was worse. Ed Kramer, whose farm had gone up in smoke earlier this week, had told her personally that folks in the thirties had gone on relief as a last resort, when the last pig had been slaughtered, the last potato eaten, the last onion peeled. Then he told her—without including himself—that half his neighbors were collecting on crop insurance or were on welfare.

It wasn't natural. And she doubted it was karma, or the alignment of the planets, or cosmic bullies. And if it was a punishment from God, why?

If Carl was right about anything, it was the drought. But she could not believe that tubby Henry Barker had anything to do with it, or any knowledge about it She couldn't picture some CIA agents and Henry Barker in the same frame unless it was him and his wife collecting autographs and having their picture taken at some kind of "Meet Your Secret Agents" day at Disneyland.

The government agencies were doing nothing about it, and on

that point, at least, Carl was right. Except denying it existed. They sent no one out to study it. No one had done anything more than take notes, and even that, not since the first year. They were in complete denial about an entire town.

Janet scared herself with the line of thought she was taking. Then she heard him on the phone. She listened at the door.

Carl kept his notes in front of him. Calm, articulate, rational. Henry Barker would know who he was up against; would know that he was cornered. He meant Henry no harm. He just wanted him to confirm what Carl already knew to be true, and then to get out of the way.

He cleared his throat and listened as the phone rang on the other end miles away, in Henry Barker's kitchen.

"Yeah," Henry's voice on the line.

"Henry," Carl said. "Carl Simpson."

"Carl! Been meaning to give you a call. How are you doing?"

"I'm calling on official business, Henry. Got some things I'd like to discuss," he said. There was a pause on the other end. Carl imagined the sweat beading up on Henry's forehead.

"Well, Carl, I was just about to leave for the office, how about I call you from there?"

"I want to talk now, Henry."

"Go ahead then, Carl," Henry said. "But I only got a couple of minutes. What's on your mind?"

Carl took a deep breath before beginning. "I've been wondering who you're working for these day, Henry." Carl's heart began to pound and he listened anxiously for the telltale click over the miles of phone lines that would indicate a tap.

"Huh? You know who I'm working for, Carl," Henry said patiently.

"I don't believe I do."

Henry let out an annoyed sigh. "Christ, Carl. I don't know what you're talking about. I don't have time for this now. Lemme call you later, from the office."

"You better talk to me now, Barker. I *saw* you last night. I *saw* you and your friend. I saw him pass you a note."

"What the hell are you talking about, Carl? Tell me straight or I'm hanging up."

"What'd the note say, Henry? Did it give a time and place? I checked the guy out, you know. Saw his map. How long you been in on it? The whole four years, Henry? Did you think no one'd ever see you? You and your *friend*? What're they doing down there at the banker's house? She in on it, too?"

Henry was struck by the frighteningly serious tone of Carl's voice. "You tell me what you're talking about and I'll give you a sane answer, which is more than I can say about this conversation, for chrissakes—"

"YOUR FRIEND! Who is he? Last night, on Parson's, I saw you following your contact, or whatever he was. I saw him drop the note, instructions, information, whatever it was. I SAW YOU. Now you give me your *sane* answer to that!" Carl lost control and shouted into the phone.

Henry rubbed his eyes. If it had been anyone else, he would have laughed and hung up the phone. But the tone of Carl's voice—and the fact that it *was* Carl—kept him from doing it.

"For chrissakes, Carl. That's goddamn police business and none of yours. I don't have bloody time for this—"

Carl shouted, "I'm not fooled! I'm not fooled! I'm going there now, and I'm collecting a few buddies along the way, Henry. We're putting a stop to this right now! The buck stops here—"

"For God's sake, Carl. I don't even know the man. He dropped a business card, for crissakes, I was following him and I picked it up. He's some kind of rainmaker. Someone must've hired him. All I did was pick up the goddamn card, had his name on it and everything, some bloody shyster trying to fleece whoever hired him to make it rain. For all the love of God—put Janet on, right now," Henry fumed.

Carl stared blankly into the air in front of him. "A *what*?" A rainmaker; Henry had said rainmaker. Carl's face stiffened into an ugly grin. "A rainmaker," he repeated, spitting out the words. There was a long pause on both ends.

Finally Carl spoke again. "I'm so stupid, am I, Henry? I'm so stupid." He paused, his face contorted with a quiet, determined rage. "I'll just bet he's got something to do with rain, and I'll bet I know who hired him. Tell yourself the lies, Barker. I'm not fooled," he said.

"Carl, listen to me. I've got it right here, hold on, I'll grab it and I'll read it to—"

"You better hope you beat me to town, Henry, because I'm going out there now, and I'm pretty sure that after I explain a few truths to some people, I won't be going out to see your rainmaker alone. You got that?"

"PUT JANET ON!" Henry's face was apoplectic with anger. He wiggled around in his chair as much as his bulk would allow, feeling with one hand to get hold of the shirt hanging over the back of the chair. It was the one he'd been wearing the night before. He fumbled around for the front pocket.

He could still hear Carl's breath on the receiver. He'd made no move to get Janet. Henry didn't think he'd do anything to his family, he was a good man, or used to be. But he wasn't that sure. Carl was not himself. He found one front pocket and felt around for the rectangular business card he'd found the night before. He found it, the paper stiff beneath the thin cotton of his shirt, the fabric damp where the card was, and strangely warm.

"Just a sec, Carl, I found it." Cradling the phone awkwardly between neck and shoulder, he finally reached behind with both hands, one hand holding the card through shirt, the other groping for the pocket opening, undoing the button, while he craned his neck to see and tried not to drop the phone. He broke out in a sweat. "Hang on," he said.

His fingers reached inside and felt their way down into the pocket. The pocket was empty. Empty. For a moment, everything stopped. His breath stopped. His fingers paused. The fingers on his other hand, the hand he thought he'd held the card in, were empty. The only thing there was the odd warmth and dampness.

Where was the goddamn card? He'd held it, in his fingers. Nearly dropping the phone, he stuttered to Carl. "Uh—put Janet on."

"Janet can't come to the phone right now," Carl said primly. Blood rushed up to Henry's face. He let go of the shirt. There was something in Carl's voice that frightened him. He took the phone in his hand, righting it on his ear and mouth.

He said quietly, "You haven't hurt her, have you, Carl?"

"Of course not!" Henry let out the breath he held. *Christ.*

"Then where is she? Why can't she talk to me?"

"Your business is with me, Henry. This is not about my wife."

The card must've been in the other pocket, he realized, his mind simply discarding the fact that he had all but held it in his fingers. Henry got hold of the other pocket and felt around. That pocket, too, was empty. His pants were in the bedroom.

"Look, I can't find the goddamn card, but when I do, I'll show it to you. It's just a prank, or a con. And I've got other business with him. He's nobody. He's not from the government and he doesn't know anything about anything. Do you hear me?"

"Then he won't mind telling me that. I'm heading to town and I'm going to get some of the guys together and we're heading out for that guy's camp. He had a good fire going last night. You think I don't know what's going on? A fire in Goodlands? Why don't you arrest him?"

"Maybe I will. If I don't arrest you for harassment first. Don't you do a goddamn thing until you see me, you understand, Carl? And you get Janet to give me a call." He was sure he had put the card in his shirt pocket, the right side. Everything he found worked its way into that pocket. He had felt it, for chrissakes. He went through the process again, feeling first one side, and then the other, holding the phone again with his shoulder, giving his voice a faraway sound at Carl's end.

"You better hope you beat me to town, Henry," Carl said. Then he hung up.

"*Shit!*" Henry said, and slammed the phone down himself.

Lilly came into the kitchen. "What's going on?" she said.

"Where's my pants from last night?"

"On the floor where you left them," she snapped.

"Well, grab them for me, will ya?" No longer impeded by the phone, Henry picked the shirt up and laid it out on the table in front of him. Maybe he'd been feeling the same pocket over and over. He got a good grab-hold of the right pocket and reached inside. It was still empty. But on the very bottom of the pocket, where he had been sure he'd held the card in his fingers, there was a rectangular shape, laid out in a damp darkness. It had been there, he knew, just as surely as he knew the card was gone. It had disappeared.

He went through the motions of checking the pants, but he knew it was gone.

Henry had a very bad feeling. In his gut. That hinky feeling a cop gets.

Confusion was the dominant emotion raging inside Vida as she was urged away from the banker's house, away from what had been the ceaseless focus of the voice since it had made its presence known. It was the confusion that frightened Vida most. The voice's assured, firm tone was gone, and in its place was a raft of other emotions, anger, and a subtle separation from its host. A loosening of the power, an uncertainty about where it would be directed.

Their bargain had not been satisfied. The confusion, coupled with the heady emotions from her confrontation with the banker, had made Vida feel shaky and panicked, and fission was taking place, not only inside of her but seemingly all around.

And something about the banker plagued her. In the cacophony inside her brain, she could not even tell if it was her plague or the other's, but the thoughts would not go away. *The banker, the banker.*

The only thing that remained clear to Vida was the overwhelming necessity to fulfill the bargain. She felt that if she didn't, she would be lost. The voice must be satisfied. In her limited access to that voice, Vida had determined its underlying need. It was revenge. She understood revenge. Revenge in Vida was a rock in hand, ready to be thrown through a window. There was another way. In fact, there were many ways. The ways and means had smoldered in Vida for years.

As she walked, the road behind her shimmered and shook in the sun, the way a puddle will seem to appear before you as you drive into the sun. It wasn't water forming in the road behind her. It was heat. It sweltered up from the asphalt, rippling upward.

Behind her, the road moved on its own. It began to crack.

She had to hurry. Just as she had sensed in the banker's yard, there had been a shift in things, a change in the air. It had become nearly unbreathable in the little yard, and was evident even as she moved farther and farther away. When she glanced furtively over her shoulder, as though being followed by something evil, she could see what was causing the change.

The sky had darkened noticeably in the west. Clouds were coming. The voice wailed. There was little time. Vida hurried her step, and arranged her intentions. The bargain would be satisfied, and she would be left alone. It was the town; the town the voice hated, as Vida did. She would hurt the town. Behind her, the road rumbled and cracked like mock thunder.

In the end, they would both have their revenge.

A short fifteen minutes after he hung up on Henry Barker, Carl Simpson walked into Rosie's Cafe. Only a few of the dozens of people having their morning coffee break didn't notice him. It was the busiest time of day at Rosie's—morning coffee lasted from ten till lunch, and didn't take a break. There was rarely a lull long enough for people to stick their heads up from the jaw-ing and gabbing of morning gossip to take note of who was walking in the door, but there was something about the way Carl walked in that made people stare.

For one thing, he looked *sick*. Normally clean-shaven, he had a near-beard of thick, dark bristle, and there were dark rings under his eyes. Others may have looked worse from lack of sleep—Goodlands hadn't been a well-rested town in years—but Simpson looked *truly* ill.

"Carl's looking bad," Betty Washington commented to Chimmy Waggles at a table near the middle of the diner. Chimmy glanced at him and shrugged. "Who doesn't?" Talk returned to whether or not Walter and Betty Sommerset's boy would marry the girl he'd met at school. The consensus was that he was crazy if he did.

Carl's eyes swept over the cafe while everyone went about their business, the talk not loud, but combined with the slap of pie plates on tables, the clatter of cutlery, and the chugging of machines, a din. He walked over to the staff table close to the front of the diner, where the group of townsmen generally gathered, away from the rest of the place. "The guys' " table. Carl bent low over the table and started talking.

Conversation at the table stopped as the guys listened to what Carl was saying, confusion on their faces.

The central thoroughfare in Goodlands, blandly called Main Street, had an old World War II statue (an anonymous soldier whose off-center nose gave him an oddly pugilistic appearance) and a bench on the sidewalk with a spindly tree planted in front of the Dry Goods to mark it as being a little more important than the others. The big tree, the oldest one on Main Street, was gone, except for the jagged, dangerous stump that kids had already started to pull apart. There was also a bench across the street from the Dry Goods, in front of the cafe, but there was no tree and the bench itself belonged to the Kushners. At Christmastime, the streetlights were festooned with strings of lights, but it was not Christmastime now, and there was nothing else really to stamp it as the main thoroughfare. The streetlights were an anomaly in themselves, as only the cafe was open at night, and it closed by eight. The need for a brightly lit main street was minimal.

There were trees up and down the street, nearly all of them suffering badly from lack of care, too much diesel, and the drought. They had all been planted by the Ladies' Auxiliary and the Jets, a sort of Masons for Goodlands farmers. Some of the trees were quite tall, though none was as thick in the trunk as the old one had been.

Vida stopped by one of the bigger trees, leaning up against it while she caught her breath. She had run nearly all the way from Parson's Road.

Her anger was a tangible thing. It had grown, rather than diminished, since she'd left Karen Grange's house, and the wreck of it, behind her. The voice was a storm inside her, urging her on, but it was supplanted by Vida's own passions, roused to fever pitch and now wholly unstoppable. The thing inside her had ceased to be a partner, a comrade in arms, and the subtle separation that she had felt was changing. She could feel it hurting her.

The two inside Vida—herself and the voice—were at odds. It was no longer a matter of the man. It was now Vida's own contest, and it was "get them." Blanket revenge for them both.

She watched the people moving in and out of Rosie's. When she caught her breath, she would follow them inside.

Karen stood facing the clearing. She breathed deeply, smelling the scent, unfamiliar and yet as knowable as her own name, of the coming rain.

And it *was* coming.

There was a distant crackle in the sky. Thunder. She pushed the girl out of her mind. The smell in the air, the crackle was all that mattered at that moment. Karen walked slowly toward the clearing, unable to think beyond wanting to *see* him do it. Wanting to be there when it happened.

So long in coming.

She moved instinctively through her yard, her face directed upward. She watched while clouds gathered so slowly that it seemed as though they had simply appeared from nowhere. Beginning in the west, where the sky had darkened from its earlier cornflower blue. They gathered in a circle around Goodlands, as far on the east as the Badlands, as far on the south as the open fields of the Hilton-Shane Dairy, and around her, Clancy's, the old Mann fields, the silos on the north side. She headed for the trees that marked the clearing.

She crawled inside the tangle of them, not wanting to give up her view of the magic happening above her, but needing to see it as it happened. Without the sky, she looked through the trees, hoping to catch a glimpse of him. As quietly as she could, she moved through the tangle of branches, keeping her head low, looking toward the clearing.

Halfway through, she caught sight of him, blurred through branches.

He stood tall, body stretched upward, as before, face turned to the sky. On his face was a look of utter blankness, as though he were not entirely there. His chest glistened with sweat or rain, or both. He looked caught in the middle of a rainstorm that had already happened. He was still, like silence. Locked in stone. He was beautiful.

She watched him. There was another crackle in the sky. She could feel the air changing around her, even sheltered as she was in the trees. She could smell it.

Karen could hear her own breathing, could hear her heart pounding slowly, could feel the saliva building up in her mouth. She swallowed. She waited.

Carl had spent the time as he drove to town choosing the right words. He chose carefully, knowing that if he came across sounding crazy, or paranoid, no one would believe him.

He had chosen well. Some of it—sorry as he was to do it, but he had to choose carefully—he made up. It was all for the Good of the People. The end justifying the means.

"Hey, listen up," he said. He bent low over the table full of men he'd known most of his adult life. People he trusted, and who, he assumed, trusted him.

"Something's going on out on Parson's Road," he began. "You guys know that I've been researching the drought, keeping up with it, right?"

Carl's ranting over the last couple of months had turned more than a few eyes glassy. The general opinion was that Carl was getting spooky. But this time, it wasn't what he said that captured their attention, but the way he was saying it, and they listened.

"What are you telling us, Carl?" Jeb Trainor asked in his steady voice.

"There's a guy staying out in the old Mann pasture, in the orchard there. I saw him. He's a strange one, but I think he might be that guy everyone's talking about, the one who might've started the Kramer fire—"

"What?" Ted Greeson said, surprised. He'd been there, volunteer fire fighting that night.

"I saw him," Carl continued. "He had his own campfire going—well, it wasn't going when I was there, but the ashes were hot," he said, and then quickly added, so that they didn't get off track, thinking about fire, "and he had a bunch of maps with him. They were maps of Goodlands. I think he's a government fellow. I think he's got something to do with the drought."

With six pairs of eyes staring holes into him, he added, for impact, "I think it's time we went out there and got some answers." His voice was so stern, so *sure*, that several heads nodded.

"How do you know all this?" Kush asked. Already a couple of the guys were standing. Bart suggested that he could carry four guys in the pickup, if a couple of them didn't mind sitting in the back.

"Does it matter?" Carl said secretively. "I'm going out there. I'm getting answers," he said. "Who's with me?"

"I'm in," Bart said, standing, not so much for the sake of getting the facts as for the adventure. Something to break up the day, he would say later.

"Me too," Jack Greeson added, also standing. He slapped Teddy Lawrence on the shoulder. "You're going too." Teddy nodded, and took a fast sip of his coffee. He stood.

Jeb stood up in the midst of it and held his hands out. "Wait a minute, wait a minute," he said. "Where on Parson's Road? That's all private property. You can't just jump in the pickup and run out to private property and rile up some guy you don't even know. How do you know he's government, Carl? Let's talk about this!" When voices got excited at the front, people in the rest of the cafe started listening in.

"You calling me a liar, Jeb?" Carl asked defensively.

"You know I'm not, I'm just saying this isn't rational. You can't just go give someone the bum's rush 'cause you *think* he *might* have *something* to do with *something else*! You'll get us all in trouble. Tell us what you know."

"I know he's got maps of the drought area! I know he's sneaking around! I know that since he got here, a goddamn bunch of pretty strange things been happening and I know he's gotta have something to do with it! What's your theory on it, Trainor? That he's the Fuller Brush Man and he's just here to clean some toilets?"

The cafe got very quiet. Carl and Jeb were standing almost nose to nose, and Teddy Lawrence nervously sat down. Grace came over to the table and Kush stood up, putting his hands between the two men and nudging them apart.

"Okay, okay, let's settle down. This is a public place and you don't want to start any fights. Jeb, just listen to what Carl's got to say. Some of us are interested."

"Now, what's going on over on Parson's?" Gracie said. She had the coffeepot in one hand and she was ready to dump it on the first one to throw a punch. If they were going to act like animals in her place of business, she would treat them as such.

"It's all right, Gracie," Kush said. "Just a difference of opinion. It's fine now. Why don't you get Carl a cup of coffee?"

From the other side of the restaurant, someone piped up, "I wanna hear what he's saying!" It was Debbie Freeman from the zoning office. "What did you say about the drought?" Her dad had a stroke last year, right on the farm. He was learning how to walk again, but sounded like a five-year-old when he talked. Debbie blamed the drought; people agreed with her, even if no one ever said it. He wasn't the only one done in physically, or emotionally, by the drought. A few people muttered in agreement. They wanted to hear what Carl was saying, too.

Carl turned so that he was addressing everyone in the cafe.

"I saw a government man messing around on the old Mann property. Where Karen Grange is living. He's set up in the orchard over there, and I just wanna take a trip over there and get some answers. I don't know about the rest of you, but I'm bloody tired of being lied to," he said loudly. "I want to know what they're doing about it. I wanna know what kind of tests they've been doing down there"—he punched the word *tests,* hoping people would get his meaning without his having to explain. "I wanna know when they're going to share it with the rest of us. It's only our town," he added, his voice heavy with sarcasm. "I'm going out there right now. Anyone who wants to, can come with me." There was general confusion and some muttered discussion, much of it in support of Carl. A couple of people stood up and moved toward the front of the restaurant.

"Hold on," Jeb called out. "We don't know who this guy is. Maybe he's a surveyor, maybe he's a drifter, camping out, maybe he's a friend of Karen Grange's. Why don't we ask *her* who he is? If he's on her property, she'll know who he is. Kush, call the bank and ask her," he said.

"She's sick," Leonard Franklin said quietly, from his table by the window. Heads all turned in his direction. "She's not in today. I was in there earlier, picking up some papers."

There was a strange silence in the cafe.

"Well, maybe she's in on it, too," Carl said,

Everyone spoke at once. Some people said they were going with Carl, others said they had to get home. Folks got nervous; one lady put a hand over her mouth and sat silent, her eyes wide and fearful.

Grace's attention was caught by the door opening and closing as a girl walked in. It took a couple of moments to place her. She stared at the girl, who stared back. Bored holes into her, more like it. The girl displayed a smile that made her look worse. Made her look crazy. Then Grace put her finger on it. It was the Whalley girl. *Did something to her hair,* she thought distractedly, and turned back to the drama going on in her restaurant.

Carl was saying, "I saw his maps. Bart, Gooner, John Livingston, the Tindals—where's Jacob?—they all saw a fellow who meets his description, walking past the fire at Kramer's calm as could be. He's out there, on private property, he's doing something, and I just want to know what—"

"I saw him, too." The words were not spoken very loudly, but the voice was peculiar. Sounded like it came from someone talking through a tunnel, people would say later. As though there were an echo coming from somewhere. Mostly everyone turned around and looked to see who had spoken. At first, people didn't recognize her, and then, like Grace, they realized it was Vida. The Whalley girl.

"You know who I'm talking about?" Carl said.

Vida nodded slowly and seriously. There was something strange about the way she was holding herself. If people noticed, they didn't mention it, although more than one person wrinkled up their noses at the sight of her.

"He had a . . . *machine,*" she lied. She knew without asking, and without having heard much of the conversation before. She could feel the energy of the crowd. She could feel their confusion and dismay. It was pleasing.

"A machine?" Grace asked.

"A *computer*," Vida said gleefully. "He was doing something with it," she added.

"Let's go," Carl said decisively, turning back to the people in the cafe. People started to move impulsively toward the door, with Carl.

Suddenly, Chimmy Waggles snorted, "You're going to take the word of a *Whalley*? She'd just as soon lie as look at you, for goodness sakes."

That was when Betty Washington reached over and slapped Chimmy Waggles across the face. It was loud enough to silence everyone in the room. Even Grace Kushner, who had seen her share of family violence in her lifetime, gasped.

No one looked more shocked than Betty Washington. "I—I don't know what happened—" She stared at her own hand, as though it belonged to someone else, then back at Chimmy, confused. "I didn't mean to hit you—I don't know what—" That was all she got out before Chimmy loaded up and fired one back. The shot was ill-timed. Betty ducked some and Chimmy caught her on the side of the head, sending her glasses flying across the room. They hit Charley Blakey on the chest and fell to the floor. John Waggles was on his feet and halfway across to where his wife was. "What the hell—" he said, when Lou McGrath stood up and put his arm out to stop him.

"Just stay out of it, buddy," Lou said gently. What he did next was not gentle. He shoved the troubled, delicate man with his massive baling arm and John went sailing into the table behind him, knocking the table flat, and everything on it to the floor, not to mention knocking over Mary Taylor and Marilyn Jorgensen. Marilyn's dress hem went flapping up until her panties showed. No one heard the pained giggle coming from the front of the restaurant.

Vida Whalley was in charge.

"Oh God, I'm sorry, John," Lou sputtered, and reached a hand down to help him up. "I don't know what came over me—" John backed away from him and got up under his own steam.

Faces, especially those of the people who committed the violence, were confused and frightened. But the fights escalated in spite of the apparent reluctance, in spite of all natural instincts. Those who tried to stop the fighting found themselves creating it, and those who were attacked fought back. It was a riot within minutes.

No one noticed the narrowed eyes or the small, effective movements of the girl at the front of the restaurant. No one heard her laugh. No one listened as she argued softly to herself. No one even noticed when she held her body tightly and grabbed on to the counter, as though trying to keep herself upright. By the time things really got hopping, no one noticed her at all.

By that time, people were spilling out onto the street.

Henry was afraid he would miss Carl. But he had to detour and drive down to his house. He had to check on Janet and the boy, just make sure they were okay.

He found the house empty. He'd knocked at the front, and tried the knob, and it was locked. It wasn't like the Simpsons to lock their doors, but Carl wasn't behaving like Carl, or Henry wouldn't be there, looking in windows and calling out Janet's name. He went around to the back door and it, too, was locked. Then he started checking windows. On the south side of the house, he found what he was looking for. A screen had been pushed from the window—he didn't know what window but he suspected, judging by the curtains, that it was a bedroom. The screen had been pushed out and the window was shoved all the way up. On the ground beneath the window, there were several footprints in the dry dirt. Someone had gone out that way. He called up through the open window, called Janet, called Butch, but got no answer. He thought about going around looking for a ladder to take a peek inside, but calculated that he'd probably find the house empty. The footprints were little, one a pair of fancy patterned running shoes, and he thought they might be Butch's. The two of them, Henry figured, the wife and the boy, had slipped out the window, maybe going after Carl. Which was just what Henry was going to do.

He wondered if he should bypass town and drive directly down to Karen Grange's place, and hope to catch Carl before he did anything stupid.

He figured he would be too late now, anyway, but he hoped he could at least prevent an uproar. He would have made better time if he hadn't been flagged down by a guy in a red pickup, coming at him just as he got into Goodlands. If there was ever a time he wished he had one of those bubble sirens with the importantly flashing lights and loud, authoritative sneers, it was then. But he didn't and the guy was flagging him, so he stopped. The two vehicles stopped in the middle of the road and the guy called through the window.

"Hey! I just tried to go down Parson's—you might want to check it out, call someone, I don't know, but the road's like, snapped in half almost! Can't drive on it worth shit, I drove partway in the ditch and partway on the road. Looks like a damn earthquake or something," he said.

"*What?*" Henry said.

"I'm telling you, I don't know who you'd call, but I'm on my way outta town or I'd help you out, Henry. Sorry." The man waved and pulled away. Henry closed his eyes for a second, trying to figure out what the hell was going on. He couldn't stop and make a phone call, he had to get out there. Goodlands was turning into a damn full-time job.

He pulled into the right-hand lane and drove at a hot clip. Even if he had no bubble or siren, he could speed if he had to. Just then, he happened to glance upward into the sky. He blinked twice, thinking he had something in his eye, maybe the sun reflected off the hood. The scene remained the same when he was done blinking and rubbing. His mouth opened and closed in sheer incredulity.

"Well, I'll be damned," he said. The speedometer on the car rose up.

She didn't know it yet, but she had made the biggest mistake while trying to fulfill her part of the bargain.

Vida had let go of the purpose. She directed what was left of the power inside her to the people. In her confusion, she did not recognize this as an error, even as it unfolded around her.

She stumbled out of the cafe with both arms wrapped around her waist. Her face was screwed up in a tight knot of pain. The voice was hurting her.

The crowd that piled up outside the cafe had taken on a life of its own. A bunch of men, many of them lifelong friends, were throwing punches at each other, some of them making contact, some not. A number of the ladies were crying. Grace Kushner was trying to pull Betty and Marilyn apart. Secrets were screamed out, old grudges brought up, all the tensions from the last four years were pouring out.

Vida had little control over the power within her, and what she did have, she used to direct that power at the crowd. She had her own grudges.

Chimmy Waggles now had a broken nose. Vida had used the person closest to her to push her from behind and she'd fallen into the bench in front of the cafe, face first. Vida imagined she'd heard the crack of bone, but she hadn't. Her blood was roaring in her ears, the thing inside her was racing her heart so fast that she grew dizzy and unable to think. Her focus on the crowd was minimal. People became shapes. The bright summer day she had woken up to seemed to darken.

Something was wrong with her insides. She was hot, burning, there was a flame where the voice used to be, and the sound of a scream rang in her ears. Her scalp was tight and getting tighter.

Much of the violence had settled down, and people were standing in small groups shouting accusations, fighting with words. Someone called Bart Eastly a faggot, an unspoken but not unthought conclusion that may or may not have been true. Bart was gape–mouthed, unable even to respond. Gooner, his friend, stepped in and pushed hard at the man who said it. The man fell on his ass. Dust flew up under him.

"Don't you EVER say nothing like that to Bart!" Gooner shouted, screamed, really. Leonard Franklin ran nervous hands through his hair. His lip was cut and blood ran down his chin from a punch that had landed against his mouth. Ed Kushner, "Kush," everybody's buddy, had hit him.

"You think I'm *lazy*? You think I'm *lazy*?" Kush repeated it several times, his face no more than an inch away from Leonard's, while Leonard tried to deny it.

"Kush—I never said—" And then Kush socked him. Grace stepped into that, and Kush whacked her one, too, although not as hard.

"*I* think you're lazy. I never met a man so lazy. You're the world's LAZIEST man, and you have no idea how many times I've sat up at night and tried to think of a way to kill—" Grace and Kush had a good old-fashioned marital screaming match. It was old hat for them, simply transferred from their bedroom to the street, with her insisting for the millionth time in their marriage that the only reason she didn't kill him was that he wasn't worth the paperwork for the insurance.

Vida was in a space of her own. The world had gone dark, even though her eyes were wide open. She was bent over at the waist and gasping for breath. The voice was speaking to her.

It's coming, it's coming! It was repetitive and unrelenting as Vida agreed. Helpless against the fury it held her in, the pain it was causing, she agreed. "Okay, okay, okay," she said. No one gave her a second glance.

Slowly, the voice let Vida stand and some of the pain diminished.

The man! Get the man! It comes!

"Okay." Both statements came through the same lips. The voices were different. But no one heard.

She stood to her full height, a mess of a person, hair and eyes wild, pain still evident in her movements, anger replaced by dismay and exhaustion on her face. She wobbled into the middle of the small mobs.

"Wait," she said. She raised a hand. She was universally ignored. "Stop," she tried. She couldn't speak, by then, much above a whisper. She tried again, her hand waving listlessly in the air. Tears ran down her cheeks.

"Wait."

That was when she felt it. On her forehead first, and then on her upraised arm. A drop fell from the sky and dribbled down her dust-grimed arm.

The people around her must have felt drops, too, because a hush fell suddenly. The fighting and yelling, shouting and recrimination stopped. George Kleinsel stopped in a bent-over position, one hand halfway to the rotary saw that Leonard was trying to stop him from grabbing. Everywhere, there was utter silence.

Faces turned up to the sky.

Teddy Lawrence uttered a garbled "Waah?"

The sky was darkened with cloud cover. Dark, low clouds hung in a strange, irrational pattern, mostly around the outskirts of the town. People shifted their gaze from upward to around, some turning in circles again and again, all of them the image of awe and wonder.

Leonard Franklin, for whom it was too late in coming, smiled.

Someone laughed. No one spoke. There was nothing to say.

In a matter of minutes, the tiny droplets increased in quantity and water poured from the sky. It was undeniable. It was a miracle. It was rain. Pure sweet rain. It hit the ground with a steady rhythm of taps, sending the layer of dust puffing up in clouds around each tiny drop. The dull thuds changed to light splashes and the asphalt on the road and the concrete on the sidewalks darkened in the persistent bath. There was more laughter. Soon everyone was laughing. The cacophony had turned from anger to joy, and the people turned blithely toward the sky, faces upturned, mouths open, eyes blinking, tears mixed with cool drops from the sky.

Tom had held on to the rain until his hands were numb, had pulled with aching muscles on the faraway wisps of rain cloud from the lush places on the outskirts of Goodlands, had pulled and tugged, yanked and begged, until they moved slowly closer to the center, where he stood, a lone, straight figure in the middle of the dying clearing.

His face was mantled in sweat that ran down into his mouth, warm and salty, then sweet, as the rain came closer.

He did not think. His mind was a photograph of the land, and that only. There were no heard thoughts, no spoken words, just the steady *uh uh uh* of his breathing.

His first sign was the taste of it. A sweet, cool taste filled his mouth and the fragrance wafted up to his nostrils. That was when he knew.

It was only moments later that it was all taken away from him. The door opened.

First there was an enormous rumble in the sky, to the west of him, followed by a crack of lightning. The power of it drummed through him, vibrating from the inside out. It built and climbed and held on to him just as he had held on to it. The next rumble came from the north, as though answering the first. Tom could feel a movement in the palms of his hands, a slipping away. A tug from above him. He opened his eyes, looking up, and there was the very nature of the skies, the black rolling clouds, closing in on all sides of him. He hung on, suddenly afraid. The control seemed to be slipping away.

The clouds began a tremendous pitch forward, and before his eyes they rolled and rumbled faster, toward the center. Toward him.

He lost control. He felt a hard yank on his hands that pulled his arms nearly from their sockets, like a rope scraping viciously against flesh.

The door opened, and the rain moved forward of its own accord, hotly, angrily, as though, as it was, a long time in coming.

Tom could not change his stance. He stood as he had all morning: eyes raised, but now open, to the heavens; body stiff and unyielding, muscles tensed; hands raised, but now in supplication to its power, the power of the sky, palms out and upward. The clouds rolled and rumbled. Faster, faster. The light all but disappeared as they covered the sun; the air around him came heavy, almost too thick to breathe, the humidity gathering on his face, thickest around his nose and mouth, dripping from him. The clouds rumbled hollowly in his ears and this was the only sound he heard, loud enough to drown out the harsh gasps of his breath, the pounding of his heart.

The first drop fell on Tom. He threw his head back and roared.

The pounding of the rain was all Karen could hear. It was a clamor of earth sounds, fast, loud, overwhelming, all around her. She stepped from her hiding place in the trees, out into the clearing, just as Tom roared, his arms up, fists clenched. It was an animal sound, deep and primal, and she felt it in her, as much as heard it.

He turned his head toward her, as though he knew she had been there all the time. There was no surprise, just recognition. And a grin spread slowly across his face, no less animalistic than his shout to the heavens.

She could feel his eyes on her, she was sure of it. They were hot.

The rain soaked her through, slicking her hair to her face and neck, pasting her clothes to her body, making her feel naked. She turned her face to the sky and closed her eyes, letting the rain fall on her, opening her mouth to it.

When she looked again, he had his arm outstretched toward her, his fingers curled in invitation.

She crossed the distance between them and reached for him. When she touched him, his hand closed around her wrist, and he pulled her against him, burying his face into her neck, tasting the rain there.

Karen crossed another divide, and let him.

His mouth was on hers, and she tasted him, then. He tasted cool like the rain, and wet.

His hands were on her back, holding her fast to him. Her own arms slipped over his skin, over his hard, muscled back, wet and slick with the rain and his sweat. He felt hot, as though fevered. His heat covered her and the rain cooled them in turn. His breath was hot, his hands scored her back with their own heat. She wanted to feel his heat on her flesh. She tugged at her clothes, not wanting to break away from him, but needing to feel his heartbeat against hers, like the pounding of the rain on her body.

All was tactile motion: hands, mouths, taste, touch. Together they lay on the ground as the rain fell around them, on them, and the sky crashed with thunder.

He did not speak. Except for once.

"Karen," he said, and it was like a rumble from the clouds.

Henry Barker stopped his car in the middle of Main Street, where everyone had gathered to watch. They stood like a collection of statues, heads thrown back, hands outstretched, the rain falling on them. He got out of the car and stood in the street about twenty feet from the crowd. He did not try to approach or join in. This was their moment. He watched from beside his car, and except for the steady sound of the rain tapping on the roof of his car and hitting the pavement, there was silence.

He watched the people watch the sky. That was how he saw the young woman first.

Out of the crowd she came spinning, fast, stumbling under the burden of the spin. Her hands covered her head, her hair wrapped around her face so that he couldn't see who it was. Instinctively, he stepped forward to help her. Her hands flew from her head and an animal wail of frustration and rage hurled its way from her throat. She clutched at her hair, the scream still sounding until her face was red with the need for air.

People heard. Their eyes pulled reluctantly away from the sky not wanting to give it up, but drawn to the screaming woman. They looked, but no one moved. They watched, confused, unable to break the spell the rain had put upon them. They looked, and looked again. Henry's arm was still outstretched, but he watched in amazement, not really able to move, as she spun out of reach, stumbling, falling, that unearthly scream still coming from her. She ran in a circle until her body fell to the ground. Not fell, really; later Henry would say to his wife that it looked like she'd been *pushed*, though no one laid a hand on her. Such was the force of her body hitting the ground. Still she did not stop, but writhed as though in horrible pain, clutching herself while a jumble of inarticulate sounds came out of her.

"Someone help her!" A woman's voice suddenly cried from the crowd. By then Henry was running to the girl, who thrashed about in the center of the road between the Dry Goods and the cafe.

He grabbed the first part of her that moved close enough to touch. Her arm. The head paused midway above the pavement, the eyes bored up at him, and a guttural, inhuman screech tore at him.

"*Let go of her!*" Henry dropped the girl's arm in alarm. As he did, the eyes, so clouded, so ignorant of what was going on around her, cleared for a second and looked up at him.

What he saw was a plea.

Her head raised itself up and slammed hard back onto the concrete. There was an appalling smack and Henry recoiled in horror as her head slammed down again. Air rushed out of her lungs with the force of the crash, followed by an odd cloud of what Henry first thought was smoke. Then she lay still, and the tightness and pain slipped from her face slowly, as though she were falling asleep again after a bad dream.

He bent over her and felt around her throat for a pulse. There was a faint blip under his thumb and then nothing.

She was dead. It took him a moment before he realized who it was, so stark was the difference between the still girl lying on the road and the cocky, angry teenager he remembered. But it was Vida Whalley. He placed a hand under her cheek, nestled against the pavement and turned it softly to look more closely at her face, not really believing it was her. As he did, her lips parted.

Another puff of smoke swooped out through her lips, seeming to settle around her mouth. He looked closer. It was not smoke, but dust. A layer of dry gray dust.

"Ah!" Henry recoiled with disgust and yanked his hand away, gawking at the girl in horror. He looked up at the people, who were already turning away. No one else seemed to have noticed. Their faces were oddly uninterested in the poor girl lying in the road.

People turned away slowly, unsure, from the sight of the girl on the pavement, some with expressions of guilt and disgust, and back to the welcome sight of the sky.

TWELVE

GOODLANDS WAS IN A STATE OF CELEBRATION. FOREVER, when someone asked, "Where were you when it rained?" memories would turn to a clear, static moment as firmly and closely remembered as yesterday.

Jennifer Bilken, teller at the CFC bank, member of the large Bilken clan, had come out of the bank to stand on the steps with Marty Shane from the dairy, one of her customers that day.

First she had come out to see what the commotion and noise were about, and had watched, shocked, as the riot unfolded in the middle of the street. That was quickly supplanted, however, by the darkening of the sky and the gathering of the clouds. When the first drops began to fall, she turned on her heel and *ran* inside the bank to call her father. The phone rang and rang and rang and rang. She listened to it ring, knowing that they weren't answering because her mother had wheeled her father outside to look at exactly what she was calling them to see. The picture of the two of them out there on the porch, staring up into the rain that would finally save them, and the farm, held fast in her mind, the telephone's futile ringing her connection to them.

She held on to the phone and listened to it ring at the other end as she looked through the big front window, no longer seeing a crowd of fighting people, but instead people staring up into the sky, hands held out to catch the drops.

Her lips pressed together in a tight line, chin wobbling with emotion, as she pictured her father's face. And did not cry.

On a farm at the other end of Goodlands, Bruce Campbell was crying. He stood in the yard with his arms strung across the shoulders of his wife and his brother, their arms in turn wrapped around him, all three of them with their faces held down, their tears mixing with the rain, falling and hitting the ground, sending up little puffs of dust at their feet.

It would be all right. They would somehow get a reprieve. They could get a loan, lease the farm back, and everything would be all right again.

Larry Watson was lying on his back under the trailer that carried the barnyard water tank, with the tank hitched to the back of his truck. The water tank was still empty, the last to be driven over to Oxburg to fill. He'd already been into Oxburg twice that day, filling tanks, coming home again. He hadn't moved the tank two feet when there was a loud *pop!* and a jerk. The left tire on the trailer had blown. Cursing, he got out of the truck to change it, only to find that the axle had snapped.

The day had started out badly, and now it looked as though it was turning right to shit. He jacked up the trailer and crawled underneath to see the damage.

Lying there, he heard a distant, tinny echo coming from the tank. He thought it was birds, dropping shit or seeds on it from the feeder that was hanging off the barn.

Larry was dragging his hand along the axle, checking the damage, when he noticed the tapping did not stop, and that it was regular, insistent. His heart caught in his throat and he would not let himself believe what his mind was beginning to say.

It couldn't be.

He lay still for a moment under the trailer, afraid of getting out from underneath, afraid to check, to even consider the possibility—

He stuck his hand out. In the midst of the tapping, he felt something hit his hand. He drew a breath in and held it, waiting for another. Another came. And another. He closed his hand into a fist and felt the cold and wet spreading inside his hand, seeping between his fingers.

Larry lay there for a full minute feeling the rain fall on his hand before crawling out and running to the house.

"*Mindy!*" he called as he ran. "Mindy!" She came out of the house wiping her hands on a towel, planting them on her hips.

"What is all the yell—" She didn't finish her sentence. She looked up and then looked at her husband running toward her, gape–mouthed.

"It's raining!" he called out, needlessly. He ran to his wife and swooped her up and the two of them spun around in the yard. His two grown sons and their hired man jumped and whooped and made merry while the rain came down around them.

Jessie Franklin packed her three-year-old into the car and stuffed her pregnant bulk behind the wheel, for once not worrying over whether or not the old beater would make it to town with the gas gauge on E. If it died on the road, she had a feeling that there would be more than enough cars to take the two of them into town.

She chattered on to Elizabeth nearly nonstop about the *rain* and what it meant. She tried to remember if Elizabeth had ever seen *rain*. It could very well have been the child's first time. She peered through the windshield as the downpour increased in intensity and drove down the road, with a half dozen other cars, all on their way into town.

As the cars, each carrying a familiar face, formed a small convoy, Jessie made note of something odd. No one had their wipers going. She realized she hadn't turned hers on either. Like them, she wanted to look at Goodlands through rain.

"Snowing, Mommy," Elizabeth said.

"No, honey, it's raining," she said, unable to keep the smile off her face. "Raining is much, much better." Jessie drove to town where her husband would be; she was not thinking, for the meantime anyway, about how little good it would do them now. In the grand scheme of things, it didn't really seem to matter.

Main Street in Goodlands was celebration incarnate, populated with more people than it saw even on Independence Day, more than it had seen in a long, long time, and they kept coming. People from as far away as Weston seemed to be coming to share the good fortune with their neighbors, perhaps as a way of apologizing for not having shared their misfortune. Oxburg, Telander, Avis, and Mountmore were all well represented, but mostly the streets of Goodlands teemed with its own.

Ed Shoop, Goodlands' mayor through thick and thin, as he liked to say, stood in front of the old World War II memorial. He was trying to make a speech. But no one was listening. He finally gave up when Jim Bean showed up with his guitar and Andy Dresner pulled out his harmonica and the music started up.

Knots of people formed and broke up and re-formed, squeezing their way around the cars parked at crazy angles, children and mothers and men jumping out of them sometimes leaving their doors wide open, not minding that the seats and floors would be saturated in the rain.

A small group of children, ranging in age from four to ten, were making up a song and chanting it loudly, laughing as they changed the words, getting it wrong, getting it right, their exuberance tolerated for once. "Rain, Rain, DON'T go away, but COME AGAIN another day!"

The door to the cafe had been propped open and people were helping themselves to the coffee. Jennifer Bilken from the bank had locked up for the day, and some of the people joked that she should open house like the cafe, but it was, for once, just a joke with no poorly hidden malice. Women kissed their husbands; kids grabbed each other and danced; husbands, some of them farmers, some of them dependent on the business of farmers, seemed dazed by the exhilaration of it all and walked about with faces cemented in lopsided grins.

There was some dancing, and even some singing, and people for sure tapped their feet, but the center of the action wasn't the musicians, or Ed Shoop glad-handing his way through the crowd as if he had made it rain himself. The center of the action came from above. In the midst of the clutches of folks, the rain displayed itself in pomp and glory, streaming down in a steady flow, disinterested, unmoved, and unchanging, going about its business without a single degree of pretension. Raining down its rain.

Leonard Franklin and Henry Barker had discreetly covered Vida's body with a blanket from the Dry Goods. It wasn't a matter of not disturbing evidence—a dozen or more people had seen that Vida Whalley, age nineteen, from Lot 27 of Plum View Road, Goodlands, North Dakota, had had some kind of seizure and died from a fall. The cause of death likely having something to do with the god-awful sound of her head hitting the concrete.

Henry wrote a few things down in his book and quietly mentioned to Leonard and Jeb that the county might want to talk to them briefly; then the three of them carried her into the Dry Goods and laid her out on the floor. Henry sat inside with Vida's body after asking John if it was okay to lock the door. He almost need not have asked: people were as uninterested as if she'd fallen and scraped her knee. He choked back the shame he felt momentarily for the people. After all, it wasn't every day in Goodlands that it rained. He did not do anything about the pity he felt for the young girl, who seemed so light and tiny when they carried her inside.

Henry called his wife and told her about the rain and only

briefly mentioned Vida Whalley. Then he called the county coroner, whose assistant, Jim Daley, said he would radio him in the car and have him down there ASAP.

"Who was it?" the assistant asked interestedly. A death in a small town brings dozens of connections, although Henry didn't think this one would.

"Vida Whalley, from out Plum View," he said.

"Oh yeah?" he said. "Kilt herself?" The funny dance she did before falling flashed through Henry's mind, followed closely by an auditory memory of her head cracking on the pavement. The dust on her lips. Henry pressed his eyes shut, and swallowed down bile, very much aware of her body laid out behind him.

"Up to the coroner, ain't it, Jim?" he said, and hung up.

There was nothing much to do after that, except avert his eyes from the shape under the blanket and listen to the rain. From inside the building he watched the people of Goodlands all but dance under the falling rain, the rain itself echoing the rhythm like a mariachi band.

Funny thing just coming like that.

He got some of the story from Leonard of a near riot that seemed to have broken out just moments before the rain fell. Leonard told Henry that Carl Simpson was off his rocker and maybe someone had better talk to him about it. Those were the exact words he'd used, "off his rocker."

"Anyway," Leonard had said, "it's all right now. It started raining and it looks like people have forgotten all about it. Tension, I guess." Then he'd slipped back out of the Dry Goods to join the rest of his community in the rain.

Henry watched as another car pulled up, practically into the square of town. It was Reverend Liesel from the Protestant, walking through the crowd, hands spread out, face beaming. He'd been one of the many who had held prayer sessions to bring on rain. As far as Henry could remember, there hadn't been a session advertised in quite a few months. Probably bad for business when rain didn't come. But the way he was walking around, smiling, shaking hands, it looked as if he was ready to take some credit. Might have some trouble with Father Grady over that; the Catholics had done much the same over the last few years. There'd been that traveling evangelist that someone had brought in last year, too, come to think of it. Maybe he'd show up and roll around on the ground some. There could be a regular Holy War over it.

Unconsciously, Henry fingered his breast pocket where the strange business card had been just the night before. It felt slightly damp, still, even these many hours later. *The rain did it. Shirt's damp from the rain,* he thought.

Maybe not.

" 'There are more things in heaven and earth than are dreamed of in your philosophy.' " Or however that goes. He realized that he'd said it aloud in the dim light of the overhead in the Dry Goods. His voice was funny and hollow in the mostly empty store. Shakespeare said that, he thought. Or Milton. For no good reason, he always got the two mixed up. School was funny, the way it filled your mind up with quotes that were completely meaningless; then out of the blue, one day, you find yourself thinking about one, and it rings true. Like that one. More things in heaven and earth than you could dream about. Like how maybe you could find a card on the road, dropped by a stranger in the middle of a town in crisis, and then the next day it would rain.

The card had said he was a rainmaker after all. Some silly little motto underneath it, too, which he couldn't remember at all. Something about exercising. No pain no gain, something like that. The card had been wet, and unless the guy showered with his wallet, he couldn't imagine why. And it had smelled damp, too—he could still, almost, smell it. Couldn't imagine, unless the guy had wanted it to be wet. Unless it was some kind of joke. Henry hadn't been drunk or dreaming. He'd had five lousy beers, and the day he got drunk on five beers, he was turning in his liver. He hadn't been drunk, and he had followed that fellow up the road from Clancy's, and he had seen him drop the card. It floated down through the air like an autumn leaf caught on the wind. Poetic as hell. Maybe Shakespeare said that too.

Poetic and coincidental, or maybe deliberate.

Henry guessed that maybe Karen Grange had hired herself a rainmaker. Sounded crazy, and Karen was not your typical crazy in Henry's opinion. In fact, he had a fairly high opinion of her. But desperate times call for desperate measures. Still, he certainly would never have imagined her lying to him. So why had she?

Because it was a secret. A surprise. A really stupid, unbelievable thing to do. So what was she supposed to do, send an announcement to the *Weston Expositor*? "Coming Soon! Rainmaker! To Banish the Evil Drought! Mann Farm, Coffee and Doughnuts, Balloons for the Kids!" No rain date supplied, of course. If she had so much as uttered it, people would have laughed, if not strung her up for her mockery.

Would they have? Maybe not. Henry would have laughed, from his comfortable, occasionally rain-soaked perch in Weston. So would the people from Oxburg, Telander, and so on. They all would have laughed. The *Expositor* would have run a story on the Rain Lady from Goodlands and the CFC brass would have quietly transferred Karen Grange and that would have been the end of that.

That question brought him back full circle to the Karen Grange question. Would she have brought in a rainmaker? But the $64,000 question was for the rainmaker himself.

How did you do it, buddy? The Shakespeare (or Milton) quote came back to him, and he wanted to leave it at that, but some of Carl Simpson's paranoia had sunk its way inside him, and he wondered about the possibilities. Because it could have just rained on its own. For chrissakes, it's bound to rain sometime, just as people had been saying for the past four years. Weather was cyclical, and it was probably, finally, Goodlands' turn. All the shit that had been said over the past four years about global warming had made more men than Henry sit up and take notice, and God knew there had to be something to it, or every frigging scientist with a degree on his wall would find something else to talk about. He didn't buy in to Carl's theories about conspiracy and weather experiments, but you had to be a fool to ignore the predictions of science.

Science was exact. There was no room in science for Shakespeare (or Milton), and funny how all kinds of strange things started happening right when Mr. Rainmaker—*rain without pain*, that was what the card had said, he remembered—showed up. The Kramer fire was not the least of it. There was also the trouble out at Revesette's, Watson's tanks, the poor Paxtons and their spooky crucifix, the car upsiding at Bell's, and for that matter the Greesons' driveway popping up like that, funny as it was later. It had all happened when Grange got her company, regardless of whether she admitted to the company or not. He wasn't about to assign some kind of magic bullet theory to the fellow, and add the Whalley girl dying like she did, but still, funny how that happened too. If you had to, you could also add to that list whatever it was that happened to the road, coincidentally, right outside the Mann farm. And all of it just happened to coincide with the first sighting of the stranger. Funny, that.

And as happy a coincidence as the rain was, he still would like to ask Karen Grange and her friend a few questions.

Suddenly Henry was very anxious for the coroner to show so he could finish up there and get home. He wanted to check the Weather Channel and see what the pictures said.

Bob Garrison, the coroner, showed up just after Henry had opened a box of Fig Newtons to help pass the time. After the coroner took and looked and asked his questions and wrote down his names, the two of them loaded Vida's body up on the truck.

Bob ducked his head in the rain. "This is something, I guess, huh?"

"I guess it is," Henry said. The people around them waved and shouted. That was all they said about it.

"Notify the family, yet? We'll need an ID."

"Nah, they don't have a phone. I'll drive out there and tell them. I'll come down later with one of the brothers, most likely. Whoever's sober," he added meanly. Bob nodded.

He was getting in the truck when Henry asked, "Bob, you know who said 'There are more things in heaven and earth than are dreamed of in your philosophy,' goes something like that?"

Bob looked at him blankly. "I promised myself that once I got my English credit, I'd never have to look at another dead guy's book." He chuckled. "Why?"

Henry shook his head. "Just can't think if it was Shakespeare or Milton," he said. Bob laughed. The laugh from the coroner inside the truck drew a few stares. The people smiled, though, believing the cop and the coroner were laughing about the fortuitous break in the weather.

"Milton?" Bob said. "He write *Paradise Lost?*"

Henry nodded, feeling foolish. "See you down there," he said. He waved for the truck to pull away, and it did, driving slowly through the crowds, which parted equally slowly.

A woman asked Henry what had happened.

"Seizure," he said simply. There was a sympathetic nod, but no real sympathy.

"Isn't this something!" she shouted at him after that.

"It is," he said, but the woman hadn't waited for his reaction. She wove her way back into the impromptu celebration that had taken over Main Street.

Henry got into his car and found he had to maneuver it out inch by inch, nearly barricaded in by other cars. He knew he should say something to people, get them to move their vehicles, but he didn't have the heart. He took the road out of town toward the Whalleys'. He would drop in and give them the news, and take someone down to meet Bob at the hospital. His was the only car leaving, amid dozens coming in. He was sorry he was missing the party. Lilly would probably drop by later, he figured. As for him, he had work to do.

Driving, he remembered something that Milton did say.

By force hath overcome but half his enemy; something to that effect. That was from *Paradise Lost*. Why it came to him at that particular moment, he did not know.

The party on Main Street started to wind down sometime in the afternoon. People were finally rained out. The wind picked up around two-thirty and turned cool. Clothes, shoes, feet were wet and soppy; the dust that had clung to everything had turned to mud that covered everything. Children, heretofore at least tidy, if not entirely clean, were caked in the stuff, having discovered a mud hole in the making behind the shops on the south side. They rolled in it, literally, and more than one mother shrieked at the sight. Not that they minded so much on that day in particular, because they weren't so tidy themselves. Women's hairdos were spoiled and sticky from their hair spray running; the minimal amount of makeup appropriate for a Goodlands woman had been washed away, and dresses were probably ruined. Cheap shoes certainly were, and since most children were wearing inexpensive versions of Keds, the soles fixed on with glue, their sneakers would be useless tomorrow. Besides the obvious physical weariness brought on by the sudden rush of the rainstorm, people were feeling anxious to get home. In some unspoken way, they wanted to share the end of it with their land, with the earth that had suffered with them, and was now, finally, to be delivered.

As people began to leave, a few of them paused and joined in the giving of thanks that was offered by the Reverend Liesel, and true to Henry Barker's prediction, by Father Grady, who had shown up after saying his own prayers in the church, with the echo of God's work pounding on the roof.

Also true to Henry's prediction, the bottleneck of cars was bad enough that it took people more than two hours to clear them all out. Several of the men got out and started directing traffic to get people home, but no one really fussed. Certainly there were no four-letter words, the way there might have been at any other time.

There were some casualties. John Livingstone, who had cut his hand on the fence out at the fire, had been on top of his barn roof adding a salvaged piece of tin in a make-work project. He was so surprised by the rain that he fell off and broke his ankle.

A few people arrived home to find that the bounty from the sky had ended up in their living rooms. Time had marched on in spite of the drought and roofs had deteriorated without anyone's having noticed.

Jeb Trainor's basement had filled up some, which would have been okay, except that he had recently stored some seed down there, optimism having given out to concern over hungry, herbivorous predators.

Not to mention that no fewer than seven babies would be conceived, thanks to numerous toasts to the sky and more general high spirits.

These things were discovered gleefully, however, and not without a certain amount of welcome, much as a hypochondriac would welcome the flu. It was something to be happily attended to.

The people of Goodlands turned in reluctantly that night, and some not until the very early hours of the morning, loath to leave the window, the door, the porch, the yard, the sweet-smelling earth.

The rain fell.

THIRTEEN

KAREN SAT ON THE PORCH AND WATCHED THE RAIN RUN OFF
the roof in great, heavy streams with no eaves trough to impede
it. It was still coming down heavily. Every wave that rolled off
the roof hit the porch railing and splashed up cold, clear, as
sweet as honey, but much louder. Like a new orchestra, depending on where in the yard you were listening, the rain rang out
different tunes: the splash of it off the rail, the hard tapping on
the roof, the solid thwack on the ground. There was also the distant rumbling of the clouds, not thunder exactly, but motion,
surely, with not a hint of lightning.

Tom was inside the house, invited finally, and sleeping in her
bed. He had been exhausted. His eyes had been heavy and over-
round, like moons, rimmed with red, and bruised in thick
pouches underneath. Karen had watched him watching the rain
after they'd made love, the ground still dry under them. While it
fell on them, hard and cool like a massage, she lay beside him,

she on her side, he on his back, looking up. The rain ran over his face, which had a look of pensive satisfaction. When he stood, naked, his shoulders had stooped slightly with exhaustion. That was when she suggested that they go back to the house. Very little had actually been said. She watched him dress silently, slipping on his jeans, stuffing his things into his pack. She'd dressed also, feeling silly, putting wet clothes on, her T-shirt clinging to her so that she might as well have stayed unclothed.

He'd held her hand gently on the way through the trees, and up to the house. She had led him, after that, and watched him fall across her bed. He had said nothing about the destruction in the front room; had only raised an eyebrow in question, tiredly at that, and she had just shrugged. "I'll explain later," she'd said. He'd nodded. She would tell him about it when she herself figured out what the hell had happened, and who the girl had been. She supposed that she should call the police. She was feeling too . . . *lazy* maybe, to do anything at all but sit in the rain and let her body throb.

It seemed impossible, like some Child's First Fantasy, but there was a man in her bed. She had twice gone to look, and he was sprawled across the big mattress on top of the bedclothes, his feet and chest bare. Both times she looked, an unfamiliar thrill had run up and down her until she had to pull herself away from the sight of him.

Her body felt hot, still, in spite of the coolness in the air. It felt *tingling* almost, as though it had been rubbed and rubbed with something rough. *Not so far from the truth,* she thought ruefully, embarrassed. She was sure her cheeks were red and hot, the way her body felt.

There were two chairs on the porch now. Karen was in the old one, and had dragged out another from the kitchen, in case Tom woke up and found her outside. Now and then she turned toward the house and once caught her reflection in the windowpane. After that she had smoothed out her hair, especially at the back where it had knotted up into a regular rat's nest, and as she did, her hands felt like impostors for his, his hands holding the back of her head. She could nearly feel his breath in her ears, the whispered use of her name; she stopped because she felt hot, hotter, hottest and the thought of his hands in her hair made her think about his hands elsewhere and then she got embarrassed and turned away from the window and didn't do *that* again. She didn't look any different. She *felt* entirely different, as if she had been Karen Grange four hours earlier, and was now someone else, someone completely foreign to her, Elizabeth Taylor maybe, into whose life she had been suddenly thrust so that she couldn't find the answers to even the simplest questions, such as where the bathroom was, or her own middle name. Just someone else.

In the midst of the good, warm body feelings, she had another, less qualifiable feeling. Not remorse. There was a better word for it. If she had been able to keep her mind on any one thing for longer than the second it would take to conquer it, she might think she was frightened. The amusement park ride, spinning out of control. She could not shake the feeling, and it interfered greatly with her need to figure this out, to add up the figures on her side of the column until they matched his. The last time she had felt this way, this overwhelming need to *make it fit,* had gotten her into a lot of trouble. What was missing was a balance. If she stood, she feared that she would list in the direction of the house. Specifically, in the direction of the man in the bedroom. When she looked deeper at it, the imbalance was not altogether unpleasant. It was, however, entirely too unfamiliar, not one that she'd had with any other lover from her less than vast assortment. Actually not an assortment at all, but variations on a theme, a theme that Tom Keatley did not fit into.

She smiled wryly. It was somewhat like buyer's remorse. Buyer's joy and remorse. The Joy of Ownership, followed by the Agony of Owing. They could be subjects in her book: "How to Use Bad Judgment for Brief Self-Fulfillment."

She could not think, right then, of exactly what she owed back. Except that you cannot go back to holding hands after you've gotten the milk for free. But she knew that was a mis-statement. A woman could say no anytime she wanted; another "time" was not what she felt she would owe. In a way, a cosmic way, Karen had just spent her last dime, and she wasn't sure what she was going to get for it. Buyer's remorse.

What did she want, anyway? Not marriage, which was the obvious extreme. Karen laughed softly at herself, as nearly embarrassed as the early afternoon had made her. Not going steady, not to be pinned—*heh heh,* as the frat boys might say—not to be owned, not to be kept, not to be had forever. The traditions of femaleness did not seem to apply, and they all implied ownership. Did she want to own? Maybe, just maybe, this was a simple rental agreement, and she needn't think beyond the fact that there was a man in her bed and she wanted him to touch her again, the way he had touched her before.

She had not yet dealt with the debris in the front room, and through the fog of her remembering the touching part, it slipped in uninvited and Karen frowned. Something about it bothered her, too, nagging at her, like the thing with Tom; an omen.

She would have to call Henry Barker. And then *that* would have to be dealt with. She had lied to him about someone being around, and now she would have to explain Tom's presence. A cousin from Ohio might cut it, as long as she didn't giggle or run her hands up his chest while she introduced them. Of course, she would control herself ably, but Henry was not a fool. Maybe she should just clean up the mess and leave it at that. Did she really need to involve the police?

Who was she, the girl who had come? Karen did not know her, even though there was something vaguely familiar about her. If she set such an experience down on paper, in her usual columns to come up with a balance, she would ask: Who was she, and is she likely to come again? The most logical assumption was that the girl was the daughter or wife of someone who had been burned by the bank. Just because Karen didn't recognize her didn't mean she wasn't from Goodlands. Would she

come back? The damage was done. Karen had been appropriately frightened, and besides all of that, there had been a miracu-
lous turn of events. It was raining. The porch was soaked
halfway to the door. Karen had slipped off her shoes out at the
clearing and they were still there, maybe two little pails of water
by then, and her feet were dirty and wet. She raised her long legs
and rested her ankles on the railing, the rain running over them
from the roof like water from a faucet. Cold, hard, wonderful.

Later she would go and see what was damaged beyond repair.
A number of picture frames, some of them antique, were destroyed. The pictures would likely be all right. The small table in
the corner had split in half, and she had paid three hundred dollars
for that table, solid oak it was, quaintly called a parlor table, originally owned by someone now dead. (A small part of her mind refused to let go of that. *Oak?* Split in *half?* How could that
happen?) Vases, many of them crystal or porcelain, expensive as
hell, of course, were shattered. A long swipe had been taken at the
sofa and the chair near the window; they could be repaired, although the repair would show. Lived in, was how it would finally
look. The museum quality of her home would be lost, and that
wasn't necessarily a bad thing. Perhaps she should find the girl and
thank her? Unlikely.

Karen was shocked by how far away her beautiful things
seemed. As though their destruction had happened to the other
Karen Grange, and she was now someone else. There was another feeling that went along with the destruction of her *stuff,*
because that's what it was, only *stuff,* and it was somewhere in
the neighborhood of relief. Bad memories that were finally, magically erased, due to some computer foul-up that awarded large
amounts of cash to someone, instead of overbilling. Like when
the instant teller spit out an extra twenty because two bills were
stuck together. A no-obligation-to-purchase bonus.

Physically, on the other hand, her feeling was *warm.* Warm
everywhere, from the inside out. A squishy, soft warm, centered
in a place that Karen did not normally think about.

There was the matter of insurance and more paper to deal with, but that was something for the future. Insurance would cover everything. Without really thinking about it, Karen calculated the amount and realized something coincidental, ironic, and really, in the scheme of things, pretty hilarious. Insurance for her precious things—which had brought her to this place, and paradoxically, to the drought, the rainmaker, and the destruction of the things—would cover Tom's fee. She smiled. If that wasn't some kind of magic, then she *was* Elizabeth Taylor. She would deal with it next week, serendipitously or not.

Next week, when Tom would be gone.

The thought hit her like a jolt.

But she had no more time, and no more presence of mind, to think about that, because from inside the house there was a rustling sound and then the back door opened and from behind there were large, warm hands on her shoulders and a breathy whisper in her ear. Her own name.

"Karen," the breath whispered. It was moist and warm and utterly, utterly arousing. The hands slipped down her arms, over bare flesh in her T-shirt, and down to her hands. The fingers of his hands tangled themselves in hers. He crouched down behind her chair, tall enough so that even when he crouched, his head was above hers. He rested his chin on her shoulder, lightly, and breathed.

She tried to think of something to say, thought indeed of many things (*Did you sleep well? How are you feeling? Hello, how are you, what's up . . . ?*) but her mouth could make none of it happen. When her lips parted to force something out, all that emerged was her own breath. In lieu of speech, she tightened her grip on his fingers and turned her head slightly so that her lips were close to his. He kissed her, tasting of rain. Her breasts seemed to swell and press against the front of her T-shirt. Her feet slipped down from the railing and hit the porch floor gently, gracefully, and she was able to turn more of her body toward him. His hands untangled from hers and slipped around her, touching her back so clearly and firmly that she felt that she was not a whole body, but just lips and back and skin. Only the parts that touched him seemed present, the rest lost somewhere in the void between who she used to be and who she had become out in the clearing.

One of his hands ran up her back and into her hair, not once leaving her body, reawakening the flesh as he dragged it slowly along. He stroked the back of her neck softly and pulled his face back from hers. She could not open her eyes at first, even though she knew he was looking at her. She was reluctant to emerge from the purely physical, knowing that opening her eyes would bring on another element. She did, though. Eventually.

He was smiling.

"Hello," he said. Her cheeks burned. He looked into her, and he, of all people, knew what they had done. What he had done to her. Shock and embarrassment, joy and anticipation, those two fun couples, arrived at the party together.

"Hi," she croaked out.

He pulled away from her casually, his hand slipping off her neck, her back, withdrawing from her skin an eighth of an inch at a time, or so it felt. He dropped into the chair that she had pulled out of the kitchen just for that purpose.

"What happened to your house? I miss an earthquake?" he said next, as though nothing had ever happened between them. As ordinary as good morning. He looked out at the rain.

She stared at him, unbelieving, her heart still thudding hotly in her blouse. She curled her arms over her breasts.

Her mouth opened and then closed. He turned to look at her and saw her eyes. His face changed. He looked into her.

There was a space of silence between them that filled suddenly with whatever it was she was feeling; then he felt it, too, and was out of the chair. He tried to chuckle but it came out like a moan. And as he stood, reaching for her, his expression changed. His eyes were hooded, sloped, sleepy.

"Karen," he said. Her name, coming from his mouth, sounding like hot, moist breath on her neck. "Karen. Karen." He exhaled heavily and pulled her from the chair, held her, buried his face in her neck, opening his mouth and tasting the place in the crook of her neck. She groaned then and felt wobbly, too weak to stand. She pressed herself into him for balance, nothing more, her head drooping back, without the energy to hold it up. His mouth moved around her neck, tasting her everywhere. It was over—whatever or whoever they were going to be after the fact, the restraint was gone. He pulled away from her only to open the door again and pull her back inside.

Together they slipped into her room and this time, fell together across her bed and tangled themselves together, still clothed, to begin what would be a very long dance.

Carl's farm was in a position to receive deliverance from the rain. Had he started right away, like many of his contemporaries, he might have had a chance. But Carl had other, more pressing items on his mind, and was not distracted by the mute possibilities.

When he arrived home, the house was empty. There was a note in Janet's legible schoolgirl handwriting saying that she was sorry, but she and Butch had left. She did not add "temporarily," although she did say that she would call him later, and that he should go and see Henry Barker immediately and leave "whatever you think is going on in the hands of people who can do something about it." After that, underlined two times, the underscore so deeply gouged in the paper that the last one had torn through to the rest of the pad, was simply, *"PLEASE,"* in capital letters.

They had gone out through the window and used the spare keys in the woodshed to get back into the house. Carl admired his wife's cunning. He wasn't angry at her; she was doing, in short, what he was doing. Looking out for herself, and Butch. By the time he had arrived home, from the deluded celebration in the town streets, having stayed only long enough to get his truck

out and going, he was beyond all reason. He was livid, horrified
and determined. The rain was obscured in his mind by the perpe-
trator. The fact of the rain, and not the possibilities of it, was
weighing greatly on his mind. It proved, he believed, that someone was playing with Goodlands, the way a nasty boy will pull
the wings off flies.

He made himself a sandwich and ate it standing up, only to
satisfy the rumbling in his stomach. He was exhausted, hungry,
and more than a little hysterical.

Have to keep my strength up. He chewed woodenly on the
sandwich, not tasting it, not feeling the cold milk as it ran down
his throat, but hearing, most definitely hearing, the thud of the
rain distantly on the roof, every drop urging him. Every drop an
accusation making him feel guilty and tired.

He felt ready to collapse.

The earlier desire to "save" Goodlands now had a red-hot lick
of urgency to it. He'd had the people in his hands, he had them
and was about to prove to them that someone was dicking with
them, and then it had come. It had come and they had believed
it. They were fools and they acted like fools, dancing around under the rain as if it were manna from heaven. It was not manna,
and Carl would have bet the farm—what was left of it—that it
was going to stop soon enough and then they would see.

It was all experiments. They were practicing. It was some kind
of weapon that would one day be used on an enemy more clearly
defined than the Russians, now that the Russians were redefining
themselves. The Cubans, the Iraqis, aliens from outer space, or
whoever they were deciding was the new enemy, the government
or its minions were designing the ultimate weapon, one wearing
nature's clothes. Dry them up. Drown them. He saw every force
of nature as suddenly belonging in a warehouse in the Arizona
desert behind a big door marked Area 51. If they could do rain
and drought, why not earthquakes, tornadoes, and floods?

The rain, therefore, had to be seen as the enemy, as much as
the man he expected to find in the clearing at the banker

woman's place punching away at a computer, a slick, satisfied smile on his government-issue Judas face.

The problem was what to *do* with the Judas man once he got hold of him. Because this time, he would be alone. The original scenario was one of confrontation by the group. Safety in numbers. If enough people stand on one side of the fence, then the lowly number opposing them will have to abide by the decisions of the greater. Democracy in a nutshell. The group confrontation in a variety of forms, be they real or implied, is how governments are elected, laws are passed and repealed; it's how a single laundry detergent gets to be number one when all others are Brand X; it is how running shoes, spaghetti sauce, and garbage bags are sold. It is the way of the people, by the people, for the people, and Carl had had some blurry notion in his mind of his group arriving en masse at the clearing and stopping the work of the military scientist by virtue of Majority Rule. The rest of it was equally vague. Beyond showing up in Grange's field, Carl had not really thought it through.

To kill him might have been the directive in a movie script, but this was not a movie script, no matter how much of the motivation had come from the running dialogue on the television set in the den. Carl still had enough of a hold on real life that anything as dramatic and irreversible as *kill him* had not yet occurred to him. Beating him up had occurred, but that was also something thought of only in passing, more a reaction than an actual possibility. The original plan had been something along the lines of a confrontation, a real-life *"Ah-HAH!"* followed by some equally cartoonish "Curses, foiled again" on the part of the bad guy. The American Way, Justice for All, Absence of Malice and all that, some schoolyard caught-you-now-you-have-to-stop. Tag, on a more formal level. Olly-olly, all-in-free.

The less vague plan (after the initial *ah-HAH!*) was to get pictures, documents, papers, whatever constituted proof and then go to the papers—not the *Weston Expositor,* or the *Avis Herald,* but something bigger. *The New York Times,* the *Chicago Tri-*

bune, Tom Brokaw, Peter Jennings, Bob Woodward. Serious Journalism.

The middle-class world that had produced Carl, his family, his neighbors, and most of the town—excluding the degenerates out in Badlands, he supposed—was still the world that steered their course. In that world there were mostly clear definitions for right and wrong, and Carl, in spite of his state of mind, would never have dreamed of doing something *physical.* If he met the man in a bar after too many drinks, he might, if provoked, have punched him. If the guy had insulted Carl's wife, tried to lure his kid into the bushes, slashed his tires or pissed in his garden, he might have been moved to violence. But so far, the damage was intellectual and, in some ways worse because of it, damage not only to his town, his land, and his livelihood, but to his perceptions of right and wrong. It wasn't something that could or would be fixed by a punch in the nose or the loss of some teeth. Government was like trying to empty one of those Hollywood swimming pools with a pail; if you scooped a pail the minute hollow you created would immediately be filled, and you were powerless to do any more than kill yourself trying to empty the pool. But if you had the whole town emptying that pool, eventually it would have to give way.

But Carl was alone now. And he was entirely unsure of his power. Alone, the situation became more elemental, and such is the way things degenerate into violence. The powerless individual taking that powerlessness to task.

As a child, and as an adult, Carl had never been abused, never been mistreated, had been, all in all, treated fairly, and that was what he had learned growing up in Goodlands. That this was fair and that was not, and it wasn't all that different now from the child's world he had once inhabited. The playground edicts of "Do over" and the black-and-white "That's not *fair!*" still sounded in his brain, however translated into rights and laws and the charter of a man's livelihood being sacrosanct, and that was the bottom line to whatever was going on in the orchard out at the banker's place. *It was not fair.* And Carl couldn't win by punching him out, and he needed the strength of numbers to shout the collective "Do over!" And he was so goddamn tired, and his wife and kid were gone somewhere, all because he had started shouting it alone. And now that the rain had come, no one was going to care. The ends justifying the means. When the faucet shut off, maybe he'd have them again.

Carl finished the last bite of his sandwich and drank milk right out of the carton, draining it, then putting it gently, tiredly, defeatedly on the kitchen counter. He put the mustard back into the fridge and the butter knife into the sink.

He went into the bedroom. The window that his wife and son had crawled out of was still open, the screen resting inside, leaning up against the wall. Janet was very tidy, apparently even in escape. The rug under the window was darkly stained with the rain that was still blowing in. The sound of it was much louder in the bedroom. Carl closed the window to muffle the sound. Briefly, he looked out into the yard, and farther into his fields, the barn with its listing south wall standing out in the middle of the picture. What he saw was his land, soaking up the water, dark, wet, the mud hole looking sticky, the trees not green yet, but looking almost green in the light, with the bubbles of water clinging and falling off. He welcomed the sight, and there was a slight leap in his heart at the sight of his land, his world, his livelihood, his son's future. Still, ultimately he knew that this was the trap that They wanted you to slip into. The blissful ignorance of antipathy for all but the immediate.

Carl clicked on the TV and turned it to the Weather Channel. He wanted to see if ET had called home. He imagined the secret conversation like something from an episode of *The X-Files*, with Cancer Man answering in dull monosyllabic code that said nothing, and everything.

His eyes closed on their own while he waited for the report for the Dakotas. He missed it by minutes, but there was nothing to see.

*   *   *

Henry Barker had also flipped on the Weather Channel, but did not fall asleep before the report came on.

He fell into the sofa with a groan. Lilly had waited supper for him and he could smell the hamburgers frying in the kitchen, all but blotting out the smell that still remained in his nostrils, that of the dead room down at the hospital where he'd taken a sober and hungover Donald Whalley, Vida Whalley's middle brother, to ID her body. "That's her all right," he had said, a trifle sickly, but Henry would never be sure if it was the sight of his little sister's body or last night's binge. Those were his only words on the subject except for a muttered "Need a beer" in the car on the way back to Plum View Road.

It was the kind of smell that took a day or so's forgetting to lose. Henry wasn't nauseated by it, just irritated. He'd be perfectly able to eat his dinner when the time came.

Not that he liked the smell, for sure, but death did not put him off the way it used to. He'd seen his share of bodies, or pictures of bodies. The worst he'd ever seen was this woman down in Mountmore who'd had her head shot nearly all the way off and then lain quietly stinking up the old privy where she'd been propped after the fact. It took more than a week before someone noticed she hadn't been to town in a while, and then a few days before someone realized that she probably wouldn't go out of town for so long without telling someone to go and water the garden, and then another couple of days of fussing and speculation before someone called a neighbor, who checked the house. Her living room had looked like there'd been a goddamn free-for-all in it. Her purse, keys, and car were all present and accounted for. The toilet in the bathroom was unflushed. Who leaves the house with a full toilet?

They checked the grounds for her and while everyone noticed the smell coming from the privy, well, for goodness sakes, it *was* a privy and it wasn't until the law got called in that a thorough search of about two minutes turned her up in the outhouse, propped up sitting over the hole as if she were taking one last crap. Henry'd tossed more than just his cookies that day. He figured later that half his stomach was in the thistles grown up along the path to the outdoor. Turned out later it was a scorned and demented boyfriend from the city who was happy enough to get caught, filled with remorse and shrugging off a bad drunk—and wasn't that an old story? No, death didn't bother Henry. Besides, the Whalley girl wasn't murdered or killed in a car crash, two of the worst ways to go. She looked like she'd died of something unhealthy, like a bad can of tuna, or the flu. Something where you throw up a lot. She looked bad.

He'd gone from there to the office, where he tried to write up a report on the whole sorry deal. He would wait for a cause of death from the coroner to fill in that part. Wouldn't hurt to leave it overnight; it wasn't as if her corpse were going to rise up and start demanding he finish the paperwork, like some nasty official in a Stephen King novel. Henry had other things on his mind.

There was the matter of Parson's Road, but he'd given the county a call and they were sending the road crew out tomorrow, so that was half taken care of, too. He'd had to lie a little bit, but that was okay. What he mostly wanted then was an end to the whole mess. He wanted to talk to Karen Grange, so surprisingly slick and closemouthed about her house guest. He had to wonder if she knew it was against the rules to lie to the law. He wanted an explanation and some closure. Wasn't that what the psychiatrists called it? Closure?

Closure as to why she lied. Closure as to whether or not the man who had been seen walking plain as day up her driveway was in fact her house guest, and whether or not he had started the fire out at Kramer's. Closure as to what the hell he had brought with him that made the town go bloody crazy the minute he arrived. Closure as to when the guy was leaving. And a few closures that were a little less on the record. Such as why he had dropped Henry the message he did, and where it went all on its own, because he knew as well as he knew his own arm that he hadn't touched it after slipping it into his pocket.

Closure as to what the hell was going on down there on that property. Karen Grange's arrival in Goodlands—if the gossips were to be believed—was also somewhat coincidental. Drought, that grisly situation with the body, everybody losing their farms. Not that he was putting any stock in any of that, he was just pissed off, not only because she lied, but because there was something hinky about the whole thing and he had no handle whatsoever on any of it.

The Whalley girl, for instance. Little tiny thing, really, but most girls that age appeared that way, before they hit twenty-five or so and started packing on the chocolates and potato chips. They all looked tiny as hell to Henry, and he liked them better when they started meating up, like his own Lilly. A man could grab on to something if he needed to (although discretion and the marriage bed demanded that he insist, "You're not *fat*, Lilly. You look good," whenever she asked). But he'd noticed something else about the girl when she was lying there under the blanket in the Dry Goods, and noticed it again when she was being ID'd by her no-good brother. Tiny little feet. Not unlike the tiny little footprint he'd seen in the mud out at Watson's place after the tanks had been so cruelly emptied. While Bob Garrison had Donald signing the forms to release the girl to the funeral home over in Avis, Henry had discreetly slipped a little sneaker off the girl's foot and taken a look inside. Size four, it was, *tiny* was right. Henry didn't think he'd ever heard of a size four, but there it was, black number inside a white circle, and just for good measure, he'd grabbed the tape measure off the shelf and gave the shoe a measure, taking note of the print, although he didn't remember a clear shoe print at Watson's—the mud had been soft and runny and he'd barely got a shot of the print before it started melting away. He'd also measured it, like a good cop. Vida's sneaker was roughly the same, if he recalled; he would check the numbers later. Funny that, too. He had a feeling he was never going to get the proper answers to any of it.

He had to take care of that, and then he was going to deal with the Carl Simpson situation. Goodlands was a full-time job and he found himself wishing they had their own goddamn sheriff.

It wasn't as if he could charge Carl with anything—inciting a riot came to mind, but he didn't think Carl had really done anything on his own. Henry had heard most of the story from Leonard, who'd seen the whole thing, and it sounded as if people were taking their own shots. Still, he was going to have a long talk with Carl about getting some help. He hadn't been able to find Janet or the boy, but they'd gone out on their own, and he was pretty sure they weren't too far off. Carl was better off on his own. If he could find the time, he'd maybe call a neighbor or two and see if anybody'd seen them.

For now, he was going to watch the weather and see what the official word was about the rain in Goodlands. Then he was going to eat some dinner, and tomorrow, when the rain likely would let up, he was going to take a drive out to Karen Grange's place and see if there was a fellow there shaking sticks at the sky, jumping around a fire, or whatever it was a man like that did to make it rain. By God, he was going to know. He waited for the official word on the unofficial rain in Goodlands.

He didn't expect there would be any.

It was full dark when Karen started doing something about the mess in the house.

Earlier, although Karen could not have said when—the day had waned since its start as one long afternoon—they had awoken and dressed covertly. They had slipped out of bed to get snacks and something to drink, each time stepping carefully around broken glass and shards of splintered wood, upturned furniture, the pieces of her former life. There was an almost comic bravado to her pointed disregard for wreckage as she lifted each leg demurely in turn and avoided stepping on any of it with her bare feet. Tom was less indifferent.

"All your stuff's wrecked," he said several times, in a variety of ways, each time trying to get a reaction.

"Yup," she would reply, and feed him a small, sly smile.

"And tell me again, what happened?" he'd ask. She'd told him that there had been a break-in while he was in the clearing.

"Vandals, I guess." She had decided on that explanation.

"And they didn't steal anything?"

"I don't think so."

They had crawled back into bed again, after eating out of the fridge—a couple of cold boiled eggs, and pickles pulled from the jar by Karen's long, slim fingers. They drank milk from the carton. Tom had stopped long enough to pull his wet denims off before getting in under the covers. His skin still wet, warmed quickly against hers. That had been hours before. In the interim, they dozed and made love again.

She woke again at dark. The bedroom was filled with shadows and phantoms. The only light coming in through the curtains was from the moon. Tom's breathing was even and deep beside her, and she got out of bed carefully, not wanting to disturb him. Holding the cover over her as long as she could, she kept her back to the wall, not wanting to expose herself to him even if he was alseep.

Her own jeans were still damp and cold. She fumbled around in her closet until she found her loose cotton sun dress, a favorite from years before, and slipped it on, enjoying the feel of the soft cloth on her naked skin.

She was about to leave the bedroom and attack the front room when he spoke, his voice loud in the dark.

"Still raining." It was a statement. She looked over at him. Her eyes had adjusted to the light in the room; a sliver of moonlight fell across his face. His eyes were open, his face unreadable.

Karen listened and could hear a gentler tapping on the roof.

The sound was hollow inside the bedroom. It would be louder in the rest of the house, where all the windows were opened wide.

"Yes," she said. In the dark, she could feel herself blushing. There was silence between them, while she wondered how long he had been awake. Had he watched her shadow dressing? His breathing sounded no different and she did not turn to face him.

"I'm going to get rid of the mess in the living room. Can I get you anything?" Her words felt oddly formal, considering, and she wished she'd said something different. *Stay with me here, forever,* maybe.

"I'll give you a hand," he said. The bedclothes shuffled as he got up. He was silhouetted in the light from the window. As she had the night he first arrived, she watched him discreetly, head turned away, eyes in his direction as he pulled on his wet jeans.

"I'll be in the kitchen," she said, and left him to dress.

The bottle of white wine that had sat in her cupboard so long was still half full, and sitting on her counter now. She pulled it down and poured it into two pretty wineglasses, suddenly glad that the girl hadn't made her way into the kitchen. Karen hoped a glass of wine might soothe the jitters she was feeling. She had had very little to eat, and her life had done a full 360-degree spin in the last twelve hours. The two glasses looked festive. Two of them. *Two.* The thought mingled with the sound of him moving around in the bedroom and again she had the strange feeling of being someone else.

He came into the startling electric light of the kitchen, blinking against it, his hair loose and full, tangled around his shoulders. His jeans clung wetly to his thighs.

"They'll dry," he said when he saw her staring. She felt the blush come up again.

"I'm sorry I don't have anything for you to put on." She was about to add that they could throw his clothes (and hers) into the dryer, when she realized that he would have to be naked through the process, and stopped.

"Not the first time I've been in wet clothes," he said. She nodded and smiled.

"Of course not. Sometimes," she added, "it feels nice. Cool, I mean. I poured you some wine," she rambled. "I'm stalling. Never liked housework, cleaning up, that sort of thing." She jabbered, feeling foolish. Tom picked up his glass and drank some. He moved to the back door and stood looking out through the screen. He flicked on the porch light, beside him. The porch lit up wetly, the light shining in sparkles on the rain that coursed off the roof, making it sound louder somehow. He sipped. The silence was filled with the rain. Karen watched him watch the rain.

"Nice wine. A good afternoon, once again?"

She giggled nervously, wondering if he was referring to the cheap, late-bottled wine, or the afternoon they had just spent in her bed. She tried to think of something else to say, realizing that they hadn't had so much as a full conversation since . . . it had started to rain. The rain, in the meantime, fell on the roof and splashed onto the porch. His eyes followed it, his face pensive, unreadable.

"Should I put on the radio?" she asked him.

He shook his head, no. "I like the rain." He stood that way a moment longer and then felt around in his back pocket. Without a word, he pushed the screen door open and stepped out onto the porch, leaving Karen alone in the kitchen.

In a moment she could smell the pungent scent of his tobacco. She let him be, getting her broom and dustpan and a big green garbage bag, and went into the living room.

She righted a table lamp and perched it atop the remaining corner table, then switched it on. It threw mostly shadows. The floor was a mess, scratched from the many broken pieces of porcelain, and glass. Two tables were in pieces. The square oak coffee table that had cost close to a thousand dollars was missing a leg, and sharp, deadly-looking spikes of splintered wood faced in her direction. Under that was the remains of a crystal vase. And then there were her frames, meticulously gathered and placed, with photographs of people she no longer gave much thought to—mostly her parents—a dog she remembered only vaguely, an old vacation scene. The frames were bent, the glass broken, the backs torn. Karen looked over the mess, and tried to gauge her emotions.

The wreckage represented thousands of dollars in goods. But there was not a thing of value.

It was okay.

She swept indiscriminately. Crystal, art, paper photographs, all into the same pile. She shoved the first of it into the dustpan, and dumped it into the bag. All together. Not once did she bend down and see if something could be saved or fixed. The work was as heady as the buying had been. Sweat popped up on her forehead, her hands dampened, her breathing was shallow, just as it all had happened when she bought the things in the first place. Her heart raced, but this time, it was to the finish line.

She rushed through the work, righting tables, adjusting pillows without care, wiping surfaces, and dragging the larger, wounded pieces to the door where they could be taken out later, in the light of day. The coffee table could be fixed, a new leg made, a nail here, glue, and it would stand sturdy and even and hold magazines again—and isn't that all that is required of a coffee table? Karen supposed she would ask George Kleinsel if he could take care of it when he was done with the Dry Goods. Sometime next week, maybe.

Next week, when the rainmaker was gone.

She dragged the big table to the doorway and leaned it up against the wall.

She looked outside at the rain falling in the moonlight and wondered who she would feel like then, when this was all over.

Tom smoked his cigarette and tried to enjoy the sound and look of the rain. His rain. He concentrated on each drop, felt it through his flesh, felt it through the porch floorboards as it fell and hit the railing and steps. He heard it and the sound came from inside of him. Closing his eyes, he felt for it. It was there, still, full. It would fall for a long time.

It didn't help.

Like the constant drone of wasps in a nest, beneath the sound of the falling rain, it was still there. The hum, the buzz. And with it was the feeling of doom.

He flicked his cigarette out past the porch rail onto the grass. The tip glowed for a second, like a lightning bug, and disappeared, drowned by the rain.

The steady hum under his feet was not drowned out by the rain. If he was not mistaken—and he was not—it was stronger now than it had been before.

There was something at work.

Karen had been vague about what had taken place in the house while he had been in the clearing. He couldn't help but wonder if it coincided with the sudden crack of the sky opening above him. It had seemed futile, that he was expending all of his energy just *holding* on to the rain, and then suddenly, almost casually, the sky opened, and the rain poured forth.

Almost ominously.

Tom downed the rest of the wine in the little glass and wished for more—in fact, wished for something stronger, fairly certain that Grange would have nothing stronger around. He could hear her moving around inside.

He wanted to go inside and take her in his arms and make love again, get lost in the warm flesh, the humid feeling of body wrapped in body. Lose himself, banish the feeling of doom, replace it with something completely physical. Use her as a barrier between him and this terrible feeling he could not shake.

Use her as he might have used a drink.

But he couldn't do it. Not like that. Not now. And it disturbed him. Tom scowled into the night. The rain, the woman, all of it somehow conspiring against him, and he did not know how.

The door creaked open behind him. Karen came out with the wine bottle and her own glass, still nearly full.

"Would you like the rest of the wine?" she asked him. He turned his head to look at her. She was smudged and looked dusty, but she was smiling. Tentatively.

"Read my mind," he said, and held his glass out.

She ducked her head shyly. "Don't you prefer the bottle?"

"Only in front of a fire."

Karen stepped closer to the rail and leaned out into the rain. She closed her eyes and let it fall on her hair and face. Her light dress settled into the curve of her back, and swelled with her hip. Tom followed the curve with his eyes. Maybe it would be all right.

She lifted her face to the sky for a moment and then pulled back under the safety of the porch.

"Mmmmmm . . . so wonderful, after so long," she said.

"The rain, you mean?" he teased. She blushed prettily.

"Of course." Her eyes were downcast, and she avoided looking up.

"Hey," he said, trying to make her look at him. She didn't. "Karen," he said. Finally she glanced up and looked away again, the blush still pink on her cheeks.

"Is everything okay?" he started, fumbling over the right words to say. "I mean . . . about my being here now, and all? You okay about it?"

"Oh God," she said. "I mean—" She blushed furiously then. "Of course it is." She looked back out at the rain and thought about when he would leave. "I don't expect you to marry me, or anything of the sort." She smiled.

He reached out to her and put his hand, warm, on her back. She did not look at him, but watched the rain. He ran his hand up her back, to her neck, and circled it gently. He grabbed a hank of hair and slipped it over his fingers.

"You have to tell me about what happened here this afternoon," he said.

"I told you."

"You lied."

She leaned over and rested her elbows on the railing. She kept her head tilted back under the roof to keep out of the rain. Her forehead creased in a frown.

"It was a girl. A kid, almost. Terrible-looking thing, like a rat, or a . . ." She struggled to find a word to describe the girl. "A victim of something. I found her in the house. She had tossed things around, I guess it looked like, and broken everything she could pick up and throw. Some kind of nut," she said, and her face clouded over for a moment, thinking herself wrong, and unable to say why. She shook the thought away. "Someone's daughter, I suspect. Some drought victim." She looked down at the ground, the light from the porch splashing over onto the wet brown grass. "And bank victim, I imagine. Indirectly—although I'm perfectly sure that's not the way they would see it," she said bitterly, "my victim."

Tom moved closer to her and gently pressed his body to her back. His hands clutched her waist lightly. She was warm. Rain dripped from her hair onto her shoulders. He pressed his lips where it was wet and tasted it.

She didn't tell him the rest. There was nothing else to tell, nothing she could put words to, and what ultimate difference would it have made to him, in any case? It was her problem, the strange feeling of recognition, the way the girl's eyes had looked into her own. The girl had been crazy; case closed. Suffering from something, maybe schizophrenia. She did not want to spoil the moment, with Tom so close to her, the delicious feeling of it. *Tell him the rest.*

He whispered in her ear, "You know, if you make love four times in one day, you win a prize."

She smiled into the backyard. "What's the prize?"

"The next time," he said. He pressed his body closer to hers and his hands began a slow motion around the rise in her belly. One hand slid slowly over her hip and lower, to where her dress ended. His hand touched the warm flesh of her leg.

She didn't tell him the rest.

FOURTEEN

T HE RAIN STOPPED JUST BEFORE DAWN.
In the seconds after that, a dark cloud began to rise up from the earth, beginning first on Parson's Road. The long, deep fissure that had gutted the pavement yielded what looked at first to be a gas. It was, in fact, a fine, brown dust, the desiccated remains of the once fertile earth, the leftovers from what had once grown and flourished in the agricultural village, dust that was at once living and dead. It rose from the fissure like a malevolent fog, sluggish and drifting at first, floating up in great dense clouds, gaining strength with elevation. As it rose to nearly a second-story level, it began to spin with unearthly, deliberate slowness.

It rose in waves and moved in all directions, eddying and waning, lurching and swelling, swirling in endless patterns, each mote departing in an imperfect dance. Every blade of brown grass, every worn rock, every flaw in the earth was overwhelmed, smothered and overcome, layer upon layer of dust clinging desperately as the cloud moved to surround everything in its path.

The cloud moved so slowly as to seem motionless. Trees, though they'd drunk the rain like drowning men, were screaming their own death knells long before the dust came, and were, finally, overcome by the arrival of this new antagonist. What might have been salvaged from the sunken, arid earth by the earlier bonanza was choked by the billows of dust as it rose and fell, making its way up the road toward town.

The rain-soaked ground, sticky with mud by late afternoon, found itself sucked dry again by the surge and swell of clouds that came up from the rifts in the earth. In dozens of fields and roads across the town, the dust came up. It blocked out the scant light, creating a sort of gray twilight that would turn into a black night darker than the heavens. But that would be later. For now, it moved methodically, wrapping itself tightly around the town, sneaking through cracks invisible to the naked eye, slipping under doors, filtering through window screens, easing its way over people as they slept, the thick smoky fog of it covering them in a blanket of the driest soot. The town, as though in a fog of its own, slept on.

Animals bayed in barns and yards and fields, unheard by the populace in its deep, cataleptic sleep. They did not cry long.

All over Goodlands, the people slept, ignorant of the stealth with which this new plague did its work. Slow, purposeful work. By true morning, any balm that might have been spread by the rain was scraped away by the grinding score of the millions upon millions of fractious motes guided by an unseen hand over the town of Goodlands, and nowhere else. The borders around the town swam in whirling clouds, from the edge of the earth itself to as high as the eye could see.

The town woke suddenly and painfully, nearly all at once, and literally choking.

*　　*　　*

Janet and Butch Simpson had escaped from Carl's lock-in to the home of a neighbor, and slept fitfully in her attic bedroom. Janet woke first, a feeling of claustrophobia so strong and so repellent that she retched in her sleep. Like so many of the people that night in Goodlands, she had been dreaming of the rain. The rain pouring down on her head first, drenching her body in its cold glory, but finally filling her eyes, her mouth, her ears, her nose, coating the palms of her hands, with a gritty, sticky heat, as though closing the pores of her body so that it could not breathe.

As her throat filled with the dream-rain, the soft, moist tissues clogged and made her cough. A small cough that she heard outside her dream sounded, and dragged her up. She existed half in dream and half out, crawling under a tarp in the dream world, escaping the rain, the air under the tarp getting closer and closer until it seemed as if the very walls of the world were closing in, and she coughed again, much louder this time, loud enough to wake herself up in time to hear the rasping, choking voice of her son.

"M-u-uh-uh—"

She opened her mouth to speak, to call out "Butch! What's wrong?" But she could not get purchase on the words. Her mouth was filled with something that bonded her tongue to the roof of her mouth.

Her eyes opened to stinging pain, the gritty scratch of moistureless lids against soft membranes. Her hands flew to her eyes, and she choked, then gasped for breath, Butch and his mangled cry all but forgotten in her desperate bid for air.

She rubbed at her eyes until some of the moisture left in her body reconnected there and she could open them to the room. Butch lay on a trundle bed in the attic room the two of them shared in Mary Tyler's neat frame house no more than half a mile from their own.

"Butch—" she choked out, and stumbled out of bed toward him, dust flying as she moved bed sheets, nightgown billowing up as she walked, sliding on the floor, the floor slippery with a coating of fine dust.

Her head swung, confused, from side to side, as the dust flew up into the weak light that filtered in through a small window. It was like a mop being shaken in the sunlight. She felt the dust under her feet, saw it coating the table beside the door. Her immediate thought was that the place was filthy. How could she have not noticed in spite of the dark when the two of them had made their way up the stairs and inside? The thought took only a moment to dismiss.

Butch was sitting up in bed, bent over, rubbing his eyes furiously, as his mother had, a whine all the noise his throat was prepared to make, dust flying out of his mouth with every cough, like the fog your breath makes on a cold winter morning.

Janet sat hard on the bed beside him and dust flew up. The boy coughed a few more times and then spoke.

"Choking—" was what he said. He gripped his mother's shoulders with both hands, surprisingly strong, given his small size, and then gasped for breath. Panic seized Janet and she did the first thing that came to mind, pounding him on the back, as the dust danced up with every swing. With her other hand, she covered her mouth and nose.

"Cover your mouth with your hand," she said, not waiting for him to do it, but physically moving his hand for him, cupping it and putting it over his nose and mouth. "Breathe through your teeth," she added, through her own gritted teeth. He looked up at her. Two round red-rimmed eyes, red from rubbing, a small scratch at the corner of one.

"What's going on?" he sputtered.

"I don't know." She pulled at him to get up off the bed. "Tuck your head down. Let's get out of here." Together they stumbled in the low light to the trapdoor of the attic room. She glanced at the window and could see nothing through it. Nothing. It was as though someone had thrown a blanket over it from the outside.

"Let's go," she said, and pulled up the hatch.

The second floor was better. The dust was not moving through the air as it had been in the attic.

"Mary?" she called out. Distantly she heard the sound of a window being slammed shut. Then footsteps.

"Janet! Is it a tornado?" The three of them stood in the hallway between the bathroom and the upstairs bedrooms.

"We have to shut the windows," Janet said. *Tornado?* She didn't think so. Her hand was still over her nose and mouth, and she was talking through her teeth. Mary was doing the same, but the air was better. Janet dropped her hand to test it. Her hand went back up to her face again. No sense in getting a lungful of dust.

"Shut the windows, yes, that's just what I'm doing," Mary said as she moved to the spare bedroom. She turned back to say, over her shoulder, "Woke up to it, thought I was going to choke to death." Janet nodded, indicating she should keep her mouth covered. Butch lingered beside her, one hand over his mouth, the other hanging on to her nightgown. His eyes were slitted.

"I'll get the bathroom window and then head downstairs for the others," Janet said. Mary nodded and disappeared into the spare room.

Downstairs, too, the rooms had a coating of thick, fine dust that clung to everything and flew up in clouds at every movement.

The three of them went around, shutting every open window in the house. The dust swirled up, filling the air with dancing clouds as they disturbed the layers that covered everything, the floor, tables, the fruit in the basket in the kitchen. Even the curtains and drapes were blankets of dust.

When the last window had been shut, the three of them gathered in the living room and tried to see out of the big picture window.

"It'll clear soon," Janet said. "In here, anyway." Outside the window, though, it looked like a snowstorm, a whiteout, except for the ugly, faded color of it, the color of dead grass. *Beige* was the best she could come up with. She could not see as far as the road; she couldn't even see the flower bed that Mary had put in at the end of the drive. That was less than twenty feet away.

"Is it a tornado?" Mary asked again. Their voices still held a hint of panic, but the closing of the windows, the *action,* had made them feel better. They were still talking through their hands and teeth. She couldn't see their tractor, even though it was presumably still parked in the field across the street, where it had been for two months, unused. Janet thought of Carl, alone, at the house.

"I don't know. I don't think so," Janet finally said.

"Mom, I need water," Butch said. His eyes looked bad; red, sore.

"You go right ahead and get it, Butch, you don't have to ask here," Mary said, patting the boy on the shoulder. "Poor thing," she added, to Janet.

"I'll come," Janet said through her hand. She would call Carl.

By silent agreement they walked slowly and carefully to the kitchen, trying to avoid the dust as much as possible. It was just beginning to settle; the inside of the house no longer resembled a sandstorm from a B-grade horror movie set in the Mojave Desert.

Janet reached up into a cupboard and got a glass for Butch. It was coated in the powder, like everything else.

"Rinse it good, first," she said. He nodded. She went to the phone and punched out her number, hearing the grit as she did, the grinding noise of it, caught between the works. She held the phone to her ear, taking her hand away from her mouth, breathing through her teeth. It wasn't too bad.

The heat was trapped in the house, just as it was on any other day—worse now, because they had shut all the windows. She was sweating. Her hand was slick and chalky and the dust was clinging to the perspiration on her back, her legs, and under her arms, especially. It was like a chalk film. When she was a kid in school, every week there was a board monitor whose job it was to bang the erasers and wash the board. The dust from the chalk stuck to the inside of your mouth and you could taste it for hours. That was how it felt now. Sick and chalky.

The phone had just begun ringing on the other end when she heard the clang and sputter of the pipes behind her. An unfortunately familiar sound.

"Mom! There's no water!" Butch cried out.

Janet closed her eyes. *Christ. What the hell was going on?*

"Get something from the fridge, honey," she said. In her ear, the phone rang and rang. Carl did not answer.

Carl could hear the phone ringing inside the house, and for a moment he wanted go in and answer it. To the safety of the house, away from the flying dust. But he didn't move. He stood on the the cement path—even though he couldn't really see it through the thick air, he could feel it under his feet, under the gritty sheet of dust that covered everything. The porch was between him and the house. The porch offered no more safety than the yard, though. He had to make it to the truck.

He had fashioned a sort of protective suit out of his windbreaker jacket, with the hood pulled up over his head and knotted tightly around his face and neck. He had his welding goggles on over the hood, and over his mouth he had tied a handkerchief. It was adequate, but hot, and the handkerchief made it hard to breathe. Didn't matter, he was taking things slowly. It would be better in the truck.

He moved forward slowly, having to move mostly by memory since he could hardly see two feet in front of himself. He had not yet thought about how he was going to drive in this, but the truck windows were up, he knew, an old habit taught him by the old man. When you got out of the vehicle, you shut the radio off, rolled up the windows, and locked it. The old man used to make it a habit to toss his keys in the air right after getting out of the truck, with the door still open, a trick to make sure he didn't lock them inside. Carl had developed the habit himself, and had

never been locked out. So the truck would be free of dust, he figured.

It would be Janet on the phone. She hadn't called during the
night, and she would likely be worried for him, but it couldn't be
helped. He felt vindicated by the call, and the storm. Frankly, if
she didn't believe him now—if *everyone* didn't believe him
now—then they were blind. And stupid.

He felt his way along the rough path to the truck, mentally
naming the things he came into contact with along the way.

Lawn mower, birdbath, fence . . . The truck was parked no
less than five feet from the end of the fence. He was nearly there
when his forearm hit the tall pole that used to support one end
of the old clothesline.

He got his keys out of his pants pocket and held them tightly
in his sweating hand, and stepped confidently forward to the
truck.

Carl was not sure what would happen, given the thickness of the
air and the question of how long the storm had been going on. He
turned the key in the ignition and it started, a little cranky, but it
started, and it ran.

He popped the lights on and felt, rather than saw, his way
down the drive. He watched for the start of the big fence
and turned lumpily onto the road, the right front tire edging
off the drive and into the decline of the ditch before he righted
it. Once on the road, he drove straight, relying on his sense of
direction.

He realized he was going to be in trouble as soon as he got to
the junction of Route 5 and the side road he took to town. The
truck began a mechanical, suffering choke, and stalled.

The air filter was clogged. He had hoped he would get much
farther, but he hadn't traveled more than three quarters of a
mile. If it was a clear day, he would be able to see his house,
maybe wave at Janet through the window (if she were home).

It would have to come off. With no air filter, he might be able
to get as far as the side road turnoff.

Carl deliberated. Then he adjusted his goggles and got out of the truck, first pulling the lever to pop the hood.

The side road was better than nothing. Then he would walk.

Tom and Karen had fallen asleep after making love one last time, in the early hours of the morning, with the sound of the rain still strong on the roof. Karen had told Tom the only joke she knew—the punchline was "It's a knick knack, Pattywhack, now give that frog a loan." They had fallen asleep quietly, chuckling. *Perfect,* was how Karen's sleepy mind saw it. They were tangled together, something funny just said, the air around them cooled with the falling rain, tiredness overcoming them on a soft, wide bed, the opportunity for more love no more than a handsbreadth away.

Morning brought something very different.

The initial moments after waking were spent gasping for breath, and then there was a frantic, panicked closing up of the house. Karen held a tea towel around her mouth and nose to filter out the pervading dust. Tom used one of his snow-white T-shirts from the knapsack that now lay beside Karen's bed.

"What is this?" she shouted to him. Tom shook his head. He didn't know what it was and hesitated to guess, concentrating on getting as much of the dust from his throat and mouth as he could with great gasping coughs.

It was her landscape; the prairie was hers.

Tom was as unfamiliar with prairie storms as he was with the prairie itself. He'd seen the results of dust storms often enough, but had never experienced one, never been in the center of it. From the whirling eddies he saw outside each window as he slammed it shut he thought it must be a tornado, or, for all he knew, a hurricane. He thought instantly of how the odd rise and fall of the wind in the wheat fields he'd passed coming into Goodlands resembled the ocean waves. A hurricane. A prairie hurricane.

Tom was stuffing a rag into the space between the bottom of

the front door and floor. As soon as the thought passed through
his mind, he stiffened, his hand stopping its work. Not a hurricane, of course, and not a tornado, either. The memory of the
strange diner on the outside of the little town of—Wellesby?
Wellbee?—occurred to him, the blank faces of the people who,
without knowing it, were already on their way to being dead. He
shifted his position to stare out the front window at the pale
light and whirling dust.

Crouched on the balls of his feet, he placed a hand on the
floorboards and held it, feeling for what he already knew would
be there. The vibration was light, hard to pick up because of the
wind outside the door. His heart beat fast in his chest. For a
short instant, he was afraid. Without even checking, without
sending his feelers out into the sky, he knew the rain was long
gone, far away from the place where he'd brought it. Overhead,
the sky was a hard, airless shell.

Karen rushed past him, rags in hand, on her way to the small
bathroom to shut the window in there. He glanced up at her, his
face drawn. She didn't seem to notice his expression. As she
passed, she shot him such a look, that he was taken aback.

"What now?" she spat at him. It was rhetorical, of course, but
her face left no room for misjudgment. She meant it for him. She
might as well have said it aloud. *What have* you *done?*

He had not misheard her. *What now?*

He heard the window slam down in the bathroom, but Karen
did not immediately emerge. His eyes went to the clock on top of
the table so recently righted after having been sent crashing to
the floor by the mysterious visitor Karen would not reveal completely. That's *quality,* she had joked to him. *Takes a licking and
keeps on ticking.* Even after its ignominious fall, she believed it
would work. *Time will tell,* she'd said. The clock read 10:00.
There was no second hand, and he couldn't tell if it was working. He took a few steps across the room to look over at the
clock in the kitchen. It claimed nearly an hour earlier. It was 9:10
in the morning. Late.

Yet the light coming into the house was dim and weak, as though it were dusk. How long had the rain been gone? There was not even the ghost of a taste of it in the air, nothing remained of it, not even inside of him. It was utterly gone.

She thinks I did it. The dust fell accusingly around him, floating slowly, as if wanting to be in evidence a little while longer.

He was surprised to find himself hurt, his sudden half grin both sheepish and wry. She had thought negatively about him, probably still did, even though by now she would have had time to wake up, to look around her and realize that this wasn't his doing. *I don't do dust,* he thought. *I do rain.*

What now, indeed. It was the hurt feelings that got to him most readily. Cumbersome baggage after years of light travel. Feelings, somehow especially for this woman, were best avoided. Did he have feelings for her? He was surprised by the revelation that he did. He had spent so much of the last few days not thinking about his feelings for her, that at that moment he was wholly unable to deal with them.

His immediate impulse was to leave, make tracks, be gone, make it a memory. The silent and ever-present vibration under his feet, coupled with the unresolved responsibility for the woman, sank inside him. He could not go. Because there was something else at work here, and even if it had nothing to do with him, even if he could do nothing to relieve it, even if the drought was something between God and Goodlands, he still had to stay. He couldn't leave her here alone, to face this. What if it got worse; what if something else happened?

Besides, now twice challenged in the same place, he was at the mercy of his ego. As arrogant as it might seem later, he felt compelled to push back.

Whatever Goodlands was in the middle of, Tom was too.

Just as the rain had stopped, the dust storm began to settle. Bit by bit, it abated around Goodlands, the swirling wind that carried it high and low over the town slowed nearly to an end, and the dust seemed to hover. Around the banker's house, however, the real storm was just beginning. Above the ground, in a cloud that shifted its shape and moved through the thick, overcast air filled with dust. The form of it was roughly elongated and curved, giving the impression of a woman, much the way a fluffy cloud will look like an old man, a poodle, a mountain range. Its billowing form moved along the roads and fields of Goodlands, with one destination in mind. No one noticed, because in the midst of the storm, everyone had his own demons to flee.

Karen was regretting her words. She'd spoken out of fear, out of panic, speaking instinctively from the only perspective she had handy. She knew she'd hurt him. The look of pain on his face had been naked and surprised. He'd quickly recovered, but it had been there all the same.

Fool. She simply had been foolish from the start, believing that someone could play with nature and get away with it. The old thought that Goodlands was being punished—and now, apparently, repunished—came back to her and for a moment she froze. It couldn't be. Her anger wouldn't let her off the hook.

Fool. Fool. Fool.

Under the anger, too small and weak to make it to the surface was the crucial question: *Why? To what end?* She ignored it in favor of a logical assumption. It was Tom's rain, ergo, Tom's dust. *Why?* was a question fools ask, stalling for time.

Still, how could he ruin what had just started? *On both counts,* she added to herself.

He was standing in the kitchen when she came out. The worst of the dust had settled. That storm, at least, was over.

She avoided his eyes. She went to the sink and turned on the tap. It groaned and sputtered, but nothing came out. It was what she had expected. Leaning over the sink, she rested her head in her hands and shook it. She didn't understand. Maybe the place was cursed. Maybe she was.

Karen was unprepared for his hand on her arm, and the force of it turning her around to face him.

"You think I did this," he said. It was a statement and not a question. "After everything. You think I did this." She still avoided his eyes.

"I don't know," she said finally. It was unconvincing.

"Why would I do this?" That was a question, but not softly asked, not pleading, not defending, but rational. He chuckled wryly. "If nothing else, there's the money . . ." he added, letting it trail off, reducing the last twenty-four hours to their original arrangement. She was shocked and—without admitting it—hurt.

"It comes back to that, then?" she said dully. She turned away from him, but he caught her, pulling her back.

"No," he said. There was a moment during which everything hung between them. Neither of them believed it was the money; neither of them was willing to withdraw the words spoken. She wanted nothing more in the world than for his face to soften, for it to lose the hard look it held. Tom wanted to say that the money was nothing at all anymore, that he would stay. That he would fix this. For her. For Goodlands, if that was what she wanted. In that space of time they made their choices.

"Can you fix it?" she said, finally.

"I don't know."

"Will you try?" Under his feet he could feel the hum, rising and falling like a heartbeat. It was more than drought and rain. The old words about Goodlands doing penance came back to him.

"Do you love me?" he asked her. For a long time, she didn't answer, didn't think she could. She shook her head, and at first he thought she meant no, she didn't. Then she answered.

"Yes," she said, and raised her eyes to his.

He nodded slowly, but did not say he loved her. "I'll try," he said, and gently let go of her arm.

Henry Barker was making Goodlands his first stop of the day. He bypassed the Weston office, having called in for messages instead. There was only one: barking dog, second warning. The be-all and end-all of crime overnight would result in a ticket. *Thank God,* he thought.

Once in the car, he realized it was a beautiful day. That, and the fact that he hadn't missed out on anything overnight, brightened his spirits. Hell, it had even rained in Goodlands. Maybe things were looking up. By noon, it would be hot as hell, but right now there was a nice light breeze to keep things bearable. He rolled down the window, hung his arm out, catching the sun, and drove to Goodlands to take care of the Carl business before something else happened. He whistled the theme from *The Andy Griffith Show,* the only tune he could whistle, and he did it well.

About four miles outside of Goodlands, the whistle died on his lips.

Up ahead, on the straight stretch of road into Goodlands, was a goddamn wall, high as the sky, and as wide on both sides as the horizon. The bloody Great Wall of China, transported overnight to Goodlands, North Dakota.

"What in hell—"

His foot instinctively let up on the gas as he approached. *Danger, danger.* His body reacted, even as his mind struggled in vain to grasp what was happening. As the car idled, he heard the slight scrape of something blowing onto the windshield. It was distinctive enough to make him squint into the bright sunshine to see. The sound reminded him of driving through the grit blown up by the street cleaners as they drove along the gravel shoulders on their way to the next town.

Flying gravel?

A clear line of dirt formed along the seam of the car where the windshield met the hood. Not dirt, dust. Road dust?

It got thicker as he approached the town limits. It blew freely in the air, tiny whorls of it spinning in the breeze, forcing him to slow his car down to a crawl.

By golly. It's thick as soup over there. He stopped the car about ten feet from where the wall stood—there was no other way to describe it, it was a goddamn wall.

He got out of the car. His head tilted back on his shoulders as he looked up in amazement. Then he turned from side to side and realized he could not see the end of it. He simply stared, aghast, his head making the up-down, side-to-side motion again and again. It was a writhing, undulating mass of something fine, gray—no, colorless, really. What? Sand? There wasn't a quarry within miles.

It was blowing in the air around him, clinging to his shirt where the perspiration had soaked through. When he finally closed his mouth, he could taste and hear the grit crunching between his teeth. It tasted dry and chalky.

Dust. Prairie dust.

He rubbed at the grit settling over his eyes. Absurdly, he wondered about the rain. *Would've thought the rain'd wash it away before this.*

He moved closer to the giant, swirling wall of motion and stared, bewildered and incredulous. Then, unable to stop himself, he reached out, ignoring the fear building inside him, that turned the perspiration on his back cold in spite of the heat.

He stuck his hand into it. It was like reaching into a bag of powder. Soft. At first, it wasn't unpleasant. But seconds later, he swore he could feel the moisture being dragged out of him, the flesh scraped from the bone, and he pulled his hand out.

He had to get in there. There had to be an evacuation. He stared at his hand, all but gone under a thick layer of dust, and his only thought was *How the hell are they breathing in there?*

As he stood there, torn between duty and fear, the wall began to grow still, and fall.

Dust choked everything from sight. No one could see the one place in town where it was thickest, where the clouds were heaviest, at the seeming source of the storm. It was an area of historical interest, though no one would have known that, either.

Ten years after William Griffen, the erstwhile doctor of Goodland's golden years, died, a prosperous family by the name of McPherson bought eighty acres of prime Goodlands land for planting—an open field guarded by a copse of sour apple trees, wild and stingy. The prime land turned out to be less so, and it was parceled and sold and sold again, this time to three different families. Joseph Mann bought the front forty, the piece that abutted on the road into town. By the time the turn of another century was approaching, the Mann family had been gone a long time, their forty parcel cut up and sold again, all but the piece with the family house, three acres near the road.

That house had been rented to two families, each of whom left their mark. After Karen Grange arrived, she decided to build a gazebo to brighten up the barren backyard.

The discarded body of Molly O'Hare had been long forgotten by the people of Goodlands by the time she was finally discovered. Dug up as unceremoniously as she had been buried, she was anonymous to those who found her. Soon after the giant machine scored and scarred the earth that had covered her body, the town of Goodlands descended into drought.

The distant hum that Tom Keatley could hear and feel under the earth was this woman's scream, unheard for a century.

Goodlands was being punished. But not by God.

FIFTEEN

As after a brawl, the dust settled.

Inside their houses, protected somewhat from the whirling dust, people stood in living rooms, or huddled in bedrooms, and watched as their views began to clear.

There were dark smudges first, then familiar shapes as the light became less muddied. It could be felt in the air inside the houses, too. The dust was settling thickly on windowsills and roofs. Cars and trucks were buried to the wheel wells, sidewalks had disappeared, and the smaller debris of everyday life had vanished.

The dust settled over yards, roads, homes, and gardens like the snow in the paperweights that tourists bought.

The devastation was only hinted at through the windows still coated in a fine film of the pale dust. It was, however, imagined, predicted—in most cases, accurately. Livestock and pets, left outside or in drafty barns and pens, were deathly silent. Wells were filled not with Oxburg or Telander water but with a sludgy, mucky clay, undrinkable, even unrecognizable.

People were afraid. Worse than that, their fear had no direction. This was not their more familiar drought, or a flood, or any of the other natural disasters that could be listed on an insurance form. This was outside their normal realm of knowing. The people of Goodlands were suddenly afraid of their town. Or whatever was in it.

When they began the long, arduous task of digging out of their homes, when they saw firsthand what had happened to their lives, they did what people do in disasters. They gathered.

Carl Simpson, the man who might have most appreciated the gathering of his fellow townsmen, did not see it.

He had walked an amazing distance, given the circumstances, and was all the way to Parson's Road when he began seriously to weaken.

Had he waited a little longer to set out, had he sought and taken shelter, he might have made it all the way. But he hadn't, and he was slowly being engulfed by the storm that was winding down by the time he stumbled.

He couldn't breathe. The handkerchief over his mouth and nose was coated in sludge, a mixture of his own moist breath and the thick dust. His lungs were full of the stuff.

He'd pushed on by will for the last mile, a man on a misguided mission. He was, he believed, saving his family, his town, and his country, in that order, and that kept him upright for a long time. When he finally fell, he thought first of the letter in his pocket, explaining where he was going, and why.

Carl stumbled on the side of the road, unsure of where he was walking. He had tried, with some success, to stay in the center of the road, feeling the solidity of the ground underneath him, adjusting his step when he felt the softness of the shoulder. But when he hit the loose murk of the ditch, his right foot lost purchase and he tumbled down.

It was like quicksand. He was buried up to his knees and it seemed to pull him down. He did not have the strength to do more than rest, and that was what he did—stay still and breathe, thinking, *I'll just rest a minute and then get up the side*—and while he was still thinking it, he leaned back and rested his body on the dust.

Above him a singular cloud floated.

It was elongated, about five and a half feet high, no more than a foot wide. It moved and undulated as though guided by a breeze, but never seemed to lose its form.

It took the shape of a woman. From the head it curved in at the neck and then broadened to include slender shoulders and a pair of arms. The arms were outstretched from the body as though waiting to embrace someone. From the arms the torso tapered narrow to a waistline, curving out into shapely hips. Carl saw all of these things in the seconds it took to identify them, and he believed, even in his indifferent spirituality and Protestant faith, that he was seeing the Virgin Mary.

The woman's shape ended in a long skirt that waved and rolled in the air. She hovered above him, as the skirts of dust gathered up and swooped over him. Grainy particles filled his mouth, his nose, his throat, as if they were being pulled down inside him, through delicate mortal flesh, effectively cutting off the scant supply of oxygen he needed to keep his heart pounding.

Just before his eyes closed for the last time, he felt her smile as she dragged the last breaths from his body.

Carl's eyes never closed while his body stopped its arduous work of staying alive. He lay faceup, sinking lower into the thick dust in the ditch, until it had covered him completely. By then his body was no more than a low mound among others. He might have been a scrub of grass or a rise in the edge of the road.

The shape above him hovered for only a moment before becoming as indistinct as the wind again, and moving forward. It was indeed smiling as it made its way down the road.

* * *

The dust had begun to settle when Henry Barker went into Goodlands on foot, his face covered with a rag, taken from the car, that smelled of cigarette smoke and gasoline.

What was most apparent was the stillness.

Outside the town limits, he had been driving in a pleasant breeze, the warm day made more comfortable by the moving air. Then he had walked into a vacuum. The air was tight and thick, hard to breathe, or even see through. He kept the rag over his mouth and nose, walking slowly.

He had barely made it to the first driveway when he heard a shout for help. It would be the first of many.

By the time he got to the Revesette ranch, there was a caravan of them with him, twenty men, women, and children, coughing and choking and wading through the dust that was thinnest on the road, since it had drifted over into the ditches, making it hard to distinguish the road from the ditch, until someone stepped too far and sunk into it.

Except for the struggled progress, and the constant coughing, there was no sound at all from the people. Even the children were silent, their eyes alternately on their parents and the world that they remembered so differently. For Henry, the scene brought to mind lines of battered, tortured, fleeing refugees as they moved from one horror to another in search of peace. Except he had never experienced their struggle firsthand, but caught it filtered through the indifference of television. This was real.

As each new straggler was met by the group, he said the same thing, looking at Henry with imploring eyes. "What's happened?" Henry had no answer. He would say that they were heading for town; that in town they would figure things out. Help would come. It wasn't far. Walk slowly. Try and keep the dust down. When the newly joined settled in, talk would stop again. Neighbors exchanged looks but had no words. People held hands. Children clung to their parents. They walked en masse.

Dave Revesette met them on the road with two of his four golden roans, survivors of the storm. They were hooked up to a small flatbed wagon. The wagon was loaded up with children and the elderly; everyone else would walk. When that was done, the caravan moved on. Dave led the horses forward, their noses covered with squares of cloth, like four-legged thieves. They shook their heads trying to shake the clothes off, snorting and coughing, like the others.

"What's happened, Henry?" Dave asked, finally.

"Dunno, Dave," he said without looking at him. "Just heading for town," he added. They said no more because the people heard them and looked up anxiously, both wanting to hear and not wanting to know. Their eyes were like saucers, their expressions hollow.

When they reached town, there were sixty of them.

Grace and Ed Kushner had watched the storm from their apartment above the cafe. When the dust had begun to settle, they moved downstairs and unlocked the door. They knew that people would come. People who lived in the town proper came there naturally, because it had always been a gathering place. They started work immediately, their intention the mundane one of opening for business, but both knew something more important was in the works. They knew the people would come. And they did.

They yelled for people to close the door each time it opened. Ed and Grace wore paper masks from the Dry Goods, masks normally used at haying time. A large open box of them sat beside the door, where John Waggles had dropped it after struggling across the street with Chimmy. The masks were as coated with the dust as everything else, but if you shook them out, they didn't seem so bad.

Ed and Grace did not sweep, but pushed the thick layer of dust on the floor to one corner, making a tall pile. Kush suggested they wet it down, but there was no water. That had scared them. Kush and the Waggles set about collecting every drop of fluid they could find. There were bottles of water in the back, and cans of pop and soda water, cartons of milk—chocolate and white—and jugs and jugs of juice. If carefully managed there would be enough for everyone. If carefully managed. That was what they said to people who asked for a drink.

They gathered. And after settling in, they talked. The talk was hard. Everyone remembered what Carl Simpson had said.

No one saw the shape, formed of light powder, that drifted around the outskirts of Goodlands. Not in the midst of the dust storm, and not afterwards, because it looked just like what it was, an itinerant cloud, floating quietly, seemingly directionless above them. The sun, still dimmed through the gritty haze, did not cast a shadow from the shape. It was undefined—sometimes round, sometimes oval, a wave, a notion, a fancy.

It wavered through town, over and around the heads of the people who had banded together in their confusion and fear. It moved without the breeze, on some kind of energy of its own. No one noticed when it curved and drifted slowly up and out of sight, moving to the end house on Parson's Road.

Henry tried to use the phone in the Kushners' upstairs apartment, not wanting to alarm the people huddled in the cafe. But it was out.

He stood there in the Kushners' neat little front room, the dust making it look like some sort of forgotten museum, with trails of footprints slowly disappearing on the floor. It moved on its own, the dust. He held the dead phone in his hand and listened for the sound of anything on the other end. It was as soundless as a lump of clay.

Slipping downstairs, he went quietly across the street to the Dry Goods and tried their phone. It, too, was dead.

While he stood impotently behind the counter at the Dry Goods, John Waggles came in on an errand, one of the haying masks hiding most of his face. He looked at Henry holding the phone, and drew his conclusions.

"Out?" he mumbled through the paper mask. Henry nodded. "Did you try the Kushners'?"

Henry nodded again. "Don't think you should mention it right off," he said, his words not impeded by a mask. He reluctantly put the phone down, not wanting John to see the panic he was beginning to feel, not wanting to betray it by the futile punching of buttons. It was dead, plain and simple, and he would not make it work by force.

"No," John agreed. Without another word, he went to the back of the store and Henry heard him moving boxes about.

When he appeared again, Henry was still behind the counter, his mind moving sluggishly over his options. John was holding a small box that looked heavy.

"You need a hand, John?"

John shook his head no. "You do what you have to do, Henry." His statement seemed loaded with meaning. Henry could feel the burden of his eyes.

Do what you have to do. What would that be?

Henry went alone. On foot, heading for the only place he thought there might be answers. The magic man on Parson's Road—he snorted even as he framed the thought. It was only a place to start; in police work, you work through a process of elimination, always starting at the end. In this case, the end of Parson's Road.

By then, the dust storm was over, but there was still something in the air, something other than the orphaned dust that floated up softly as he walked through it. The air had a taste like sulfur, almost the way it will taste when a big storm is coming. Dry lightning. An electrical taste. He saw nothing to indicate that a storm was on the way, but felt a surge of hope. Maybe they would get some more of the rain they had yesterday.

There were unrecognizable mounds along the roads, some of them with vaguely familiar shapes about them. The air was so still and the light so muted that he couldn't be sure what he was looking at. He passed houses with the doors swung open, yawning cavities, the windows like eyes. The dust made everything the same strange noncolor, accentuated by the thin light and the still air. Everything looked dead; as though it had been dead a long time, like pictures of ghost towns. The stillness, the empty houses with their staring eyes, the taste of the air: it was all giving Henry the creeps.

He turned onto Parson's and immediately he saw the rent in the road that he had heard about before the big rain. It was massive.

The dust lay in mounds on either side of it, but as far up as the road stretched, as far as Henry could see, there was a depression running almost dead center, filled to about the last five inches with dust. He walked carefully alongside. A man could fall in and disappear in that ditch, gravity pulling him down while dust clogged his tissues, filled first his mouth and then his nostrils, sank into his pores, covered his eyes. The last breaths he took would be desperate and terrified, filling his lungs with powder until they burst—

Henry's heart pounded. He collected himself and set his eyes on the horizon, giving them a gentle rub, closing them carefully and pulling downward on the lids, getting rid of the errant dust that collected in the corners. It was gritty.

There was a large, long mound up ahead on the side of the road, being swallowed with slowly drifting dust. He would concentrate on that as a landmark; focus on one foot in front of the other.

Behind him, his steps disappeared. He felt a change around him; as he moved farther up Parson's, the air was no longer still, but moving. A breeze had picked up from somewhere. He looked down from where he had come, squinting against the dust. He could see, ever so small, the bits of dust swirling in the air behind him, and when he turned, ahead of him. Just a bit. Far up ahead, it looked worse.

He drew closer to the long mound. He focused on the shape oddly placed beside the road, and walked determinedly toward it. After he passed it, he would pick something else. Farther up he could see something poking out of the dust, a mailbox probably, although the air was too thick to be sure. After he passed the mound, he would focus on the mailbox and concentrate on making it that far. After that, it would be something else, and then he would be at Karen Grange's house.

Whatever he was looking at was buried completely. As he trudged, he wondered about it—too small to be machinery, too big to be something tossed out a car window, too oddly shaped to be—

Something inside his head clicked, like a light coming on; there was something eerily familiar about the shape of it. His scalp drew up tight; his skin prickled. He slowed his step, almost stopped. *Swallowed.* It was just long enough to be—an image of Vida Whalley appeared in his mind, not of her alive but of the way she looked under the blanket, flat on her back and motionless. Henry was suddenly quite aware of what was *probably* under the dust.

When he was only a couple of feet off, he crouched to look, not wanting to get too close. His mouth was drier than he could ever remember it having been. The mound did not move.

"Oh for chrissakes," he muttered. He stood and took the two steps forward.

It was about six feet long but curled toward the road. The dust had effectively covered every part of it and was swallowing its way into the ditch. The thinnest part of the mound was very likely—very *obviously*, he told himself—a limb; probably an arm. Probably the arm of someone who had tried to walk the distance to the neighbors' for safety and comfort.

Slightly repulsed, he reached out to touch it.

There is a terrible weight to the dead, Henry knew. A hard feeling, an unmistakable rigidity even before rigor mortis sets in. As soon as you touch something dead, you know it.

His hand sank through the dust and felt that terrible cold, hard flesh and grabbed fabric. He pulled. At first he thought something grotesque had happened, the guy had no hand, and then some dust fell off, revealing fingers. The flesh had taken on the color of the dust, and looked as if it had been formed of it, like a sand sculpture. Fighting his stomach's impulse to retch, he stood precariously on the edge of the road and finally puked.

Blue jacket. Goggles, coated in fine dust, impossible to see the eyes through it. Handkerchief covering the mouth. He'd been as prepared as he could have been, Henry thought. He looked as if he'd set out on a long trip, not one to the neighbors'—

A watch glittered on the wrist as he held it up. One of those fake gold watches. The dust shook off, revealing a crack in the crystal face.

"*Goddamn thing kicked me.*" In his mind's eye, Henry saw the arm raised in front of him, the smile on the familiar face. "*Would've broke my wrist, too, but hit my watch—*" The laugh, from long ago, sitting in the cafe shooting the shit.

His heart sank. Henry reached down and tugged on the goggles. As the dust slipped out from under them, it revealed two round blue eyes.

"Carl," he said, his voice dead.

He let Carl's arm down gently. He shook his head and pressed his eyes closed against the sight of him, not a friend exactly, but as much a part of the landscape of Goodlands as anyone could be. Guilt came then. Henry had known and should have stopped him.

"Goddamn it, Carl." He stood for moment over the corpse, wondering if he should check for a pulse. The dust blew lightly over Carl's face, clinging to the flesh around his still-open eyes. Henry used his fingers to shut the eyes. Then he turned his face away and stood up.

Nothing else could be done right then. Henry couldn't even call the body wagon. There had to be worse than lying dead in a ditch on the side of the road, but he didn't know what it would be. Disgusted with his helplessness, Henry steeled himself against it. He would do what he could later. But he had no idea when that would be.

"Sorry, buddy, but I gotta leave you here," he said out loud into the dusty air. "No helping it."

He stood back a little bit, to the hard, solid road, before he realized that he really couldn't just leave him there like that, lying half in the ditch. He kicked the dust back onto the body, and when it could no longer be seen, he turned and walked in a straight line down Parson's Road. Later, he'd make sure Carl got his dignity back. Henry's eyes could make out a taller shape in the swirling dust about two hundred yards in the distance. It was Karen Grange's mailbox, closer than he'd thought. He guessed her buddy would be there, the *rainmaker*. If he had anything to do with this—with the dust storm, with the rain—he was going to supply Henry with some answers for it. Or fix it, at the very least. He felt foolish, paying lip service to all this magic mumbo jumbo, and yet, at the same time, he felt *right*. He felt he was being drawn in.

There was tension in the house while Tom and Karen waited for the storm to die out. They did not speak and rarely exchanged looks. A subtle change was taking place in Tom, something about what he was going to do, and Karen had accepted it. She had given up everything by then. She'd said she loved him.

Tom paced through the house, moving from window to window until he made a complete pass of the house, only to begin again. It was as though he was measuring things, weighing the world outside the windows on some mental scale, against himself.

Karen sat in a chair by the big picture window and tried to see what he was seeing. He seemed so far away that she was worried. If her face was pale and lined with concern, his was in full color, his expression excited. He seemed to be in a state of anticipation. He was in a world of his own.

When the storm had settled enough so that the mailbox at the end of the driveway could be seen, he went out without a word. At the door, he had paused and looked at her, his face determined.

There was a small smile on his lips, and he nodded. Then he walked out and was gone, a shadowy figure in the pervading haze.

Karen stayed inside. She watched through closed windows while he moved about the yard, as he had in the house, stopping and crouching close to the ground, leaning into it as though smelling it, tilting his head awkwardly in the air, as though listening for something, every motion of his body agitated, excited, full of purpose. He strolled in a circle around the gazebo. He seemed to settle on the place around there, and now and then, he looked up at the sky. That posture, at least, was familiar to Karen. The way he stood, the expression, even at that distance, familiar. He was looking for the rain.

All of her attention was directed out the window. All of Tom's attention was directed elsewhere. Neither of them heard or saw what happened next.

Karen didn't hear the sliding grit coming through the crack under the doors. She did not feel the very slight motion that changed the air in the house, shifting it, nudging a molecule here, another there. Then the air began to swirl in earnest. A rotating cloud of dust and energy starting in the living room, moved forward through the house, searching.

By the time she felt the grit crawling up her back, sinking inside her, it was too late. Karen Grange was buried deep inside her former self.

She had been overcome.

Tom realized immediately that outside, everything was clearer, closer. He was hyperaware of the air, the ground, the living, breathing entity that was the earth. Under his feet, the vibration that he had felt from the beginning had increased in strength. Directed by an inner compass, he searched for the place where the vibration was strongest. The place he'd avoided all along.

He stood in the yard in back of the house, just east of the gazebo. The gothic structure was buried up to posts with the gray, gritty dust. He turned his back to it.

Tom found he was no longer tired. A surge of something rose up from under him. It was the energy coming from the earth. The vibration. Finally, he closed his eyes and looked for the rain. He was not surprised when he found it easily.

It was there, right outside the barrier, waiting for him. He could connect with it through the shell. It waited for him. The sky was no longer fathomless, but finite. Something had been dropped over Goodlands, keeping him in as much as it kept the rain out. He stood on the spot, and let the hum from the ground, buffered by a foot of dust, run up his body.

There was a crackle of static electricity—he could feel it criss-crossing his flesh, drawing over him, could nearly see it in the faded light in the yard. Everything was on him at once; every molecule of the sky, every blade of grass, every ounce of energy from the earth, was his for the taking now.

He was afraid. But he also wanted to *know*.

Before Tom raised himself above the little town of Goodlands, he glanced once toward the house, toward Karen. He looked into the black hole of the kitchen window, but could not see her. He didn't know if she watched; he didn't know if she believed him this time. If she thought he could fix it. But he could. He *would*. And it would be as much for her as for himself.

In his chest he sensed the unfamiliar feeling of challenge. There was something in this town that wanted to be defeated, or at least fought, and he thought it wanted him to fight it. That, more than anything else, was what he wanted to do. End it. He had found his purpose, the reason he was the rainmaker.

Outside the barrier, the sky was ugly. Beyond the thin veil that covered Goodlands, the lightning raged and the storm gathered, as though, they too, were ready to do battle.

Tom reached upward.

S I X T E E N

About a hundred feet from where he had left Carl's body, Henry realized he could no longer see the mailbox at the Grange place. Just moments before, it had been visible. Then it was gone. He strained his eyes into the filtered light, and saw nothing.

Momentarily confused, he tried to get his bearings, wondering if he had gotten turned around somehow. Behind him he saw the morbid mound of Carl's body, and knew he was facing in the right direction. But now it seemed as though the house had disappeared. Then he realized why.

The storm that had all but gone from the rest of Goodlands seemed to be reawakened up ahead in the road. There was a wall of dust around Karen's house, swirling with fury.

Impossible.

Henry was afraid. He held hard to his ground, his feet rooted to the spot.

He had to go there. His reasons for wanting to talk to Karen and her friend were more urgent than ever. There was some kind of hot rock in his belly that he would have liked to fool himself into believing was his cop's intuition. And some very strange circumstantial evidence.

But as he looked at the place where the house should have been, the place where the line of the earth was smudged and wavering, the hot rock of *knowing* in his belly could be easily mistaken for fear. Walking into the unknown was the province of any cop, be it on mean urban streets, or the kinder, gentler streets of rural Goodlands. *You never know.*

He was stalling, his eyes following the up, down, around motion of the dust that swirled so far—so safely far—away. It was all probably foolishness; he did not have a reason, good or otherwise, for going there. He was just doing it. Better judgment aside, he was drawn to the site. *Whatever evil was in Goodlands, was there.*

Forcing one foot in front of the other, Henry walked resolutely toward the Grange house.

The swirling seemed to worsen as he got closer. He covered his mouth and nose with his handkerchief, as he had before. The dust was moving fast, angrily. When he reached the mailbox, he grabbed hold of it, glad to have something concrete, something *real* to touch, in the midst of the unreal storm. Over the grounds beyond, the storm had thickened to the point where the house was no more than a shadow through the dust. He couldn't go in there. It would be certain death. The wind ripped at his clothes, dust billowing inside his shirt, under his skin, it seemed, sinking into his body through his flesh. They would be dead. No one could survive inside. The house, if it was still standing, would be torn to pieces. It was madness.

Even as he thought this, he proceeded by feel, moving through the storm by tucking his head low and shutting his eyes against the dust.

The dust filled his ears, painfully, and all sound became echo, a hollow wail of the wind. He crawled over the dust in the yard, his feet sinking in the soft powder and coming back up only with difficulty. He stumbled more than walked, until in mid-step, he whacked his leg hard against something solid. The porch. Twice he lost his footing before getting close enough to grab purchase on the railing. The dust was slippery and his hand, coated with it, threatened to slip and send him flailing into the stairs. He pulled himself up, wishing he were thirty pounds lighter and twenty years younger, his heart pounding, his lungs screaming for a big breath of fresh, clean air.

He flailed outward with both hands, closing his lips tight in a thin line, not breathing. He moved to the left of the railing, feeling along with both hands, still not breathing, afraid he would swallow enough of the dust to finally choke off the last of the air in his lungs. He had to find the door. It would be better inside. It had to be.

He scrambled on all fours until he was upright and then went forward, still stumbling, until he found a break in the wall. The door. The knob. He pulled.

Henry crashed into the house, unable to hold his breath for another second. He held his handkerchief hard over his mouth. With his other hand he pulled himself up on the doorknob and slammed the door shut, just as his lungs could take no more.

He leaned against the closed door and concentrated on breathing, trying to calm himself.

He felt safer inside the house than out there, in what was surely death. While he stood in the foyer, he forgot everything but breathing, the air flowing in and out of his body like a sweet nectar. He was dizzy with it. Very slowly, his heartbeat returned to normal.

With the scream of the wind out of his ears, the house seemed preternaturally quiet, with only the scrape of the dust on the windows for sound. He leaned hard against the door, his knees shaking.

Get it together, Barker, he thought.

His eyes adjusted to the dim light in the room. It was quiet enough that he thought he was alone. Dimly, he saw the outline of a table in the corner. A dark table. The large front window was letting in what light it could, and in the path of the light, he saw motes of dust floating lazily around. There was the sofa. A cabinet of some sort. Past that there was only shadow, brightening slightly as an archway opened up into the kitchen. Except for the dust, nothing moved.

They're dead. If Karen Grange was in here, she must be dead. It was that much worse in the banker's house. Madness.

"Hello?" he croaked out, just above a whisper. What did he hope to accomplish anyway? The house was empty. And even if it wasn't, what was he going to do? *Hello, Sheriff! Please stop this nonsense right now, in the name of the law.*

"Hello—" he repeated again. The word caught in his throat as a shadow moved into the doorway, between the darkness of the living room and the slightly brighter kitchen. It filled the archway between the two rooms, a distinctly feminine shape. Henry let a held breath out.

"Karen!" he said, relieved, "I thought you were—"

"I'm sorry," the shadow said slowly, "Karen Grange can't come to the door right now." The shadow raised a hand.

"Ashes to ashes!" it shrieked.

Henry was thrown sideways, his bulk hitting something hard and sharp. His breath, what little was there, came out in an *ooomph!* Bright light flickered at the sides of his vision and then everything was gone.

"Dust to dust," the shadow added.

"It's stopped," Jeb announced from the window. He needn't have said anything. Everyone was watching. Those who couldn't get a space at the window were standing in a thick knot behind those who could.

People had filled the cafe, and the overflow was across the street at the Dry Goods. The town office was also full of people.

Those who weren't in one of the four or five buildings that made up the town proper were locked up in either their houses or their cars. If they were outside, they were dead.

Once the storm began to abate, it settled quickly. The sun reflected off the dust as it descended, making it look like snowflakes in the middle of June. Some people had even said so, maybe even thinking it was. A snowfall in June was almost easier to accept.

The air inside the cafe was close, crowded as it was with maybe eighty people, all standing body to body. Young children wriggled and cried against the confines, but the older ones were silent with fear, which was fed constantly by the white, still faces of their parents, who shushed them when they spoke. The only sounds were muffled whispers, some fearful, and the calming voices of those who were sure that it would be over soon.

"I'm getting out of here, I can't stand it no more," Bart said. He started pushing through to the door, and started a near stampede, with only a few of the folks stampeding in the other direction, too afraid yet to venture out. The door opened and stayed open while a flood of people rushed out into the cleared air, the dust flying up with their feet, the storm past, the air still.

The same thing happened across the street, at the Dry Goods. The people gathered in the main street, as they had the day before under happier circumstances. That already seemed a long time ago.

People broke off into smaller groups, families and neighbors and friends. The main topic of discussion was, overwhelmingly, *What should we do?* Gossip was collected: the phones were still out; what about water? The power had gone out about twenty minutes before the storm quit. People wondered out loud and argued among themselves. They should send someone out to Oxburg, the closest town, get to the phone at the Esso on Route 55. Call for help. There were people missing. Someone was going to have to go from house to house to look for the missing— Beth, Teddy, Joe, Alice, Jim, Carl, a slew of names.

There were more than one hundred people in town, but even

that left a whole lot unaccounted for. Leonard Franklin climbed up on the bench in front of the Dry Goods and stuck two fingers in his mouth to whistle for quiet. People quieted down and looked in his direction, their faces relieved that someone was taking charge. Leonard was widely respected, and they waited for him to speak. Leonard would know what to do.

"Listen up! It's very important that all of you stay where you are! Do you hear me? Don't go home! You're safer here.

"The phones are out, the power's out. The important thing now is that we stay calm.

"There's no vehicles that are going to run, the engines'll be covered with dust. We're going to have to do what we can on foot," he said. There was a mutter of fear.

"Don't panic!" he called out. "We have to figure our way out of this, and panic's not the way!"

"I know there's folks missing!" Leonard said. "If they stayed inside, they'll be fine." He did not want to set people to worrying any more than they already were. He was wishing he felt more sure himself. "You have to stay here. There's water here. There won't be at your homes. The cafe has a generator and they're working on cleaning it up enough to get it going. That's why I say it's safer here than—" Leonard was cut off suddenly.

There was a loud rumble in the sky, a vibration so strong the ground shook with it.

There was silence and then screams. Every head turned in the direction of the sound. It was coming from the west. Eyes turned upward, to the darkening sky. Far off in the distance, they could see something moving.

Black, black clouds. They moved swiftly, like a thick, enormous swarm of bats, blocking out the light. Suddenly, in the midst of day, Goodlands went dark.

Tom's concentration on the skies was so intense that when the storm rose up for the second time that day, when it began to rage its way around him, he didn't notice. His face was trained up-

ward, into the light of the sky, beyond the barrier between
Goodlands and the heavens. In the arid heat of the summer, his
body was as dry as the air around him. Outside the barrier, so
close he could almost touch it, was a storm of another kind, an
antithesis to the close, hot place he was inhabiting. He could feel
the electricity generated just outside the wall that held Goodlands dry underneath.

His eyes were all but closed in concentration but though his
feet touched the earth, he was far above it. Then he heard his
own name, called out, close to his ear. Very quietly.

Tom, it whispered, tugging him away.

The sound of it pulled at him again. *Tom. Tom.* Then he realized it came not from around him, not whispered beside his ear,
but from *inside* his head, insistent, constant.

His neck, as though on a swivel, turned against his will.

The dust was thick. He could not see. He was pulled, dragged
away from his work by the persistent call of a woman's voice.
His eyes squinted and blinked, his face a wild mask, only par-
tially aware. The need to shoo the fly. Shoo fly.

Out of the dust storm came a shape. A woman.

Karen?

She seemed to rise out of it, gliding toward him. Her hair and
dress whipped about her slowly, delicately framing her in a soft,
curling mass. In Karen, there was no dark place for the entity to
take hold of. There was no well of thick anger. Through her, the
entity glowed with an ethereal beauty.

His eyes were riveted upon her, taken quite suddenly by the
unexpected beauty of her. Karen's lips were a deep red, as though
painted, but soft, moistly holding a slight smile, a smile promis-
ing dark, wet things. Her cheeks were flushed with color. Her
hair was dark as pitch, framing the whiteness of her brow and
face. She held out her arms. As she moved, her dress swayed, the
light fabric pressing against her body and pulling away, each
time revealing pink, naked flesh underneath, the darkness of her
nipples pressing through. She was a vision.

"Tom," she whispered. Her voice echoed rhythmically inside his mind, hypnotically demanding his attention, arousing
him.

He stood there dumbly, unable to turn back from her as she
approached. He raised his arms to pull her in, his head thick and
thoughtless, save for the woman in front of him.

She smiled widely, and held her arms open for his embrace.
His mouth came down on hers. She felt warm, moist, soft. He
pulled her body into his, pressing himself against the length of
her, lost completely in the fact of her, wanting only to feel himself inside her. The rain pattered distantly in his head.

His lips pressed against hers, and he was drowning in her
mouth, her body's wetness. She was soft, pliable, moist. His
arousal was devastating. Her mouth drew him into her. He felt
himself melting into her, disappearing. Slipping.

Behind him, like a warning, the sky rumbled deeply. He heard
it; it wrenched him back to awareness. He tried to twist his head
upward, and could not.

He tried to pull away. The arms that held him would not give.

He opened his mouth to speak, and couldn't get breath. His
eyes flew open and he stared into eyes that were Karen's.

Not Karen's.

The face was hers, softer, somehow, but hers, familiar and unfamiliar at the same time. He pulled back, and the feel of her changed
abruptly in his arms, with that awareness. Her flesh went from
warm to cold. Now he was repulsed by the feel of her body in his
arms, like a bag of rodents, a sack of something awful. The pulse-
beats, the in-out breath, all seeming at once to be false, terrible.

Then she laughed. A sly laugh, as if she had pulled off a successful trick. Tom struggled to free himself. Karen's eyes were
blank, her face twisted. The only animated part of her was her
laugh.

"Karen!" he shouted.

"Karen!" the voice screamed senselessly back at him, eyes
widening. "Karen!" it called again.

Tom stumbled backward, away from her, his mind racing, ears hearing a voice that was not Karen's coming from a body that was.

"What's happened to you?" he cried, trying to back up, faltering in the heavy dust that whirled about them. He coughed.

"Karen's in here, with me. And she's not safe," the voice said with mock concern.

"What? What's wrong with you?"

"I have to stop you now," the voice said, and Karen's body moved toward him again.

The sky rumbled and crashed. All at once the sky darkened.

The two of them looked upward, at the blackness, spreading thickly. Karen looked away first, her face growing fierce and angry. She lunged at him, grabbing with both hands, catching him off-guard.

The ground shook. The fissure that had begun out on Parson's Road had spread, breaking off into arms that reached into the driveway. It cracked along the ground until they could see it opening up between them.

He jerked his hands away from her, pushing her backward. She fell and hit the ground with an inaudible thud that was lost in the rumbling groan of the sky. Tom lost sight of her in the blackness that followed the lightning. Then it crashed again, illuminating the yard. There was a long, deep crevice in the earth between them. Karen lay on her back, with her eyes closed, out cold.

Tom felt it first.

"It's the rain! It's coming!" he screamed, his eyes heavenward. The dust that hovered in the air between them grew saturated with water.

The earth that had opened between the two of them, separating them, was still breaking up. Before long it had grown to more than two feet across, and the sound of the earth cracking all but drowned out the fight in the sky. Lightning continued to light up the sky at intervals. It was close.

Tom yanked his eyes away from the woman lying prone, the crater in the earth separating the two of them. He sent himself upward into the sky, feeling very much as if he was running out of time.

They gathered up flashlights and oil lamps and lit torches dunked in kerosene. They divvied up and decided who would go, and as it turned out, nearly all of them did.

Everyone remembered what Carl Simpson had said about the banker's place, and what was going on out there. To head in that direction was the logical next step for a large group of people caught in a maelstrom.

They dispersed rapidly. The Dry Goods, the cafe, and Bart's garage were looted for weapons. There were few guns, but they managed to find four. It was like a scene from a horror movie— the scene when the villagers stormed the castle, Grace Kushner privately thought, and the thought gave her the heebie-jeebies, and made her feel guilty as the ugliest sin. She was having a good many private thoughts and was more contemplative than usual. For no real reason guilt had plagued her since she got up that day and faced the storm, as though she herself was responsible for what went on in the heavens over the town. It was ridiculous, but she was unable to shake the feeling.

"We're not going there to hurt anyone," Jeb called out loudly to the crowd, back on his perch on the bench beside the monument. "We're just going to talk to whoever's out there. We just want answers, right? And no one is going to get hurt, right?" he repeated firmly. There were mumbled agreements from the crowd, and several raised baseball bats, rakes and shovels that belied the murmurs.

"Stay together!" he called out. He looked over the crowd, hoping they could see the look on his face, calm and reassuring, knowing full well that once he became another anonymous figure at the front of the line, all hell might break loose.

He pointed into the west. "We'll head out past the bank and walk up Parson's Road," he called. "When we get there, let me do the talking. Let's go!" He jumped down off the bench, and cradling his rifle in just the way his father taught him forty years before, he moved to the unofficial front of the line and started walking. The crowd followed, walking west, in the direction of the storm.

Henry opened his eyes and blinked them blindly. His head pounded with pain. Slowly, as he regained consciousness, he felt around for blood and found none.

He tried shaking his head to clear it, but it hurt too badly to move just yet. He tried to wrap his mind around what had happened.

Karen Grange. In the doorway. *Hit me.*

Except, unless he hit his head worse than he thought, he couldn't recall her moving. Something else must have hit him. Someone else. He'd been ambushed, he guessed, by the fella hiding in the corner of the room.

He played possum, listening. All he could hear was the whistle of wind and the scratch of the soft dust as it fluttered around the window directly behind him. He drew his eyes into slits that let in a minimum of dust. The house was dark. Then he heard a loud, distant rumbling crack, and everything lit up for a split second.

Henry jumped, letting out a little scream.

Lightning. Distantly, he could hear the sky rumbling, readying for more. He shook his head. He wondered if *this* was going to make it onto the Weather Channel. Freak storms in Goodlands. *No,* he thought, *not freak.* What was the word the kids used? *Freaky.* He almost smiled.

He listened for a few more minutes, trying to shake the fuzzies from his head. He tried to stand, gave up, rested and tried again. He knew only that he had to get out of the house, get outside, and for once, he did not question his gut.

Henry stumbled to his feet, feeling around blindly, all the while wondering what he was going to lay hands on, thinking nasty thoughts about people hiding in the dark, about his hand reaching out and grabbing flesh, terrible things for a grown man to be thinking, making his balls crawl up his sack. He grabbed the table he must have hit when he fell. G*onna have a helluva lot of bruises, Lilly'll think I was in a fight.* Half crouching, he found an overturned chair and used it as cover.

He listened. Nothing. The room was empty. But it was dark. He moved slowly, as quietly as he could.

That woman had hit him without ever coming near him. But it couldn't have happened like that; the fella had to have been there, too. Just because he didn't see him . . . *"There are more things in heaven and earth,"* he thought foolishly.

By force hath overcome but half his foe.

"Hit my head harder than I thought," he muttered.

In his half crouch, he made his way through the living room and into the kitchen, where it was a little brighter, the table and chairs outlined faintly, the door just barely visible. In midday. June. One for the books.

The thundering sound still pounded in his head. *Helluva a headache to go with the bruises.*

The kitchen was empty. He rose up carefully at the open door and peered through the screen, noticing a difference in the air for the first time. The smell.

Humidity. Like before a storm.

Karen's head had hit the ground hard enough to render her unconscious, burying her will deeper within her own body. It was something else that forced her body to standing.

Whatever the entity could do to Karen, it could not seem to touch the rainmaker. When she tried to stop him the way she had stopped others, she hit a wall. It forced her to let go of the dust storm that was raging around the house, around the site of her last, worst memory. Slowly, the howl of the wind diminished. Karen's own thoughts were hidden in silence, buried in her unconscious. The entity did not listen for them. At that moment Karen was not important. Her focus was on the rainmaker.

There was another change in the air. It could be felt as the dust drifted downward around the body. It could be smelled.

Outlined under the sky was the rainmaker. He stood alone, upraised. He did not glance in their direction. She could not touch him, but she had the woman.

The entity inside Karen forced her to rise in a lurching, bobbing motion. She wavered, threatened to tumble back down, and then stood tall, balanced between will and force. There she stood, her eyes pinpointing the rainmaker through the subsiding storm.

It was still there, the rain, waiting just outside the barrier. This time, he knew without looking that there was no door. There would have to be another way. There was power, massive power, beyond the veil, and it had to be somehow harnessed. It ran through him, thrumming his muscles and nerve endings like the sharp touch of needles. His skin vibrated with the force that was just barely held at bay.

He could feel all of the authority of nature above him, held back only by a fragile shroud. The rain it held back had darkened it with moisture, but could not yet come through.

Tom's thoughts shifted to Karen. And penance.

The people of Goodlands walked past the body of Carl Simpson, their dead and unavenged hero, in a long and purposeful line, without ever knowing it was there. Not even a rise in the landscape gave him away. All around them the dust had left swells and drifts, rising slightly and falling away until the landscape looked like a desert. They trudged through it, tossing it up with their feet.

There was a terrible *crrrack!* from above. Like a dark room in a flicker of lights, the world lit up around them, and they saw the place ahead, lit up momentarily, the lightning reflecting eerily on the white house like a beacon. The crack had come from the sky above the house. Without discussion, they increased their speed. Afraid and determined to confront what was there.

When the first of them were close enough to touch the mail-box that marked the end of the driveway, the crowd thinned into a longer line.

Henry watched from the doorway, unable to see through the murky darkness except during the fleeting lightning strikes that hit and illuminated the yard at increasingly shorter intervals.

What he saw was the rainmaker, who stood stock-still under the center of the storm, arms upraised, his face too far away to read.

Then the woman screamed.

As the lightning cracked, Henry could see Karen Grange in a half crouch, her head thrown back in pain. Her eyes were clamped shut, and her arms were folded against her chest as if to ward off blows.

"*Hey!*" Henry called out. He pushed the door hard and jumped out on the back porch, nearly falling into an overturned chair. His movements seemed sluggish and in slow motion, a trick of the lightning. "*Hey!*" he called out again, but the man had already turned toward the woman.

"She's in here with me, Tom Keatley!"

The voice was not Karen's. Tom yanked his attention away from the shuddering skies in time to witness the last of the agonized scream that was *indeed* Karen's voice. His body swung in her direction, his arms dropping from above and reaching out to her.

As he did, her face retreated into blankness, although her body was clearly in continued pain. And he stopped, suddenly unsure.

"She's with me! I feel her dying!" the oddly echoing voice screamed at him, over the rumbling noise of the thunder. One of her hands jerked out unnaturally and made a feeble attempt to point at him. "Only you can get her back!"

Then, in the flicker of a blink, Tom saw Karen's face change.

Her features grew muddy, unsure, and another image implanted itself on them. An unfamiliar face. That was when he knew.

The barrier. The veil.

"It's you." It was a statement. Clarification only for him. Then, Karen—very much Karen again—screamed in agony once more.

"*Karen!*" he cried out. A flash of lightning lit up the sky, and then darkness.

He had to strain to hear over the rolling sky.

"Come over to us," the voice said.

Tom was riveted to the ground, held there by the promise of the rain, so close. He did not move at first, torn between heaven and earth. Lightning flashed silently then, and out of the corner of his eye, he saw a figure rushing toward Karen. A man. The cop?

"Hey!" called the man.

There was another flicker of lightning, and then the three of them were thrown again into the dark. A vibration thundered the ground under Tom's feet, and it was not coming from the sky.

Karen's body did not listen, and so, did not hear.

Henry was off the step and running toward Karen, hearing only her tormented scream, hardly registering the dark crack in the earth as he ran. The hole was on the man's side, and Henry was closer to the woman. Unable to think of anything to say, he continued to call "Hey!"

The next time the lightning struck and the light faded away, after the silence began to creep back under his skin, he heard a quieter thunder that didn't sound like thunder at all, but seemed to move the ground under him. From the side of the house light glowed, like a lamp in another room. From there this new rumbling came. The light grew brighter and there was a swarm of people rounding the corner.

First Henry saw Jeb Trainor. Followed by Leonard, and Bart Eastly, and a crowd of others.

As the swarm moved into the yard and spread out in a semicircle, Henry stopped dead in his tracks. "What the hell—" he said.

They had guns. He squinted into the dim light, waiting for another crack and flash of thunder and lightning—they were coming so quickly now that the place looked as if it were under one of those strobe lights Clancy used to use on Saturday nights. When he could see again, he saw only Jeb, his rifle held up against his shoulder with just one hand. Cocked and ready maybe, but held cautiously.

"Jeb!" he called. Jeb turned toward him and nodded acknowledgment.

"It's our business now, Henry. Stay out of the way." Jeb's finger curled around the rifle trigger and he raised the muzzle up, toward the sky, and pulled. The crack of the rifle was barely distinguishable from the lightning. The man, the rainmaker, was looking at the crowd, but the woman seemed only barely there.

"All right, mister! You better tell us what's going on," Jeb shouted above the sky's racket.

The woman screamed again, and took Tom's attention away.

Behind him the sky still raged. He could feel the weight of it on his shoulders, just as he could see the bright flash of lightning on the faces of the people.

It was starting.

Between his shoulder blades came the familiar, tickling rise of what could be sweat, but was not. Even as he stood there, caught between land and sky, the moisture trickled down between his shoulders and soaked into his T-shirt. The remainder of it—and there would be more, he thought with a small smile—slipped down his spine and into the tops of his jeans.

It was close enough to see, misting in the air around them.

Then Karen screamed, that high-pitched, agonizing scream, as though someone had taken hold of her heart.

"No!" he cried. *Not yet! Not now.* He stepped in her direction, not seeing the wide, mirthless smile, or the huge split in the yard. He lost his footing and slipped to the ground, his ankle twisting painfully, even as he tried to pull himself back up.

There was a scornful laugh coming from Karen's tormented body.

Her arms reached forward, across the divide between them.

"Reach for her!" the voice that was not Karen's called to him. Her face was twisted into an expression of pain and delight.

Jeb readjusted the rifle on his shoulder and hooked his finger back on the trigger. Behind him, people had spread out around Karen and the rainmaker. Henry was fast approaching on his left.

"Stop, Jeb!" he called, and ran stumblingly toward him.

Henry could not know what was going on, but he had a feeling it had to play itself out. There was something wrong with the woman, but it was hard to understand just what; some kind of madness clearly had overtaken her. In the dim glow let off by the dozens of flashlights, the hanging lamps, and the ridiculously surreal torches the people carried, he could see something else. He had a feeling he was looking at the wrong enemy when he looked at the rainmaker.

Henry reached for Jeb. He grabbed the barrel end of the rifle and pushed it down as gently as he could, given his awkward footing. A quick, furtive glance at the people around Jeb confirmed his own feelings. There was nothing around but confusion and fear. There was something in the air. People knew.

"Henry, I said—"

"Jeb, that's enough. It's not what you think. Wait it out." He pointed to the two of them at the center of the yard.

* * *

"Take her and I'll let go—or she'll die," the woman's voice said. For good measure she closed her eyes and let Karen's voice come forward. Her hair was loose and flying around her face like snakes.

"Karen," he said, his voice full of pain. He reached out, thinking only for a moment about the sky. He let it go. He had made a choice.

The lightning flashed once more overhead, and in the blinding light, his eyes fixed on her face. This time it was Karen, his Karen. Her eyes open and aware; afraid.

With one hand held out behind him for balance, he reached for her.

"No, Tom. Don't do it," Karen said, in her own exhausted voice.

It was too late. As she spoke his fingers brushed against hers. From that same mouth came a cackle of triumph.

"Ashes to ashes," it began, "dust to—" The voice was cut off by the alarmingly loud crackle of electricity. There was a loud *pop!* followed by the smell of burning flesh. Smoke billowed up between the two of them, their hands seemingly welded together.

And then, rain.

Two voices came out of Karen's mouth simultaneously, each screaming in a distinctive way. Tom's hand curled tightly around Karen's and as he pulled, he felt the burning sensation coming through him.

The sky lit up like a searchlight, brighter than the sun, as it popped with electricity. The light seemed to spread, arms of it snaking out from a central point. Behind him Tom heard something fall, and then the crackle of flames.

Still the screams came, joined by the voices of the crowd that had gathered beyond them. He listened to them screaming from a distance, seeing nothing.

The images shifted on Karen's face, hers and then the other one, each a mask composed entirely of pain. He held on until he felt a sure grip from her hand. He fell to his knees.

"Karen! Hang on to me!" The grip on his hand tightened and then grew slack. She cried out in horror, whether from the burning flesh—*Me, it's coming from me!*—or from whatever was happening inside her, he could not tell. But he pulled, hanging on as best he could. He had to pull her over.

The light was flooding the sky, running brightly in many lines that emerged from a central scar, like veins.

He pulled her until her body fell, half in, half out of the crevice, and then he grabbed at her arm as it flailed the air for balance. He was using his strength to pull, to *will* her over. She hung impotently in the crater, fading in and out of awareness, the other strangely absent, until he managed to haul the weight of her over the edge and pull her up onto his side.

"Some kind of goddamn earthquake split us in two, what the fuck is next, a hurricane?" Bart said.

Tom pulled Karen close to him and held her, still grasping her hand. She whispered in his ear.

"Karen's no longer among us," and then she laughed. As the laugh rang in his head, he could feel her claws sinking into him, digging through his shirt at the back, where the rain had so recently, so closely gathered. So close.

He pushed her away, but he could not let go of her hand, which burned in his. He shook at it in vain. Karen had gone limp, and her breath when she spoke bore a sweet-sick smell of decay so thick it felt wet on his cheek. So sweet, it was compelling.

Under the horror smell of the thing, was the smell of rain.

He gulped at the air, and could taste it. Thick, sweet, not sick-sweet, but new, fresh sweet. Humidity. He noticed for the first time the way Karen's dress clung to her, the dampness under her, the clammy feel of her cold skin under it.

It was his turn now. "It's too late!" he brayed. His head swung in the direction of the crowd. "Can't you feel it? It's coming, *feel it!*"

There was a murmuring sound over the rumble in the sky.

People looked upward, and saw the opening veins that spread out, the electrical light that poured from them. They began to notice the way their clothes stuck to them, the uncomfortable, wonderful cling of sweat to skin, the thick, hot, textured taste of the air. The crowd's mumbling shifted into cries of delight. They knew, they smelled it. It was coming.

Karen's body went stiff in his arms.

Then the thing let out a squeal, not of delight at all, and he heard it, not just inside his head but inside his whole *body,* as though she had reached in and pulled at the core of him. His breath was sucked out of his body, making him gasp and gulp for air, tasting each time a mixture of the dead smell of her and of the sweet, renewing taste of the coming storm.

Lightning flashed down on them. Tom felt it strike his back, spreading in threads over the rain gathered there. It pumped along his body and through him, into Karen's body.

The woman's voice screamed loudly, and as it did, the dead smell took form. Out of Karen's mouth flew dust. Hot, dry dust. Tom turned his head away.

The sky cracked one final time, like a tear in the fabric of heaven, and the sky opened up. Light flooded over the yard.

The rain poured down, a great rushing river, gushing in buckets and barrels, in tanks.

Karen slipped from Tom's arms, and as he bent to catch her he was suddenly pushed away by the great billow of dust that flew from her. It swirled around her, her face and body disappearing momentarily in a fog of dust.

The rain fell around her, steady and loud, and washed the dust away, rinsing it into puddles that drained into the crevice in the earth.

"Karen?" Tom whispered. He kneeled beside her. When she made no response, he slid his hands under her shoulders and raised her to him. Her head hung limply back.

"Karen?" Under his hands he could feel the faint beat of her heart. He cradled her head, shielding it from the incessant fall of the rain, and pushed her hair out of her eyes.

Her eyelids flickered, then flew open terrified. When she focused she saw Tom, and relaxed.

Rain fell from his soaked hair and dropped onto her face. She blinked twice, and tried to see past him, but the effort was too much for her. She found it easier just to smile. He smiled back.

"You made it rain," she said.

GOODLANDS FINALLY CAUGHT THE ATTENTION OF THE MEDIA, four years too late.

The media in the case of Goodlands' big rain was a lone camera crew from the tabloid show *Thirty*—best known for celebrities caught *in flagrante delicto* and mysteries of the unexplained. That day they were half lost and looking for breakfast after having spent the night in the bush outside of Goodlands, hoping to catch a glimpse of the infamous "Vanishing Boy" of Arbor Road. They had not been successful. Their quest immediately after that had been large bacon-and-eggs breakfasts, and they drove up Arbor into what they described later on camera as "a disaster zone." They hit the last of the dust storm, their van getting stuck just inside the town limits, and they waited, awestruck, while all hell broke loose. They did, however, get it on tape.

Angela Coltrain, former spokesmodel for No Problemo Jeans, wanted to press onward.

"We'll walk," she said. She was outnumbered by the two men who made up the crew. Jake, the cameraman, insisted that the dust would render the equipment inoperable. Pissed off, Angela spent the remainder of the morning putting a face on. When the storm began its leisurely drop back, they taped that, too.

When Jake decided it was safe to drive in, the dust storm was nearly finished, but the dust on the roads was high enough to stall them several times. The two men pushed while Angela gunned the engine, hurling clouds of the stuff up into their faces. The fourth time, with a mutiny close at hand, the three decided to abandon the van and walk in.

They were not sorry. They were silenced.

The unearthly beauty of the storm-ravaged houses, fields, and vehicles urged them on. They were nearly in town when the lights went out. Snuffed suddenly and quickly, as though someone had thrown a switch somewhere.

They had their infrared camera with them, and they used it to shoot frightening, eerie footage of what Angela later dubbed One Town's Apocalypse. The images, Angela said, would make them all rich and famous.

By the time the dry lightning began, and the earth vibrated as if with aftershocks from an earthquake, all three former Los Angelenos became very, very afraid. Lacking the shelter of the van, they looked for a house. Angela insisted that Jake continue to shoot as they walked up a long driveway and banged at the door of the first house they came to. After a few polite minutes without an answer, they broke in.

There they stayed while the world seemed to rage out of control in front of them, through the picture window.

When the skies opened up and the rain poured down like a waterfall, they waited for only an hour before setting out again. The house had been spooky, quiet and filled with dust, the occupants out of town, they all agreed, without really believing it. A room-to-room search was out of the question. The lights were out, and the phone in the dining room was dead.

Around three o'clock, after wrapping the cameras in plastic, they forged ahead. Angela searched for an umbrella in the front hall closet and came up with one, coated with dust and stuck way in the back of the closet, behind shoes, winter boots, and a pair of gum boots that Brad, the audio guy, put on his feet.

"Christ! Doesn't it ever rain here?" she said, just before finding the umbrella.

They headed for town through the pouring rain, and when they got there, they found the people who had been missing from the silent, invisible streets leading into town.

"It was like some kind of . . . um, satanic ritual was going on," Angela explained later to her producers, trying to justify the extra day they had been gone. Jake and Brad nodded, but the tapes belied Angela's description.

"Keep shooting, I'll round up victims," Angela told Jake, meaning interview subjects. He did.

The crew of *Thirty* shot four more hours of footage.

They never got to talk to the banker. But standing on the porch of the little house at the end of some godforsaken road, they found the man everyone was talking about.

Angela saw him first.

Tall, broad-shouldered, with long, wet hair pulled back and tied and wet clothes clinging to a hard-muscled body, he made Angela lose her professional spokesmodel training for only a moment. She smiled her prettiest smile, the one that got her the interview with Jack Nicholson, and led the crew up the driveway. About halfway, the man on the porch raised his hand and spoke.

"Far enough," he called out.

The three of them stopped politely.

Angela smiled and tilted her head appealingly. "Hello," she called out. "I'm Angela Coltrain from the newsmagazine show *Thirty.* This is quite a day you've had here. We'd like a few minutes of your time to talk about it." As she spoke, she took a couple of small steps forward. Behind her, Jake's camera whirred.

"Sorry," the man on the porch said, he too flashing a smile, white and startling on his tanned face. Angela felt heat rushing through her. "There's really nothing to say."

"Is Karen Grange in the house? I understand that this is her place. We'd like to talk to her, if you don't mind." Angela's smile never once wavered as she walked slowly toward the porch. "I'll just knock for her, unless you'll call her for us."

"Stop there," he said, his smile fading. "She's resting. So if you don't mind, Angela"—he drawled out her name with exaggerated slowness—"I think it would be best if you moved on." He turned his back and reached for the door.

"Wait!" Angela called out. "You're not going to let us stand out here in the rain, are you?" She widened her eyes and used her most simpering smile, and took four or five quick steps in the direction of the porch, getting that much closer to the man.

He smiled down at her slowly, his smile broadening, and he looked into her eyes. His smile was infectious and her television smile was replaced by one more natural; the muscles around her mouth softened and she felt, oddly, like giggling.

Several seconds passed before Angela realized she wasn't saying anything, just standing there like a teenager, smiling. Behind her, Jake whispered her name sharply. It startled her. She blinked.

"Please," she began, "I want to ask you about the rain . . . There are people who say you did some kind of a—" She hesitated, embarrassed. Her cheeks flushed red then, at having to say such a *silly* thing to such an . . . *intense* man.

"Um . . . a rain dance," she finished. A tiny giggle escaped through her lips. Jake heard it and the camera moved a little bit as he pulled his eye away from the viewfinder and shot a confused look at Brad. Brad shrugged.

Tom did not break his gaze. He chuckled low. "There was no dance. No magic"—he spread his arms—"just a rain shower. A little rain. Right?"

Angela nodded. "Yes," she agreed happily.

"Good. Well, it was nice to meet you, Angela," he said finally. She nodded again.

Tom turned with a small wave and went into the house. The door snapped closed on the spring, a knock of wood against wood sounding muffled in the rain.

Angela still held the mike out in front of her, the smile still on her face.

"What the fuck was that?" Jake said angrily, shutting off the camera. "Where the hell were you?"

Angela blinked again, her face confused for a moment, then cheeks blushing, this time just embarrassed. She pressed her lips together briefly and turned abruptly, pushing past Jake to the borrowed truck.

"Fuck him," she said. "We've got hours of the other stuff. We can cover this with voiceover." She pulled the passenger side door open and stepped inside.

"Let's *go*," she snapped.

The three of them got a ride back to the van, which was then unstuck with a good push from Bart's truck.

"When'll this be on TV?" Gooner asked her.

"We'll let you know," Angela told him, dazzling him with a smile that disappeared as soon as she got into the van. The van pulled away and started the long drive back to New York.

Angela couldn't wait to see the stuff they'd shot with the infrared. About two minutes outside of Goodlands, Jake set it up for her. She screamed. It was not with delight.

"The fucking camera malfunctioned!" she screamed. Jake looked through the viewer. The footage was of the lonely and empty road outside of Goodlands, Arbor Road, where the Vanishing Boy never showed.

"It's just a wrong tape or something," he said uneasily, setting up another tape. It showed the same thing. Panic didn't really take hold until they looked at the interview tapes.

All blank. Every one.

*   *   *

All in all, it rained for two weeks. The passion and fury of the original rainfall let up somewhat after the first couple of days and settled into an even, steady rain that was absorbed with equal vigor by the earth, the trees, and the people. For a few days folks had their suspicions about this particular rain, after having been so disappointed with the last. But this one seemed right, somehow, and that was what people said to each other.

Angela Coltrain was scooped by the *Weston Expositor,* which ran a lead story that week with the headline FREAK STORM BRINGS RAIN TO GOODLANDS. No one else covered it.

Henry Barker told his wife the whole thing and never once turned on the Weather Channel to see if the story had shown up. Lilly did, when Henry was back at the office, but the coverage only showed rain in the centermost part of North Dakota. Business as usual. She never mentioned it.

Henry's report for that day was a belated one on a barking dog. A second warning had been issued and the subject turned over to animal control. He pulled the Baggie that contained the butt of a hand-rolled cigarette (not a controlled substance) out of his pocket where it had been for days, and dropped it into the trash bucket beside his desk. Case closed. He let the Simpson matter drop from his mind, believing it better that way, knowing he couldn't explain everything, and especially not that part of it. He left Goodlands to their own.

Larry Watson, the Campbells, the Bilkens, both Greeson brothers, the Sommersets, the Paxtons, the Trainors, and nearly everyone else in town spent the weeks that it rained planning and getting ready for reseeding. Everyone came down with a summer cold. They spent a lot of time outside, happily catching a chill.

George Kleinsel barely got the front of the Dry Goods fixed before having an arm-long list of repairs to do at people's homes all around Goodlands. The storm had wreaked its havoc—shingles mostly, but in a couple of cases, light buildings had fallen, and farmers were busy with other things. George and his partner had their summer planned.

Ed Clancy did not do a booming business. He watched *The Guiding Light* and helped himself to a few cold ones now and then.

The manner of Carl Simpson's death caused some consternation for a couple of days before Bob Garrison ruled that he had died of asphyxiation. Carl's lungs were dirtier than a miner's, the coroner told his colleague, but kept it simpler on the official report. After the funeral, Janet and Butch returned to Minnesota, where she had family, and mourned Carl from there.

A lot of people left Goodlands, in spite of their town's change of fortune. The Franklins had their auction sale, and in spite of the circumstances, it was a happy afternoon. Someone from Telander did indeed get the John Deere, but paid nearly what Leonard had, brand-new, for the privilege.

Near the end of the two weeks of rain, when it was beginning to be dismal and inconvenient, the talk turned from how it had arrived to more mundane matters, like seed prices, planting, and gardening. Life was returning to normal.

Karen's left hand was still bandaged, but Dr. Bell had said that in two more days he would take the bandage off her wrist. Tom's ankle, sprained but not broken, had lost its stiffness after the first week.

Tom was the only one Karen talked to about what had happened to her the day it rained. He held her close and she told him between sobs. There were nightmares, but by the time Tom was walking without a limp, they too, were subsiding.

On the fifth day of the rain, Tom told her that he loved her. He wouldn't leave, if she didn't want him to.

The rain continued to fall. Midway through the second week, when their injuries were healing, and their feelings spoken, Tom started to get restless.

He spent a lot of time outside those days, while Karen, on a leave of absence from the bank, read and slept. She slept a lot those first days after the rain—the nightmares were worse when it was dark and her sleep was interrupted constantly. Sometimes she would watch him through the window. He often stood inside the gazebo, leaning out so that his head was in the rain. He could do it for hours.

People came in droves. They brought money, food, and gifts. They said little, wanting only to express their gratitude. Karen told them it was him. But it was her hand they shook first.

Except for fifty bucks, Tom wouldn't take any money. Not the money people brought, and not the $2,500 that was still in Karen's purse, where she had left it, what seemed like months before. He wouldn't even discuss it. She gave up trying to make him see.

Something had changed in him, and they both felt it.

Karen could almost hear him trying to wrap himself around what had happened, even as she tried to discard the memories of that afternoon from her mind. In the first hours and days after the rain had come, when she lay in bed, curled around herself, trying to ward off night terrors and day terrors, she would hear Tom get up from where he sat and pace around the room, not unlike the way he had paced the day it happened. She would hear the back door squeak and he would disappear into the rain for hours at a time.

Karen had been right; Tom was trying to make sense of it. All the years he had spent making rain had not prepared him for the things that had happened in Goodlands, the magnitude of nature that had flowed *through* him. It had passed through him and into Karen, and at that moment, he had felt it, as though for the first time. Tom needed to know if something else had been at work that day. If he had been a mere catalyst, or the rain itself. He had to know who he was. What he was. And it frightened him.

They made love as they had before, with the added bonus of something that was more than physical. They talked, and near the end, even laughed. They watched TV. Ate in the living room. Sat on the porch. All the while, there was the unspoken reality of when the rain would stop.

One night, Tom asked her if she wanted him to stay. There was such pleading in his voice that she was unable to answer him.

The next day, they woke up to silence on the roof, and sunshine.

"It's stopped," Karen said. She felt heavy and tired. Tom nodded.

They had coffee on the front porch, drinking it dutifully, but Karen didn't even taste it. Residing just inside her skin was a terrible pain that had not come out, and maybe wouldn't. But it was there just the same, keeping all other feelings at bay, making her feel numb.

They talked lightly. Karen said she would be going back to work the next week. Tom took her hand in his and looked closely at the fresh, pink skin that would be a scar later. He held her hand gently, running a thumb over the soft part of her fingers, sending, even then, a small thrill through her. She knew she had to say something.

"Tom—" she started, her mouth suddenly dry. He looked at her and did not speak, the words hanging in the air between them.

"I think you should go," she said, finally. In the space of time it took her to say it, she wished the words back. But she had said them.

"I wouldn't stay away long," he said, looking away from her when he said it. "Six months, maybe." She did not ask him what it was that he had to do, where he had to go; she was certain that he didn't know, himself. Only that he couldn't stay. Not then, anyway.

"Will you be all right?" he asked.

"Yes," she said, smiling a little. The last two weeks had seen her welcomed back into the fold of Goodlands. She would be all right, that way, anyway. She couldn't help herself. "Where will you go?" she asked.

He shrugged, "I got fifty bucks," he said, smiling. He drank the last sip of his coffee and went into her bedroom to pack.

He found her sitting on the back porch steps. She did not turn around when she heard the door open. Tom threw his bag onto the ground in front of them. Karen laughed. He had taken her navy Louis Vuitton backpack. It was stuffed full, his blanket tied to the bottom with the dirty hockey laces.

"I'll want that back," she said.

"I left mine on the bed for you. In case you need to go somewhere."

"Thanks," she said. He sat down beside her and took her good hand in his. He pressed it to his lips and kissed her fingers.

"I'll think about you," he said.

"Every day?"

"Every night," he whispered close to her ear.

I won't cry, she thought. She turned toward him and wrapped her arms around him, burying her face in the warm part of his neck. "Good-bye," she said.

"Six months," he said. "No more. Maybe less." She nodded. Tom got up and walked down the last step, scooping the bag off the ground and shouldering it. He looked exactly as he had the first night she saw him.

He smiled and pushed his cap back on his head.

"Riding off into the sunset, like a hero."

"It's ten-thirty in the morning," she reminded him.

"Sunset somewhere," he said, his smile fading. He paused and looked up, squinting into the sky. "Won't rain again for a while. Maybe a week." He pointed off into the west. "It's there," he told her, looking back to see if she knew.

Karen closed her eyes and felt the sky. She could feel it. Six, seven days to the west.

"Yes," she said.

She did not stand when he turned and walked to the corner of the house. Instead she watched him from her perch on the porch steps. At the corner of the house, he looked back once, unsurely, and saw her there. He gave her a half smile before turning his direction to the road.

Karen listened to his boots crunch on the gravel driveway until she couldn't hear them anymore. When he was likely no more than a speck on the landscape, she closed her eyes again and turned toward the sky, and felt the sun on her face, and the rain in the distance.